Bridget—
May your roots always find water

Barry Alexander Brown

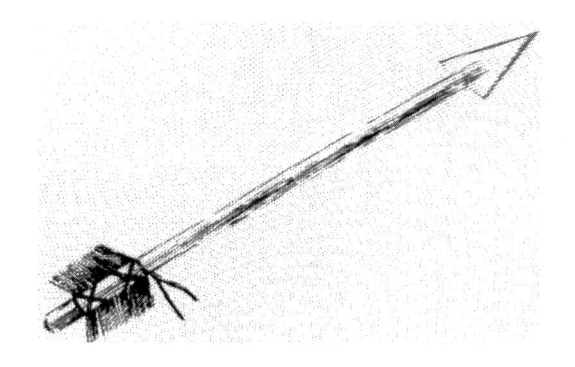

THE SONS
GOLDEN RIVER
SOOS
EIN
SIRE RIVER
ORZAMOND
SEA of SUMON
MERNARES MTS
LUL
J'KAI
FOULLANDS
PENINSULA
DIVUL
O'BIR SEA

WIND

TOR'OC TRILOGY
BOOK 1

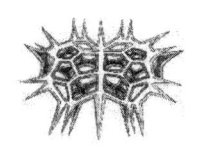

Barry Alexander Brown

©Copyright 2025,
Text & Illustrations, Barry Alexander Brown

ISBN: 978-1-969589-00-3 Paperback
ISBN: 978-1-969589-01-0 Hardback

Cover Design: Juan Villar Padron
Illustrations: Sasha George
Illustration Ch 11: Barry Brown
Editing, Book Design, Map, Alphabet: Anne Kent Rush
Text Font: Palatino

All rights reserved under International and Pan-American Copyright Convention. Without limiting the rights of copyright reserved above, no part of this book may be reproduced or transmitted in any form or by any means (electrical or mechanical, including photocopying, recording, or by any information storage and retrieval system) without prior written permission of both the copyright owner and the publisher of this book.

FV-24

Visit the Wind Website:
www.WindTrilogy.com

Intellect Publishing, LLC
www.IntellectPublishing.com

Dedication

To my darling Verane

for whom this book was written

Barry Alexander Brown

CONTENTS

GREETING – Page 3

PART ONE: *The Trees*

Song of Long Beginnings

CHAPTER 1– Page 11
CHAPTER 2 – Page 41
CHAPTER 3 – Page 83
CHAPTER 4 – Page 123
CHAPTER 5 – Page 163

PART TWO: *The Cities*

CHAPTER 6 – Page 209
CHAPTER 7 – Page 247
CHAPTER 8 – Page 285
CHAPTER 9 – Page 327

PART THREE: Blood Moon

CHAPTER 10 – Page 363
CHAPTER 11 – Page 401
CHAPTER 12 – Page 439
CHAPTER 13 – Page 463

REFERENCES

THE AUTHOR – Page 495
GLOSSARY – Page 499
ALPHABET – Page 511
CONTACTS – Page 515

Book 1

Barry Alexander Brown

GREETING

...For as you know, or do not know, worlds are always built upon worlds – the new crushing the old, layers upon layers, evolving, diverting, same and different, converging into one another, into ever-flowing, ever-ebbing rivers, through singing deserts, across time and sound. As you stand in the river now, feel it flowing backwards, your present flowing world flows upstream, back through circling worlds and times of nature and creatures of land, water, wind, and fire. Feel several layers folding oceans above and skies below, spinning time around to one of those layers where you started, to ten thousand ones and zeros of your time when the world was already a world, and spirit was already a spirit held in human flesh. The land and water had many dances to twirl before landing as they now are beneath your feet. As always, all the players and all possible plays were already in flight, constantly rolling out lands, creatures, riddles, journeys just as they are doing now, to carry you across loving time, along azure trails of shady waterways, and into one particular long forgotten delta.

Welcome.

Barry Alexander Brown

A Kollokk

PART ONE
THE TREES

∕ᖴᗪᗪ✶

Barry Alexander Brown

Wind

⠀⠀⠀⠀⠀‖⊦◇⋀└⊓F✲

Song of Long Beginnings

Morla

I am the daughter who became the mother
I am the one born not in the land from far and far but on the journey from it
I am the true daughter of Sumon, the Warrior Chief
I am of the people who came
The people named Tor'oc
To be Tor'oc was to be born to battle
We were not born to rule
We were born to conquer
If you fought us, we ended you
If we did not end you, you did our labor until we traveled on
We were born with the wanderlust
It was the wanderlust and our greed that led us to the Peninsula
It was the lie of wealth that led us to the Peninsula
And it was the Peninsula that kept us
It was the Earth that broke and gave birth to the river Divul that kept us from leaving
It was the flooding water that came next to end us
Ended Sumon and Ended the Tor'oc Nation
It was the trees that saved me and the two hundred and two
As the water took me, the trees reached out and whispered
"Come to us"
The trees are our haven and our home
As true as breathing, Tor'ocs do not harm Tor'ocs
The trees are as Tor'ocs to us now

Barry Alexander Brown
In the boughs of the trees we build

We build by growing and twisting
In my life we began the City in the Trees
And we watch from above as the rushing water comes back
Seeking to end us when the light is short and cold

Oroleia

I am the daughter who became the mother
I was born and have only known the Peninsula
I am the true daughter of Morla, the Great One, the Savior
I am known as the second mother but I am not the ruler
Tor'ocs are not born to be ruled
Tor'ocs are born to battle and survive
The generations before us knew nothing but how to fight
They did not know how to raise crops to eat
They did not know where the metals for their knives came from
They did not know how to make the cloths to wear
We had to learn from no one
The Tor'ocs before us knew how to ride beautiful animals that ran swift and wind like
We only had the oryx and Morla said the oryx was not the beautiful animal they rode,
oryx were too savage, she said
We learned from no one to raise crops, make metal and sew cloths
From the same no one, we learned that Tor'ocs make great oryx riders
We are the learners who teach ourselves
The ones before us did teach the younger ones how to fight
Before Morla left us, she taught us what she remembered and she remembered much

Wind

We had no one to fight
As mother, I made the games of fighting
Our bodies wanted the games and hungered for the fight
We are the people who ride savage animals
We are the people who fight but do not end each other
We are not the people lost and left behind
We are Tor'ocs still

O'bir

I am the daughter who became the mother
I am the one Morla named the southern sea after
I am the true daughter of Oroleia
I am the mother of O'jolique the seer
We had learned and she wanted us to keep what we knew
O'jolique visioned the marks for our words
She saw we could grow the vines to make a way to walk in the trees
She visioned the hanging ways
The trees had taught us how to speak their language, WIND
The trees knew much from their long lives
The trees knew what their brothers and sisters know in the Out World
One of us will go back into the Out World
We have to be prepared
We have to keep what we knew from before the Peninsula
We have to keep what we learned
We have to know the way of fighting
We have to know the way not to
We no longer know the need to conquer
We know how to be Tor'ocs of the Peninsula

Barry Alexander Brown

Wind

1

The trees are screaming. That's what wakes Aeon the Leaf, me – from my swimming dream. I am not drowning as any other of my people would be if they found themselves, even in a dream, deep in the water where fear and death wait for us. We live where water surrounds us on every side, and the water is not our friend; it is vicious and vengeful, and something in its nature aims to drag us below. More of a barrier than any wall built, the water is the border of our existence.

However, dreaming, I, Aeon, can move through the liquid as a sea creature, undulating, speeding, flying, free of the force that holds me to the ground, sliding up and down and around and laughing silently. This is not my first time underwater. I dream of this often, though I don't recall how many times. I forget these dreams upon waking, but the easy movement, the freedom from the earth, and the fun of it remain with me, anchoring just behind my heart. There is even a smell here, a clean, blue smell that doesn't exist outside the water. And I am not alone. Someone, something – some many things are swimming with me. I can feel their presence, but I cannot see them. Perhaps they are such a part of this place that they and the water are one.

My swimming has a direction, even though there is no place I am swimming toward. And so, I swim, shooting through the water past nothing until light glows from the deeps of the place that feels bottomless. This light is warm but not inviting. It glows and flows and burns, and I swim at it. What could this be, this brilliant, burning light - so brilliant that it is difficult to see the source? What burns?

Still, there is the screaming. The trees are screaming, and the burning thing at the bottom of the water has limbs and branches and leaves, all on fire, so much fire that the water burns as well. What completely engulfs me are the cries and the aroma of the fire. The trees are screaming, and their screams reach me in the depths of sleep; they grab and yank me back from the water. This screaming is not just in dreaming.

Wind

In the landed world, the trees were screaming. I was born in the trees, and I knew the smell of the scream was real, and its alarm shook me from dreaming to waking, to jumping to my feet, to running. Sleep slipped quickly from me as I ran along the hanging way, away from the sounds and smell of trees in panic. I ran toward the water. It was the water we needed, and I was the only one not afraid to wade waist deep into the river that could extinguish the fire.

"Sleeping?" a voice barked at me, as I jumped down from the hanging way and approached the line of men and women already waiting by the river. "The city burns - and you sleep!"

The voice belonged to Uthiriul, two years younger than I, and braver and tougher, yet no less afraid of the water than the rest of the line. She shoved a bucket into my hands as I moved down the line of Tor'ocs to the last one standing at the edge of the water. He was hanging over the edge of the embankment, dangling a bucket, trying to reach the water without tempting the anger of the river.

I crossed over him and slid into the mild but threatening current, a current that whispered, "We can take you if we want." To me, the current was more welcoming than frightening; but as I stepped farther into it, the line of Tor'ocs drew in their breath as one and held it, expecting the river to grab me and pull me under as it would have done to anyone else who came into it. No one else does because it was known that it was the desire of the river to drown us.

The river was the boundary that kept us from the Out World, and the boundary was very good at its job. Still, whenever there was a reason for me to be in the river, I was glad to be in it, though along with that sense, there was a part of me that feared and resisted staying in the water. As I descended into the current, there was a part of me that floated high above and away with such a fascination for height that it could take in the whole Peninsula, the river, and the horizon of the Out World beyond the river.

In the first breath high above, I could see the fire that was burning a tree at the very edge of the city. It was just one tree that had caught fire, but the fire had grown large enough to threaten the trees surrounding the burning one. The screaming trees were pulling water out of the ground and filling themselves, their limbs, their branches, their leaves with as much moisture as they could to help save themselves from the flames. But the trees were thick, so the water ran slowly into them; and the fire was fast.

Below I could see me, Aeon the Leaf, scooping a bucket into the river, the water spilling over its edges as my body pushed it into the hands of a Tor'oc on the riverbank. The buckets came one after another, and the Leaf pulled them through the current in a single motion, pushing them back into hands above that were always there to grab them. I could see as the water buckets sped from the river hand to hand, up through the city in the trees, along the hanging way, and to the end of the far branches of a Bent Tree that stood tall above the one burning. Wanting to drown the fire, the water landed

Wind

on its mark; but the fire had fight in it and swallowed the early water as if it were thirsty for it. I was high above my own body so I could not feel the muscles of my arms and I could not feel the many and many breathes that passed as the dark reached closer to the sunrise, as myself below scooped the endless water into endless buckets. It was probably through laziness that I had learned this trick of leaving my body during unrelenting work. Enduring pain and hardship had been a last remnant of my ancestors' skills; but I did not want to endure hardship, and that was why I was called, 'the Leaf.'

Gradually, morning light rose high enough to show clearly the forest where the fire burned. Smoke spread, and smoke was the only thing that could be seen. The aroma of the trees told us that the fire had lost its fight and was near its own death. It was a good smell even if it was mingled with the odor of the burned wood. Below, the buckets stopped coming to Aeon, and the Leaf stood in the river looking lost, holding one final bucket, and reaching for others that were no longer coming.

I let myself fall back into my body. Exhaustion hit me with the force of a wind that could knock me down. I was able to hold my arms up, but my chest heaved for air, and my legs gave out under me. I fell, and as in the dream, the water was around me. But this time hands grabbed and pulled me, and I was out of the water before knowing it had swallowed me. In the next breath I was on land. Land felt wrong to me, too solid; I wanted it to give in a little under my weight. That somehow would have helped me, would have restored me; but the land had no give, and I lay there thoughtless until a head of hair blocked the light.

Uthiriul was above me on her hands and knees, her face inches away; her eyes were hard and suspicious.

"How do you do it?" she smiled – a smile with no warmth in it. "How does a body as scared of everything as you run into that and stand in it for hours and hours?"

"Someone had to do it," was the only thing I could think to say, though I could hardly get that out with the little breath I had.

"And somebody is always you and you don't seem to mind it. Just tell me, how do you do it?" Her grin grew larger but not friendlier.

I rolled away from her and found that I was still holding a bucket full of water. Its bottom rested on the ground so that I was more lying against the thing than holding it. I used the stability of the bucket to pull myself into a sitting position.

"You're a funny one, Aeon, last of the line of Morla. What would the Great One think of the Leaf, I wonder. I wager she would think you are as strange as I know you are."

Uthiriul spun a two-bladed finnif knife a finger's length away from my skin, slicing off a lock of hair that had fallen across my forehead. The action was so fast that it was over before I flinched and shut my eyes. My eyes were still closed tight when I heard her laugh, and I opened them to find that she was staring at me, looking for some kind of clue to my mystery, her mouth held in disgust and consternation.

"Fentesimal," she grunted as she stood and then stopped as something caught her eye. She gazed down into the bucket of water, her eyes narrowing. She held the stare a moment longer, softening only as much as she allowed, and then turned and walked away carrying the hair as a trophy.

I sat longer, waiting until the embankment was free of people. They all must have returned to their own kollokks to catch the sleep that they had lost in the last hours of the dark. My own kollokk was nearby. It was not the oldest in the trees, but it was old, tended eight hundred years ago by a Tor'oc with a talent for growing and bending and strengthening. It looked more like the natural cocoons that it was designed after than the kollokks of the last four hundred years, those in my view resembled squashed, oblong melons. I liked my cocoon; it might appear too small to allow free movement, but the interior was surprisingly large and tall. I liked lying in my bed sling, staring at the vines above me that formed a conical point where they hung from the tree. The vines within the walls had grown so tight that wind and rain and cold were kept outside where they belonged. It had taken years for the vines to want one another enough that they grew into one fabric. After eight hundred years, they had even forgotten that they once hung swaying, each by itself, from the limbs above.

I pulled myself to my feet and walked along the spiral ledge of steps that had been carved around the trunk of a tree that led to the hanging way. The hanging way was the bridge that connected all of the City in the Trees - made of vines like the kollokks. The tendrils were carefully urged to grow around the trunk of a tree and then guided to spread across the expanses between trees until they grabbed another tree creating a path between the two where no path had lived before. The way was older than my kollokk, older than some of the trees it connected, older than the memory of those who had twisted the first walk. It was a bent and living thing that the entire city relied upon to make it a city. The lowest point grew near the ground but was still high enough to be above the flood that came every year when the days were small.

The tallest point had grown higher each season to take advantage of the new branches at the top of the trees, branches that finally had become big enough to support the weight of the bridge carrying the Tor'ocs who crossed it. At points, the bridge ran high and free enough that it allowed a view encompassing all the Peninsula, out to the point where the oceans met. We called them the two oceans because that was what they looked like to us, two oceans with distinct personalities. Named after the War Chief, the Sumon Sea to the north was a mad, wild, churning grey water with waves that had pounded the land into cliffs. The O'bir Sea, named after the War Chief's great granddaughter, was to the south and was calm and blue, but with treachery in its undercurrents. It would pull anyone down who dared to wander far into it and drag them out a distance too far to make it back to land.   We Tor'ocs could not swim, so that distance was not far and far.

The third body of water was the river that we called the Divul. It was the child of the two seas. It had both qualities, a raging surface as well as undercurrents that, unlike the Obir Sea, never let you go, no matter how far it took you.

We had not built our City in the Trees on a Peninsula but on an island. We called it the Peninsula because that was what it was when our ancestors charged onto it a thousand years ago, attacking and slaughtering the native people to no more. We knew little about the people who lived here, but we knew that they did not live in the trees because nature wasn't a threat to them as it was to us. We took to the trees because of the Mad'la. The Mad'la is what we call the moment when the two seas rose and the water rushed across the land to the Divul and then washed back again taking the Tor'ocs with it. The Mad'la was the great flood and then there were the lesser floods that came every year. The floods only came when we did, and only after the Four Mothers had created the river. The Divul was made to cut us off from the Out World and the Mad'la was made to wipe us from the earth. I reason the lesser floods were there to try to finish what the Mad'la could not. It was Morla, the Great One, who took us into the trees.

I was the last of the line of the Great One. Her father was Sumon, the legendary war chief, who led us here. Originally, we had been a warrior people, a warrior nation always on the move - every man, woman, and child. A nation that had ruled no lands and lived to eat and sleep, to conquer a nation of people. We were without the skills to farm or build or weave or design or write or read. We were a storm that crossed the land devastating any society that was unfortunate enough to be in our path. Once a people found themselves inside the storm and under the rule of Sumon - if you could call him a ruler - they cooked, cleaned, made our cloths and the saddles for the epus we rode, sewed the tents we lived in and the tallums they slept on, raised the crops, and forged the weapons that were used to dominate them. That was a thousand years ago, so I only knew what was passed down from generation to generation; and what I knew was that we lived to kill, to conquer, to maim and to battle; and when the land was so devastated that its people could give no more or die no more, we moved on. The hunger for slaughter was the thing that drove us.

It was Morla, the Great One, the Savior, our Mother, daughter of Sumon, who took to the trees. It's said that she was carried over four long arpents by the first great Mad'la, before grabbing a branch and pulling herself to safety. She cried to others to follow and it was the children who mimicked her and took to the trees with her. Just like the yearly floods that take after it, the Mad'la was quick and vicious and clever.

She named their refuge the Forest of the Bent Trees because the limbs were bent and twisted into one another, which in places seemed to form one enormous tree reaching almost twenty to thirty Tor'ocs above the ground.

Wind

They passed the first dark, huddled together for warmth and spent the light moving through the trees, exploring a territory that welcomed them on the condition of peace and harmony. I don't reason that my ancestors were easy minders of rules; but if they wanted to survive, they had to learn. And they did, led by Morla, who was just 480 moons old when the flood took her father and all the rest.

The people stayed in the trees for weeks until another miracle, the arrival of the oryx. The great antelopes appeared below them one day, grazing on fire bush that had withstood the waters. Had the Four Mothers decided to repopulate the land thinking that all the Tor'ocs were gone? Did the oryx swim across in some miraculous way? Whatever had occurred, the presence of the oryx inspired the survivors to venture out of the trees. If these animals were not afraid, then why should the Tor'ocs be? At first, the oryx were seen only as a source of fresh meat. In time, my people learned to ride them like epus, eventually breeding them into three separate species – smaller oryx that they named anilees and used for meat; jiooiun that they raised to provide milk; and then the giant oryx, that they rode, and over centuries to come, trained to plow land and do other heavy work. The need for the oryx pulled the people out of the trees, but it was to the sheltering trees that they returned every dark to sleep. They had already grown too used to the sway of the boughs to want to dream anywhere else.

Our cocoon homes, the kollokks had first been twisted and shaped in the generation of Morla's daughter, Orl'isjud. None of these kollokks have survived to the present. It was my understanding that they were crude and uncomfortable dwellings, without floors or flaps. They provided some protection, but only a little more than the natural defenses already existing in the Bent Trees. The first generation of kollokks twisted and shaped to give comfort were formed a hundred and fifty years after the original ones. Of that time, my kollokk was a one-person-sized pod that early on may have had to house a family. The outer vine walls were thick and solid of a beautiful dusty brown hue. The inside was smooth, shiny, as the resin of centuries of fire bush smoke had sealed its vines with a burnt red color. The most wonderful thing about it was its scent, the odor of a lived-in, living thing.

    I walked along the hanging way which itself was made of vines that had been grown, twisted, and shaped into a pathway that connected every vessel in the trees. A kollokk can take months and months to shape, but any section of the way takes years, and in the decades that follow, a soft green moss grows to cover the bridge, bottom, floor, and sides. It was a pleasure to walk along the way, and I took my time as I walked toward my kollokk, the bucket full of water still in my hand.

    The bed sling that I had slept in was turned inside out, left that way in my surprise and panic when I awoke to the fires. Returning, I hung the bucket on a sturdy branch that grew into my home, across it, and back out again. The branch had taken advantage of a careless former in-dweller who had let its rooting happen, but it had turned out to be a handy line for hanging a variety of objects. As I straightened my bed sling and lay down, I steadied the bucket that was still moving from when I'd hung it on the branch. My muscles ached, and a deep exhaustion ran to my core. I closed my eyes hoping that sleep would take me, but above me, there was a movement causing enough disturbance to worry me. Looking up, I saw that the bucket was moving, swaying -- and more disturbingly, it was surrounded by unusual marks that appeared to move along with it. Marks – a voice in my head named them 'sybils'. I had seen these marks, these sybils, in the air before, and over recent weeks, I had seen them more and more. I had always been able to watch them in the half-light, and knew they were never there for anyone else; but now I saw them in every light, and they called to me. This time, these sybil markings around the bucket were clearer than ever.

    I reached up, steadied the bucket again, and closed my eyes. My body relaxed into the web of the sling. Then there was the swaying again, and, unbelievably, I sensed that it was increasing its movement, as though a wind were howling outside, pushing the tree - but really, there was no wind, and neither the tree nor anything else was swaying. When I placed my hand against the bottom of the bucket to stop it, I felt motion coming from inside. I stopped the bucket again, but as soon as I'd let it go, the bucket shook, jumped a hair, and began swaying. The marks swirled and lingered around the bucket whenever it moved.

    I reasoned that I was not truly seeing what I saw. The simplest thing to do seemed to be to take the bucket down, stare into it, and try to see if anything was inside.

Surely, I must have scooped up something from the Divul when I had been submerged in it. I stared. I could see nothing but clear, clean water, all the way to the bottom of a not very deep bucket.

"You have lost your reason," I said out loud, in my bad habit of talking to myself, as though I couldn't grasp my own thoughts unless I voiced them.

"Please," the water in the bucket bubbled.

My eyes were fixed on the water as I considered whether the words really could have come from it.

"Reasonless," I scolded myself, certain that leaving the sense of my body for as long as I had today while pushing it beyond exhaustion was having a very bad result. "Absolutely reasonless."

"This is reason," the water bubbled again. "Please, take me out."

Was the water actually asking me to take it back to the river? Understandable if it had, but surely it couldn't make a request - it was water. This was a conversation I was having in my head; I was probably asleep and dreaming, yes, asleep and dreaming. I decided to lie back down and steer this dream in another direction, a calm, beautiful direction where water doesn't talk, and buckets don't sway on their own. I moved back toward the bed sling when the water bubbled a third time.

"Not a dream," it said.

I was sure I hadn't said anything about dreaming and sleeping out loud. So, was the water reading my thoughts now? What was I reasoning? Even if I had spoken aloud, water can't hear or speak or read a mind, though in a dream, maybe it could. That was a pleasant thought - that dreams have the capability of everything, and this relaxed me.

"Put your hand in and take me out," the water pleaded.

"As you command, dream water! Let's see what you have for me," I said, as I plunged my hand into the still cold water.

Something moved into my palm and wrapped itself around my fingers, holding tight. I yanked my hand back, and my hand didn't come out alone. A creature made of water was attached to me – a creature with a head, torso, arms, hands, legs, feet, and what appeared to be wings. It turned its tiny head to look at me with sadness and fear and apology in its expression.

"Iz," I thought it said.

"Dream, please speak in a language I understand," I replied.

It spat a stream of water that hit me. I was awake. This was real, and I was holding water that was solid and liquid and that could speak, spit, and grasp my hand.

"My name, it is Iz. I am sorry for the visit and the fright and setting the trees on fire."

"You set the trees on fire?" It all made less and less sense.

"Not me, but us," the water creature said and looked even sorrier. "We had to draw you into the river."

I knew for certain that I should throw the creature back into the bucket, then take the bucket, and toss it and all its contents into the Divul. Perhaps after that, my reason would come back to me. But I didn't do it. I stood there looking at this little monster. I was awake; it was here, holding on. I could feel its grip.

"What are you?" I finally found my tongue to say.

"I am a fee – a water fee," it said, as though I should already have known.

"A fee? You are not a fee. They don't exist. Fees are figments in stories."

"I, a myth?" it replied, with all the shock in its voice that it could summon. "My, my – the myth accuses me of not existing." It swallowed and looked at me as though it were sorry for being harsh. It continued with a kinder tone, "You know what you are, back where all the other men live? You are the biggest myth of all. You're the thing that goes bump in the night, the thing parents use to scare their children into behaving." Then it bent over as though talking to a smaller person as it imitated a human parent, "You'd better stop that or the Tor'ocs are going to get you. They eat naughty children." Finishing the imitation, the water fee looked embarrassed but carried on. "You are the evil spirit that lives in the shadow, that cowers behind the chairs in the lonely hour, that waits in the corners and under beds to snatch them. There isn't a child under five where the other men live who isn't petrified of you, and not one over eight who knows for certain you don't exist. You, Tor'oc, are the myth. Now, what is your name? I gave you mine."

That was much and much to take in, but I answered, "Aeon."

"Do you have a personifer?"

"They call me 'the Leaf'."

"And are you, in fact, of the blood of Sumon?"

"Yes...I am."

"So, the infamous war chief and murderer has been, over time, reduced to a Tor'oc named, the Leaf. Well, I suppose that's just. Can you put me down?" It indicated that it wanted to be taken to a natural ledge in the wall. I did as I was told and placed the water fee so it could sit and face me.

"Could I have the wrong blood descendant?" the water fee asked someone, but not me.

"No, there are no others. There is only me," I told the figment of a thing that I had started to accept as not a figment at all.

"Then, you are the one," Iz said to himself.

"The one?" I asked.

"The one we have come for," Iz answered.

"But you didn't even know me, know my name...how am I the one?"

"They said you would be the one who entered the river."

I walked as far away from the water thing as I could. I needed to reason.

"You set the trees on fire to get me to the river," I said, as this was beginning to make some kind of sense to me.

"It was not me who set the woods on fire. It was others." It was pleading for me to understand that it was not to blame. "But, yes, the fire was our doing. We would have put it out if you had not come at all."

"But I did come. And it was us. We drowned the fire, not you," I said, angry. "Why are you here?"

Iz didn't want to answer the question of why; it changed the topic, "Aeon the Leaf, is there anything you're good at?"

"I'm good with the oro bow."

"Oh, good, good," it said, and it smiled in the way a thing made of water can smile; the smile rippled.

"What is it that you want?" The truth of talking to a water creature lit my mind with wonder and suspicion.

Iz let out a sigh, reached into itself, and pulled out a tube that became crystalized as soon as it hit the air. It opened the tube and took out a scroll that it unfurled. I could see right through this creature of water to the wall behind it, and there had been no tube or scroll visible inside of it to pull out a moment ago.

"I've come to take you," it said. I took a quick step back, ready to fight it.

"To retrieve you," and that sounded no better. Iz held up the scroll and shook it in my direction. "It's an invitation, of sorts."

I craned my head to grab a view of the words, but the letters looked like the marks of birds' feet on the ground.

"You won't be able to read it," Iz said, pulling the scroll around so that he could. The water fee made a gargle sound before it began.

"Blood of Sumon, with great consideration, respect and fear, your presence is required at the Camarod of Susceptible Nations as representative of the Tor'ocs of the Eastern Prison Island. You are granted an escort through and across the Boundary Waters and safe passage on all the lands from the Boundary to the city of Orzamund. This is not a pardon or forgiveness of crimes but is the first step in a journey for partial and full reemergence. It is to all our benefits – yours and ours - that the Blood of Sumon is to appear and participate in compliance with the nature and peaceful intentions of the Camarod. In All Susceptibility, signed: Hasmapludi III, Gerent of the Middle and High Bosagin"

Iz rolled up the scroll and handed it to me, waiting for my response. I stared at the scroll, that somehow had become just as large in proportion to my hands as it had been in Iz's; in other words, the scroll took a size that was right for whoever held it. I turned it around in my hands to give myself enough time to let all this settle in me. Then I looked at my guest, if I could call him that. I had to reason all this.

"I have questions," is what I uttered, as much to myself as to Iz.

"Oh, questions – yes, of course," the water fee nodded. Iz had captured more than a sizable amount of my curiosity. Though I had no intentions of going anywhere or doing anything far away from my kollokk, I wanted to know more than I knew.

"First, a Camarod – what is that?"

"There has not been a Camarod, a true Camarod, in a millennium, not since the Four Mothers imprisoned you and yours, and attempted by drowning to finally rid the earth of the Tor'oc nation. It was at the last Camarod that all the Susceptible Nations -- meaning lands and people who had or could be attacked, enslaved, and slaughtered by the Wandering War Nation of Tor'oc -- tried the Tor'ocs and found you guilty of every and all crimes that one man could do to another, including murder, thievery, slavery, terror both mental and psychical, rape, arson, and simple assault. There is more on the list, but no reason to go on. A Camarod is called to find a meeting of the minds and to resolve a plan against an exterior threat. Until now, no one has needed a defense since you were taken out of the question."

"So, the line about this not being a pardon means that I was born into a prison as a child, where I became legally a prisoner, guilty of crimes committed one thousand years ago." I wanted to make it obvious that

Wind

this was ridiculousness. How could anyone be guilty of crimes made by others long and long dead?

"That's right...you're a Tor'oc – born guilty." It was clear that Iz had no problem with that.

"And if I'm such a terror, why do they want me?"

"If they could see you, I'm sure they would strike that word 'fear' from the document. But, in all consideration, that is unknown to me," the fee replied, indicating an apology in its watery body for not knowing, or perhaps, for lying to me about not knowing.

The water fee had not won me, and it knew it. Then Iz stated, "You've seen the marks; I know you have; and more you will. Those marks are Tor'oc sybils. The ancient sybils beckon to you. They want you in the world."

Iz's words tipped me off balance. This was true. Ever since I'd been young, I had felt their pull, felt the marks ever steering me toward the Out World. How did it know this?

"How far is this place, Orzamund, and do they have Bent Trees there to sleep in, or is it a horror of ugly square kollokks built on the ground so close on top of one another that a person can't breathe? It's in our legends that this is what the cities of the Out World look like. This sounds more like a prison to me than my life here. So, in all consideration, I will decline the invitation and stay here in my cell. Perhaps in another thousand years, you can try again," I said, trying to hand the scroll back to Iz who refused to take it.

"The Out World," Iz said, moving the word around in its mouth as though tasting it. He looked in the direction of the river and across and nodded, "Alright, I see," it said turning back to me. "The people there call it 'Aemira'."

"Whatever they want to call it, I am not going." I pushed the scroll back at it.

"You must go."

"And if I don't?"

"The Out World, as you call it, and all its people need you. You and your kind slaughtered them and terrorized them for moons and moons and many moons. Your very name means terror in many of the languages of Aemira, and there is a balance that even after a thousand years should be set right. I do not know why they need you; and, as water is my witness, they would not let a Tor'oc, especially the Blood of Sumon, back into the land if that need could be met by anyone else. You must go. You have owed this debt from your birth, as you pointed out."

"I didn't point out any such thing; I was making reason," I said firmly. Still, some of his words had found their mark.

Iz smiled the rippling smile, and arched its little shoulders in a manner that I think was supposed to imply fun.

"It will be an adventure," the water fee said, smacking its lips for an effect I reasoned it thought would draw all the wonder of the adventure into my kollokk. "Consider it, Aeon. Don't you want to see off this island? Of course, this is not a prison, as they call it. You Tor'ocs have done something remarkable here in the trees. It has an earthy charm that, if you are land-bound, must be delightful. But this is an adventure, Aeon, Blood of Sumon! Go out and see where your great ancestors burned and plundered -- or perhaps that's not the best way to name it. But the Out World, as I understand, is a wondrous place; and you will be the first Tor'oc to see it again. That's got to be worth something."

"There are wonders here. I answer, 'nc'. Shall I put you back in the bucket?" I asked, trying to be cordial while leaving no space for argument.

"So, you won't go," Iz barely made a question out of this.

"No. I have my own balance that I listen to; and that balance tells me not to fly out into the far unknown where, an insulting little sprout tells me, they hate me."

"You have good reason, but you also have a debt," the water fee countered.

"I'll go!" a voice from outside cried, as a body connected to the voice swung in through an opening near the trunk of the tree.

Uthiriul landed on all fours like a wild cat in the space between me and the water fee. Standing, she looked about the room, seeing Iz but not seeing him. She turned herself around, still spotting nothing that she hadn't seen before.

"You were talking to someone -- or were you?" she asked. "Was it just you?" Her eyes narrowed, trying to see what she couldn't.

"How long have you been there?" I pointed at the limb just outside my home's flap.

"It could not have been just you. Where is he?" She looked about again to catch what she had missed. I let her spin her head, and then nodded at the sitting fee. She followed the nod, and her eyes allowed her to see it and take it in, but she wouldn't believe it.

"It is a fee, a water fee," I told her in the most casual way I could find.

Turning to look at me, not believing me or her own eyes, she simply said, "A fee?"

"They exist. There is one right there. It even has a name – 'Iz'."

"Iz," she repeated, turning back to look at the water fee who had patiently been waiting for her to understand.

"It is not exactly pronounced that way, but yes, my name is Iz," the water fee said, meeting her eyes with a look that invited her in.

"I saw you in the pail of water," she said. I was surprised to hear it.

"You did," it said, knowing she had.

"And you are real," she said, more to hear herself say it than to make a statement to Iz.

"Real as you." It felt the need to make it clear.

Uthiriul made a quick recovery and straightened herself, crossing to face Iz as she pulled the scroll out of my hands. "You must take me. I am the one you have come for."

"Uthiriul!" I yelled, but not loud and loud. I did not want any more Tor'ocs to witness this water fee.

"He has made a decision on what he reasons is a reason," Uthiriul said pointing at me. "But that is a mistruth. Aeon refused to go because he's full of fear." She leaned into Iz, "And even though they say that Aeon is the last of the line of Morla, which means he is the Blood of Sumon, I reason he may not be. How can any of us be absolutely certain that such a claim of blood is fentesimal? We are talking about a long ago and ago, even before the written word. Who knows who was born of whom? If you or anyone had to guess the likelihood of the Blood of Sumon passing through the ages to the Leaf or to me, what would they reason?"

Iz smiled, and his smile beamed as he saw the way out, a course toward success.

"You are saying that you are also the Blood of Sumon?" Iz was almost laughing.

"I have felt it since girlhood. The blood boils in me as they say was true in the Tor'ocs before the trees."

"You are a branch keeper," I accused her, "sitting with all ears open. How much did you hear?" I screamed.

"Enough of it. I know what a Camarod is, and I know they want us there…"

"Me," I interrupted. "They want me there."

"No, they want the blood there, and I am offering mine," Uthiriul said, fiercely enough that the smell of blood rose into my senses. She turned back to her new friend, Iz, "The trees tamed us, as you can see with this specimen that everyone calls 'the Leaf'.   The trees treat him like a pet.   Is this the one they had in mind when they summoned a Tor'oc to the Camarod?"

"It's hard to imagine," Iz nodded.

"Then it's fentesimal – settled and set.   We bend and bond," she said, pushing forward her hand toward its extended arm.

"Don't you dare!" I pushed her hand away from Iz's.

"This is a request, and I accept it," she spat back at me.

"To go into the unknown?"

"To embrace the unknown!   I welcome it. I have breathed for it since you told me of your dreams. You saw my days to come, but you did not understand what you saw. I did," she said, holding up the scroll. "This is for me.   What do you think brought me to sit outside your window?"

"You've always been sly," I said.

"I was pulled here by your dreams.   This is my finality. Aren't you struck by that?"   She came to face me, a breath away.

"Look at this," I gestured toward the water fee. "How can you so quickly trust it or go with it or listen to it?   It's a monster from the waters that has come to trick us."

"It's not a trick," Iz interrupted.

"It is not a trick," she echoed.   "You told me in your dreams seeing that I don't grow older in the trees;

and I don't remain peaceful; and I don't ride oryx. I ride another beast that is lean and beautiful like the epus in our stories. Just now, I fell to sleep, for just a moment, and in that moment, I dreamed of that beast, the one you told me. I woke and I knew where to go, and this is what I found," gesturing to Iz. "There has been nothing clearer to me in all my breaths than that this is my finality, and I am not afraid of it. I go."

"Reasonless you go. I'm you're elder..."

"Only by a breath!" she said, and I was silent.

I turned to Iz. "You've won," I said, giving Iz a look that said I might still harm it if the reason came to me. "You have me – bent and bonded. Give that to me," I said to Uthiriul pointing to the scroll.

"Take us both," Uthiriul made this a demand rather than a plea to the water fee.

"That's not possible. That is a grant for one traveler in one direction."

"You mean there isn't a return?" I was shocked by the thought of it.

"I'm sure they would like to put you back in this prison when what they need to be finished is finished; but that is a business for the future and for some other poor fee in that time. But for me, I can only take one of you," Iz looked up to Uthiriul. "I would trade all the water in the oceans to bring you because you are truer than the tides, but my spirit tells me that he is the Blood of Sumon. The mystery is, they must have him; and I do believe he will break their hearts, where you would either bring darkness or light; and I think it is the sun you have in you. Give him the scroll. We leave at day end."

The fight hadn't left Uthiriul, but she reasoned that she had lost the advantage, and capitulation was her best option for now. I didn't trust her. She handed the scroll back, never actually looking at me, only gazing at Iz.

"Change your mind," she hissed to the water fee as she disappeared through the doorway.

I found myself staring at Iz, wondering how my life could have spun away from my control so quickly. "Take this thing to the river; throw it back in. Climb up to your comfortable sling; fall asleep. And when you wake, this will be just a dream upset." Those were the thoughts getting the most attention inside my head. But others were there. There were the marks and sybils still stirring in my head. They were quieter, but they held power.

"How far away is this city?" I asked, hopeful that within my words was the message that I was not convinced to go. "How many darks will it take to get there?"

"Darks? You must mean nights and days – yes, that's how I would put it – it will take days to get there. How many, hard to say exactly," Iz responded, his whole body moving with each sound. It takes effort to voice a mistruth, even for something made of water.

"If I go – I will return with a grant of safe passage," I told the water fee.

"Meaning what?" he asked, trying to hide the fear in his voice.

I said, "Meaning that when I reach again the Divul's edge, you will escort me back through the river, without drowning me. We will bond on this, or I'll put you back in the river, and we'll be done."

It was silent while considering the simple proposal. "You have my bond," it said with reluctance. and again, I wondered what it was hiding from me. I could feel the secrets so nearby, they could have touched me.

"Water fee, what is it that you're not telling me?"

"Nothing," it squirmed again. "Aemira is almost as much a mystery to me as it is to you. Exactly what you will find on the other side, I can't tell you. I live in the water, and I could describe everything about that; but you will be on land, and once across, you are beyond my knowledge. You are big; you are strong; you are skilled, as you say. You should be fine. As the invitation puts it, the Out World is more wary of you than you should be of it."

I was not convinced. I reasoned that it had not told me all that it knew. But now there was Uthiriul. Uthiriul was headstrong. Being her elder meant that I was first before her, and that meant responsibility. I could not let her race into the unknown, as she desired.

"I will bathe and eat and gather my things, and then we go," I heard myself say, and realized that I actually meant to do this.

"It's not any time close to day end. You can sleep," Iz said to me, with the first sound of consideration in its voice.

"We can't wait to day end," I was certain of that. "I know her spirit, and Uthiriul has not given up or given in. She is hiding in wait. If we stay until day end, I won't be leaving. I will be left unconscious somewhere, probably at the river edge, and you will have to take her. She will force you. She will find your weakness, and you will be the one bent and bonded."

Iz nodded. "Do you need to take much?" the water fee asked, as someone who travels with things invisibly tucked inside itself.

"Not much – an anilee satchel, my finnif knife, the oro bow, a bed sling, a watchet to cover my chest, and these sit-upons."

"And soles?" Iz asked.

"I would take it if I knew what it was. Is it needed?"

"It's what men wear on their feet," it told me.

"For what purpose? I don't reason they can help with climbing."

"The Out World people must have softer feet," the water fee was reasoning aloud. "And I don't think they do much climbing – at least, not in trees."

Wind

2

I moved through the trees along the hanging way, carrying the bucket with Iz back inside -- the water fee and the water were one again. I headed toward a section of the city that was close to the river and where few Tor'ocs wanted to live. Only a few could be seen moving about the city as I headed to the water. They were recovering from the night of burning, which was exactly what I felt like doing—sleeping away the soreness in my body and the emotions caused by listening to the screaming trees. I was wondering when I would be able to sleep peacefully again. I was not certain if I would keep my promise and go journeying. I was making a bond to myself that if I did, the going would be short. However, maybe it would be better to throw the water with the fee inside of it back into the river. What could it do to me if I did that? Maybe it would grab me and drown me the next time a fire erupted in the forest when I was entering the river to save the trees. Yes, I reasoned it could do that.

The river and the trees had grown since the farthest kollokk had been shaped hundreds of years ago. They now met one another, and the oldest limbs reached beyond the embankment. That ancient kollokk hung over the river, and it was a mash of vines that had grown tighter and tighter. With no one to tend them, the vines had squeezed the kollokk into a long thin cocoon that birds used for protection to build their nests. The hanging way had stopped long before we reached this last kollokk, but the limb it hung from was big and sturdy and broad enough that it formed the essence of a bridge. There I crossed to what once had been the entrance to the kollokk. I looked down, and below me the river was deep and swift. The energy of the current was pulling at the bucket in my hands. I reached into the water bucket and felt the fee cling to my palm and fingers. I pulled my hand out, and the fee was once again a thing I could see.

Iz looked about—first up into the trees and then to the ruined kollokk and finally down to the water below us.

"Good, good," it said, frowning. "I was thinking and rethinking that you were not really bent and bonded, that I could find myself mid-air flying back home…alone, without my prize."

"What makes you think that won't happen?"

"Because you have reasoned this—not coming is more dangerous than coming," Iz said, the threat lingering after the words.

"Because I will go back into the river one day," I said nodding. "And what if I never go into the river again?"

"And who would, if not you? You won't let the trees burn, and there will be a fire again, natural, or unnatural. You wouldn't let them burn any more than you would let the girl take your place. There is a game the land folks play called Round Ribbon, and I believe you've been tied." The fee concluded its argument by folding its hands together in front of it.

"But there you're wrong. If I go with you, then who would go into the Divul when the fire comes? And then the trees and perhaps the whole city would burn." I had found my way out.

"If you go, someone will replace you, as has always happened. If you stay but refuse to go back into the water, everyone will be even more afraid of the river, and no one will stop the burning. The fire this morning was a mystery, but we know they started it. Maybe next time it will be dozens of trees, some in the city itself, and you think you won't go in the river to save your trees and your city? I think you will, and I think you know what will happen then. Reason this, Aeon," he said, knowing my response by the look on my face.

It was right. I knew it was right, and yet, I did not want to give in—and I did not want to go. I knew the game Round Ribbon, and it did have me tied.

"How does this happen? I cannot swim across this river." I admit I was saying this in hopes that there was a fault in the fee's plans that would keep me safe and dry at home.

"You don't have to swim. We will take you." Iz finished the last four words in song. Its song continued and lifted into high, beautiful tones that vibrated from the center of its body and melted into music that rose out of the water beneath us. The water was churning and changing. The current was madly swirling in more directions than I could follow, and the music drove it about and shaped it into forms. The forms were fees, countless fees, and as soon as they appeared they clung to one another to mold a bowl of water, a Tor'oc length away and directly under me.

The bowl was growing long and wide enough to hold my body; and from the memory of Iz's grip, I could reason it had the strength to carry me, not as water but something solid - not exactly dry, but not wet, a thing in between. Iz hopped from my hand and tossed itself into the bowl, disappearing into the mass of fees, its arm

Wind

rising up out of the mass to signal me to follow, to trust, to fall as it had.

I held back, touching the wood to ask its advice, and the tree whispered to me to go—let go—fall. What did it know that I didn't? Much is the answer; we were taught to trust the trees. I moved my fingers along the rough bark, feeling the energy of the tree pushing me away. Over and over, it was telling me to let go, fall, and fall forward into the unknown. I pulled one last breath of air in the world I knew and fell. The distance was no longer than myself, but the fear in me elongated through every falling moment.

I didn't so much hit the bowl of water as become swallowed up by it. It enveloped me. The fees moved around to close the bowl to make it tight with air. Then they let themselves sink into the body of the river holding me inside. Once underwater, the bowl spun faster and tighter and moved itself in the direction my feet were facing—toward the opposite embankment, across the river. I raised my head and looked down beyond my body to see if I could make out the river ahead, but it was a blur the same color and density and light as the bowl. I could feel we were flying, but my eyes told me that the only movements were the spinning fees. I couldn't see the water passing by or anything in the water that told me how fast we were flying. I wiggled and pushed at the wall of fees. I was able to twist and look to my right and then back behind me to see the white path that we were making as the water passed around us and left us, churning like the angry

Sumon Sea. That water was being left behind at a rate that was fast, faster than a Tor'oc could have travelled, except by falling.

We Tor'ocs all fell once in our childhoods. To fall was part of growing, of becoming. At each child's hundred-and-one Acu, or full moon, a ritual was undertaken to teach respect for the trees and overcome fear of living in them. The ritual, called Lijkose Iant An Acu, was performed on the eve of that moon. Each child was taken to the origin of our city, the balcony where Morla had called the survivors to her. Below the east entrance to the balcony, there was a natural opening through the limbs that reached to the ground without obstruction. On the ground at the very bottom of the opening, moss had grown over itself for centuries, creating a bed that seemed to have no bottom. Once one of the original children fell through this opening when they had first taken to the balcony. When she survived the fall without any harm and climbed back to the top, back to her people, they witnessed a new person without fear of the height or the trees. She was nimble and had a balance that was free and sure. Her name was Lijkose, and she was exactly a hundred-and-one moons-old when she fell.

After Lijkose, we all had ceremonially fallen, not slowly like my slipping into the bowl of fees, but fast and furious. Each part of the tree they passed changed the faller, filling them with the manna of the tree, connecting and linking them to the core of the wood. It was almost impossible to be without fear before falling

Wind

as we had been taught up until this time to be careful in the trees, watch our steps, our hand grips, and see the tree just in front and below us. Living in the trees was a dangerous thing, and a fall for a child could kill them. I tried to refuse my Iant An Acu and grabbed at a leaf, which tore away as my mother pushed me forward. The fall for me has been a memory in fragments, remembering more a sense of falling rather than witnessing with my eyes or ears, though there were colors in that fall that I saw and still can see when I recall it. At the bottom as I lay on the bed of moss, looking up at the faces that gazed down at me from so far above, I realized I had survived it as everyone before me had. I had seen a shimmering of dying light that the trees emitted during my fall. I had stood above this place many times before; but looking down, I never once had seen the light. I believe that light was only for the fallen one.

Flying through the water felt like falling, but with no special light or sense of connection to the water when flying through it. There was just speed, a smooth flying speed. The foamy white water behind us created an illusion that there was something darker on the other side of it, flying just as fast as we were, perhaps something following us. I imagined it was some large fish that took us for good things to eat, but my reason told me it was just a play of light showing through the foam. Whatever it was—fish, water, light—it would not catch us. Our speed was increasing.

Music—it rose around me. Until then, the only

sound had been a whirling, spinning sound like wind passing through a tiny crack where a dried leaf was wedged. I turned back to see beyond my feet, to make out whatever might be seen in the direction we were heading. The water in front was lighter and getting brighter, and I thought I could see the bottom of the river reaching up. We were coming to the other side. No longer moving forward, we were moving upward out of the water. The bowl opened again, and the sky was above me. My world was back on the other side of the river. I sat up.

The water here was a calm, smooth, welcoming current, quite unlike the embankment I had known all my life. The music felt farther away, no longer surrounding me. The bowl was disappearing from under me. The fees one by one were becoming themselves again and part of the water, each appearing and melting away a moment later. Once my legs came free, I stepped down and felt the soft sandy river bottom that the cool water pushed around my toes. The river was to my knees, the bowl completely gone. At one of my calves, there was a familiar grip, and I pushed my hand down into the water to receive Iz back into my palm. I lifted it out.

Iz was speaking even as it entered the air. "This is where I leave you. Your companions are near. They will guide you to Far Road and perhaps beyond. May your journey last no longer than it must. Be brave and trust your footing."

The fee said nothing more, before slipping away

and back into the water.

I lingered, standing in the river looking about, not eager to enter the unknown world ahead of me. I turned and gazed back across the water to see the land there and to say something that might mean farewell. We had no word for a good-bye because we had had no use for it. I was the first to need to say it. I brought my oro bow forward, opening it into the X-shape that would give it the most power. I took an arrow from the drawstring bale on my back, laid it in the notch, pulled back the bow string, and fired the arrow across the river. It arched high beautifully over the water and, as I had aimed, it reached the other shore and beyond, striking the ground in front of the nearest tree. Someone would find the arrow and by its markings know that it was mine. They would see how the arrow was angled into the ground and look across the river from where the arrow must have flown. By that, I hoped they would know that was where I had disappeared. No one except Uthiriul knew what had happened to me, and she would tell a fantastic story that would be impossible to believe. The arrow would be her proof.

Now, I turned to find myself staring at the new land. I folded my bow, hooked it around the bale on my back and left the water. The land under my feet felt just the same as the land on the other side. Somehow, I had thought it would be different—colder or warmer or softer or harder, anything but the same. The sameness was not reassuring but disappointing. I thought the newness would put me on my guard, but I was lulled into the feeling that all was the same and all safe once again, that there was nothing new to fear -- even as my reason told me everything was new, and nothing was the same, to be afraid, be on guard. I forced my hand around the handle of my finnif knife but kept it sheathed. I moved forward along a beaten-earth path that animals had formed over long time as they walked between the bushes down to the river to drink.

The path opened into a clearing of tall grass surrounded by trees. There was nothing there but the life of the forest. No one was there to meet me. Perhaps the trees are to be my companions, I thought. I wondered if they spoke the same language, so I spoke to them in the wind language we Tor'ocs knew. I blew the air softly through my open mouth and moved my arms to sway like branches, my fingers shaking like leaves. I simply told them I was here as they were, a common greeting. I told them my name and asked if they would take me to Far Road and admitted I knew nothing of that place or in which direction it might be.

One near and very large, very old Bent Tree took the light wind that was circling around it, forced the currents through itself, and blew, "Aeon the Leaf—a good name. We are here as you are," repeating what I had blown, and it chuckled. "I have not heard that greeting in many, many rings. You must be very old or simply speak an ancient wind. 'We know you, and you may grow here,' is what we say, and have said since I was first in the ground. So, I say to you, 'You may grow here.'

Wind

"I am young and probably do speak an ancient wind," I heard myself sway an apology, embarrassment implicit in the movement of my fingers. "My people have been separated from the World for a thousand years. Your cousins on the other side of the river taught us their wind, so that is what we speak. I am honored and pleased to grow here. Are you my companions and do you know Far Road?"

"We know Far Road, which is on the away side of our brothers and sisters—away and away." The old tree indicated the direction of the inland. The tips of its highest branches pointed out and up, which told me that it was away and away and away, farther than I had imagined. "But we are not your companions. They are here and not of us and cannot speak as you can. In all my rings, I have never heard an animal speak the wind."

At that, all the trees around the clearing rustled every single leaf, and I threw my arms in the air and rustled my fingers back to meet their smiles and turned to smile at each and every one. This made them laugh, never having seen a smile returned from a thing that could spin so freely.

"You are a seed—free and flying. How do you get your roots to dance like that?" a younger evergreen whistled out to me.

"My roots are free of the earth, and I have to drink my water through the highest parts of me rather than the lowest," I said, indicating my mouth without losing the sense of my meaning. The wind moved through the forest in an "Ahhhh" as they understood the remarkable and unlikely meaning of what I was telling them.

"I move along the ground like any other animal, and I sleep in the trees that let me." I bowed in a way that asked for them to allow me to do this.

"You are welcome in every and all," the old tree told me without a breath of wind between my words and his; and he swayed the lowest, heaviest branches in a way that asked me to approach.

I walked under the canopy of his branches and limbs and leaves and knelt at the foot of the old tree, placing my forehead against the thick bark of its base. "Thank you, Father," I whispered in my own language and swayed in his.

"Who is your father?" The question was asked not by the tree, but by something or someone in the shadows around me. Very unsettling, the words came in a single sentence as anyone would say it, but from three different directions. My knife slipped into my hand, and I spun to catch the speaker, only to see no one but the shadow and the light, and beyond that light, the field of grass. It is my imagination, is what I reasoned.

"We ask you again, who is the father you are thanking?" the three directions asked.

I fell back against the tree for support and to reassure myself that there was no space for attack from behind. It seemed to me that it was the shadow itself that was asking questions.

Wind

"Show yourself," I demanded, trying to bury the fear that was obvious in my trembling voice. "You surround me, but I am armed," I said with more firmness than I meant, while I spun the knife into view. "I will sheath this, but you must show yourself first."

Into the dappled light beneath the tree, three figures stepped, identical to one another and cloaked in long clothes the same color as the shadow itself. Was this the way of this new world, where everything appeared and disappeared into the fabric of the world?

"Ancient wood, how am I going to defend myself on this land?" I blew.

The old tree above me laughed, as I had swayed the last thought out loud without being aware. "These are your companions," he said between laughs. "They have been waiting a dew light, late light, a dark and dew again."

"My companions are shadow beings?" I blew back, overawed by the strangeness of companions like this.

"No, they are hiders…very good hiders," the tree replied.

"Tell us of this father," the hiders asked gently, but in a fashion that told me they were unsure and disliked the meaning of me talking and thanking my father as if he were there. Now I saw them as individuals in the half-light where they stood and was even more undone by the way they spoke the words, each one speaking a sound in the process of the sentence, as though they were one being. They did not hold a posture of violence, and I was deciding to save for later the understanding of their way of talking.

"This tree is 'Father.' We had been speaking and knowing each other, and I thanked him for his offer," I said, putting my knife away. "Who are you?"

"We are Jannanons, but we thought you would have guessed that. Do you not know of us?" This they asked in their three-way talk, with a surprise in their voices that indicated this was unheard of.

"Where I come from, there is no knowledge of you. You are my companions; the tree told me. The water fee said you are taking me to Far Road."

"Far Road and beyond," the three replied.

"I still cannot quite see you in this shadow," I admitted to the three. "Can you walk from under and into the light?"

Without an answer, the three moved simultaneously into full sunlight, and I followed them. Perhaps because I was startled and afraid of them at first, it had not struck me that their voices came from below me. They were much, much smaller than I, and all the same height, their heads reaching to the mid of my torso. I had been taught that Tor'ocs were large by the measurements of the World, but now I felt that we must seem giants, not giants like trees, but certainly large. The fee had fit into my palm, and these Jannanons were half my height and a quarter my weight. Each had a distinguishable face, but their hair was the same color and length, a dark wood brown falling around their heads and down onto their shoulders. As on my face, there was no hair on their faces, but there was a darkness that came from under their skin that covered their jaws and under and above their lips. Other than that, they were quite different from one another. One had light purple eyes, the second forest green, and the third the same yellow that flowers have when the weather first warms, but in this one's eyes there was a ring of brown that diminished the sense of yellow. Even the shapes of their faces and noses and cheeks and lips were not a match. One had a large nose, another a small nose, the third a pointed nose. One had thin lips, the others full lips. One had sunken cheeks, and the other two had fat cheeks. One had lines that crisscrossed the forehead, while the young one had a head that was smooth like mine, and the third's was in-between. They talked as one and moved as one and at first looked the same, but they were not. Each held his own individual expression as I took them in, and I reasoned that if I could commune with each separately, I could find out about each on his own.

"Are you hungry?" Three words in one sentence, spoken in three distinct voices; yet I was already getting accustomed to it.

"No," I said, having eaten before I'd been sent spinning through the water.

"Then you're ready," they said as a question and a statement.

"To go to Far Road, is your meaning," I said, also as a question and a statement.

"Beyond," said the wrinkled older one with the yellow eyes.

"It is away, away from here, and that's why they call it Far Road," I reasoned out loud so they would tell me.

"No. They call it Far Road because it is the last road that ends at Foul Lands. No one would clear a road beyond that border because, as the saying goes, "No one but a Tor'oc would want to cross it." But you are a Tor'oc…"

"So, I can cross it."

"As the saying goes."

I looked back at the Divul and beyond to my home. Was this the last I would see it? Would I end somewhere away and away? I wanted to return. That was my thought. I did not want to cross Foul Lands and walk on Far Roads. I wanted the trees I knew. I wanted my kollokk. I wanted my people. And I turned back to the Jannanons.

"I can't go with you," I said. The three little ones were not large enough to make me.

As one, the Jannanons looked across the river, as I did.

"You want to return?" they said in their together way.

"I have to go back," I said.

The three turned and looked away – away to the Far Road.

"The only way back from here is forward," they said and pointed away from the Peninsula. "That is the only way back."

"It is the way forward – not back," I replied.

"It is both," they said turning back to me.

I walked away from them and circled the Father Tree and sat to lean against the large, warm, dark wood. I was not happy with this choice, and it was my only choice. I could not live alone on the far side of the river, so I could not stay where I was. I could not cross the fierce Divul without the water fees. I could not go back.

"I am reasoning that we must come to Foul Lands and through it. So, when and where do we find this land?" I asked.

"We are standing at the edge of it," they responded.

"Well, if this is Foul, I am ready to begin," I laughed, looking around at the trees and their smiling leaves.

I looked around the Father Tree to grin at the Jannanons.

"Yes, this is pleasant, pleasant, pleasant," each one of Jannanons said the last word. "The last arpents of the land are beautiful, as you see, but there are dangers in the shadows. The legends tell us that the Four Mothers could not believe the gift that luck had given them. Your ancestors rode onto a land that could be cut off from the World, and that land was soon enclosed by such a hostile territory that even if individual Tor'ocs could cross back from their island prison, they would probably not survive Foul Lands."

"If that's so, why did my ancestors cross it at all?" Reason told me they wouldn't.

"They were tricked into it," the three informed me. "Sumon was given a map that convinced him that there was a wealthy nation beyond Foul Lands, a nation of boundless resources. He was told of great black horses with golden manes that could outrun the wind, of a people that forged arrows as strong as iron, of herds of beasts that had the tenderest meat, of trees that bore fruit in every season, and that even the lizards in this land could be boiled into strong, tasty wine."

"Fantastic." I marveled that my great ancestor could swallow a lie as big as that, and then it struck me that I might be swallowing one as well. "They tricked him, and now the trick is on me."

"How? What have you been promised?"

"Nothing," I admitted.

"Then where is the trick?"

"The trick is to make me cross back to here."

"It is not a trick; it is a task, an undertaking that any of us may breathe long enough to tell," they said, with a warning deep in the sounds of the words.

"But didn't you cross those Foul Lands to get here?" I asked.

"We did, and yes, we survived. But we can move silently, and we have the talent to blend, as you have seen. However, you walk with us now, and we must protect you. Soon and soon, you will expose us."

"To what?" I asked.

"To harm."

"Well, I will try not to bring harm down around our ears," I said, conveying my willingness not to be a burden, though for reason's sake, I don't know why I felt obligated. After all, they were part of the plan to yank me from my home.

"Impossible," the youngest one with the purple eyes said.

"But I was told by the water fee that Tor'ocs were the greatest horror in the memory of man, and I am a Tor'oc, so what do I have to fear?"

"There are worse things than Tor'ocs, but they don't travel beyond the boundaries of Foul Land; the light is too bright for them outside."

"Your version of the future doesn't make me want to go into it. Why don't I just stay here?"

"Because you are not safe here either and you won't survive without us."

There was something in their voices that told me there was more truth in their words than the words themselves, but I didn't like being trapped into a decision already made for me. I walked away from the three and back to the shadow the old tree was casting.

"The hiders tell me there is danger in the lands before the Far Road," I blew and swayed to the old tree. "Can you tell me what the wind has told you?"

"On your path, there are disturbed, spiteful natures and great beasts, both on ground and under the earth. There will even be a burning earth that is angry and where trees cannot grow. Until then, our brothers and sisters will be with you and will aid the hiders and you, especially you—we have blown your worth to them."

"The hiders said I am not even safe here."

"They said true—after the light, the dark will come, and so will an animal that moves freely in ways as you do and whom you will not want to meet, but who will want to meet you. You can climb up into us, and we will keep you safe; but on ground, there is no protection. It can smell you, catch you, shred you, and devour you. It eats everything that is animal," the old tree warned.

"By my understanding, I will be bigger than this beast," I said, thinking back to the water fees and the hiders.

"Untrue. You are smaller," the old tree swayed his branches lower to indicate just how much smaller, and one far branch swayed down to touch the top of a sapling.

"Sail away with the hiders before any further fading light," the old tree advised. "Keep close to the trees. Nest in them in the dark and beware of the nest where the roots tangle."

"The nest? A nest of what?" I asked.

"It is many lower beasts that should not live together but do. Poisoned things that even turn the trees whose roots have grown around them into infested wood, and we trees no longer count them—they are living and dead at once."

"When and where will I find this nest?"

"It lies underneath where the land burns. If the wind wishes, you will sail by it before another dark and dark."

"I see by the leaves that I should take care not to pass the nest in the dark if I do not want to join them," I said. I'd noticed several branches close by with leaves that had turned in. Mixed with the aroma coming from the tree, this delivered a message that was visual in and outside my head. The language of trees was much more complicated and sophisticated than man's tongue. Not all of it was in the sound of the wind that carried only a fraction of their meaning. It was the smells that were twisted into the wind that added pictures to the words, images that danced across your inner eyes. What I was seeing from them was a desolate place where the shadows slithered as well as walked in a crouched fashion under trees full of brown, dead, dried leaves.

"Do not meet them in the dark. Do not trust the trees with the dead leaves that do not fall -- and look to the sky."

"And what will be in the sky?" I asked.

"Your advantage." The old tree seemed to know nothing more than that. "You should sail now along the way," the tree said, indicating a direction into the deepest part of the forest. "There is a grove of Dairs that you can meet before the dark comes. The Dairs have tricks that the beasts of the dark have never mastered. The Dairs will keep you safe."

I bowed to the old tree in thanks, and the lower branches moved in response.

"May your roots always find water, Aeon the Leaf."

"And may you grow as high as the light, Father," I responded, with what I hoped was not too ancient a goodbye.

"Sail now," the old tree ordered me.

I took my steps backward and away, finding myself in full light and again in the company of the Jannanons before I turned my back to the Father Tree. Even though he'd warned me of dangers that I couldn't yet understand, my feeling was that this world was not so different. I felt that as long as there were trees, I would be safe and well and happy. I looked to my companions, and the comfort of this thought disappeared like smoke when they spoke in their three-voice manner.

"Do you want to stay longer?" Their tone clearly warned that we should start moving now.

"We can go. I've learned and I have said my farewell. I will be back again," I said, trying to translate the last phrase into a sign to the trees.

"In all good spirits, you will," responded the three. This was a phrase I had never heard and didn't quite know if I liked.

"Are spirits what we will meet here and beyond?" I asked the Jannanons.

"No, not here," they said in a way that did not make me feel safe. Then they moved, once again in unison, crossing the field of grass that buried them in the tall stems. I followed, slowly spinning once more, addressing the trees with a final parting, yet never losing a step or falling behind. The trees moved the wind through their boughs and down toward me, embracing me with an image of swaying my body among their branches. I smiled and was content to follow the three strange little humans who were so much like me but who hadn't a dewdrop of understanding of me or my friends who stood among and around us and welcomed us into their shadows.

The forest that we walked through was crowded with an underbrush that grew easily in the shadows of the giants that loomed above us, without a break from one tree to another, grown so tightly that I could not see the sky. In our forest across the river, the floor under the woods was clean and neat, and the underbrush was kept from overgrowing; but there were no Tor'ocs to make that happen here. There were stumps here and rotting dead trees, impassable bog lands full of ferns, scavenger plants, and black magic taro, mushroom villages that grew as high as my knees, and fields of moss-covered rocks, some big enough to be boulders, but still hidden until they blocked the way. Still, nothing blocked our way as annoyingly as the passageways of twisted thorns and vines that had reached the ground. They made it so we had nowhere to go but around and around and through the many vines, and then around again.

The Jannanons walked through this world without making a sound, walking apart but in unison, each of their steps and each arm movement exact, even when one came to a boulder or had to switch around a bush or cross a small stream. When one of them looked toward a far-away sound, they all looked in the same moment with the same movement of their necks and heads and eyes. For small people, they moved fast. I found myself lagging behind and had to hurry to keep from losing them. They never looked back to see whether I was there or not, probably because they could hear my every step. I was not as quiet as the three and didn't see reason to be.

In spite of all the trouble of moving through this land, I liked its wildness. This must have been what the

Wind

Peninsula was like when Sumon rode onto it, and the way it was when Morla took to the trees, before the generations that followed built the city and cleaned the forest floor. We moved through these woods, without stopping. I wanted to breathe in this old world longer. The Jannanons wanted to walk faster, to leave the wild woods behind and return to what they knew. There was a coming world that we would breathe in soon enough, and reason told me that it would be more difficult to move through than this wild, overgrown, ancient forest. That world would be even harder and stranger and more impossible to see the boulders in the pathways. If we had lingered longer here, I would not have minded, no matter the danger of the things that wanted to hunt me. Of course, I had never been hunted, so how would I know?

The light was near where it meets the land—it was day's end—when the forest opened and the trees kept enough distance from one another to let late light through; and the floor was clear of the great depths of plant life that had, until then, choked our way. The ground was covered with the same green velvet moss that grew on the hanging way. I looked up, expecting to find a city in the trees, as it all felt familiar; but there was none. There would be no City in the Trees again in this new world.

As one, the Jannanons stopped at the edge of a field of moss that spread out over an even larger opening in the trees. It seemed that the moss moved, undulating in the slightest way. Yet, when I concentrated on any part of the moss field, it was as steady and unmoving as moss should be. The Jannanons turned to look at me. In one set of their eyes there was concern, in another wary anticipation, and in the third was impatience.

"Do not be frightened." The three leaned in toward me to make their point stronger.

"There is nothing to be frightened of," I told them. "These are woods. This is more known to me than to you."

The oldest one smiled. The middle one's concern turned into a grimace. The youngest one leaned toward me as they said, "You have no idea what you're talking about."

"It is not harmful, and they will not harm you," the three added, and stepped onto the moss that lay ahead of us.

As their feet touched and sank slightly into the green velvet, a light, white with gold mixed in it, circled their feet, glowing strongly enough to illuminate their bodies from below. They did not take another step but turned and looked at me again to see if I understood.

"They will not harm you," they said again.

I was not afraid and never considered that the light could be harmful. The exact opposite was true. I marveled at the wonder and without hesitation stepped into it—one, two, three steps in, and unlike the light around their feet, my light was blue tinged with dark purple specks. There was a feeling on the bottom of my feet of warmth and something pushing back against me. I looked down and around my feet and smiled at whoever or whatever made this happen, and then looked up like a grinning fool at the three faces that stared at me all with the gaze that seemed to say, "Is he okay?"

"What is this?" I said, breaking the silence.

"They are called, 'spillets'," they said, as though they were still trying to ease me into the experience.

"Spillets," I repeated, mainly to hear myself say it.

"Impossibly small creatures, too small to see just one, but when many and many and many beyond counting, come together, they can do marvelous things."

"And so, I am stepping on them now." The realization hit that my weight must be crushing them. "They aren't harmful to me, but me, aren't I killing them now?"

"No, you cannot kill them; they are much too small to be killed that way. They are feeding."

"Off me?" I didn't like what that meant.

"In their way, but they are not eating you. None of us end at the skin. We all project beyond what we think of as our bodies," they said, as if talking to a child. "In the quality that surrounds us, there are stimulations that are us but not us. These stimulations can feed the spillets. They thrive on it."

"Well, then—eat," I commanded the little things, as

I ran across the field, at once falling and rolling. The blue and purple light was sparking and glowing as I played in the moss; and at one moment the entire field exploded in an instant into purple as I rolled and rolled. I stopped my rolling with my belly against the moss, my arms and legs spread out as far out as I could make them. I looked down into the moss, the spillets' blue light blinding me until I turned my face up to the Jannanons. They had not moved—their feet were still planted where they had made their first steps.

"How is it that the light here is blue, and the light at your feet is white?" I asked.

"Different stimulations create different light. Blue with purple, very strong, very good for them. White is good, positive, but nothing like blue."

Liking this very much and not wanting to leave it, I asked, "Is this the only field of spillets in the world?"

The three laughed, and their laughs were delightful. For the first time each had become its own being, and though their laughs married nicely together, each laugh was a laugh on its own. Still laughing, they said, "There are spillets nearly everywhere."

"And fees?" I wondered.

"Fees more than spillets—fees of all kinds and natures. We don't doubt that we are surrounded by fees right now."

I moved my eyes about in an attempt to catch sight of one but saw nothing like Iz. "Where are they and can they live outside water?"

"Water fees cannot, but there are fees of air, earth, wood, fire, of all the elements, on and on."

"And are they all as strange as Iz?" I asked, wanting to hear that they are not.

"Each fee is as different as each man," they said in a knowing way, "though the water fees can have tempers, even more than the fire fees."

The three took another step into the moss and onto spillets, that lit each of their steps as they came toward me. I sat up to take in the sight as much as I could, each step new and wondrous. I could have watched it infinitesimally, as Uthiriul would have said, had she been here.

"We should stop soon to eat and make our arrangements for the dark," and as they spoke, the light became golden on each word.

"Shouldn't we wait until the Dair Grove?" I looked off in the direction that the Father Tree had pointed.

"How do you know of the Dairs?" Alarm was in their voices, as though I had been hiding secrets.

"The Father Tree told me," I said, and their faces relaxed.

They reached me, and the lights merged, blue and purple spilling into white and gold. I swished my hand through their lights, and again the entire field exploded in a moment of purple and gold.

"You are right. We should get to the Dairs; it is not far," they said, clearly annoyed at my playing. "Get up, please. We must move before the dark."

I took my time getting up, moving and touching the moss with as many parts of my body as I could. To make a test, I swirled the edge of my oro bow across the surface—there was no light. The three Jannanons encircled me, and I could feel their impatience; even the light at their feet lessened and became darker.

"These fields of spillets continue onto and past the Dairs. You will not be leaving them, but we must go," they said. I felt a small hand at my back, nudging me in that direction. I nodded, and we walked on. I liked the walking so much that I didn't look up when the trees turned from one type to another and then to another. After a while, I felt the hard, true rhythm of Dair Trees, which not only used the wind but also the ground to talk. Even when they were silent, their core beat so strongly, it felt as though words were forming.

When I did look up, we were on a ridge overlooking a shallow valley where the Dairs grew, many and many of them. To the surprise of my companions, I stopped and stomped my feet. It was a greeting stomp that the Dairs would understand, a greeting that asked permission to come near. There was a small patch of Dairs on the Peninsula, but no one dared to grow a kollokk in one. The Dairs were well known for their sense of superiority and sensitivity. One needed to show respect or accept that the Dairs might punish you. I would hate to climb into a Dair that I had insulted. In that case, as you walked, their branches would twist just enough to make you lose your footing. As you climbed, a leaf at the end of a twig could poke you in an eye to blind you. Then as you slept, their limbs would become too weak to hold you. So, I stomped and waited for their welcome.

They knew the stomp came from a stranger, a stranger who could move unlike a tree. Momentarily, the Dair beats in the earth became a jumble of confusion and curiosity, which was one of their weaknesses.

"Who?" This one-word question meant, 'Explain yourself'.

I took two steps in their direction and stomped that I must approach to explain, that my language was ancient and odd, and I could be mistaken from my stomps alone.

"Carefully." They meant to approach slowly and with reverence.

I turned to the three. "Walk behind me in a line as silently as you know how. Stop when I stop. Kneel when I kneel. Do not say a word."

I started down the hill toward the grove, and the Jannanons gracefully came behind, silent as stars. We headed slowly down, my eyes to the earth where the spillets were busy lighting my way. My eyes lowered not to see the light but to show respect; and, somehow, I could feel the three little heads behind me bent toward the ground as well.

"Enough." The Dairs meant that this was close enough and that they could hear and see me from there. I stopped and knelt, and the Jannanons did the same.

"May I grow here?" I blew and swayed, hoping that the Bent Tree expression was known there.

"You are the beast that speaks and whose roots are not in the earth. The wind has brought news of you. You may grow here."

I stood in order to be more eloquent and blew, "I am a man beast, and these three are also man beasts. We wish to spend the dark among your boughs."

"You wish to sleep in us?" one of the Dairs blew back. I could not tell which tree to address. Their voices seemed to come from every direction and no direction, especially when a word came through the ground and up through my feet.

"We wish to sleep in your limbs and branches. I carry a bed sling, but the other man beasts have nothing. If they sleep on the ground, I was told they will be harmed."

The Dairs sank into a conversation of low rumbles that I could not follow or understand, but it was evident they were considering the request and attempting to find a way to help. What I had smelled was a concern for our safety. They were rough, and I felt small among them, not because of their size but because of their temperament. If they would allow us to climb up into them, we would be safe. I was certain they had ways to defend against any beasts. The rumble slowed and stopped; then one tree spoke.

"There are bird dwellings not used for long and long, but still having their form. We will lead you to them."

"My friends are small, but not so small as birds," I pointed out.

"These were woven by the Great Rods," the trees answered. "Each man beast can fit in one. There are three dwellings still strong enough."

"I will tell and make them know," I told the trees so they would be patient with us.

I turned about to face the Jannanons, all three still kneeling, their heads bent, listening to my strange conversation with the Dairs that they couldn't follow but had been trying to understand. They looked up in unison with placid faces.

"We can stay in the trees tonight," I said. The three took in my words and looked to each other, concerned and anxious. "They have giant bird nests for the three of you. I don't think you can hide from anything on this ground with the spillets underneath you."

The Jannanons looked down and around them, and the reason was obvious that what I said was true. They didn't want to climb into the trees or sleep in a nest of a giant bird, though I could see that they understood that they had no choice.

"Even the lowest branches are high. How can we

even begin to climb into those trees?" they asked, wishing that I had no answer.

"Near there." I pointed to trees a short distance away, "There are trees that still grow low. We will climb into them and walk across the branches, tree to tree. The Dairs will lead us through to the nests, and I will find a bough to make my sling. You have never slept in a tree, and I have never slept on the ground; but I can't dream that sleeping on this hard earth could be anywhere near as comforting as sleeping in the arms of a tree. You may never want to come back down again."

"We want to be down already," the sad little men said, relenting. "But let's have our meal first. We will try to sleep there but we refuse to prepare food and eat up there."

I explained to the trees that we would accept their generous offer of protection among their limbs, but that we would have our meal on the ground before climbing into the lowest branches. I asked if it would be safe to wait, and they assured me that we had time before the hunting beast came to find us. It would have smelled us, and it would have followed us. But it was not near yet; they made that clear. As I spun around to tell the Jannanons that the trees would be waiting, I saw that they had already spread a cloth upon which were dried meats, dried fruits, stalks of green edible plants, and four empty cups. The youngest Jannanon grabbed the cups and stood. On my face must have been enough wonder for them to explain to me.

Wind

"There is a stream just ahead. Fresh water," they said, as the youngest held the cups up. The cups were nothing like we had across the river. These had intricate designs, were made of metal, and were impossibly thin yet sturdy. Our knives were metal, but metal for us was so difficult to make that we never wasted it on something to drink from; everything we ate off was wood, wood given to us by the trees.

The youngest, purple-eyed one ran in the direction of the stream that we all could hear. Each of his footsteps was punctuated by white light that I still enjoyed and thought I would never stop liking. The spillet light that came from under us as we sat lit the meal in a soft, underbelly way. My first meal away from the Peninsula had not one part of it that I could have imagined that dew light. Where had they kept the food on their little bodies? Under their long cloths, surely, but I never saw anything as they walked or knelt or sat. And the cloth itself, what was it made of? I took the end of the spread on the ground and felt it between two fingers. It was completely different from the animal hide watchets and sit upons we made for our ourselves to wear, and nothing like the grass-woven bed sling or bale that carried my arrows. I rubbed and stared at it, trying to see what plant or animal could have formed this.

"Have you never felt cotton?" the two Jannanons asked, and it was strange now to hear a sentence from just two voices.

"No," I replied, making it plain that I understood that what they wore and the cloth on which we were about to eat was something called cotton. "What sort of animal is cotton?" I wanted to know.

"Not an animal, it's a plant. A plant that blooms into tiny white balls that can be woven into strings like the one on your bow, but small and smaller."

I took a closer look at the cloth and could see the strings, marvelous little strings that intertwined into a whole that moved and flowed like water. Our weaving--the weaving of grass into bed slings, bales, bonnets, bands, and straps that took my ancestors generations to learn--was crude set against the delicacy of the cotton.

"This is coarse cotton, but you will see finer cloth when we come to the villages and towns and cities on our way," the two said, apologizing for the beautiful, wondrous cotton I held in my hands. "There is cloth where we are going that is made of worm threads, soft and strong like liquid metal, lighter than the wind that keeps the wearer cool in the hot months." My mind went numb trying to reason what could be finer than this cotton, which I now felt was too beautiful to place food upon. I looked at my own rough coverings and, for the first time, was not happy with what I saw.

"What will these people in the cities think of me?" I said, indicating the hides that I was wearing.

"They will be impressed by you, frightened of you, wary of you, and they will not come close to you." My question back was written on my face—Why? The two looked at one another, making a hard decision of some kind. Finally, the older one nodded. "You have an aroma that makes it difficult to breathe."

"You say I have a bad odor about me?" I shook my head in disbelief. "I've always been told I smell sweetly."

"Perhaps to another Tor'oc, and to us it is passable; but we have been on the road and in the fields and the woods for weeks and we must have an aroma, too."

"I look like an animal, and I have the odor of an animal. How can I be a part of this Camarod, or even walk on the road of the most humble village?" I asked.

"We will bathe you when we can, and what you're wearing can be aired and perfumed—perhaps for several days," they said meekly, not wanting to insult or upset me any further.

I nodded to myself, "That will have to do, I guess."

The young Jannanon returned, and we ate in silence. I didn't want to hear anything more about myself. The three ate carelessly, whereas I was anxious not to drop a crumb or a drip on the cotton. As I ate, one word in their talk annoyed and frightened me—'weeks' is what they talked about. Iz had told me the city of the Camarod was days away. Yes, weeks were made of days, but now I knew it would be enough days to make weeks, and maybe enough weeks to make months. I had been tricked; it was a tricky world this side of the river. I reasoned that would not be the last time I would be tricked.

At the end of the silent meal, the food, the cups,

and the cotton were folded away and hidden under the long cloths they wore. There wasn't a bulge or bump to see, considering that the three small men were carrying so much around their bodies. I signaled that it was time for us to climb into the trees. They stood and followed behind me until I reached a low branch of a young Dair that I could grab and pull myself onto. The three gazed up at the branch that was still too high for them.

"I will hoist each of you up, and you will climb to the middle of the trunk where there is a safe place to sit until we are all in the tree," I said, pointing to the path along the branch that I wanted them to take and to the place I wanted them to stay and wait for me. This was the first time that I had spoken since understanding that I smelled bad to them, and my voice was sterner than I wanted it to be.

I grabbed the youngest one because I believed he would be more willing to climb along the branch, and that might give the other two the confidence to follow him. As I picked him up and lifted him past my face and up to the branch, I saw that he was holding his breath, and in an instant, I became angry and I wanted to drop him, preferably on his head. But it was not his fault that he could not breathe my smell; and I had to admit that this close, I didn't like his aroma either. I pushed him up a little faster than was necessary, and he hit the tree hard with the top of his head, making a cracking noise. I apologized to the tree but said nothing to the little man, feeling ashamed that I was acting like a child.

"Hang onto the branch and pull up your feet," I

said, softening my emotions. He followed my words and got onto the branch surprisingly quickly, scooting along to make room for his companions. I waited until he was far along and close to the trunk before picking up the next one. This time, I stared above us to where I was about to put him, in order not to see his mouth closed, his chest tight, and his nose scrunched up in a way to allow in as little accidental air as possible. The third one was up soon after the second. All three made their way to the trunk before I thanked the tree for accepting my companions and asking permission for myself to climb.

The young Dair thumped, "Come."

Once I joined the three, I told them to stay with me and that I would travel through the trees slowly enough for them to be able to follow. The trees blew a path to me; the smells inside the wind were a map on which I could see each branch to take, leading me higher, higher, and farther into the grove where the tallest trees stood, whose lowest branches were five Tor'ocs from the ground. The scent map also showed where we would find the Great Rod nests and a safe place for me to sling my bed.

The path through these great trees was easily done before I could think of it, but the little men behind me were wet from head to feet in their own moisture and breathing hard. The light from the moon and the stars was enough to show us the branches we walked and crawled on, but not bright enough to show us the ground when we stopped at the first nest. All four of us examined where the great birds had laid their eggs and grown their young. The nest was large enough for a single Jannanon to sleep in. These birds must be giants, I thought. They would dwarf the largest birds of prey on the Peninsula. It was hard to imagine what they must look like. I very much wanted to see one, just not now, and did not want one to come back to these nests that looked old and abandoned but strong. The trees blew to me the places to find the other two nests, surprisingly and happily close. We made our way to the second nest where we settled the Jannanon with the green eyes. The youngest one then followed me to the highest nest at a spot where the branches split into three boughs heavy enough to support my sling. We made our beds, the young one in his nest, and me in my sling.

I lay down and smiled, smiled to feel the comfort of a tree that swayed in a gentle warm breeze. I closed my eyes and imagined that I was home in my kollokk, safe among other Tor'ocs, my body at last releasing the exhaustion that had been building since the fire.

The fire – I had woken to the fire and was already not the same Aeon the Leaf, he who fought the fire and now came to lie in the Out World, trying to calm himself to sleep. There had unfolded the dream of the fire, and then the waking fire, and entering the threatening water, then taking back a water fee from the river, and the thing convincing me to leave my steady life, then flying through the Divul in a bowl of fees, and talking to the old Bent Tree, then meeting the shadowy Jannanons with their visions of a Far Road beyond something

Wind

called Foul Lands, and wading through the glowing spillets, and finding the nests of the giant birds. These events had the feeling of moons and moons of experiencing and changing. How could it all have happened in the selfsame day? That was a wonder. I feared that the Out World would unveil itself to be a place offering no end to wonders.

Barry Alexander Brown

3

Black earth burning; burning, smoking, steaming, shuddering black earth; hard, angry black earth. I am walking, running across the flat open plain of black earth, fleeing is how it feels, and the Jannanons are with me, not wearing their long cloths now but wearing watchets made of tiny flat, silver pebbles sewn together that cover their necks, torsos and arms. The silver on the watchets reflect the bright white light and the flames we are running past. They don't move in unison but separately like any man would. They have weapons - a short, fat sword, a hide sling, and a flat, small, sideways bow that fires arrows from holding the bow across the forearm. We are not alone on this black earth; there are shadows.

    The earth is black and the shadows are blacker; the shadows are running, surrounding us - shadow teeth, shadow claws, shadows unattached to any beasts but they are beasts themselves. The shadows snap and lunge and the Jannanons fight and I fight, striking at the shadows with my bow but not as a bow, as a stick or a club. Shadows, more shadows, so many shadows, out of the ground they jump, and there is no way to fight them all and I am afraid of becoming a shadow myself — I have to keep them away, have to beat them back. There is a secret to defeating them and I don't know it. Then they are screaming, screaming a beast scream and I wake.

    As in the dark before, the scream was not in the dream only - it was in the World. A real scream. The scream bounced through the tree where I was surprised to find myself swinging. Then I remembered some events of yesterday and realized that, although I was in my own bed sling, I was not in my own tree or my home kollokk. I was a Tor'oc away from his home. Confused, my body wanting more sleep, I looked about to find the screamer, and discovered it was not with us in the trees--but down below. I grabbed the sides of the bed sling and pulled myself upright, spotting a young, purple-eyed Jannanon, peering down at the ground. When he sensed me, he looked up, his face serious and sleepy, but alert. As the screamer screamed again, he looked down, and I followed his look. About ten Tor'ocs below us, there was something large and red, screaming and

Wind

thrashing at the trunk of the tree; and it sensed me too. The big, red thing looked up; it looked into my eyes, and I jumped back.

It was a man and a beast, and it had the wild, crazed look of a beast that could smell its prey but could not have it. Lying back in my sling, I felt its nails dig into the trunk of the tree that touched the earth and went into it. The skin of the Dair was thick and wasn't being harmed by this beast, but the tree was displeased at the thing and was considering what to do about it. I smelled all that in the aroma of the tree, carried by the breeze. I again rose as the beast stopped its useless attempt to climb.

"What is that?" I asked the Jannanon, who was still looking down.

"It's a Muon," he said simply, as if I should know, then realized how little knowledge I had of anything. "It's part of the Damnation Legend," as if that explained everything.

"It looks like a man," I said, taking in the huge body, that was not red but bathed in the red light from below it, the red light the spillets were glowing as the man-beast moved about on top of them in small, frustrated circles, glancing up and smelling and wanting me just as the Father Tree had warned. I could now see and judge how large it must be—I would be like a Jannanon to it.

"Yes, the Muon are men, or once were men," Weoduye scrunched his face, remembering something. "They were hunters, a race who learned from the great cats to hunt in darkness. Their eyes became like cats' eyes, and they saw in dark as though it were day; then day to them became an impossibility."

The Jannanon fell silent, never taking his eyes off the Muon who thrashed, snarled, and twitched. I had already gotten used to the three-voiced sentences of my companions, and listening to the young one's solitary voice was offbeat and strange because the words came out more halting. I would have thought the opposite would have been true, but without the other Jannanons, each Jannanon had to think and talk on its own, something that probably felt strange to them.

I studied the Muon beneath us. It moved like an animal on all fours but could stand like a man, though it never stood entirely upright. It bent forward in a crouch, craning its neck around whenever it wanted to look up. The muscles of its arms and legs and back moved as an animal moved, and the lines around each muscle were clear to see. This beast was as strong as any wild hunter, stronger and bigger than any Tor'oc. It was naked and hairless like a man, with hair on its head and face, but no hair on the rest of its body. It was dirty; caked mud covered its white skin, white skin that was so unlike the brown of a Tor'oc. My thoughts were that Tor'ocs might become just as white if we never saw light, only dark.

"Are there many of these Muons?" I asked, and it struck me that if this was a race, we might never be rid of them.

"There are very few, and I thought I would never see one," the Jannanon almost stuttered. "When they got the taste for man blood, they were driven into Foul Lands—lifetimes ago. Most died there, but, as you can see, some did not, and those who lived fought their way to this forest. They have never recovered their numbers, and why is not known. It's said they are as rare as the sun and moon in the sky at once."

I stared down at the Muon, thinking of its past, its ancestors' past, which like my own had fled here and had been kept here.

"They hunted and ate men; and they are so large that I can't understand how they were driven out by the men they hunted," I said, but it was a question.

"Their weakness was day, and the strength of our people was daylight. They were found in their hiding places, killed at times, but mainly pushed out into the light, and in blindness they fled across the land into the place where we will come soon," he said, concern in his words.

"This happened lifetimes ago. How do you know this story?" I asked.

"As I said, they are part of the Damnation Legends, and one doesn't grow and reach full height without knowing the Legends," he said, attempting to hide the shock of my ignorance, but it was there in his voice.

"And are the Tor'ocs part of the Damnation Legends?" I wanted to know and not know in the same breath.

"You are the first and greatest and most frightening part." The words came quickly, and the

Jannanon was embarrassed at having to say them. "The Tor'ocs were worse than the hunters who hunted and ate men." I did not like that thought.

"Do all of the Legends end here, on this side of Foul Lands?" I asked.

"No, only two," The purple-eyed one said, and nodded at me and then toward the thing below. "You and him. Foul Lands was the end of the third legend."

"Yoooooouuuuuu!" was the scream that came from the beast on the ground. Had it really screamed "you" at me, or did I put that sound in the scream? I looked down to see it, and its hateful eyes tore into me even from that distance.

A short distance away, a small animal ran across the edge of the moss, lighting the spillets in greens and yellows. The Muon saw it as I saw it, and with no more than a glance in our direction, it ran on hands and feet, covering the distance between itself and the little animal. I could still see the green and yellow flashes that were being followed by red explosions as the Muon hit the moss, using its greatest weapons—speed and hunger. The green and yellow flashes zigged and zagged, while the red explosions kept a steady line, closing in. The little animal must have left the moss with the spillets as the green and yellow flashes disappeared, though the red line of explosions continued for another few counts, and then were gone. In an even shorter count, a screech bounced through the trees, the screech of an animal caught in the teeth of a hunter, no doubt shredded into bits, bits swallowed whole—muscle, hair, and bone. I looked in the direction of the screech, searching the air for other sounds, sounds of the Muon, but it was silent. Perhaps Muons drag their meals somewhere and eat in a private place. It was not returning, and I didn't think that it would, not that dark.

I turned back to the young Jannanon, who was gazing off in the same direction, the direction of the kill. He looked back at me, but his look was far away as well as inward, and he whispered, "This is a rare, rare day."

"For me, every moment is rare since I left my trees," I said, to break him out of his thoughts.

"I have seen a Muon." He glanced toward me as he came out of his reverie. "I have seen a Muon hunt and heard its kill as I sat in the nest of a Great Rod, while close to and talking to a Tor'oc. I was told when I was chosen that I would see and hear jiffies that were beyond my familiarities and understandings and that would alter me, separately and alone. I did not believe them, and in the first day and dark with you, it has already happened." There was fear and wonder and sadness in those words.

I waited for him to continue, but he didn't; he just sat as he was, staring past me off into the dark where the green, yellow, and red flashes had disappeared. The Jannanons were connected to one another, by their strength and their comfort, but they also had the experience to be their own.

"Do you have a name separate from the others?" I was wondering for the first time about him as a man.

He looked at me, surprised at the question or that I was talking at all. "Do you have your own name?"

"Yes, of course," the young one replied, still not giving me his name.

"What is it—your name. Or is it really just a personifier, like The Leaf?"

"We do not have personifiers. That would be against the current of what it is to be a Jannanon. My name is Weoduye Jannanon."

"Weoduye—does that mean something?" I asked.

"It's a name of my family. No two living Jannanons can have the same name; it is part of the way we know one another." I guessed that he meant connected to one another. "There was a Weoduye generations before me. That Weoduye Jannanon has his name recorded in the Damnation Legends."

This made me sit up straighter, and I smiled; the Tor'ocs and the Muons are not alone as damned things. "So, the Jannanons are in the Damnation Legends as well."

Weoduye looked at me, clearly not liking my smile that included him. "We are in the Legends....as heroes, not as the damned. After these days, my name may be there, too."

"The Legends are not finished and over and old?" What kind of legend is that? I was wondering.

"They were, but now the story has continued."

"What story?" I asked, hoping for a real answer.

"The one we are living," he said with finality, and with that he slid back down into his nest.

He was hidden, but I knew he could still hear me. "Is there a city that you're from?"

"Yes." The voice traveled over the edge of the nest.

"Is it just Jannanons?"

"Yes, just Jannanons."

"Will I see this Jannanon city?" I asked, hoping that I would.

"It is the second to last city on the Far Road, so you will see another city first," his voice answered.

I settled back into my sling, wanting to ask one more thing before giving myself to sleep. "Can I call you Weoduye?"

"Yes, now that you know it."

"And call me Aeon...not The Leaf."

"Aeon," was his last response.

I didn't know how, but, in that instant, I knew that each Jannanon had to tell you his name. I could not get the name of a Jannanon from someone else; and out of respect, normally I would not tell Weoduye's name without his permission. I used it in my telling because later, when he was still breathing, he told me I could. After that thought, I let myself relax into the woven grass of my bed and sank deeply into sleep and dream.

When the dew was already dry, I woke abruptly. A hazy memory emerged of a dream in which I was walking across the moss-covered spillets, walking carefully, but their white and blue glow illuminated and exposed me. I tried not to make a sound or draw attention. In the dream I tried to climb a tree but couldn't – very unsettling.

When I woke, I searched the Great Rod's nest for Woeduye and found it empty. Directly below me, I saw the three Jannanons sitting and waiting, a meal spread on the beautiful cloth that I would never have dared place on the ground. I rose, folded my bed sling, and, carrying all that I had in this land, made my way through the trees down to them. As I moved along the branches and limbs, I thanked the many Dairs for their comfort and for their protection. The trees blew back their pleasure of having me among them.

I approached my three companions and greeted them the way I would friends on the Peninsula, "Dew light finds you dry and fed."

They nodded back to me in unison. I nodded to each of them individually, coming to the youngest, I said, "Weoduye." The other two, jolted and shocked, spun their heads to look at Weoduye and then back to me, a question in their eyes—"How did this happen?" I had never seen the three of them, so close to one another, move without all three moving together. Weoduye sat removed from the others, his eyes lowered, his body expressing the sorrow he felt for his betrayal of protocol.

"We were all hunted the last dark," Weoduye began alone; and I believed he was saying these words so I could hear them as well. "As you know, it will not be the last dark or day that we are the prey. We will be traveling with Aeon the Tor'oc for days beyond we know. We will fight together, and we may die together. He should know our names."

The two sat and looked at Weoduye in their stern, silent way. They held that same stare for many counts until the older Jannanon turned his eyes to me and stood, an action he did alone.

"Sheios." He bowed and sat back down.

The last Jannanon stood. "Goyel," he almost whispered, bowed as his friend had, and took his place again on the ground.

"Weoduye, Sheios, Goyel," I nodded to each as I said their names. "I look to the days and darks and I am glad to be among you. May we grow strong together." I used the word day – we Tor'os know the word day but rarely use it except to say 'day end'. We use the word light.

Sheios was the first to smile, and then Weoduye and finally Goyel. They smiled with their entire bodies; it's the only way I know how to relate this. It was a force like the wind; it came from them, embraced me, and welcomed me for the first time. I sat down among them, smiling back and wishing it could be with my entire body. Then we ate our meal.

I made my farewell to the Dairs and thanked them again. They rumbled back, inviting me to return to them, indicating that they would much enjoy if, when I did return, that I'd stay and grow there with them in their boughs. I laughed with my fingers and said that was a pleasure to hear. Then my companions and I -

they were really my companions now - set off for Far Road.

As we left the moss and the light of the spillets, the Jannanons assured me it wouldn't be the last field of spillets that I would walk on. I had turned and was taking my steps backwards, looking back at the moss when they said this. I had to believe them, but still I didn't want to leave the magic of this invisible life that gave light.

The land of this dew light was much like the land back across the river. There were the sorts of trees that I knew, land that rolled away, folding down and up, animal paths beaten down by generations and generations that made it easy to walk through the under bush; and just like in the high earth at home, the bird song was the same bird song. It felt so similar that I could forget that this was not the Peninsula, that I had not slept in my own kollokk, that I was traveling to cities that were not built in trees, and from which I might not return. At times, I walked with my eyes closed to just smell the familiarity; and then I was sure I was home, until I heard a rarely audible footstep by one of the Jannanons.

Jannanons were stepping into bushes and picking seed pouches off a plant—the one plant I did not know. They picked the pouches, and then those dry, little, brown pouches would disappear into a place under their long cloths. They picked without losing their rhythm or missing a step and they picked with reverence to the plant, trying not to hurt it any more than necessary. I wondered if we would be eating them later and I picked one, brought it to my nose, lowered the seed sack to my lips, and opened my mouth to take a bite -- when a hand swatted the pouch away. The three Jannanons had stopped and were staring at me.

"Do not eat that; it would kill you," they said, then turned and walked on.

I was almost too surprised to even form the question, "Then why are you picking them?" They did not bother to answer but turned and walked. I continued following them along the animal path, certain that by day end, I would find out why the Jannanons wanted so many non-edible seeds. I was curious to hear the name of the plant, but I also could wait to find out later.

I smelled water and that made reason to me — most animal paths led to water. The path led down a hill, and I could see in my inner eye a beautiful small lake like the ones with fresh water on the Peninsula. These lakes were always cold and clear, and the water was fresher than any other water on the land; but we were shy of water at home and never went far into a lake. Tor'ocs could not swim, or try to swim, or want to try to swim. However, I liked the water and was tempted to go farther and try, but the first thought of how to do it was a mystery that I couldn't solve. When alone, I would walk farther and farther into a lake, nearly far enough for the water to cover my body, and then I would go no farther, my mind a white light with nothing in it, nothing emerging to tell me how to move the water so it would lift me. I was certain that it could, but how to make it happen was not known to me. I asked the trees, and they knew less than I did.

We came out from under the trees that formed the edge of the forest we had walked through since leaving the Dairs. Before us was a lake, as I knew there would be, but this lake was not like any I had grown with—this water stretched and stretched, and I could not see its end. I could see something across but even that was only recognizable by small outlines of rocks or so I thought it might be rocks, maybe islands. Was this a lake or perhaps a calm sea? I walked down to the edge, put my hand in the water, and it felt like a lake. I scooped water into my hand and tasted—it tasted like a lake and not salty like the seas and the river. Maybe this is a new sea or new river that was fresh, but I could not reason how we could cross it.

"What kind of water is this?" I asked the Jannanons, who must have crossed it and knew it already.

"A lake. Don't you have lakes in the Eastern prison?"

"We do, but nothing so big as this." I marveled that a lake could grow so large. "I don't see the path that leads us around it."

"This lake is larger than you can reason, and we cannot go around it; we have to cross it," they explained.

"And how do we do that? Fees?" I asked, wondering if that was something I wanted to do again.

"The water is deep, and there are no fees. You will see soon, but at this jiff, we have something else for you," they said, smiling and walking along the edge of the lake and then back in away from the water. They were moving toward a light smoky mist that was rising beyond a short wall of bushes. We found a way around the bushes, only to be stopped at the rock end of a small pool that was full of steaming water. I could see that water bubbled up from beneath, and the steam was greatest where the bubbled water hit the surface. At the other end, the water spilled over its edge, forming a stream that flowed into the lake.

I was taking in this little, steaming lake when the Jannanons passed me, wearing nothing, but holding the dry, brown seed pouches in their hands and hurrying into the water. Each sat as soon as they found a place. They weren't smiling, but their faces relaxed into a dreamy state. They looked up at me, waiting for me to join them. I thought that if little Jannanons weren't afraid of the steaming water, how could a Tor'oc hesitate? I did what they did—took off my watchet and sit upons and walked into the pool, found a spot, and sat.

This was not water; this was liquid light. I had never felt warm or hot water in such abundance, enough water to lie in, to move about like flying; and this water lifted me without being tricked into doing it. I could relax even more in this water than I could in my bed sling, and where the water came from beneath, the force of it could hold me more as easily. I looked toward the three to see if they were as happy as a Tor'oc in this steam water and found that they were rubbing the seed pouches in their hands. The seeds were turning into froth, like the foam left at the edge of land by the O'bir

Sea. Weoduye made his way to me, holding out the froth for me to take.

"Aeon, this is soap. Rub this into you, all over," he said, pushing the white froth, that was thicker and heavier than it looked, into my hands.

"What will it do to me?" I asked and held the froth away and up from the water.

"It cleans you. You need cleaning. We all do."

"Will that make my odor better to you?"

The three Jannanons smiled a 'yes' back to me. I rubbed my hands together as they did, increasing the size of the froth; and then, following how they put it on their own bodies, I smeared it on myself and rubbed as hard as they were rubbing. It felt nice, not as nice as the liquid light, but my skin liked the cleaning and the froth, and liked everything about being in the steaming pool. I didn't know how we were going to get across the great water in front of us and didn't care, as long as I could stay in this water longer and longer.

"Is this the only small, hot lake in Aemira?" I asked, and if the answer was to be yes, I didn't know if I wanted to go any further.

"Like the spillets, there are many more," they assured me. "There is even hot water in large, man-made bowls that would even fit you to sit." I was certain this was not a true thing they were telling me but thought that they had sensed I might not go on with them unless my visions could be filled with the hope of this steaming water again.

Wind

They rose from the pool in unison, and I stayed while they made the mid-meal. There were many disturbing things in this new world, like the Muons and Foul Lands that we were heading toward, but there were marvelous things as well, and my reason was that there were more marvels to come beyond my reason. I would have to get out of this wonderful water to find the other marvels. If that thought had not come to me, I think I might still be in that pool, or near it.

I stood naked at the edge of the pool looking for my coverings, but they were not where I had left them. I was certain the Jannanons had done something with them and walked out to a large flat rock where I could lie down and dry myself in the light. I was still tired from my last two darks of rudely wakened sleep, and I let myself fall into a rest where I hoped I would not dream, dreams being more unsettling these past two darks.

They let me sleep, and when I woke my watchet and sit upons were next to me and folded around tiny, light blue flowers that perfumed the coverings with their scents. I slid my legs into the sit upons and my arms through the watchet, smelling the hide as it fell over my face and down across my chest and stomach. They had never smelled so sweet, and this aroma would melt into my skin as well. I could sense the Jannanons nearby, waiting for me to join them for the mid-meal. They wouldn't eat until we all could eat; that was the Jannanon way.

I sat and chewed the dried meat and fruit and a new kind of leaf that they wrapped around the meat to make it taste different. This must be a plant that grew along the lake, as I hadn't seen them pick anything but seed pouches, and this leaf was fresh. As I finished, all three approached to take my empty, metal cup, but they really came to smell me. They were hiders and they hid this intention well, even when they moved too close, aiming their noses over my body. I let them.

"Is it pleasing enough?" I asked, and the three looked at me with the innocence of children, as if not knowing my meaning. "Could I lift you into a tree without you closing your noses?"

"Oh...yes, yes, yes," they each said. "Your coverings will need more flowers, but your aroma is much kinder—much kinder."

The steaming water, the sleep on the rock in the light, and then the mid-meal had relaxed me to my bones. I leaned back on an elbow and looked out across the water that showed no end to our left or right.

"If there are no fees, and the water is deep, and I cannot swim, then how do we cross?" I asked, looking from one to another of the short men.

"We have a boyt," they answered.

"A what?"

"A boyt—it floats on water, and we get in it," they explained, thinking this would be enough for me.

"It floats on water like a water bird does, and we get in it?" I asked, not seeing at all this boyt they were talking about.

"No, not like a water bird. It is more a long bowl made from the body of a tree."

"And where do we find this boyt?" I could not reason how such a thing could be made or found.

"We carved it before on the far side of the lake and moved across the lake in it. We hid it where we could find it."

They had killed a tree in order to make their boyt to get to me. I felt responsible and angry that they had needlessly hurt a tree. "The tree did not have to die for me. You should not have carved your boyt," I said, and they could hear the anger in my words.

"The tree was dead, which is why we chose it." They were telling a truth; I could hear that. "Burned by some fire, probably the fire from the sky. That wood makes the best boyt—dry, easier to carve, and better to hold back the water. We dragged the body of the burned tree for many arpents because we knew of the lake and knew we needed a boyt."

"Can I see this boyt?" I believed them that the tree had been burned and dead before they carved it, but I wasn't certain I would get in it and move out onto that water.

The tree trunk was lying on its side, hidden under dead branches and dead leaves the Jannanons had gathered from the ground nearby. They pulled the trunk out, turned it over, and I saw what they had done—dug out the other side where the fire had ended the tree, dug it down deep and wide enough for a man to sit down in it, even a man as big as I was. They let me touch the body of the tree—the boyt—long enough to see that I was satisfied that everything they had told me was true.

They pulled the trunk to the water and pushed it out to show that it would not go beneath the water but stay on top, like a water bird.

"We will have to go soon. The Muon will smell us here, and there are no large Dairs to sleep in at this water's edge," they told me, as though I had not noticed.

"The light is low already," I said, looking at the sky. "Can this boyt take us across before the dark?"

"No."

I waited to hear more. I was not going to get into this dead tree and stay floating in it in the dark in the mid of that great water. I started to walk away to find a tree that would be safe to spend the dark in.

"There is an island that we can make before the dark," they said, all three pointing toward a black patch of something far away in the lake. "The Muon can swim but it won't because it won't know we are there. Once it loses our smell at the water's edge, it will turn back," they said, and they could read on my face that I didn't believe them. "It can't reason where we have gone. It won't search for us. It will go hunt for an easier prey."

I looked at the black patch, trying to make it out. "Is there a tree on that island?"

They hesitated before answering, "Maybe a small one."

"You are telling me it's not big enough to sleep in."

"We did not sleep there on the way across. There is a tree; we don't know how big, but not big," they said, hoping that what will be will be.

"Then let's find out how big it is," I said, moving back to get my bow, knife, and satchel.

They kept the boyt near the land for me to step into it in my awkward way, nearly rolling the entire tree boyt over and me over with it. I finally threw the oro bow and bale of arrows into the boyt first, and then dove over the edge, landing at the bottom of it with a grunt. The Jannanons, who were so much smaller, slipped into the boyt without trouble. Weoduye was in the front, Goyel in the middle, and Sheios in the back where I lay, still trying to find the balance of the thing. I thought that if I looked to the bottom of the hollowed-out trunk, then I could find the balance; maybe it was there. We were moving, gliding. I felt that, and I looked up past Goyel to Weoduye, who was standing, leaning forward and pulling something through the water, and that something was what moved us. I looked around, and Sheios, on his knees, was doing the same motion with something in his hand that looked like the handle of long wooden blade. He pulled back, lifted, pushed forward, and back again in rhythm with Weoduye. They pushed the water backwards to move the boyt forwards. I pulled myself up by holding onto the edges of the boyt and was amazed at how far we had already traveled away from the land.

"You have never been on the water before." Sheios made it both a question and a statement.

"Until two lights ago, I had never been deeper than my chest, and until this breath I had never been awake and wholly in water," I replied, looking about and out to the water that passed to our sides and under us. "Gliding on top of water has never even appeared in my dreams."

"But you Tor'ocs on the Eastern Prison Island are surrounded by water—how did you not conquer it the way you did everything else?" He was talking without the other two even taking notice or joining with their voices.

"Sheios, how are you talking alone with Goyel and Weoduye so close?"

"It's the lake. There's a confusion on the water, and the touch between us is broken." He gazed across the water. "If we three were in the water together, the touch would be the strongest, stronger than land. It is the fight between the air and the water that creates the confusion of sound. But what is the problem between the water and you?"

"The water around our Peninsula is deadly," I replied, and that seemed to be all Sheios had to hear. "Can you show me how to work the blade? I would like to learn to move the boyt forward."

Sheios pulled the blade out of the water, and I was surprised at the length of it and how far the blade must have been driven into the lake. He handed me the blade to show me how to hold it and how to push it through. When I knelt as he had and pushed the other end into the water, my arms struggled to pull the blade back. I glanced at Sheios—he was more powerful than I had thought.

"At the end of the stroke, raise the paddle out of the water to put it forward," Sheios instructed and I did.

He showed me how to use my whole body to pull and not just my arms. In a short count, I understood, and the boyt took on speed. Weoduye turned back to see why we had taken more speed. We were fast enough then that the island was coming more and more quickly to us.

When we reached the island, I thought that we should push on past it and to the other edge of the lake; but the edge was away and away, much farther than we had already come. Weoduye guided us onto the island, jumping out as the land came close and pulling the boyt to the edge. The water was only at his mid, which meant it would be at my knees. I jumped into the water to push the boyt all the way onto the land. I then looked around at our home for the dark. There was a single tree, a tree that might be strong enough for my bed sling and me. I would ask to see if it would welcome me.

The island was big for just one tree. A grove could have grown in the open space of short grass, bushes, and rocks; but there was only the one, crooked tree that had grown to the size of three Tor'ocs and looked as though it would grow no higher. I walked to the nearest branch that twisted and bent down then up again, and I knelt as I did before the Dairs. I stretched my arms out and blew, "I am called The Leaf. May I grow here for the dark?"

The tree was silent—not a thump, not a breeze, not an aroma. I was thinking that perhaps it could not speak or could not understand me. I stood, walked closer, and put my hands around the thin but tough trunk. It was alive and knew I was there. Perhaps it had been alone for so long that it had forgotten how to speak or maybe never learned; it was on an island in mid-lake far from any other trees. I did not want to climb into the tree without its permission, so I chose to try one more time.

I gestured to myself while I blew and thumped, "The Leaf. I am here as you are."

The leaves of the tree tingled and turned toward me, the roots creaked and thumped back, "Leaf, here as you are."

So, it was a thumper and maybe a thumper only. I thumped the request to climb and know it. It thumped back, "Welcome."

I climbed into the twisted old thing, and I say that not out of disrespect but because it was old, generations and generations old. It was thin and short, and the skin of the tree was hard and sharp, but there was strength in the limbs; the wood had iron in it. I climbed about the tree, and my weight barely moved the branches, even the thinnest ones. Still, the tree had a sway in it as a tree should. I would be happy to sleep in it that coming dark, was my thought, when I felt it thump.

"You are not tree or seed. What are you?"

Wind

I was in the tree and so couldn't use the ground, so I thumped using my hands. "I am man."

"Man—yes," it thumped, and there was consideration of something in that. "There was a man here, here time ago before I was seed and grew."

"What happened to the man?" I thumped.

"Nothing happened. Man is here, still here where my roots near touch it," the tree responded.

I looked about the island, all of which I could see from the tree, but there was no sign of any man-like thing in the earth or on top of it, except for the Jannanons who were setting up their camp. The twisted tree had thumped that the man was where its roots nearly touched it, so the man must be in the earth and had been in the earth when the tree took root to grow as a seed. The tree was talking of a buried man.

"Where is this man?" I asked the tree.

For the first time, the tree used aroma to talk, showing me the bones of the man beneath the earth, and I knew where the buried man was and that the man had been buried with his cloths and his weapons. I climbed down from the tree, feeling myself pulled toward the spot of the dead man, steps away but not so many, and at the center, the highest point of the island. I stood at the edge of the grave of the buried man, knowing it was the edge and looking for any sign of him. He must be buried deep; the land was the same across the entire island, low grass, rocks, a small wild berry bush that had fought to keep its grip in the soil. The wind must be fierce across the island at times and hard on little plants like this. Beneath a branch of the bush, there was a rock that looked different from all the others; it was rust brown with a ruined quality to it. I bent, brushed it off, pulled it from the ground and picked it up. It was not a rock but a man-made iron half bowl with an odd handle that had mostly rusted away. I felt someone at my elbow.

"You have found a helmet," Weoduye said.

"What kind of bowl is a helmet?" I asked, turning the thing in my hands and knocking the dirt out from the hollow.

"It's not a bowl. It's for the head, a warrior's head." He knew exactly what it was.

"Then it's a warrior buried here." I moved my hand to show the spot where I knew he lay.

"Look," Weoduye said, pointing to something that also looked like metal sticking up from the ground and hidden by a clump of wild onions—it was the butt of something that did not belong there. I reached down and touched it, smooth, cold, and with none of the pocks and pits as were on the helmet. It was still smooth, though hard wind and rain and the earth had been at it for all this long and long. I pulled at the end of this metal thing, but it was dug in as though it had grown there. I could only get one hand around it. I grabbed the piece and, with the strength of my arms and legs, I pulled back and up, and the earth rose beneath me. I was standing on it; the shape was long and wide and rested just under the surface of the ground. I widened my feet to give this buried metal space to be tugged out of the earth. I bent back over the butt, grabbed with both hands, as now enough of it was showing from its grave, and pulled. The earth let go--and I tumbled, hitting the island earth with my back; the thing flew at me and struck me across the head as we both landed.

Still on my back, I lifted the thing up and away to see what I had unearthed. It was a long metal stick, nearly as long as I was, around which were bones of an animal that were tied together, and strips of hide pulled over the bones where hide still existed. It was a type of large plate or shallow bowl, and the long stick had been under this and tied to it at the bone plate's flat end. Weoduye was over me and gazing down at the stick and plate. I looked at him, wondering if he knew what it was, and by his expression I believed he did. He saw the question on my face.

"It's a shield," he said in his halting way. Away at the camp, not far away, Sheios and Goyel looked up and over to us and said together, "A shield?" They stood and in unison came our way. "It's a shield and a spear," Weoduye was talking as much to himself and the other Jannanons as he was to me.

I sat up, and as I did, this thing Wecduye had called a shield crumbled into pieces of bone, rotten hide, and strips of leather that were barely more than dust. I stood, still holding the long metal stick he called a spear, and wiped the dirt off it as best I could with just my hand. The metal of the spear was nothing like the helmet. Except for some dirt, the spear looked untouched by wind or rain or earth. It was longer than the Jannanons but not as long as me. Bordering the lean, long sides there were inscriptions and marks that seemed too smooth to have been carved. In the mid of the spear, there was a grip for a hand. As I touched the grip, my fingers found their way around it. The thing had a balance to it that made it feel light and easy in my hand.

"May we see it?" the three Jannanons asked, again talking as one. They reached out and took the spear from me, holding it with their six hands, gazing down at it, each one of them taking in the part of the spear that was directly below their eyes.

"Do you know what this is, this spear?" I asked them, looking from one face to the next to the next, none of them looking back up but rather examining the long metal stick.

"Yes," they replied, not wanting to say much more than that for the moment as the spear seemingly caused them to be agitated. "It was made for a Warrior Chief, long long ago." Sheios pointed at a symbol in the part that he was holding.

"Do you think the warrior is buried here, then?" I asked, nodding at the hole where the spear and shield had rested.

The three handed the spear back to me, knelt down where the earth was loose and soft, and opened and moved the dirt away with their hands, exposing the once white, now brown bones of a man. They carefully brushed more dirt away until looking up at us, was a skull of a small person. But how could someone handle this spear that would have been longer than itself?

"Is this the Warrior Chief?" I asked, knowing that it wasn't but wanting the Jannanons to tell me what they knew, what they were too disturbed not to know, and what they knew but did not want to tell.

"This is a child, a boy—look at his cloth," they said, indicating the rags of the cloth that barely covered the dead boy's chest of bones.

"What else do you see?" Sensing they knew even more and were not saying what they knew and did not want to tell me what they saw.

"He was a Tor'oc."

"A Tor'oc," I said to myself, bending down to the dirt of the open grave, reaching my left hand in to touch the forehead of the skull. "Do you know how he was buried here?"

"This ground is old. He has been here generations and generations and generations." They were fighting to keep something from me.

"He was a Tor'oc who died here," I said, understanding the meaning of generations and generations.

The Jannanons said, in their way when they would prefer not to say anything, "A thousand years ago, he died crossing this lake to get to the Peninsula."

I moved my hand across the skull and down to the threads of cloth that remained, feeling them in my fingers, feeling my nation's past when we were warriors. It had all been a myth to me, the warrior nation, the flight to the Peninsula, the flood, the birth of the Divul, the Mad'la, the taking to the trees, the generations who built the city in the trees, the change in the character of my people. Deeply, I believed that none of this was true, that we had always lived in the trees and always had been peaceful and thoughtful and had always known how to shape and grow a kollokk, how to farm, how to forge iron, and that our cloths had always been made of hides, our bed slings made of woven grass. Here, I was touching cloth that was like the smooth cloth of the Jannanon's, and holding a long spear made not of iron but of some fine metal that time and earth could not alter. He was a Tor'oc, and yet so different from me.

"This is a boy." I looked down and across the spear. "If not the Warrior Chief, then why would he have this buried with him?" I asked, looking at the Jannanons for an answer.

I could see in their expressions that they were not sure, but they thought they knew. The three sat in silence, considering what they knew with certainty, what they thought could be, and what they might wish to tell me. With a sigh, they gave in to telling me everything. "The Warrior Chief placed the shield and the spear here. We think this was his son."

"You are Jannanons; how do you know any of this? And do not tell me this was all in the Damnation Legends." My voice rose louder as emotions gripped me, tossing me about inside. "Or is this one of the legends—a famous chief and a famous boy?"

"No, we have reasoned this—it is not part of the Legends, not a story that is known, at least." Their eyes turned and rested on the upper part of the spear that was in my hand. "The Warrior Chief, you know him."

They were right; I did, and I said under my breath, "Sumon." I was holding the spear of Sumon, my blood; and in the grave was his son, Morla's brother, my blood. They had good reason to be careful with me. This was a blow. I felt I didn't know anything at that moment, and inside of me there was turmoil. Some part of me that always had been me was tearing, shredding, dissolving; and a new part was growing, forming something in me I didn't know and didn't want. I tossed the spear away.

"How do you know it was Sumon?" I asked, pleading for them to tell me that they were not certain, that they were wishing or guessing.

"We have many Tor'oc weapons and shields and cloths saved from the long and long. They cover the walls of the rooms of the consuls where anyone can go and study them." They paused, allowing the words to penetrate. "All children are versed in the weapons and symbols of the Tor'ocs. If we weren't, we wouldn't understand the Legends. What we know is that every Tor'oc warrior, which was in essence every Tor'oc, had a symbol that they earned in battle, and that symbol became forged into each warrior's weapons.

"Sybils, is what I reason you mean," I said

The Jannanons nodded as they thought this out, "Sybils - symbols - the same, understood. They continued, "Well, the most famous 'sybil' was Sumon's. His was the one woven into the flags that others made and that were flown over their conquered nations. The symbol was carved into gates of their cities, the halls of the fastholds, and even in these days, can be seen in some ancient walls that still stand."

"Do you yourself have Tor'oc weapons?" I asked.

"It is against the law to own a Tor'oc weapon. If one is found, like this one, it must be given to the consuls." They were talking as though this was news that would upset me. "No one has ever found a weapon of Sumon himself. The legends tell us he never lost one, and none were ever taken from him. This is rare, rare."

The three moved to take the spear, which they took from the place I had thrown it and laid it across their three laps. I was glad for them to have it now. I did not want it, did not want to see it, did not want to touch it again. They must have guessed that I felt this. They stood and turned, walking the spear back toward the camp where they wrapped it in the cloth on which we ate, the only cloth long enough to cover it. I joined them later, not wanting to see where they had put the spear, but I could feel it and knew where it lay.

They had made a fire and were cooking white meat over the flames. It was an aroma that I had never experienced, and it made me come back from my thoughts and know that I was hungry, very hungry for cooked meat, even white meat like this that I couldn't recognize.

"What kind of animal is this and when did you hunt it?" I truly didn't know when they could have hunted without me knowing on this small island, and there were no signs of animals besides birds here. I had looked.

"We did not hunt. This is fish from the lake." They saw me grimace as I looked back at the meat over the fire. We had all seen shapes in the water around the Peninsula and knew the name of fish, but no Tor'oc had ever tried to catch one and eat it. The light was low when the fish was done, and we began to eat. It had an unusual taste that I did not like at first bite, but that I liked very much by the time there was no more fish. I asked them to show me how to hunt for fish.

"You don't hunt fish, you fish for fish," they replied.

"Fish for fish, that's against reason," I said. "It is like saying you don't hunt an antelope; you antelope an antelope."

They laughed their three-voiced laugh, which had different notes in it, notes that fit on top of one another like in a song. "Good reason, Aeon, but still the language says that you fish for fish."

I thought to myself that I would come up with a word for it, which is what we do on the Peninsula when we discover that we don't have a name for a thing. I will watch them get their fish, which I am curious to see, and how they do it will give me the word. That is the way it is done, and any Tor'oc can do this, but some are better at it than others; and I was always very skilled. From eating the fish and thinking of how to name the catching of it, my spirits had risen from the depth of the disturbance I felt with the grave and the spear. The

Jannanons built the fire to be higher and warmer, and the four of us lay down around it, gazing into the flames— calm and peace is what each of us felt. The light fell behind the end of the land, and dark was taking the sky.

"Yooooouuuuuu," was the scream that flew across the lake to us from the land where we had taken the warm waters. Unmistakable, it was the Muon crying out for us. The fire would tell it where to find us. There was the lake between us and him, but the Jannanons had said the Muon could swim. The Muon would swim that lake, I thought, and he would have no problem climbing the tree, and we could not leave in dark.

"We have to put out the fire," I said, tossing dirt on it.

"No! Stop. Don't," they yelled back, no fear in their voices.

"It's the Muon. He knows we're here. The fire will give him the sight to swim to." I pointed out what they should have known.

"The Muon doesn't know fire, except for wildfire." They again talked as though to a child. "He is not a man anymore. He is a beast, and all beasts are afraid of fire. He doesn't know that this is us; he doesn't know that we would light a fire to have a fire. Our smell ended in the water. To him, we disappeared like a spirit. He is hunting something else."

The idea of the Muon swimming at us, finding the island, running out of the lake, and attacking made me want the spear back in hand. I had the thought, and my hand grabbed for the spear as if it were next to me and ready to be used by me. How could this have been my instinct? I wanted the dew light to arrive without a Muon coming. I wanted that whatever it was hunting would take the beast away from the lake and that the animal would escape the beast. Later, there was thrashing in the trees across the water as I hung my bed sling in the bough of the island tree, but there was no more yelling; and when I lay down in my bed, I fell to sleep quickly, as usual.

It is the dark, and I am still on the island, but there is no tree and no lake; and the island is a low mountain in the mid of a valley. I am not alone; around me are Tor'ocs. They are strange men in strange cloths, holding long, body-size plates in front of them with one hand, carrying weapons of many different sizes and shapes in the other. On their heads are the metal bowls that Weoduye had named helmets. Most are on foot, but some are riding as we rode oryx; but these animals are the ones from our myths that are called epus. They are beautiful, sleek and tall, and the Tor'ocs on them are the fearful things of legend. All the Tor'ocs, on foot or on epus, are gazing down the mountain, their eyes not shifting from what is moving up at them.

The men in the army below look quite large and terrifying, but at the same time, look ragged and unorganized, unlike the calm men who wait for them. The brutes are screaming and running up the slope of the mountain, while the Tor'ocs above wait, silent, strong, unafraid, waiting for the fight. The ragged soldiers look like men, wear cloths like men, but they are

Muons, an army of Muons. The Muon army hits the top of the mountain in an explosion of violence—swords, spears, arrows, blood, death, cries, men strangling men. The Muons are large enough to bring down the epus with their hands. The Tor'ocs are slashing and maiming and fighting—born to the art of fighting and killing. Even though each man in the army of the Muons is broader and taller than any of the Tor'ocs, they are not equal to the skilled speed of the Tor'oc blades and the arrows and the spears. The Muons are not a match for the lack of fear in their enemy. The Tor'ocs love the battle and the blood. It is not the idea of fighting to the last man; the idea of fighting is enough. There are so many Muon dead that the fighting becomes difficult, like fighting in a field of boulders growing more and more boulders.

The Muons who have not died see their own deaths flying down on them. The ones who can, run. The Tor'ocs do not chase after them; it is not the Tor'oc way. They know if they meet these Muons again, they will end them then. The battle is done, over so quickly that I feel it did not happen at all; but the top of the mountain, my island, is covered with the dead, not all but mostly Muon. The small count of Tor'ocs who have died are being lifted from the battlefield and carried away. The Muon dead are doused in a liquid and set on fire, a fire that blazes hot and consumes everything—hair, skin, bone.

In the center of this burning field of the dead, an imposing man kneels over a small body that is covered in the armor of the Tor'ocs. The face of this man—this

Wind

Tor'oc—is flooded with pain, loss and pain and bewilderment and anguish and failure and hopeless hurt. He removes the helmet from the dead boy on the ground and places it carefully to the side, bringing his fingers back to gently touch the forehead, as I had done. The man cries out for the boy, his dead boy.

I turn to view the field around me and I see that it holds the smoking remains of the Muons, reduced to piles of ashes that the wind will carry away. I turn back, and there is a hole dug; and men are lowering the body of the boy into the grave. They place the body down carefully, with reverence, and arrange the arms across the chest, the hands folded into each other. The man takes the hands and places a spear in them, and then he lays his shield across the boy, covering him from head to foot. The shield is marked by the same sybol the Jannanons had shown me that marks the spear. I kneel next to the warrior to look at him closer. This is Sumon, and the boy is his son, my blood.

I gaze down to where the boy lies under the shield, the tip of the spear showing itself above, displaying the part that marks it as the Spear of Sumon. I reach down and touch the sybol. At the moment of my touch, Sumon, looks up with a jolt and into my eyes. As I see him, he sees me.

I woke struggling. It took many counts to find myself and bring my mind back to the island and the lake and my time. It was light, but the light was still new. I located the Jannanons on the ground not far away, still sleeping. It was true about the Muon in my time; it was a beast that was afraid of fire, but his ancestors were once men, and the last of them had been burned to ashes. Maybe it had reason to fear fire.

I slowly left my bed sling and climbed my way out of the tree. I walked to where the Jannanons slept, walked past them to the place where they had hidden the spear from me. They had slid it under low bushes, bushes that were just wide enough to conceal the ancient weapon. I pulled the fabric-wrapped spear out, unrolled it, and draped the cloth across the bushes where recently the sword lay hidden. Any unnerving sensations I'd had the day before were gone. I grasped the spear by the handhold that was made for my great ancestor and felt that it was made for me. I wanted to aim it and throw it, but there was so little on the island; the only aims besides the bushes and the ground were the Jannanons and the trees--but of course, I was not going to use any of these friends for aims.

I heard water slap against the end of the boyt that was sitting in the lake; and I wondered, could I hit the boyt with the spear from where I stood? I thought that surely I would miss, so I didn't consider if I would damage the boyt or not. I had never even seen a spear before yesterday. I had never watched a spear thrown except inside my dream. Yet, the feel of it in my hand was natural, and it demanded to be used. I set my feet as I would shooting my bow, brought my arm back as though preparing to throw a large rock, aimed at the boyt that was too far to hit with a rock, and threw. The spear took the air better than any arrow I had fired; it gained the air and caught it; and the wind took the spear too, pushing it through the sky and aiming for its mark.

Wind

The spear struck the boyt with such a thud that the Jannanons jumped out of sleep. They looked at me, and I looked at the boyt. They turned to see what I was seeing; the spear was sticking part way through the top half of the hollowed-out trunk. They did not at first understand that it was the spear and that I had thrown it. Slowly they rose, walked to the boyt, touched the spear, and then gazed back at me. I walked to them, knowing it would be impossible to explain what I did and why I had to do it. I wasn't certain myself.

No one spoke as I reached the boyt, took hold of the spear, and pulled it back through the hole it had made. I held it in my hand again and felt the weight of it and the balance. They could see that I had changed, and that the meaning of the spear for me had changed too.

Holding the spear out in front of me I said as an explanation, "It called to me."

"You can't keep it," they responded.

"But I think I will," I said looking at the weapon with a warmth, though I didn't understand the meaning or the source.

"It's the law that you can't keep an ancient Tor'oc weapon. You'll have to give this to a consul when we reach the nearest town," they told me, this time not quite talking as though to a child.

"The law is for your world, not for here, not for me," I said, still looking up from the spear, not wanting to really challenge them but wanting to make it clear. "This was the spear of Sumon, my blood. Now it's mine."

"You may keep it for now," they said, as if they had the power, "But later…"

"It is not by chance that we are here," I said, knowing that this was such a truth that the Jannanons could have nothing more to say. "The spear is mine. No one will take it from me, certainly not a consul."

I walked back to the tree and climbed up to get my bed sling, bow, bale of arrows, finnif knife, and satchel. When I was back on the ground, I found that there was a way to position the straps of the bale so I could carry the spear securely across my back. Later, I thought, the moment when my friends concluded that I should hand this spear over to a consul, I'd create a firmer hold for the spear.

There was one more thing to be done before leaving the top of the mountain, on the island that I didn't see as just an island anymore. I found myself back at the grave of a great-uncle who had been merely a boy. I replaced the remains of Sumon's shield on top of him, covered the shield and small bones with earth, and knelt at the head of the grave to sing the mourning song. There were ancient words in the song that I did not understand fully, but the song still carried the hurt and the pain and longing. I sang the song, and my companions left me alone to sing and to finish.

When I was done, I found that they had prepared the boyt. It was not sinking because its new spear hole was safely above the water line. We pushed off into the lake toward the far edge.

4

Sitting mid-boyt, I did not offer to help row, as the Jannanons called it, but watched the cool water slide beneath us, allowing my feelings about the Tor'oc past to wash over me. My ancestors had lived and fought, and some had died, in the land at the bottom of this lake, a battleground that we now glided over. Something of their warrior spirit was in the water of this lake, not that the water was vicious—it was just the opposite. There was some brightness that the water gave to the air, something that I was breathing in from the water. I almost felt the tip of Sumon's spear pushing against my back, urging me to pay attention. Whatever it was that I was supposed to learn from this water and this land, I knew would live deep in me, something that I could not reason, something that would rest in the place that governed me though it was still unknown to me.

I was lost in my thoughts when a voice asked a question. It asked it several times before I understood that it was not in my head but a voice in the boyt.

"The bow you carry, did you hunt with it in the prison?"

The voice was coming from Goyel, who had taken the back position in order to handle the blade and relieve Sheios. I did not turn around; I did not care to look at him, though I didn't mind talking.

"Yes, we hunted, but it was for the games more than anything," I said. I gestured to the bow. "This is too powerful for most animals; it would rip them apart."

"The games?" He didn't need to say more.

"The games are very old, from the beginning when Morla began to teach the young ones the skills of Tor'oc." I had the realization that this talk would not be my last history lesson. No one knew about us; we were a myth. "Before the flood we call the Mad'la, before the trees, young Tor'ocs learned from watching the battles and then being in battles; but after Divul cut us off from the world there were no more killings, and Morla saw that there would be no path for them to learn the bow or the knife or sword for battle. Still, she did not want these skills to be lost, so she founded the games."

"You kill each other in the games?" Goyel asked in his innocence.

"Tor'ocs do not kill Tor'ocs," I replied, and I would never be able to convey how deep in us this rule lived. "The games are there just to give reason to train…"

"…to kill," Goyel finished my sentence.

"No, to do well in the games," I said slowly, his words had made me feel uneasy.

"So, tell us about the games."

"We have games of the oro bow—first with the bow as a single for the short arrow, and then the bow crossed double for the long arrow, and then shooting from the back of an oryx running as fast as it can."

"You ride oryx?" It was question inside of an exclamation of surprise.

"Yes, in our land they are what we have, and the best oryx move as smoothly as water." I moved my hand in motion to demonstrate the running oryx. "Do you have oryx on this side of the river?"

"Oh, we have them, but they are wild beasts. Nobody rides them." His eyebrows arched expressing awe just imagining the possibility.

"If you have them, I will catch one and I will ride it."

"We have another animal we ride that you may find easier to catch."

"I think I've seen the animal in dreams," I said, thinking back to Uthiriul riding something black and sleek. "I will prefer the oryx. I'll just have to have a saddle made for it if you don't ride them."

"A saddle for an oryx!" He marveled at the idea. "I hope you have some as'ash—that will cost you a lot."

"Cost?" A new word for me. "And what are as'ash?" I gestured to everything I had. "I don't have much with me. I don't think I have that."

"As'ash is what we use to buy things," he said, so matter-of-factly, it seemed that I should understand everything he just told me. He saw that I understood none of it. He reached into a pocket; his hand came out holding flat copper circles on which someone had crafted the head of a man and words that I could not read. He handed me a circle. "That's a ten lurm as'ash."

"What do you do with it?" I could not reason how it could be useful.

"Enough of those would buy you an oryx saddle, if you could find one," he said.

I twisted this copper circle around and around, lost in the reason of how a saddle could be made from this or many and many of these. I tossed it back to Goyel and said, "It would make a very bad saddle."

"You wouldn't make a saddle of it; you'd use it to pay someone to make a saddle," he said. Seeing the expression of lost-in-understanding that I must have had, he continued, "This as'ash is used to give to someone; and they give you something back, the thing you want."

"I give the saddle maker this, and he will make and give me a saddle?" I laughed hard, thinking what a world we are going to where men take a small round piece of copper for a whole saddle. "You must think I am a fool to believe in that."

"I tell true."

"It cannot be," I finally said, after laughing more and more.

"In Aemira, we have all agreed that this—" he held up the as'ash again for me to see —"is worth something. We all know what it is worth; and if you have many and many of these, you can have everything."

"And if you have none, like me?" I asked.

"Well, you will need to have some."

"Do they fall from the skies," I gestured rain falling, "or do I pick them up on the ground, or dig for them?"

"No, you must earn them."

"Doing what?"

"Something of value."

"My coming to the Camarod, is that value?"

"Yes, I think so, yes—definitely so," Goyel said.

"They will give me many as'ash for coming?"

Goyel frowned, and his forehead wrinkled as he thought before saying, "No, I don't think so."

This made me laugh the hardest. "So, value is a slippery snake in Aemira." I liked his joke, but I didn't want him to think I was such a fool as to believe everything he told me. I reached over and touched his knee. "When I do something that is of value, you will let me know."

He grimaced and smiled, realizing that I was not going to be easily fooled, and I could see that he decided not to take the joke further. He put the copper circle away. "You have copper on the island?"

I nodded and said, "Made from the green rocks, very difficult to make. We wouldn't waste our copper to make little round circles." I smiled again, thinking they must have so much copper that they can use it for jokes. "We use it for the blades of our knives and for the forks that turn the ground for planting."

"And of all your weapons, are just the knives copper?" Goyel seemed as if he thought I was teasing him as he had me.

"For the weapons, yes, but also for hooks. Look at this satchel." I held up my bag so he could see its clasp. "You must have large fields of green rocks here for your copper as'ash."

"No, we find it inside rocks deep in the earth." He moved his hand to indicate that the rocks were far down in the ground. "We must dig for it. But I want to know more about the games."

I nodded that I would tell him more, "The games last for one cycle of the moon. They are games of skill and strength, such as throwing the finnif knife from as many positions as you can reason. I told you about the oro bow; and there are sword battles—one on one. Our swords are made of wood, which leaves your skin marked blue and hurt, but no one is hurt too badly." I decided to tell him one more thing about the swords, so he didn't think that I had no knowledge. "We do have three ancient swords made of metal. No one uses them; except that they are on display during the games. They are beautiful, and we have tried to make metal for swords like those, but we have never accomplished that. The iron swords are too heavy, and the copper swords are too precious and too weak."

"So, you throw knives and shoot arrows?" Goyel waited a moment, and I could see he was trying to find the right words. "Into what?"

"We have aims."

"And what does the aim look like?"

"They look like people but smaller than us," and as I said it, I saw how this was going to be perceived by him.

"People...made out of what?" he asked, looking very uneasy.

"They are made of grass, but they are just aims."

"No, they've kept you on the ready, for a thousand years, kept you on the ready," he said, with a hint of fear in that voice.

"We are a peaceful people now, not like before." I was certain of this. "We live in the trees; and the trees have taught us, and we have learned from our own selves. When my people took to the trees, we were warriors and only warriors, only trained for that. Now we are farmers; we are builders; we make cloths and tools; we cook; we grow kollokks and hanging ways and have built a city in the trees. We provide for everything that we need."

"You may be more dangerous than before then," he said sadly.

Wanting to help him see that we were not what he imagined, I told him, "We also have the Last Man Run." Goyel looked up interested. "It is a race along the length and width of the Peninsula, and it ends when there is only one runner left racing. The race can be long and long. I was once the fifth man, and you may not think it, but that is not easy. We are a people of runners."

"Yes, predators have to be good runners." Goyel's remark hit a tender spot in me. How was I to make him see that we were not predators any more than he was?

"Perhaps it thinks that you're the predator when you fish the fish."

He understood that he hunted, and that made him no different from me, but he wanted it to be different. After a count of many breaths, he asked, "And so you have different games and races for the women from the men?"

"No, why would we?"

"Because of size and strength—women being smaller," he stated what he thought I should already know.

"Are they smaller where you are from? The women are even smaller than you?" I replied, not wanting to insult.

"Women everywhere are smaller."

"Not Tor'ocs." I shook my head. "The men and women are the same. Our bodies are shaped differently, but the women are strong, and just as many times a woman wins the games as a man does."

"They win with the bow and the knife and the sword and the running?" He said, as though he didn't believe me.

"Yes, and our women are especially good with the knife, something in their fingers handles it better." Nobody knows why that is, but it has always been hard for men to win the knife games.

"So, why do you need the spear?" He was looking at me in a hard way. "It sounds as though you didn't even have spears on the island."

"We had no spears," I admitted.

"Then why do you want it now?"

I wasn't certain that I could explain to him, or even to myself, why I wanted it, why I had to have it. The spear was mine -- that I knew. I could not give it up to let it be hung on a wall for others to look at and imagine what horrors Sumon had committed with that spear. I could not have it put on a wall for any reason. The spear had life in it and needed to be held. My hand needed to hold it, and my back needed to feel the spear pressed against it, tied tight to my oro bow. The spear had been waiting on the island before it was an island — sleeping, waiting for me. I wouldn't betray the spear or myself by giving it up. I would need it and I did not know for what. I was not going to kill with it; I couldn't do that. But it was mine. If challenged, they would have to take it from me by force; and I reasoned that nobody could.

"It's mine," I said, and Goyel knew that the talk was over.

The edge of the other side of the lake was near, and I was glad to be soon out of the boyt and away from the talk, though at first, I had liked the talk with Goyel. The bottom of the lake was close to the boyt, even this far away from the edge. I saw this and jumped out before anyone else took notice. The water was to my mid, and it was good to be in the water. I could see the fish, small ones that were curious about me and who kissed my legs to taste me. I grabbed the boyt and pushed it to the edge where it hit the lake bottom before the waters ended. Weoduye jumped out; and the two of us pushed and pulled the boyt to the land—land that was white, crystal white, until it disappeared into a line of bushes and grasses that were different from any of the grasses before, tall, thin wisps.

I was staring at the white earth when the Jannanons told me, "It's called sand. It comes from the bottom of the lake. It is what water does over time to earth and bone."

"We have the same with the seas around the Peninsula, but not as white as this," I replied.

The Jannanons carried the boyt to a place of hiding, and I was surprised by that, thinking that I would be the only one to return to this lake. I was glad for it being there so that I could boyt back to the island, back to the other edge. I would probably have to fight a Muon who surely would be waiting for me, even though now it didn't know what it was waiting for. I had been thinking about the fight with the Muon since my dream. The dream had taught me how to end it. There was a deep part of me that wanted this fight, a part of me that I had had no reason to feel before.

"Are there Muons on this edge?" I asked the Jannanons.

"No, here there are no Muons, only across the lake."

"But there are oryx," I said, smiling and looking down, seeing dung that had to have come from an oryx not long ago.

The Jannanons had a silent exchange between them as Goyel told the others of my plan. The three gazed back at me. "You want to catch an oryx and ride it?"

"I will catch one," I said, pointing. "It headed that way."

"But that is not the way we must go. That will take us away from Far Road."

"I will catch this oryx this dark," I said, not wanting to explain that the oryx would get us to Far Road and beyond more quickly than their short steps.

"And then we will have a wild oryx." They were in shock that I had a plan to take a wild animal prisoner.

"It will not be wild after two days, two darks," I told them in a fashion that did not invite any more questions.

"We will lose time, two days."

"We will gain time," I reasoned. "We can all ride the oryx, as small as you are. It will walk much faster. We will gain time in time."

"No, an oryx is not needed," they replied, thinking that this would be enough for me to give in. "We are going on, not chasing something to ride that cannot be ridden."

"Then, go!" I waved at them, in a manner that said I knew they wanted to travel a way that was not my way at that moment. I turned and headed after the oryx.

If I were going to find it before dark, I was going to have to hurry. My steps increased as I followed the trail. The animal had been there but perhaps not recently. I didn't need to look behind me to know that the Jannanons were following; they had no choice, but they could not keep up with me. I was on the hunt, and running was the only way I was going to meet and catch my oryx. It would not be hard for the Jannanons to track me. Eventually they would find me, and they were quiet, and would not disturb the oryx when they arrived. I thanked the wind for that.

We crossed the land, the oryx and I. By his tracks, I saw that he was walking. I was running and I was certain that I would catch sight of him by the time the light began to cast its long shadows. As I ran, I looked to see signs of other big beasts, including man, and saw

Wind

nothing. I began to feel that the oryx was the king of this land; and that was a good feeling—kings are not afraid.

The ground of this land was different than any I had run on before; it was hard and white, and the bushes and grass and trees that grew in it were not as strong as the life that grew in rich, dark brown dirt. The plants here were brave fighters; but the earth itself was not giving, and that was not a fault; it had little to give. Like most lands, it rolled, grew high, and plunged again and again. After days of walking, it felt good to run, to feel this strange white earth give under me as my feet hit it and hit it. There were counts when I forgot why and to what purpose I was running — I was running and that was enough.

During one of these counts, I gained a hill; and in the far part of the short valley where I was headed, I saw a large brown thing moving, slowly. Not a reasoned thought, but a voice told me to stop. As I slowed to a walk, my body screamed for the pleasure to run again, run down the hill and to the valley and across it, and on and on. I forced myself to stand -- to be still, to look. The large brown shape was an animal; it was far away and stepped into a group of trees that hid much of it. I could not see horns or much of the body, but the size was right. I took steps that gently led me down to the edge of the field that opened to the wide valley.

I stopped again at the field. When they wanted to announce themselves, oryx made a sound that came from deep in their chests, a grumble that undulated out of their closed mouths. We had learned to mimic this sound on the Peninsula; it calmed the oryx, even the tamed oryx we rode. I knelt and hid myself in the grass and flowers, then grumbled from my chest. It didn't need to be loud. The sound would carry in this place. I waited, but neither heard nor saw anything in reply. I grumbled again, waited, and saw movement where the large brown beast had disappeared into bushes that grew large enough to hide it; but it did not come out of its hiding place and did not reply to me. Maybe I had been wrong, and this was not an oryx but something else that had wandered into my path. I grumbled one more time. In no count at all, a low grumble was returned; and the oryx stepped out to see who was calling to it.

It could not see me, but it knew where the sound had come from and stood, staring. I carefully raised myself just high enough to show my head and shoulders as I grumbled again. There was a quick tick of the neck of the beast as its eyes locked onto me. It had seen many things in its life but had never seen this, a thing that was not an oryx but sounded like one. I sat back down and disappeared from its view. I grumbled. My grumble was returned.

After waiting through ten counts, I raised myself. The oryx was not moving now, but it had come twenty steps closer and stared. I lowered and waited, longer this time, and when I reappeared the oryx had come to the mid field, again stopping and staring. Maybe it had felt me about to rise and stopped to watch. I held the look; we could see each other well now. His nostrils twitched as a light breeze blew from behind me, delivering my scent to him. I sat back down, leaned onto my back, and then twisted onto my stomach. From this level, I crawled away from the oryx and toward a rock big enough for me to sit on, but still be situated lower than the oryx's neck.

Once I reached the rock, I took off my oro bow, spear, and bale, and left them as I climbed slowly up and grumbled as I flattened against the rock. I looked over my shoulder, and the oryx was walking, slowly walking at me. I turned around, sat on the rock, and watched him walk. His eyes never left mine—he meant to find out what this animal was that kept calling. He stopped two Tor'ocs away. I could smell him now, and it was a good clean, musty smell, a smell I knew. We met each other's look. I could see that he was not quite sure what to do. I hoped he had not decided that I wasn't an animal he would like; then he might walk away, or worse, run far. I turned my back to the oryx and rolled slowly off the rock, letting the ground cradle me as I disappeared from his sight again behind the rock. I stayed against the earth and waited, silently waited, my face deep in the crushed grass.

I heard it and felt it at the same count. The oryx's nose was touching my back.

He was smelling me, examining me in a way it couldn't manage even from a close distance. It wanted to take its time with this odd smell, and I was glad to wait. I moved my hand and felt the leg closest to me, my fingers reaching up carefully, softly, tracing their way. My body rose to follow the fingers that found its chest between the front legs. Kneeling, I could not remember how I came to kneel. My hand was pressed against the chest, feeling the sound of the heart, keeping my head lowered; and I was smiling. The nose of the beast smelled my head, my hair; and I raised my face so it could smell that too. I blew my breath into its nostrils and looked up into its eyes.

Keeping the stare and holding the oryx with my look, I stood. My hands moved along its neck and around the head to stroke the long face. These were all new tingles for the oryx, and I wanted him to learn to want the touch. I moved a hand to the center bridge between his eyes, and my fingers stroked the hair and skin. I whispered now so that he could hear my voice, "My name is Aeon the Leaf. Will you tell me your name later?"

I waited another count for the oryx to take in my sound, and then said, "Can we see where you stopped to eat? It must be a good place."

I took steps in that direction, picking up the bow, bale, and spear. I did not want to look back—if I were to catch this oryx, it would be now. This was the count when it would let itself be caught. It had stayed, watching me, and then took steps to follow, and then to walk beside me. We crossed the field and entered the grove of trees where the oryx had been eating when I'd first seen it. The trees and thorn bushes that the oryx liked were different from those I had known on the Peninsula, but I could see they were close cousins. I tore a branch and fed the leaves to the oryx, who accepted them with mild surprise.

Wind

As the oryx ate, I turned to the trees and walked into a small clearing in the mid of the grove. "I am Aeon the Leaf," I blew. "May I grow here?"

They blew back a welcome at once and moved the wind through their leaves to make me feel truly invited.

"I am here with the beast that eats the thorn bush," I said, waiting to sense if they knew the beast. They told me that they knew the oryx. "I must keep him here with me for this dark and two more darks. Can you aid me in this?"

"We can keep him among us," they blew back. "As long as the rain falls elsewhere, we can keep him."

"During these two darks, may I rest among your boughs?" I asked, keeping my words as humble as I could.

"You may," they blew back in a fashion that made me feel very welcome. "There are sweet roots in the ground. Bring your beast back; we will lead you to them."

What good fortune—sweet roots. As long as these were in the ground, I barely needed the trees' help. I went back to the grazing oryx, tore another branch of thorns and leaves, and stood in front of the beast, waiting for it to finish and look to me. As soon as its head raised to see the branch in my hand, I turned and walked, holding the branch a short way off the ground. The oryx followed. We entered the grove of trees, and they sent me their aroma. At this trigger, the images in my inner eye showed me the way to the nearest ground where the sweet roots grew. I laid the branch of the thorn bush across the ground and stepped back.

The oryx could smell the sweet root, and its hooves kicked away the guide branch. It dug into the ground with hooves and nose and found a jalap growing just below the surface of the dirt. Grabbing the brown root, it tore it out of the ground. Oryx love the taste of jalap, and I had eaten it once to find out why. It was bitter to me, and it had made me shit until I thought I would die of shitting.

I climbed into a tree to gain its feeling. I could view the land from where I had come. The Jannanons were following, I was certain; but I could not see them on the trail I had taken following the oryx. The Jannanons would be here at light end, or not. I would see them soon, and they would be surprised to see that I already had my oryx. I thought how very surprised they would be to see me riding it, and even more surprised to be riding an oryx soon themselves. Goyel had formed a bad sense of me. They were all connected, so I reasoned that Sheios and Weoduye mistrusted me now as well. Riding on the oryx might heal the mistrust. I could not see how it would not.

I climbed back down through the tree and found a bough where I could hang my bed sling. I hung it and left my bow, bale, and spear there in the tree. I was hungry for meat but would not hunt it or eat it while I was winning the oryx. There were plants I had seen on the edge of the grove that I could eat and a bush with fruit. That would have to be enough for me until after I had ridden the oryx. I ate it near the oryx while he

Wind

finished the underground field of sweet roots, that were many and large. He was not going to stop until there were no more.

I lay back on the ground, propping myself up on one arm and staring at the oryx, trying to hear his name. "I hear Bol over and over, but I don't know if that is your name or just a sound the wind is blowing," I said to the oryx, who paid me no attention. He still had sweet roots to eat. "Let's try something," I said, thinking that I would say the names that swirled in my head. "Oodjei." No reaction. "Dhoiej." Again, nothing. "Kaeroi." All good oryx names, but this oryx didn't know them and didn't want them.

"Bol," I said, and he looked up with a jerk of his neck. "So, Bol is your name. I cannot say I like it much, but if it is your name, I will call you Bol." There was no reason to call him a name that was not his. "Do you remember mine? It's Aeon...you don't have to call me the Leaf. I don't like it any more than I like Bol, but we're both stuck with them, I reason."

It was good to talk to Bol; he was a good listener, and he liked the sound of my voice. An oryx who didn't like your voice would not stay close no matter how many sweet roots there were left to eat.

"You live in a beautiful land. I am sorry that I am going to take you away from it." I thought I should get that said before long. "But I am told it will be a great adventure that we will be going to. I did not expect it any more than you did, but you see I'm here and making the best." I ate some fruit that grew nearby and thought about what else I should tell Bol. "You will meet my companions tomorrow, I reason; and you must show patience with them. They understand almost nothing, but their hearts are good. They are very small, so be careful not to step on them. You would hurt them, not meaning to, but you would hurt them. Me, you can be carefree with, Bol." He gazed at me again when his name was spoken—it was his name.

Dark settled in around us; and the trees released an aroma that was calming, inviting, and made a person—and I hoped an oryx—want to stay, to sleep, and feel safe. I reasoned that the Jannanons had found a place along the trail to rest until the next day. They were great hiders, and they would be safe in this world without great cats or Muons or other men. I was glad to have a dark with simply Bol and me and the trees. I would sleep well and wake happy to see this oryx that I was winning. I climbed into the tree and through the limbs to my sling. Tomorrow I would have to twist the twine that would keep Bol safe once we leave the grove. He would not be happy to be tied nor I happy to tie him, but it is a thing that had to be—he would not be safe without it.

I fell to sleep quickly and did not remember dreams, if I had any. When I woke, my first thought was of Bol. I looked down, and he stood there, near where I had left him the dark before. I wondered if I had won him already, but I had to be careful.

This light was going to be our walking light, the day we would leave the grove to see the land together. I wanted to start out soon so that we would miss the

Jannanons' arrival and not meet them until sometime later. When they had caught up, they would see my bed sling in the tree and know that I had been there and to wait for me.

The trees had shown me where a small field of sweet root had grown and where a better, tastier root was that I could use to entice Bol back to the grove. I led Bol to the sweet root and let him eat before I stood, pulled the rest of the sweet roots out of the ground, and walked away with them in my hands. Bol followed. I walked, feeding Bol from my hands.

I was not interested in the land. I was interested in Bol; and I cannot say where we walked, across what kind of land, under what trees, through which bushes or grassland. We walked, and when Bol had finished the sweet root, I moved the hand he had eaten from, moved it across his nose, his face, past his ears, down his neck. I rested that hand on his shoulders as we continued, and I let him lead me. When I reasoned we had gone far and far, I turned us with a light touch from my hand; and we headed back toward our grove, a path Bol would not have taken on his own.

We came upon a thorn bush that I knew he would like, and we stopped to let him eat. I was hungry but had not seen anything I could eat, though I reasoned we had passed many plants and fruits. I sat and watched Bol. Nearby, I heard a stream. The sound of water rolling over the rocks brought to my attention that I also was thirsty. The stream was close, and I found it in two breathes. I leaned over the water and drank. Then, reaching to the bottom of the stream and pushing my hands into the mud, I brought them up shaped into a bowl and sealed by the mud wedged between my fingers. I walked back to Bol and offered him the stream water. He drank, and he was thankful for the water and thankful for me. It was not enough water for him, and we both walked to the stream and drank more and more.

It was time we returned to the grove. I led the way, my hand resting along his haunches, and sometimes touching his horns; he would have to get used to that. Though I had no wide knowledge of the land or our path, I did know the way back. We walked slowly, more slowly than when we'd left—the Jannanons would be there, and I was not sure how Bol would feel about them. I did not think he would feel good.

I kept my eyes focused on where the grove should appear. When it did, the three Jannanons were standing, waiting for me. As soon as I saw them, I stopped; and Bol stopped with me. We both looked at the Jannanons, though he saw them more clearly than I did. I did not move and did not show that I was going to move. I stared at them without a wave, without a motion; they would have to read what to do from my inactivity. I wished that I could have been as connected to them as they were to one another. I would have told them to hide, to let me do what I needed to do. They would feel awe and wonder that I was standing with my hand on an oryx. And they must have reasoned that I had caught it and was winning it, just as I told Goyel I would. But they hadn't thought it would be this soon. I reasoned they had not thought it would be ever.

They did not move, and I did not move. Some counts had passed, and they had not moved. I still did not want to take one step closer to them with Bol, so I held my free hand up and pushed it as though I were pushing them back into the trees.

They stood a count longer, and then turned, walking into the trees; and I knew that they would be there when we returned. I gave them time to disappear, and Bol and I took our next steps toward the grove. On our return, Bol would know they were there; but he would not worry about them—kings are never afraid.

Once back in the trees, I showed Bol where the new roots were that he would like better than sweet root. I dug up the first one myself and laid it on the ground for him to eat. I lightly stroked his body from head to tail as he dug up the good things to eat so he would think of the smell and touch of me when he thought of good roots. This was enough new for this light. I would let him eat and be. I would find the Jannanons.

On the far side of the grove, I located the three of them where they had chosen a place upwind from the oryx—maybe they knew more than I had thought. They were eating, and I was glad to see food prepared and ready. Sitting down, I began to eat without explaining anything that had happened since we last had seen one another. I could feel their eyes on me, but I was really hungry.

"Go ahead; ask me," I said, my mouth full of stalks of a plant I did not know.

"How?" They said this one word together.

"Luck," I said, and looked up at them with a smile.

"Yes, you are the one with the wind to his back," they said, smiling back.

"You must see and know that this is not my first oryx," I said, in my way that also said that they should have trusted me. "I could feel him, even on the boyt. I knew I would find him, and he would find me. If he lets me, I will ride him tomorrow. Once ridden, I will give him one more dark and dew light to say goodbye to his land. It would be best if you stayed upwind until you see me ride him back."

They said nothing but they nodded, understanding what had to be done, though not knowing how I would do it. I stood and nodded back and walked away from them toward Bol, who was happily eating the new roots. I spent the rest of our time together not touching him but telling him the story of my life and my people. It would be best and fair if he knew everything before letting me ride.

Once I gauged that he knew enough, I walked through the field and chose the grass I would twist into twine that could hold Bol, and spent what was left of the light braiding the twine.

That dark, the trees filled the air with the aroma of calm and safety, and I slept as I had the dark before.

Wind

    I woke to find Bol beneath me again in the dew light -- he was waiting for me. That dew light, we ran and ran a reasonless run. Bol led us across the land; and I touched him as we ran, letting my reason visit some other place. We crossed fields, ran through a thick forest and along a path beaten down by many numbers of oryx who had lived long before Bol. Bol knew this path, and I think he wanted to show me. He was running, running because I wanted to, but he was also leading us to a place to stop and eat and rest. We ran onto a ridge that looked out over the land, and there grew the thorn bushes Bol had been imagining.

    This was the highest land from which I had ever seen across the world. As Bol tore at the bush and ate, I walked to see what there was. In the far and far, I thought that I could just make out the Peninsula. If I had had the eyes of an oryx, I would have been able to see it clearly; but, in my sight, it was a shady line on the horizon, a sliver of cloud that I knew held my people and my city in it. "That is where I am from, Bol." I pointed, and he paid no attention.

    "We have oryx there, like you," I said as he ate. "They would be jealous. You are more handsome than the handsomest oryx there." Bol didn't care. "Ready to run?"

    We ran down from the ridge. This incline offered my best chance of an advantageous position to mount Bol. He could run on flat ground and uphill faster than I, but running downhill was more difficult. At this angle, I could easily run beside him, then hold back a step or two so he would be lower than I would on the hill. I breathed to calm myself; my heart felt ready to explode from fear. If I missed the jump or stumbled, and this frightened Bol, he could throw me off when I mounted and—thinking that I meant him harm—even impale me with his horns. Also, if he were as smart as I thought, he could run at full speed under a low branch to knock me off. That had happened to me before. But this was no time to hesitate.

My moment arrived—a steep drop where Bol had to slow to a near walk to maneuver down the ledge. My legs pushed; my arms pulled; and I was up, landing just behind his hump. In a breath he stopped – not another step. He didn't want to move. He was too surprised that I was now on top of him, and he wanted to decide what this meant. The earth was shifting. To keep balance, he allowed his legs to maintain a halting, cautious walk. I leaned back from his head and, without letting go of the horns, stretched across his back. Steady now, I breathed into his skin and grumbled softly as an oryx might, a calming sound he felt coming through my body and into his. He seemed to remember then who I was and what I was. Filling himself with air, he blew it out at once. I didn't know what that meant, but it felt like an acceptance, though I kept tight against him, waiting for something unexpected to happen.

It was a long walk down from the high land. He took his time, and I was glad. He was getting used to having a man on him. When he came onto the flat land, then we would see how it would go. Anything could happen then.

Wind

Reaching the bottom of the hill, he did something I had never seen an oryx do—he turned in a tight circle and looked back. I think he wanted to see whether or not I was also behind him. Now, he knew for certain that I was on top, completely on top of him.

Softly into his ear I said, "Bol, run with me." I squeezed my legs into his sides, dug the rounds of my feet into the bowl at the top of his back legs, then projected my spirit out in front. He jumped--and landed in a full run. The earth below him became a blur of grass and stones and dirt. He was running as fast as any oryx on the Peninsula, and I felt that he was faster. I pushed myself low on him, my head against the hump, my legs squeezing. The grass twine I had been making for reins would enable me to sit up; but for that first run, I simply had to grip and stay on, knowing that he would have to run until exhausted. That would break his fear; then he would be mine.

I didn't care where he ran and did not look up to see. At this pace, I could have lost my balance or my grip and fallen off. This was his run. He ran across the first field, into a forest, across a stream, up a small hill, down a path walled with fire bushes, then past smooth red rocks rising like mirrored cliffs on either side. We jumped a boulder nearly as big he was at the end of that pass, ran along a furrow of loose stones and rocks, onto a dried riverbed of caked, hard mud, and then hit the white earth that was the border of the lake. He had run so fast and so far that I would not have been surprised to find us at the Divul with the Peninsula on the other shore. Instead, when he slowed down to begin to ease into a walk, I looked up and found that we were at the lake, at the end of the lake where a river poured itself into the great body of water. The river ran fast, tumbling and tossing itself into a white fury over the large rocks before it reached the lake. It would have been impossible to cross that river, and this was where finally Bol came to a stop.

He was breathing hard, and I knew he must be thirsty. I was not the one who had run, but my own throat was dry; and Bol's must have been drier. I slid off him, and brushing my body against his side as I walked up to his large head, I rubbed his face, especially the velvet ridge between his eyes. A light rain began to fall, and I looked up, smiling—rain was a foretoken of good, a blessing from the sky. I kept my body touching his, already damp with his own moisture and the rain, and our scents melted together. I let him smell me, then I turned and walked to the river. He followed, and we drank together as the rain fell.

I had my fill of water before he did, and I used the jiff to win Bol a little further. My hand stroked his powerful neck as he swallowed a constant stream of water. The rain clouds were moving away from us, the rain becoming lighter and lighter; and by the time Bol had finished drinking, the rain was gone.

"We are far and far, Bol," I said, straining to see just how far. "I crossed this great lake but cannot view the place of the crossing from here. We will make our way back along the edge of the lake until I can see the island. I know you are not lost, but I am. We must return to my companions. You may have smelled them back where the sweet roots grow."

I stood up and, knowing Bol would want to eat, I searched for thorn bushes that were likely growing near the river. On a nearby rise, I spotted the top of a single thorn bush. If there were only one, that one would do. I walked toward it to see if Bol would follow—this would be a key test of our bond. He remained at the river while I took several steps away from him. He turned his head to watch me; and when he felt I had gone far enough, he made his own steps to follow.

Looking back, I said, "Then, it's settled and set; I'm yours and you're mine. We're going to have great adventures--and when they're over, I will take you to the Peninsula where you will be the king of the oryx."

But he was already king in this part of the Out World. What would he care to be king on the Peninsula? These thoughts were interrupted by a rustle in the brush to my left that caused me to turn sharply. The sound was of something big and heavy and fast charging--at me, at us. I had no defenses with me—no bow, no spear, no knife. I had wanted to be free of all of these for my leap onto Bol. My hands searched for the weapons that were not there as the large wild aper exploded from the bush--head down, tusks high, aimed at my mid. I fell back and hit the ground. The huge pig ran over me, stopped, spun around in a half breath and charged - its giant tusks pitched down to pin me. I put up my hands in a feeble way to protect myself, just as the tusker was smashed by a force large and powerful. Bol's head hit the aper across its mid, sending it flying, and Bol chasing. The aper hit the ground hard but it was up again after rolling across the earth three times. It was shaken, angry, and unsteady when Bol came up fast from behind. Two long horns punctured the aper's hairy body, through one side and out the other. Bol's giant head tossed the aper as if it had been a piglet. I was flat on my back against the earth, as the aper flipped high over my head. The huge pig hit the earth and did not move, dead by the time it struck the ground only three Tor'ocs away from me. I lay still on the ground as Bol bent down to make sure that I was breathing and good. Reaching up, I grabbed his head; and he pulled me to standing.

Kissing the nose of the big, wonderful beast, I sighed, "I am bent and bonded to you, Bol. Harm will not come to you as long as I am able."

Bol snorted, and I released him—oryx never liked being thanked. He turned away from me, took steps to cross to the unmoving aper and lowered his head to the body. He nudged it with his nose to make sure the aper was not going to stand to fight again. Certain that it wouldn't, he straightened, and breathed in heavily, taking in the clean air.

Bol was hungry, and I took him to eat at the thorn bushes I had seen from the river. We had surprised the aper in its hiding place. What had it been doing? Perhaps digging for the roots that Bol also desired. Pigs were the best hunters for roots in the wild. I walked to the bush and crawled under it. The aper had dug a hole that exposed the tops of several sweet roots. I pulled them out and took them to Bol, a better reward for saving me than any words.

I let Bol eat and rest until it was time for us to head back to our camp. He was done and ready to walk when I leaped back on him, and he let me, shivering his muscles once I was up and sitting. I put slight pressure on one of his horns to turn him and show him the way back along the edge of the lake. When I could spot the island in the far, far, we would move inland and find our way to the grove and the Jannanons. We had enough light in the sky to make our way back.

During the walk back, I sat with my hands resting on the hump against which I was pressed. The sway of an oryx was familiar and good, and I could gaze at this Out World feeling as though I were home. Bol had made everything better. There was something inside me that was easing into this life. I was not aware that I had held doubt and fear, but they were leaving me. I rubbed Bol's neck and thanked whatever powers that had sent me to him and him to me.

The lake was long and long, but sooner than I had reasoned, the island with the single tree could be seen in the far; and it was the time to find our way along the land to our camp. We would be back sooner than I wanted, but it would be good to let Bol rest long and well before tomorrow.

The grove of trees that hid the camp appeared in the near, and the Jannanons were again standing just outside the edge of it, staring at us, waiting for me to give them a signal to remain or to hide. I gave them no signal, and they stood where they were. Bol saw them and smelled them and didn't mind that they were there. I believed he already understood that they were with me. We walked up to them, and as I put my hands against the base of Bol's horns, he came to a stop. The Jannanons gazed at me and at Bol and tried to form a reasoned thought but were too clouded with amazement.

"His name is Bol," I told them plainly.

"How did you do it?"

"I told you I would and that I could." I rubbed Bol along his hump, "The next time, you should believe in the things that you do not know, if I tell you I do. My knowledge of the Out World is none. Your knowledge of the Tor'ocs is the same. I will learn and learn, but the Out World will learn as well. You need to let him smell you."

I moved a hand slightly and shifted my weight and my soles toward Weoduye, who would be the safest of the Jannanons for Bol to smell first. Bol took steps to the youngest Jannanon, and Weoduye kept his ground. The beautiful oryx bent his head and took in the odor of Weoduye. He then moved to Sheios and Goyel, and they all acted with respect and awe; and though they were frightened, they held the fear inside, and Bol did not mind that they were afraid.

I slid off Bol, and the Jannanons took steps back, no longer hiding their fear. "Is that necessary?" they asked. "Isn't it better if you stay on him?"

Wind

"Let's walk; I'm hungry," I said, realizing just how hungry I was after a light of riding and not eating.

I walked, and the Jannanons, their eyes turned to the oryx, walked with me as Bol followed. When we had reached a flat clearing under the trees, I saw the Jannanons had the cloth on the ground and food ready to eat. They understood more than I had reasoned, and I was glad. Before I could eat, I asked the trees to show me where the rest of the roots were growing. They sent their aroma back to me, and I led Bol to the spot, digging the first root out myself and handing it to Bol. He took it, and I hoped he knew that he would always eat before I did. Then I sat down and, as before, began to devour the food without waiting.

The Jannanons, still staring at Bol, said, "Are you going to tie him?"

I glanced at Bol and then to the three. "He won't be going anywhere. We are settled and set." That was enough explanation. I turned back and kept eating.

The Jannanons believed that Bol would not be there in the dew light when we rose and secretly thought I had wasted three good days. On purpose, I slept later than they did so that they could see my oryx waiting on the ground below my sling.

I had worked braiding the twine until I fell to sleep, making enough line for the Jannanons to hold when they rode Bol. Bol wouldn't like the twine, but coming from me, he would accept it. I looped the twine around his neck just in front of the horns and laid the long end on his back.

"It's time to go," I said, facing Weoduye, Goyel, and Sheios. "Let me lift you. Hold the twine in both hands but don't pull it. He will be good; don't be afraid."

None of them wanted to be on the back of what they saw as a wild animal only recently settled by a Tor'oc. But this was the plan, though none of them had agreed to it completely or thought it was even possible. I reached down for Weoduye, who was always the most open to new ideas. He stiffened as I lifted him.

"Swing your leg around," I said, seeing that he was not going to do it instinctively. He pulled up his short leg, and I sat him behind the hump where I had sat before. Bol rippled his muscles--and I thought Weoduye was going to scream and dive off. "He is just getting used to you," I said to calm the young Jannanon.

"You next," I said, looking at Goyel. He was stiff as well but pulled his leg over as he had seen Weoduye do; and then Sheios followed. The three were on top of an oryx, the twine dangling around their feet. I lifted the twine that surrounded them and told them to hold it. I touched Bol along his side, his neck, his face. I leaned down to my oryx and, as gently as I could, told him, "Let's go."

"Wait, wait...you're not getting on?" The Jannanons were in a panic.

"At first, I will walk; he needs to feel you."

Though the Jannanons had not come this way, they knew the route, the way that would take us to Foul Lands. Their fear of Bol was so great that they could barely speak to tell which way was the way. But I coaxed them and little and little they spoke more clearly. The vision the Father Tree had given me sat heavily inside me. We followed an animal path that took us toward what I was certain was the worst part of our journey. We wouldn't get close to it that light; I was going to make certain that we did not. We would find a grove of trees to bed in and wait for the dew light.

As we walked, I told them about the aper and how Bol had saved me. That had a great calming effect on my companions, and the sway of Bol had an even greater effect. I think they were starting to like the oryx. I wanted them to love him as I did but reasoned that they couldn't—they were not Tor'ocs who had lived and loved oryx since before they could remember. Liking Bol was enough for me to ask of the Jannanons.

When the light was high and above us, we stopped for mid meal in a beautiful small gully with bushes for Bol to eat and a stream and flat land for our meal to be laid. I could see by the way the Jannanons walked or tried to walk that the ride on Bol had not been easy for them, but we were definitely traveling faster than they could have walked. And after riding Bol they could hardly walk at all. In a few days, their bodies would be used to riding, and they would not get so sore. They did not complain, and quietly I thanked them. They were good men. I saw that they were brave and willing and sturdy, and I liked them as my companions.

We journeyed on after the meal, and as the light moved down behind us, there was a shift in the wind-- or more true, there was something in the wind that had not been there before. Bol felt it before any of us. He was on guard; his muscles twitched; his ears bent back; and his head turned to see what was in the wind. I felt it next, and then the Jannanons, who never looked about but straight ahead as if they could see it in front of them. It was unsettling, disturbing, and was coming from the direction we were walking. There was a greyness settling into everything—the earth, the grass, the trees, the bushes; and there were no flowers. Until now, the Out World had been filled with flowers, flowers in colors and sizes I had never seen on the Peninsula. The flowers had been seen in all directions, and they were a constant—even trees that I thought did not have flowers had flowers that bloomed on the vines that wound around them. Now, we had entered a land where the flowers would not go. However, there were thorn bushes aplenty, and that was good. I hoped that the leaves were still good to the taste for Bol.

"We should not go much farther in this light," the Jannanons said, not looking at me but ahead.

"I will look for a grove to make camp," I said, not wanting to stop walking and not wanting to make camp in this place.

"How far are Foul Lands?" I asked.

"We will reach the edge in the early light before mid meal," the Jannanons said, tension threaded through their words and voices.

In a very few counts, I spotted a grove of Dairs not far, and we made our way to them. Once we had entered among the trees, I knelt and, showing full respect, asked to be welcomed.

"You." The word was a slap from an old tree. "Who are you?"

"I am Aeon the Leaf." Not feeling a look up would be liked, I bent my head lower.

"You are not a Dair; you are no kind of tree. You are a beast that has come to trick us."

"I am a beast and no tree, yet I come honest. We wish to grow here only for this dark."

"And in the dark what will you do—cut us, burn us, eat us?"

"We are too small to eat something so great." I looked up now and spread my arms. "We have nothing to cut you with and we are not carrying fire."

"Why are you here?" another tree thumped. If it was possible to be less inviting, this one was.

"We are on our way to Foul Lands and beyond." I could not have replied with anything that would have had a greater effect. The Dairs shivered at the words 'Foul Lands'.

"You're Foul Land creatures," the old tree accused, but he was not certain of that.

"I have never been to Foul Lands, but we must go there and fully cross in the next light." I gestured to the Jannanons and Bol. "The oryx is from near; I am from the far edge of the river." I pointed toward the Peninsula and then to the Jannanons. "They are creatures from far beyond Foul Lands. We have no wish for Foul Lands, but it is on the path to the place we must go."

"You will never get there. Foul Lands will take you. Turn back and leave us."

"These three have already passed through Foul Lands and know the way," I stood up and took two steps toward the old tree. "Has the wind not brought news of us to you?"

The entire grove was quiet for many counts, and then the tree farthest away from Foul Lands and nearest where the wind would have come answered, "Yes, we knew of you and knew you would arrive soon and soon."

"Then let us grow here for the dark."

Again, there was silence until the same tree rumbled, "If no others will let you, you can come into my boughs. I am young and not as large, but I can hold you."

I turned to the Jannanons to explain. "The grove does not want us here, but there is one tree that has given us welcome. We should go to it."

The Jannanons nodded in agreement, and I led Bol to the far tree, where I knelt again and thanked her for her welcome.

"Do not be angry at the others. It is not easy growing this close to Foul Lands," the tree blew to me. "I am protected, a little, by them, and they get less of the fresh wind."

Wind

I told her about Bol and asked if there were any sweet roots growing nearby. She said there were but warned that they may not be sweet enough. I dug where she showed me and found the roots. They were darker than I had ever seen before and shriveled. Bol was at my shoulder. He looked at the roots, smelled them, then turned away. He walked out from under the tree to a thorn bush that grew on the wind's fresher side of the grove. There was a stream that ran close, but we were unsure of drinking from it.

Without discussing it, we had all decided not to eat or drink anything from the land until we were on the other side of Foul Lands. Over that dark, none of us slept well. No happy travelers would be gathering in the next dew light.

Barry Alexander Brown

5

Dew light—the sky was grey, not from cloud or rain, simply grey, a sorrowful grey sky. I could see in the far and far where we had traveled from, where the grey met the blue and melted into it, but above us there was no blue where blue should be, and in the direction where we would be heading, the grey continued and darkened. The feeling among our group was, 'Turn back, we don't need to go into this country, we were happy where we were.' I could feel that we were one in wanting to turn in any direction but straight ahead. Our first meal was done, and we only had one light to cross what they called Foul Lands and get out from under the grey sky.

Before our departure, our host tree described aids to help us survive Foul Lands. She directed me to grasses, bushes, and small trees from which I gathered bark, sap, and leaves that would nurture us. She asked permission from each green tree to allow us what we needed. They used a different language than the one that I understood and spoke. The asking was made through the ground, and I could feel the slight rumble as our host tree talked to each one of them. To me, she explained when, with what, and how to use all that I was tucking into my satchel. These instructions were conveyed in the form of an aroma that would be easy for me to see as images in my inner eye when the time came. Our host was kind, gentle, thoughtful, and cared for us. I wondered just how beautiful she would be if she could grow in a better land.

I made my farewells, gave her my thanks, and I promised on my return to take seeds from her tree back home to the Peninsula where they could grow into trees of beauty and strength.

With each arpent we crossed, the land lost more color and life. The air moved less and had a stagnant weight to it, a heaviness that replaced the fresh lightness of the air in the earlier lands. These trees in the forest where we now walked were bent, but they were not Bent Trees. They were Dairs, Firs, and Weepers unnaturally twisted and blackened. Barks that should have been brown, green, and white were all black. The smell of pain rose out of everything--and that smell was growing.

Wind

The Jannanons had traveled through this land before; yet, while I was certain that riding on the back of a great bull oryx made it a better experience, they still looked unhappy, tense, nervous. As I walked beside Bol, each time my foot touched the earth there was a feeling of being held or pulled to the ground, as though the ground didn't want to let go. It wasn't like sink mud that sucked one down; it seemed as though the force that everything feels was stronger here.

This land was strange in many ways. Its texture was wrinkled and rippled the way the O'bir Sea would have been if the water had instantly frozen. Constantly walking up and down the small waves in the ground gave me the sense of approaching the edge of something. Bol, however, was steady; the Jannanons on his back rocking with the false waves and his own steps helped to keep them even and calm.

"When we get close to Foul Lands, we will walk." I was surprised to hear the Jannanons speak. "It will be necessary. You should consider riding then."

"Why should I ride?"

"It will be a benefit." The Jannanons were certain of this.

Their tone had convinced me of their seriousness, but I couldn't see myself taking their place on Bol. "I don't see how…"

"You have fought from the back of an oryx, in your games," they interrupted. "We have not. We would be useless up here."

"Will we have to fight, then?"

The Jannanons sighed and looked troubled, "We did not fight when we came across. We know how to blend, even in the most unpleasant lands. The shadow creatures here sensed us, sensed something, but never could find the sight of us to know for certain. That way, they never knew how to attack. Now, they will know."

"But we can make it across before the next dark," I said, remembering what the Father Tree had shown me.

"We have no choice but to cross before the dark comes. The dark is even more their world than it is the Muon's. They own the dark and they will take us if we are still there."

An odor with a burnt, unpleasant smell stung our noses. I could feel the odor stinging my skin. I wasn't aware of exactly when the odor had settled in; it may have arrived along with the trees that grew dead leaves—brown, dry leaves that didn't fall from the limbs. I didn't speak to those trees. They were not our friends or friends to anything. Nothing looked alive about them, but they were not dead. I could feel their life and that life was as dark as the grey sky.

The low valleys between the earth waves were now filling with ink-dark water. When this fluid first appeared, it stood barely a toenail high; but by the tenth dip, it was to my ankles. Bol reacted badly to the dark water on his hoofs. He grunted every third or fourth step to let me know he was unhappy with this walking and that he was doing this for me. I laid my hand against his neck and stroked him. 'Thank you, old beast;

we will get through this,' was the meaning I hoped came through my touch.

The water stopped rising, but there was always some in the dips, staining Bol's and my feet. I looked at the feet of my three companions dangling over the sides of Bol, but they were hidden inside what they wore—I reasoned they were the thing called 'soles' that Iz had asked me to bring. Still, when I had seen their feet, they were unstained. How could they have made it through this without walking in the ink water? Was there a secret that they could have easily told us? Sheios saw me wondering and gazing at their feet.

"It comes off in two days," the Jannanons said, reading my thoughts. "But you have to walk through hard grass for that entire time and scrape your feet with every footfall. There's enough hard grass that grows on the other side."

I had never heard it called hard grass, but I was certain I knew the grass they said we would need to clean our feet. It was short, close to the ground and had soft leaves but many leaves. What made it hard was the type of stems the leaves grew out of, which were solid, tough, and unforgiving, and the place where the stems met was a knot of hardness, unpleasant to walk on. I was careful never to walk across them if there were another way to go. Even beasts with hooves as tough as Bol's avoided these particular grass fields. I don't remember ever seeing a path beaten down through one and I never thought I would look forward to making such a path. There was a Tor'oc saying that everything was good for something; you just had to live long enough to find out what that was. Now, I had lived long enough to know what hard grass was good for.

"Was this land the same a thousand years ago?" I asked, wondering if my ancestors had seen what I saw.

"No, this land was green a thousand years ago."

"Is it in your Legends—what happened here?"

"It is." The Jannanons breathed in as one, as people do when they're readying themselves to tell a long story. "The Muons were the first to be driven to this part of Aemira. There were no men here then, except on the far reaches, on your Peninsula," the Jannanons said, as if reciting a lesson. "It was the Four Mothers who saw the advantage of killing the Muons and the Tor'ocs, or rather, having them kill one another. The Muons were routed and forced to this place, that was already far from the nearest towns. That time was before the Tor'oc Nation rained down on Aemira. It was thought that the Muons had been our curse; but to our shock, the Tor'ocs were a curse unimaginable. Muons hunted and killed, but the Tor'ocs slaughtered for the fear and power that killing many gave them. The Four Mothers devised the lie that would lure the Tor'ocs across the land where the Muons had settled. There were battles and one great battle was at the top of a mountain that has since disappeared."

"It has not; we slept on the top of it." I surprised the Jannanons with the knowledge.

"When?" they asked together; I realized that I had come to like the song of their voices when they spoke a single word together.

"It was the island. The grave was the marking of the battle. I saw it in my dream."

Knowing that I wanted to know how their story led to making of Foul Lands, they took this in and continued. "The Tor'ocs nearly wiped out the Muons in that battle and kept killing them whenever they were found. The few Muons that survived became what we saw—horrid animal creatures that deep in their souls were afraid, even of one another. Muons bred, and how has remained a mystery because in living memory one Muon has never been seen with another."

"But why Foul Lands?" I said, getting back to my original wondering.

"Foul Lands were a mistake," they said, allowing that to sink into me. "The Four Mothers confined the Tor'ocs with a raging river, which we do not have to tell you much about; you could tell us more than we know. The Mothers were satisfied that was enough shield; but there were others who feared the Tor'ocs so much that the Mothers then agreed to bring the flood, what you call the Mad'la. Even that did not kill all the Tor'ocs or satisfy the people. It was thought that you could survive anything, and one day you might make it back across the river and, in rage and revenge, kill every man, woman, and child. The Four Mothers were certain that you were imprisoned by waters you would not and could not defeat; and they told the people of Aemira that they had done what they would, and had not been honored or thanked enough by the Ungratefuls, their name for the people, our ancestors included.

"A delegation was selected to call the Four Mothers to a Camarod in which the Mothers would be asked to do one more thing to ensure the safety of the people. The Mothers came and that was the worst thing that could have happened."

This was the part in the tradition of oral history tales in which a child, whom I was the stand-in for, was supposed to ask, "Why was that the worst thing?" So, I played my role and asked the question.

"The Mothers were already ill-tempered and angry by the time they arrived at the Camarod. The delegation first asked and then demanded that the Four do one more thing to safeguard Aemira.

"You are immortals and powerful and you have the responsibility to protect us mortals in our short lives." The delegation had the awfulness to preach to the Mothers.

Diluhao, who always spoke for the Four, asked them, "If you were immortal and had a power that even Tor'ocs could not resist, would you put yourselves as the last defense against the Murdering Nation? That is what they called you in secret."

"Why do you keep saying 'you' as if I were there?"

"You are a Tor'oc, and we have not found a way to unthink of you as we always thought of Tor'ocs," they said, shyly and apologetically. "We will try to exclude you."

"Good, because this is not a story about me."

Wind

"The delegation, not truly understanding the meaning of what was being asked of them, said they gladly and with all their hearts would be that last defense if they were immortals."

"So, the Four Mothers made them immortals, but cursed them," I whispered 'cursed' to myself, guessing at the dire conclusion to the story.

The Jannanons nodded. "Yes, cursed—immortals but not alive; and because they were immortals, they were not dead."

"And they had a power?"

"...the horror--to make everyone the same as they were—not alive, not dead."

"So, the Four Mothers waved their hands, or sticks, or whatever they had, and turned the delegation into cursed immortals?" I asked, not quite picturing the scene.

"No, it is never as easy as that." The story was making the Jannanons sadder at each turn, as if this were something that had happened to them and only recently. "For the curse to work, the delegation had to offer themselves one more time. The delegation was told that if they truly wanted this last defense, they would have to come to a ceremony where each person willing would become an immortal, not like the Mothers, but immortal. They were given three days to consider all that it would mean to never die, to outlive everyone they knew and loved, to outlive their own time.

"After the Four Mothers had departed, the delegation met secretly in one of the homes. They argued over what it all meant, and finally came to the conclusion that this was a test, that the Mothers didn't have the power to make anyone immortal, and if they tricked the Mothers to agree that the immortals would be the last defense, then the Mothers themselves would have to be that last wall.

"The third day came, and a cassion, a sort of ancient coach, large enough to hold the Umbrare of Thirteen, as they were later called, was waiting in the square of the town. It was an ornate wagon that had no wheels, instead it had six posts that rose up from its four corners and two of its sides, and the posts ended in large iron circles. The thirteen delegates took seats that were made of cloth unknown to man, cloth that was soft but firm, cloth that made the riders feel a sense of comfort and calm and ease that made any fear or misgivings that they had evaporate through the top of their heads. It was in the midst of this well-being that six Great Rods flew down from the high clouds, took the cassion by the iron rods and pulled the wagon with its cargo into the sky.

"They were flown to the cliff-side alcazar of Keoen Fam, who held all the ceremonies for the Four Mothers. She invited the delegation in and led them to a hall where a table was set with goblets and drink. The three other Mothers were there waiting, sitting in the mid of each side. Keoen Fam took her seat in the mid of the last open side and asked the thirteen to take their seats. Once they were all seated, Diluhao asked them if they had thought and if they had decided what they wanted to do. She told them a final time that a last defense was not needed. This was what they were sure she would say, and it was final proof that all of this was a charade; but the delegation was also certain a last defense was absolutely necessary, and that they were clever enough to turn the Four Mothers permanently into that defense.

"We do not know who spoke for the delegation, but whoever it was told the Mothers that they wanted the defense, that they wanted the immortality, and they wanted it as a bond that the immortals would forever be that defense. The Four Mothers agreed. The goblets that sat in front of the Mothers and their guests were there to bond this agreement with drink. The seventeen of them held the goblets and drank as one. Afterwards, Diluhao told them, 'You are not immortals yet. The drink was for the bond alone. A blood ceremony is needed for immortality.'

"Once again, Keoen Fam led the group through her alcazar to the open balcony that looked across the wide expanse of Eastern Aemira. The delegation had never seen so much of their own world. Diluhao pointed out the direction of the Tor'oc prison, too far to see, but they stood and gazed as though the last defense were merely an arm's length away.

"A green fire was lit in the mid of the balcony by Viem Hels, who performed all rituals for the Four Mothers. Viem Hels called the thirteen to surround the pit of fire and asked them to hold their hands, palms up, over the flames. They were all nervous that they would be burned—the fire was high, and their hands held out straight would not be just over the fire, but in the mid of it. 'You must do this,' she told them. The first to put their hand into the fire was the Jannanon delegate; we know this. She held her hand there, and it did not burn—the fire was cold and cooling. She smiled with relief, and the other twelve followed her, pushing their hands into the green flames and smiling the same smile of wonder and relief.

"A blade appeared in the hand of Liuf, and she told them not to be afraid and to hold steady. She threw the small blade without a handle into the air while mouthing ancient words of a spell, and the blade flew across all outstretched palms, marking each palm with a cut, clean and deep enough to produce a flow of blood. There was shock and there was pain; it was the pain that really was their bond but it was the drink that held them in their place. They wanted to pull their cut and bleeding hands out of the fire but they could not. Viem Hels saw that enough blood had gathered in each and every palm, she instructed them to turn their hands over and let the blood fall into the fire. They did, and the fire burst into flames of yellow and blue; and the quick sharp heat made the thirteen pull their hands out.

"Each one of their palms had been burned a dark shade of purple, the skin ugly from the burn; but the cuts from the knife were sealed. The thirteen were in a state of great pain from the cuts and the fire. The Four Mothers grabbed each of the thirteen to rub a salve into their palms; a salve to hold in the pain, not to soothe it; the pain was never released. The pain was trapped in their bodies. You can smell that pain here; it is trapped in the land where we walk."

I could smell the pain they talked of. We walked on in silence, and I waited for the Jannanons to continue the story. They were looking ahead at the land where the pain might be a living thing.

"We have a word in Aemira - 'umbrare' - which means 'cast into shadow'. The thirteen were cast into shadow, but it was days upon days before they fully understood. The pain grew and changed them; they disappeared into shadows of themselves. Dark grew from their hands, took their arms and torsos, their legs, their feet. When the only parts left of them were their heads and faces, the Four Mothers reappeared. The people had become afraid of the delegation, and they were forced to hide away in the Grand Room where the Camarods were held. That is where the Mothers came to find them.

'What have you done to us?" the delegation screamed in anger at the Four Mothers, who smiled back; and Diluhao told them, 'This is the price of immortality.'

'But you don't look like this,' someone from the delegation pointed out.

'We are not immortal. Where did you get that idea?' Diluhao replied.

'You are; you have been since before anyone can remember.'

'We live ten thousand years; and after us our daughters will live ten thousand years,' Diluhao informed them, 'It only appears like immortality to you who live but a short, short time. You thirteen will be the only immortals as soon as the change is complete.'

'What can we do with immortality when we look like this?'

'You are the last defense.' Diluhao wondered why they hadn't understood that by then. 'It will be necessary for you to live your immortality at the edge of the world to guard us from Tor'ocs, if they ever escape their prison.'

'You've tricked us,' the delegation wailed.

'You tricked yourself,' she screamed back. 'You little specks who live and die as quick as that—' She snapped her fingers. 'You thought you could fool us. You thought we would fall into your ridiculous little trap. You were the hunters and the prey—this was all your doing. We only helped you realize your deepest desire—to protect yourself—and you thirteen will be the most protected creatures who ever lived.'

"There was something in her words that made the delegation uneasy. They asked her what she meant.

"Once you are immortal and you are just the shadows, any living creature you can hold and keep for an entire dark will become like you—shadows, immortal shadows.

'What's to keep us from holding and keeping you, then?' a delegate wanted to know.

'You will be shadows, but you will still feel pain,' Diluhao said, as the fourth Mother, Liuf, who was the one who carried out the physical feats of the Mothers, produced a small dart from the air around her right hand. She aimed and threw it into the leg of a now shadowy delegate, who howled and crawled away to recover in the darkest part of the room. 'So, you see, with our magic you will never be able to touch us, much less hold us for an entire dark. It would be an excruciating experience for you, if you were to try.'

'What now, then?' the delegates wanted to know, understanding that they had been outwitted and defeated and that their fate was as terrible as any nightmare.

'Time is small for you in this world. We must get you to the Far Lands where you will exist,' Diluhao bent into them for emphasis. 'I say exist because it won't feel like life to you, though you are immortal. You will not have to eat or sleep. You will be on guard, forever on guard for the attack that will never come. The cassion is outside waiting,' and she pointed in the direction they should exit. 'It is time for you to go.'

"They had not cared to eat or sleep since they had been in the Grand Hall, so they knew what Diluhao said was true. There was nothing left of their lives, and nothing left to do but flee to the Far Lands where no one would see them, and no one would know them."

The Jannanons stopped as though this were the end of the story, but I had to know, "The Great Rods flew them here and dropped them, but what happened?" I gestured to the land around us to say something bad must have taken place after the shadows were dropped.

"Nothing at first happened," the Jannanons threw this bit out. "But as time grew on time, they became angry and wanted to punish something, anything. They began to hold captive the beasts that were here, men and women who were traveling past or through, Muons who were attempting to make their way back into the world. They also discovered that the light was harsh for them and that the pain they lived with increased in the light. They took to building an underworld of tunnels, and as their numbers increased, the tunnels grew longer and wider. The land above the tunnels became hot from their pain, and life in this land died."

"That's what the Mothers wanted to create - Foul Lands," I said, understating that missing piece.

"No," the Jannanons said, shaking their heads. "That was the mistake! They had misjudged the outcome and the result. Once they knew, they set a boundary on all four sides that runs twice as wide as you are tall and flows deep into the earth. It is a boundary of rock, called tourmaline."

"Why don't the shadows just go beyond the tourmaline?" I asked.

"They don't like it. It repels them, perhaps it makes their pain unbearable, and they have no desires left but to punish and to hold."

"How do the shadows hold you?"

"We don't know," replied the Jannanons. "The only creatures that know are those that have now become shadows themselves. In defense, we can only inflict pain on them and hope that it will be enough to get us across Foul Lands."

"Did you see the shadows when you crossed before?"

"We saw them, but we know nothing more about them."

As the Jannanons told their story, and we had walked closer to Foul Lands, the burnt stench had grown stronger; the trees and plants and bushes were few; and the ground beneath us was dry, cracked, and darker than before. Bol stopped as we came to the top of another wave. Out before us, not far, was a wide strip of land that smoldered as though a fire had recently burnt it. The land stretched to left and right beyond the distance we could see, but the land far beyond we could recognize, with trees in the far and far.

"This is where we walk, and you ride," said the Jannanons, as they toppled off Bol and landed on their feet.

I did not feel like riding. I pulled Bol forward, and our group marched toward the burnt ground, the Jannanons not walking together. Sheios was on my left, Weoduye just on the other side of Bol, and Goyel on the other side of him. We walked like that in a line until we reached the edge of Foul Lands. We stopped. The smell of burning earth with something else inside it—the pain they talked about—was strong, overwhelming my senses. We gazed out over the ground that we had to cross.

Sheios turned to me and said, "When you think of it, the shadows are finally doing the job they were sent here to do." He looked me up and down. It was clear that I did not get his meaning. "The Last Defense — stopping Tor'ocs."

I tried to force a smile back at the joke, but I think I only accomplished a grimace. I pulled my satchel around to a place where I could open it and take out the items I had gathered at the last friendly tree.

"I have a sap we should put on the bottoms of our feet, and leaves we should bind them in. I don't know exactly what it does, but it will help to protect us."

First, I lifted the hooves of my oryx and rubbed the sap into the hard shell of his hooves. He would not like the leaves, and I reasoned that he didn't need them. I put the sap on myself and wrapped the leaves around my feet. The sap acted like a bind that kept the leaves in place; and the leaves softened with the sap and took the form of my foot, like a second skin. The Jannanons had watched me, and I went to each one to show them and to apply the sap and bind their feet with the leaves. I had thought having leaves wrapped around my feet would be uncomfortable, but it was soothing and cool.

"You should ride," Weoduye yelled from the other side of Bol. The Jannanons were talking as individuals.

Sheios nodded. "It would be better."

They had reasons for this knowing that I had to trust. I climbed onto Bol, and his muscles rippled underneath me. I think he was glad to feel life on his back again. I squeezed my legs into his sides, and he took a step onto the smoldering ground. The dry earth cracked under the weight. We kept walking.

The Jannanons fanned out farther from us. I don't know if it was an illusion of the place, but they seemed to have become smaller. They were crouched down but walking at the same speed as Bol. I took my orc bow out from behind my back and readied an arrow to fire, not knowing what might come at us or from where. The land was silent. Nothing lived or moved on it. Everywhere around us there were holes, giant holes, some of which were black pits; others emitted whiffs of smoke from something burning deep below. The edges of the holes were flat against the ground, unlike the holes of the small beasts that lived in the ground on the Peninsula who deposited the earth from below, making ridges around the openings of their homes. I wondered if these holes were so ancient that the earth had been blown flat over the centuries. I wondered also if it ever rained here, as it was dry in a way that gave the sense that rain would be afraid to fall on such a ground.

We had gone far into Foul Lands without a sign of any moving thing. Just when I had the thought that we might make it across this desecrated land, a sound rose from a nearby hole—the sound of sticks scratching against one another. The sound must have risen from somewhere deep because it had an echo to it. Bol must have also heard this sound, as his ears had twitched and twitched for the past twenty steps. The Jannanons too heard the sound, and their steps took on a slower, more careful, more alert tempo.

We walked on, and the sound grew, multiplied—a forest of sticks was heard scratching, snapping, clicking beneath us, rising out of every hole. Bol jerked his head from hole to hole as the sound grew, and individual cracks and snaps, louder and more distinct, burst out of a hole here and a hole there. Yet there was nothing to see, no movement. The land was as still as any dead thing.

Movement shuddered in the distance. A black shape dragged itself against the black ground. It was not completely black but dark, dark grey against even darker grey, so that when I stared at it, my reason told me there was nothing there, but I could feel it--and it could feel me. The shadows seemed wary of us and only came out of the ground at a distance; this was not a new phenomenon. I had seen it before.

The Father Tree had shown me this moment, though I had reasoned it was to give me a view of what we were heading toward, but it had been a warning. What was it in the vision that had happened next? I relaxed, letting my mind drift back to the first light after the river, letting myself smell the vision. I was back at the Father Tree, and the view of this moment came to me: there were dark things everywhere, underground, in front, but especially behind. In the vision, I turned to look to see what was at my back, and there, legions of shadows were closing in. Out of the vision, back in the real place, I turned to look as I had in my mind, and it was the same--legions of shadows, dark grey shadows of animals, man, bird, creeping along the burnt ground, creeping fast enough to catch us at our speed. We had been tricked by the sounds and the few shadows we could see. The danger had silently made its way to take us and was close to success.

I yelled out, and the Jannanons turned as one. With a battle cry new to me, they charged into the shapes, their long cloths flying back off their bodies, exposing a sheet of metal that fell over their torsos but moved like cloth; and in their hands were weapons that they had been holding in readiness. Weoduye swung a rope that also looked like metal with a hook at the end that tore into the things and made them screech and scream and run. These screeches came from the undead who didn't fear the end of life but feared the pain of life. They were always in pain, as the story told us; but this new pain must have been fearsome and beyond my reason.

Sheois had a double-edged sword that he swung around him, cutting into the shadows that couldn't get away fast enough to end their misery. Goyel held weapons in both hands—a double-bladed silver hatchet in one, and on the other hand, there was a glove-like ball that shot a kind of lightning whenever shadows lunged at him. When the lightning touched the shadows, it caused them to scream in a higher pitch – that pain sounded the worse. Bol and I sat back from the fight—I was watching as if it were a shadow show put on just for us; and I wondered why we didn't all have the glove-ball, since it did its job so well. Later, I would discover this glove was heavier than seemed possible, and every lightning strike sent a searing jolt up the arm. Goyel was strong and tough—much tougher than I was.

I came back to reason as I felt something behind me. Swinging around, I glimpsed a shadow loping toward us, readying to pounce. By instinct I pulled the bow string with an arrow already loaded in it and fired. The arrow flew from me, striking the shadow mid-chest and sticking there. The shadow's hands grabbed at the shaft of arrow that appeared now to be part of its body and yelled. It tried to pull the arrow out, and that only increased the pain. I turned back to my friends and the fight.

I squeezed my legs against Bol and yelled, "Yaaow!" Bol charged, lowering his head so that the giant horns would be the first things the shadows would meet when we hit them. I reached back, felt for the spear, and pulled it around, pressing and holding the end under my arm as my hand gripped it to point down and forward. We struck the shadows at full oryx speed, Bol's horns tearing through shadow bodies and my spear hitting mark after mark, sometimes piercing a body so thoroughly the shadow was pulled up into the air where I shook the spear to free it. They were surprisingly light. Shadows that were not mere flat nothings against the ground, but that had shape and depth, I had assumed would have weight to them, but they didn't.

We appeared to be winning. The shadows were fewer and fewer around us, though a shadow would not retreat until it felt a blow, until it felt enough pain for it to run, crawl, or simply fall back into a hole, where it faded into the depths and did not reappear. The huge mass of shadows that had outnumbered us one hundred to one had dwindled down to only a few. By the exceptional skill of the Jannanons, who were quick and sure, those few would be gone soon, leaving us alone on the field of battle—my first field of battle.

Weoduye, Sheios, and Goyel struck at the last three shadows simultaneously, sending them scuttling into holes and underground where the pain would consume them long enough to allow us to get across. We all looked around and then at one another, marveling that the onslaught seemed over, and the battle won.

"We must move." Newly alert, the Jannanons spoke as one. "Stay on Bol and go!" they said, pointing in a direction that would take us across the grim terrain.

"Come up here with me," I said, extending my arm for them to grab. "We can all ride."

"No—go!" They urged in a brusque voice that communicated to leave them and get gone as quickly as possible.

They turned their backs to me, looked about, and began walking quickly in the direction of getting across. Given Bol's speed, I could have ridden away and been safely across soon, but I didn't feel that the Jannanons would be safe without us, even though they had outfought me and dispatched many, many more shadows. Bol and I stayed walking beside them, and each would glance at us, impatient and angry that we were still there with them.

Bursting from the holes around us came a loud cracking noise. It was the sound of an entire great tree being ripped apart from bottom to top. Because the crack met our ears from the many holes surrounding us, it seemed as though it came from the ground right under our feet. The sound stopped us in our tracks—something was heading toward us.

Out of the dark holes rose more shadow bodies, in groups of about three to one of us. They were being pushed up, surrounding, facing us, held from beneath by the hands and bodies of other shadows that were still whimpering and crying from the pain. As they reached the surface the new shadows stepped out onto the ruined ground, and the shadows still in pain withdrew. They formed a circle around us, and I counted the shadows that made up the circle—thirteen--the cursed thirteen Umbrare that had fouled the land and turned its creatures into dark things like themselves. I had not noticed the faces of the ones we had fought and injured, but I had time to look at these. They did have faces with features--eyes wide open, frightening in their looks of madness and purpose; mouths held in grimaces of dark grey teeth; and noses, cheeks, jaws that looked nearly human, yet distorted, broken. They walked slowly, turning the circle, coming closer, closer. The sound of the ripping tree came from them.

They looked at each of us in turn, examining us. The thirteen had never seen a group like us. One said in a harsh whisper, "It's a Tor'oc." And all those horrible eyes were on me.

I did not feel brave, but I said, "Let us pass. You are no match for a Tor'oc."

Wind

They laughed—a hideous laugh that lacked everything a laugh should have and contained everything that shouldn't be there.

"Once, that was true," the shortest shadow said, and I saw this had a strange effect on my companions, who all three convulsed as if the words had touched them in a way, and I think it had touched them. The shortest shadow was the ruined Jannanon from the story.

"Day out of days, and you have finally come," another of the thirteen shadows said.

"What a beautiful thing you are." One that felt close to my side almost seemed to be breathing this into my ear.

"You give us purpose," hissed one from behind me, and the delegates howled.

My friends warned them, "We have dispatched thirty times your number and we will inflict such pain on you, it will take another thousand years to forget us."

A tall shadow that seemed to be a leader tried on a smile but failed. "We did not expect them to hold you. We just wanted to see who—and what—you were."

They had been moving continuously, and the circle had tightened. I wondered if Weoduye, Sheios, and Goyel were as aware of this as I had just become. My sense was that we should not wait until striking distance was reached; somehow, I reasoned that would give the Umbrare the advantage.

"Have you seen this before?" I held the spear above my head. The Umbrare looked at it but did not recognize it. "It is the spear of Sumon, and I am the blood of Sumon."

The Jannanons looked at me as if I had gone mad—how was this boasting doing any good?

"We knew Sumon," the Jannanon shadow said, sending out another convulsion among my friends. "It is good that his blood has come to us."

"You will not have blood, but I am going to take your immortality."

This caused another ripple of that horrible laughter.

"We will cross this Foul Land and we will reach the Four Mothers. They will tell me how to end you."

"Immortal is absolute," the tall one said.

"I was taught that there is a cycle and end to all things, without exception. And you are not an exception. The Four Mothers know how to end you and they will tell me."

My Jannanons now knew I had gone mad—boasting at the same time enraging the things. 'How is this helpful?' their faces said.

"No!" the tall one cried out. "You will be us."

As I talked, I had pulled the spear back, and on his words, I threw it through him. He folded in agony, and the rest screamed and moved at us, fast. This was what I wanted, to be back in the fight. The desire bubbled in my blood. Bol jumped and twisted and turned. A creature was at our backs, but Bol's horns knocked it back; and another shadow leapt in from my side. I swung my finnif knife and missed. A shadow thing grabbed me. The other shadows we had fought were like aims set up to be knocked down—these were quick and subtle and knew the fight. One swiftly pulled me from Bol, and I hit the ground with the dark thing on top of me.

Its hands and body were cold, winter cold; there was no weight to it, but it was strong and held me against the ground. Wherever the shadow creature touched, shocks of pain charged into me, tentacles of pain that ran through my body, seeking some deep part of me. The thing bared its grey-black teeth, and I think it meant to sink those teeth into me, but Bol's back hooves kicked with a force that knocked its body three Tor'oc lengths away from me. Impossibly quick, Bol jumped across me and speared the shadow with both horns; and a high-pitched cry was the last we would hear from it. It slithered to a hole and was gone.

I lay on the ground and looked across to the sound of the struggle. The Jannanons were fighting with their backs to one another, holding the things off; and it looked as though there were as many of the shadows as before. The shadows dashed in and out, avoiding the sting of the weapons. There was a method to it; they had a plan, but I couldn't grasp what it was. The shadow pain inside of me was waning now that the creature was off, but I still couldn't move. Bol was back, and he stood over me. The creatures would look to us, but none came—they weren't certain what the oryx was, and they weren't sure what it could do to them.

Whatever else it was they now wanted most, they were trying to get it from the Jannanons.

I couldn't hear clearly, but the shadow creature that once had been a Jannanon was talking, and as she talked, Weoduye, Sheios, and Goyel jerked slightly— they were fighting the shadows without, and fighting her words within. But they kept the fight at a balance, not losing, not gaining—the creatures were not beaten; the creatures were not winning. Feeling and movement were coming back into my arms. I felt for my oro bow and found my arrows. Slowly, I fitted an arrow in place, not wanting to draw attention to myself or to what I was about to do. Pressing my body flat against the ground, I raised the bow, aimed through the open legs of Bol, and fired. The arrow flew, hitting the Jannanon's shadow, splitting her head, flying through it and past. It seemed that they were made of nothing but the lack of light.

She cried out in the pain I knew the arrow had inflicted, but I wasn't prepared for my Jannanons to cry as well. They had all been connected, maybe through her words, and when the arrow struck, it wounded them, too. They collapsed and the shadows rushed, covering the Jannanons with their cold and their pain. I found my feet and was in the fight again, the finnif knife blades slashing and cutting at dark grey bodies that howled, trying to grab me and the arm that held the knife. Bol was there as well—I felt him more than saw him.

I stepped across the body of Sheios, who was lying, body curled, arms and hands across his face, but now free of the shadows. His face was contorted with the shocks that were still running through him. There were fewer shadows now, and they were busy with the Jannanons beneath them. Bol caught one of the shadows with a horn, lifting it off Goyel and running with it, trying to throw it off. Sumon's spear was stuck in the ground not far, and I wanted the spear and wanted to use it. I raced to it, took it from the ground and charged back at the single shadow over Goyel, who was face down and curled like Sheios had been. The spear struck the shadow in its mid, shoving through the body and reappearing on the other side. The shadow let go of Goyel, wriggling and screaming at a pitch that hurt the inside of my head. I braced my foot against its body and pulled the spear out. Its crawl turned into a run that took it to a hole, where it was gone like the wounded shadows before.

    I turned back to my companions, who were lying on the ground but no longer curled. Theirs were the only bodies remaining in the burnt land—no more shadows and, to my shock--no Weoduye. The second battle was over. I would never get accustomed to both how slow and how fast battles were; they happened as though time was slowed to a stop; and at the same, they took no time at all.

    I ran to Goyel to see how he was. He was breathing heavily and holding his mid, trying to ease the shocks away. His mouth moved, attempting speech, but the pain inside him was still too great for him to speak.

    "They took the young one," Sheios said, struggling to form words.

I moved over to him, "Do you know where?"

Sheios pointed down, his finger pushing the burnt soil.

"Did you see into which hole they took him?"

Sheios nodded and looked at a hole about two Tor'ocs away.

I placed my hand on him—the first time I had touched any of their bodies like this. He was muscle-hard, strong, and tough. "I will get him back," I said, feeling that it was my fault that Weoduye was taken.

"Don't! You must not, no!" he spat out. It's you they want."

"They won't have me, and I will get him back."

He grabbed my wrist and stopped me from moving away from him. "I know this from that thing that once was."

"The Jannanon that I shot?"

"Helkvin—her name." He rested to catch breath. "From her we know they took him to get you. You cannot go."

"We have no time," I said, gesturing toward Goyel to show what state the other Jannanon was in. "I am the only chance he has. I have to go." I tore my wrist away from the grip.

Bol had returned without a shadow dangling from his horns. I could see that Sheios was recovering quickly, but Goyel had had the shadows on him longer, and it would take him longer to come back to himself. I lifted Goyel onto Bol and handed him my oro bow and the spear.

"Ride to the far edge. We will join you there."

Goyel shook his head, meaning to be defiant. I smiled at him and petted the neck of my oryx. "Take care of him, Bol."

I took the glove from Goyel, discovering just how heavy it was, and ran to the hole before my friends could react. I jumped in, my feet expecting to fall a distance, but the floor met my footing only two Tor'ocs deep. It first appeared as dark as my reason had told me it would be, but soon I saw that there was some light, though little. Light it was, dim and coming from spots in the walls that steadily burned and filled the tunnel with a pale haze that choked the breath.

I fitted the glove as best as I could to my much larger hand. I could only get three fingers into it and decided to hold it as I would a satchel. The metal cloth was pliable enough to let me grab it like that. Taking a few steps into the haze-filled tunnel, I held the glove chest-high in front of me, wondering how long I could keep my arm lifted—how had he been able to fight so freely with this weight attached to his hand?

The tunnel walls were high, its width narrow, and I could often touch the sides. Besides up and out, the only way to move was down; I felt as though I was descending a hill that slowly fell away. The warm, sometimes hot walls were charred rock, grown brittle over years and years of burning. It came to me that this had been how they were able to carve their tunnels, softening the rock with fire, and why the land was burnt on top. At times I came to other tunnels that ran up to openings, but the shadows had not gone those ways, and I kept down as my direction. If they wanted me, this route would also be easy to follow.

As my eyes became more accustomed, I saw that the walls of the tunnels were not quite black but deep dark purple, and the floor looked polished, smooth, and shiny from long use. Beyond the smell of the fire, there was nothing—it smelled of emptiness. I tried to imagine what it would be like to live long and long, but not be alive, to just exist as these things have been existing, stretching out the endless time in the pits where these tunnels were no doubt leading me. I reasoned that they didn't need to sleep or eat or fill their days with the activities that we do to keep alive, and we do these things as much for the enjoyment of them as for the need of them. They needed nothing but to wait for the hordes of Tor'ocs who were not coming.

Those were my thoughts as I made my way down and down, listening for the sounds of shadows that I hoped could warn me they were near. The tunnel was silent but for me. I was the only thing making noise, and each footfall sounded like the crash of a tree. They would hear me long before I would hear them, so I didn't attempt to soften my steps. I would have to hurt and hurt them and hope that the pain they had suffered earlier was enough to weaken them long enough for me to take Weoduye.

I don't know what made me look into the ceiling's darkness—a movement or a sound or just a sense? I looked, and the ceiling above was heavy with shadows who had been watching, waiting for their moment to fall on me, or perhaps waiting for a signal. My instinct was to run, but there were shadows in that dark ceiling from beginning to end, and I could not outrun them. I pushed my hand up, the hand holding Goyel's glove, and the lightning jumped from it, hitting shadow after shadow as I ran, creating a wail of screams that filled the emptiness of the tunnel with that flood of pain. Even though each jolt shot a short sharp pain up my arm, each hit of lighting lessened the weight of the glove, as if hitting these things pulled it up from my hand. For that reason alone, I wanted to hit as many of them as possible. Once hit, they fell to the polished floor, turned and tossed a moment in their agony, then got up and ran past me at an impressive speed, trying to avoid my glove. They were trying to reach somewhere before I did.

I ran like this for a distance I could not guess, until there was no more tunnel around me. It seemed as though nothing was around me but space. I had entered a room, a large room the shape of a bird's egg laid out on its side. Countless tunnels opened into this room, each leading up. Unlike in the narrow tunnel, the burning lights in the walls of the room were many colors—some a deep orange-red, others blue, others green, others burned yellow-white. Each fire was not bright, but there were so many that the room was lit enough to see—a magical swirl of color.

A mass of shadows swarmed in the center of the floor of the room. I pressed myself against the wall next to the opening of the tunnel I had just left and looked around me to see if I could make out any shadows nearby. It appeared that the entire population was down in front of me. They were moving, moving in tight circles that spun out from a center point. The circles spun in both directions. They were like the rings of tree—a circle of shadows bound tight was spinning one direction; the next ring spun the opposite way. If there had not been such a wailing in the tunnel before, I would have been able to hear them ahead of me. They were moaning, whimpering. In the very center of the circles, the point around which they spun, Weoduye was pinned down by four of the original thirteen. The four held him by his arms and legs. In the light, I couldn't tell what was happening to him, but there was a horrible change taking place. A mist rose off him; his head was pushed back; his mouth opened as if screaming; but he made no sound. The four were not looking at him; they were looking at me.

"I will trade myself for him," I screamed at them. "Let him go."

The one holding an arm replied, "You have nothing to trade. We will have you anyway. Nothing leaves the Seap but as a shadow."

There is a saying on the Peninsula – 'The ones who reason they can never be beaten have already lost.' And I had a plan. If the plan came to a good end, I would still have to find the tunnel to take us out of this place and to the far side of Foul Lands. I needed to center myself, to know where I was and where I would go. The shadows were waiting for me, knowing I would attack, and since time was no longer an obstacle for them, they were waiting for me to move first. I relaxed myself and let go. Like the time in the Divul, I sent my vision high again, traveling through the ruined ground above me, out through it, and back to the top of Foul Lands, and higher still. Just as the Father Tree had told me, this was my advantage. I could look in the air above the place that they called the Seap and see across it, while my body faced them below. Holes were visible, so many holes everywhere. I could see across Foul Lands and pick an opening to a tunnel that was as close to the edge as any, one that I was nearly certain I could find after I had Weoduye. What I liked especially about this tunnel was that I saw Bol and Goyel in the green space just past it. I could see that they had made it across; they were safe. What surprised me was that Sheios was there, standing on the ground directly above the mid of the Seap, directly above Weoduye. They could still feel each other, and that was a luck for us; he would feel when I had him and feel which way we would be escaping.

    I gazed at the opening that would give us freedom and thought I should make certain I could find it from below. When I'm in my soul body, I merely have to think of the place or direction I want to go, and I move, sometimes too quickly, which confuses and disorients me. I have learned to control it, to move slower, as I do in my flesh. This state is faster than the flesh, but the senses are the same. I looked to the opening, and I moved across, still high above the burnt land. With a quick thought, I flew down into it.

This was a tunnel like the other, lit by the burning walls; and it ran down in a long, easy way—down to the Seap. I tried to pay attention to particular marks or lights in the walls that could help me, to guide me back up, and realized that there was nothing that made that path special. However, if I took another tunnel, one that ran off this one, it would take us up and out as all of them did. We might emerge further away from the land's edge, but we would be out, and we would get to the edge, if we could escape the shadows' tentacles below.

For a jiff, I lost the thought of why I was there. I was having fun flying down through the tunnel, the light passing by in swirls and streaks. I thought, 'I want to do this again,' but my reason grabbed me and shook me and pulled me back to the job at hand. That was where my mind was when I flew out of the tunnel and back into the Seap. I stopped and looked about, turned to see the marks around the opening I had just exited. I took in the light around it, noting the blue and green slashes that surrounded the entire opening. It was different from the others near it. This must have been an important path for them. Perhaps it was the one they used to snatch prey that had wandered in from the world.

I twisted my soul body back around. The Seap was as I had left it—the circles turning in opposite directions, Weoduye held down in the mid by the four, who were still staring at me across the large hall. I was leaning against a wall and staring back at the four who were unaware that the eyes in the body before them were not seeing and the head was not making new thoughts. They could have taken me while I had been gone, but I looked fierce in my frozen state.

I floated above the circles of moaning shadows, glad that they had not yet fully recovered from the pain of the battle. I floated to Weoduye and let myself fall just above him. His head was in that odd angle, thrown back, the eyes pinched closed, the mouth open in a scream with no sound. But what I had not seen from far away was that his lips quivered, the mouth moving to close slightly and open again. It was from the lightning shocks of pain moving into him from the four. They had stripped him of the metal sheet, but his long cloth was still tied around his neck, and he lay on it. His white body was turning another color—or a lack of color.

Greyness rippled through him, appearing, and disappearing on his skin, sometimes as stretches of crooked lines, or in other places, as patches that caused his skin to welt. Where the four held him, his body was the darkest grey, almost black. In places where they touched him, his body tremored and throbbed in ways that bodies should not, the skin folding and curling, the muscles beneath breaking like waves hitting land, and all of this in minute patterns, which made it more disturbing.

The four were unaware of me. I moved to take them in, to see them close. It was clear that they were truly once human—eyes, nose, mouth, head, expression—but now they had broken looks. The eyes were the most unsettling; they were silvery grey, unlike the rest of their bodies, and in the mid were pupils, pitch black centers that appeared like bottomless pits.

I knew enough now, and felt it was the time to act. I willed my senses to return to my body. I was falling back into it, snapping back into myself. I started moving my arms and my legs that were tingling from lack of movement. I gave my flesh some moments to come back to life and I studied that hall in front of me one last time.

"Keep breathing," I whispered to myself.

Then I charged forward, running, catching my quickest speed by the time I hit the outer circle, keeping Goyel's glove stretched in front of me. The lightning jumped from the glove as we collided. A cracking sound and an arc of light lit the room in such whiteness that I was blinded. My sense was that the shadow bodies were so tightly twisted and bound to one another that the lightning hit them as though striking one large thing rather than many small ones. The light was blinding, but the shadows' sounds were worse. Their cries bounced around the walls of the Seap at such a pitch, it felt as though their screaming was coming from inside me. The blazing light and piercing screams fused together like a curled fist that knocked me flat on the floor and drained all sensation from me.

My plan had been to cut a path through the circles, reach the four, inflict as much pain as quickly as I could--and take Weoduye to escape. Instead, I was on the floor of the Seap among bodies and bodies of the shadow creatures twisting in agony and confusion, my own eyes unseeing, my ears ringing.

As my eyes cleared, I rolled onto my knees. The floor of the Seap appeared as a black mass that wouldn't keep still with shadows continuously undulating and crying. In the mid, the four held their victim. Their heads all tilted down to avoid the light that had blinded them, too. That presented a bit of luck. The shadows' eyes were even more sensitive to the light than mine, and it might take them considerable time to see again. Still, I had to hurry. I had no choice but to cross the dark bodies to get to Weoduye. I stepped and was thankful to feel that the salve and the leaf were still protecting me – I stepped onto the next. It was like walking across water solid enough to lift me, but with an undercurrent that never quit moving, pushing, disappearing underfoot, and then pushing back again. I fell over and over, always trying to hit any shadows below with Goyel's glove. I surely didn't want to touch them with my free hand. Each strike with the glove triggered more high-pitched screams, plus more fear and confusion on the floor around me.

As the creatures began to anticipate my coming, they pushed away to get clear of me, and unwittingly opened a path. Moving through without creatures underfoot, I made some headway; but the constant, overwhelming screams caused me to be slower than I should have been. It had the effect of strong drink on me. My sense of balance was shaky. In a surge of energy, I sprinted as fast as I could and reached the central four, their heads still bent away from the faded light. One nearest me had hold of Weoduye's leg. Raising Goyel's glove, I shoved it against the creature's head, and dragged a streak of lightning down its torso. The charge seemed to jump straight through its shadow body, and it let loose of Weoduye's leg in attempt to push away the pain-making thing, which only gave the lightning a new chance to strike its hands and arms. Its agonized shrieking was swallowed up in the swirl of the countless howls and cries in the room. The shadow that held Weoduye's other leg tilted its head up. It had not recovered its full sight, but it was trying to see what was wrong.

    I lunged forward to drive the glove into its mid, knocking it back and to the floor. Not waiting to watch its agony, I turned to the remaining shadow creatures that had pinned Weoduye's arms. I fell on the first with the ball of lightning, electrifying its back. Two quick steps around my friend's head brought me to the last one. As its face blazed with lightening from the glove, its wail sank into a low, quavering, rumbling. Pulling the glove back, I saw glowing hands of the creature grab its own head as though it wanted to tear the burning part from its body. It stumbled backward and fell onto the floor of writhing shadows it couldn't cross.

    Weoduye was breathing heavily. His eyes were rolled up into his head, his mouth open, and his reason elsewhere. He was lying on a low table where the kneeling shadows had surrounded him. With my free hand, I grabbed him around his mid, pulled him up and tossed him over my opposite shoulder. Was it my imagining or was he lighter than he'd been before?

Wind

My plan had not only gone the way I had envisioned but had gone better. There was still a path cleared in front of me, a path that opened to the tunnel I wanted. If I ran fast with Weoduye, we could be out the Seap in a wink of time, up the tunnel, and across Foul Lands. We had nearly escaped, of that I was certain.

Just as we reached the opening and grabbed its uneven edges, a sharp pain hit my leg--and I tumbled, as Weoduye rolled away from me.

I had to ignore the pain, I must get to Weoduye again, must get myself out with him on my shoulder or in my arms. I crawled toward him, and he was close enough to touch when a sharp pain struck my arm wearing Goyel's glove. This was pain beyond my experience, though perhaps I had felt similar injury in the battle above; but now the pain was alive with tentacles spreading fire through my flesh. Screams of agony shot from me to become buried among the wailing of the myriad other sufferers.

What was this? Where had the pain come from? I looked about and saw them, three creatures on me. I thought I had seen all the shadows, but I must have missed these who had been waiting in one of the many dark pockets of the Seap. One had me by the arm that once had held my glove. Another had attached itself to my back where shocks were just beginning to strike, starting to find their way deeper into me than the pain in my arm could hold. The third creature was grabbing both my legs, turning them into some weak injured things that could not get up and run. The shadows were fast and could have made their way across the room quickly, or perhaps they had hidden nearby knowing I would choose that tunnel to get away. However, it had unfolded, they had me now. The shadows were working their darkness on me; and I was desperately trying to save the little reason I had left to figure a way out.

If it were possible, the pain increased. I understood what it was—it was the original pain, the pain the Four Mothers inflicted a thousand years ago. It was an alchemist's pain, a transformative pain—a pain that could burn me into a shadow. My reason was fast leaving me. It didn't want to be there when they turned me into a shadow, a creature that would exist only in the Seap, exist as part of one of those ever-churning circles.

I was face down and close to Weoduye, who didn't move. His hand had fallen away from his body, fallen close enough that I could touch him. I knew my reason would be gone beyond return, soon and soon.

"I'm sorry," I said to him as I reached out to his hand. I had failed him and failed myself.

I forced myself to look up, to see these shadows that were poisoning me, and for a flash the face looked like Sheios, Sheios who was still on the land high above us. I was going, and in my going I must have been having visions. But maybe this was not delirium; the image made sense because Sheios and Weoduye were connected, and with Weoduye stretched out next to me, I had grabbed his hand. Would Sheios now know what had happened to us, that we had lost? More than anything, he needed to be away from this place. My wish was that he knew and would not wait. Then his face was before me again.

"Go!" I said to the vision, hoping the message would be delivered.

Instead of going, the vision struck the thing on my back, and it howled--and with its howl, pain surged through every part of me, pain that took me and kept me. It was the last pain I would feel. I was leaving; I was going; I was gone.

As blackness dragged me down, I thought I heard Sheios command, "Take Aeon!" Then, something much larger than a Jannanon grabbed me.

Barry Alexander Brown

PART TWO

THE CITIES

くｲ∧ワ✶

Barry Alexander Brown

6

In the nothingness, she is there, wearing a long white drape made of cloth woven like a spider's web but thicker and, if possible, more delicate. Through the open spaces in the cloth, I can see parts of her skin, brown skin like mine. She is small, half my size, and beautiful. Her black-brown hair falls to her shoulders. Her eyes, an impossible shade of green, nearly inhuman—though she makes them human—stare into me and through me. Her lips are set perfectly in that face; they make no commitment; they do not hold a smile. The smile is in her eyes, her ears, nose, neck, torso, breasts, legs, everything. The lips do not need to add some brand of falseness that lips can easily have.

"You are Soaad, one of the Mothers," I hear someone say; and I think it's me. How do I know this, I wonder. "But you are not one of the Mothers in the story."

"No, I am not in the Legends—at least not clearly or named." She seems not to care, but it seems that I do by the way she reacts to my expression. "They don't recognize me," and in an afterthought she adds, "—the way you do. But they can't do many things that you can do."

"Like being a Tor'oc," I say, in spite of knowing that I've misunderstood her.

"Being a Tor'oc is the least of it."

I think, 'What is the rest of it?' I look around me, and there is nothing. Even the nothing we are in has a blackness that black never has.

"Where are we?"

"You are in the pain," she says. "I have come to see you."

I nod, understanding, "The original pain."

"If you want to call it that." She acknowledges my ignorance. "You don't feel pain now."

I admit, "No." And I wonder at this, thinking that I should.

"You will not feel it when you are in it and of it," she says.

"Is there a purpose to this, to all this?" I reason there must be if I am here, but I can't reason what it could be. Her lips smile for the first time, and her eyes light in a way that wasn't there before.

"Indeed, yes," she can barely say through her smile.

Again, I realize something without understanding how I know it, "...but I can't be told the purpose."

She shakes her head, no, and attempts to frown sorrowfully at not telling me the purpose or my purpose. The frown never quite forms. The smile is too present; she is enjoying herself. I want to be angry at her for liking my confusion but can't be. Her entire being is too pleasant; and somehow, I understand that it's not my confusion she enjoys so much as that I am knowing something. I wish that I knew what I seem to, but it's just out of my reach. I want to ask her to help me, but even before I can form the words, I know she won't and can't, and that it would be the wrong thing for her to do for me. These thoughts and emotions collide inside me, forcing me to feel even more that I am in nothingness.

"Why?" I finally say.

"Why are you here? Why have we gone through so much to bring you—to pull you, Aeon the Leaf, into Aemira?"

I nod, yes; that is what I want to know and have not asked.

"I could give you an answer, a simple answer, but it wouldn't clear things for you. You would be more confused."

"So, I just submit," I say, and feel I don't want to.

"No, submitting is useless to us. Live by your heart."

Did she move or did I? We seem to be floating, but in that nothingness, maybe she moved, while I stayed where I was—if that's possible to do in nothing—but I sense that I am moving, that I am floating, and she is floating.

"Can you see?" she asks, waving her arms as though there were things around us.

"There is nothing, and that is all I see."

"You were born with the Eye—the Observer's Eye. So, tell me, can you see?" And again, she indicates the space around us.

I sigh. There is nothing in the nothingness—nothing to see. Why is she playing this game? Then, drops form; they appear, or perhaps were always there. At first, a few, then more, more, and more. The drops are colors, all colors; and they move, shift, and merge from several into one, divide from one into many. Each drop is driven to spread, to take up the most space; but the others are dancing the same dance, charging into the same space, sometimes destroying the drop, sometimes merging with it. Now I see that I have no defined body in the nothing; my body is forming in the same way as the sights around and below me; it's being formed by the drops.

"Life," Soaad says.

It is a world that is taking shape, and we are above it and in it as the air itself is part of the world. It is all life—the rocks, the ground, the water, the trees, the animals, the air, the insects, even the dead things—all made of the drops, as I am made of the drops. And I understand. We are not moving across the land; we are merging through it. Experiences from my life are telling me that this is flying, but I am wrong in that. It's only a way for me to accept how my soul is travelling.

"And what of the pain?" I say, reminding myself that she says that we are in the pain.

"Pain has brought you; it is a path."

"But all things alive feel pain, and everything is life. I don't reason that this is a path for everyone and everything."

"You reason wrong. It is a path for everything and everyone," she says so easily, as if this is a truth that is known and never questioned. "Pain will always lead and always transform."

"But not always in a good way," I saw her meaning.

"No, not always." She nods in agreement. "But in the pain, there is always knowledge, always the knowing, whether one chooses to see it or not. You have the Eye, and because of the Eye, you were born on the Path, and you can see."

"Did you know I had the Eye at my birth?" Why I ask this question is unknown to me, but it is important that I ask.

"Yes," she says, looking at me with love in those deep green eyes.

"How? I was born away from you and away from this world."

"I knew because I am your mother. I was there at your birth; and you have never been away from the World, as you should understand now."

This collides with my reason. I know she is wrong, mistaken, and I scream at her like a child who would who is hurt and frightened. "You are not my mother. I know her, and you are not my mother." I am angry because my mother died when I was young, taken away from me, and this woman is trying to take more of her away.

Soaad softens as she feels the pain I feel. "We all have two mothers. She was your earth mother and gave you much and much, but not all. I am the mother of your spirit. She gave you your body and all that means. From me, you received the rest. You always feel the difference between you and the others. Do you not wonder why? It is because you are my son, my beloved one." She is seeing me as a mother sees her child, and there is love that flows from her to me.

"The Four Mothers, this is what it means," I say to myself, but loud enough that she hears. The more I learn, the more I know that I do not know. The world has become a mystery to me; and in the mystery, I am the biggest question, at least to myself.

"And what is my purpose?" I return to my early question.

"For now?" she asks, wanting me to set the limit of what I can receive.

"Yes, for now."

"To learn, to know."

"And how long will that last?"

"It never ends, but there are plateaus." All along, she gazes at me with much love and kindness. I could only accept this in amazement from a mother who loves me.

"I am willing, but I am afraid. As Iz pointed out, I will disappoint you."

She smiles with a smile that lights every drop in the world. "You are a wonder," she says, and touches my face, caressing it with her fingers. At this, I wake.

I woke into pain, in me and outside of me, striking from all directions but mainly from inside, seizing and attacking deeper and deeper. The pain was throughout, worst in my arms and legs. It was a pain that had a thousand jaws with a million teeth, pain that was eating me yet not devouring me, chewing away but leaving what it chewed in order to be able to chew more, breaking me. I was awake but I had not opened my eyes. I thought it all would get worse if I opened them.

I heard a woman's voice. "He's back."

I don't know how I could have heard her voice through the noise of the pain in my hearing. Then I heard another voice, Goyel's, I thought.

"He still looks gone to me," the voice said.

"No, look at him more closely. He's awake," said a woman's voice.

Something cool moved across my face and down it. There was comfort there. More coolness was spread onto my legs, on my arms, and finally onto my torso. The pain jerked away from the source of coolness; then the pull of the source forced some of the pain up through me, out of me, and into it. It was enough release to allow me to breathe. I must have been breathing, though after those first easy breaths, I had the feeling I hadn't inhaled since before I was lost. I let my eyes open a little.

The world was soft, no sharp lines. There was a woman, though I couldn't make out her face. I thought it was Soaad at first; but her skin was too light, and the eyes were wrong. As the lines began to sharpen, I saw that she was not Soaad, but another woman who looked nothing like her. This woman was rounder, just as young if not younger, and much taller. Her skin was very light, and her eyes were a golden brown that matched her hair. She had a large nose that somehow fit her face. Everything was large about her face—her eyes, her cheeks, her mouth, her chin, and her nose—but it all fit together in a pleasant way. I had opened my eyes, yet she was looking at me as if I had not, as if I were still gone. She looked worried.

"Where..." My voice cracked, and I said no more.

"Shhhhhh," her lips blew. She put a finger against my lips. "You are safe."

Wind

I looked about. We were in a place that was green. We were no longer in Foul Lands. I lay on a soft thing on the ground. Raising my arm, I looked at what was covering my skin--mud of some kind. They had smeared this mud on me, on my entire body. I touched my face, and it was covered with it, too. I looked at her and asked with my eyes.

"It's a salve I made from the leaves of the junjun bush that you had in your satchel," she said softly, as if her words could hurt me. "I crushed it and mixed it with water and dirt. It is very lucky you were carrying those leaves."

It wasn't luck; it was the tree that knew I would need it. The luck was that whoever she was, she knew the leaves and knew what to do with them.

"Weo..." My voice cracked and stopped again.

She indicated something behind me on the ground, a place I couldn't turn to see. "He is here but he is still gone."

I pointed to the mud on my arm.

"We can't use the salve until he comes back." She saw that I didn't understand. "If it is put on too early, he may never come back. It's the pain that brings you back."

'What does she know of the pain?' I wondered. She knew much, as she had shown. I liked her voice; it was soft and deep, with something scratchy in it. Had she been waiting here for us? It seemed to be too much luck that she was there and knew so much.

"How…" Again, I could do one word and no more.

A voice behind me answered, "Didn't you see me down there? I came and got you." Sheios walked around so I could see him. And my eyes again asked him how. "We had help." And he looked at the woman.

I could see her more clearly. She was taller than the Jannanons, but nowhere as tall as I or any other Tor'oc, and she didn't look strong enough to pull me out of the Seap. I thought that she must be surprisingly strong for her look. Sheios had to have taken Weoduye, and she must have taken me. I was looking at her, taking her in, thinking I wanted to ask her something. She leaned into me. I wanted to touch her to feel her muscles—they had to be taught and thick. I raised my hand and laid it against the top of her arm, the broad part of her arm. She had wonderfully silky skin, and the muscles underneath were firm but not impressive. How had she lifted me? How did she pull me out and along that tunnel? Bodies in the Out World must work quite a bit differently than bodies on the Peninsula. At home, someone built like her would not have been able to do anything but the lightest work. Maybe Goyel had helped her. Yes, that was it. Even that answer was missing something. When I was gone, I must have weighed twice what I weigh, and the way out was uphill. I would have to ask how they did it.

I became aware that there was something lying next to me. I turned my head slowly so that I wouldn't call back the pain. It was large and grey and smelled like an oryx. Bol's eyes met mine. His legs were tucked

Wind

under him, and his head rested against the top of his front leg nearest my head. I had never seen an oryx lie down and always thought, without questioning it, that they couldn't. He raised his head and moved it so that he could breathe into my nose and inhale my breath afterwards. I raised my other hand and touched him on his mouth that opened, and his tongue licked the inside of my hand that had no mud on it. Among all of them, he was the most glad that I was back.

I was able to make the grumble of the oryx, and he grumbled back. Of all of them, I was most glad to see him. As with the connection the Jannanons shared, Bol and I knew each other.

Goyel appeared with food and drink and knelt next to me.

"Can you sit to eat?" he asked.

"There," I said, and my eyes pointed to Bol's large side that lay flat against the ground.

He put down the food, and with the help of the woman and Sheios, gently pulled me around and raised me enough to lean my back against my oryx. They struggled with this and could barely do it, even when I helped as much as I could. But I did help. The movement hurt me, yet what kept my reason was that if propping me up was nearly impossible, even with me helping and the three of them pulling together, and then how did they get me out? It's said that in times of danger people can do remarkable things. That must be the answer, yet it didn't feel like the truth.

I ate and I drank, and feeling my back against this beautiful beast, I felt better and breathed more easily. Now, I could see Weoduye, who was lying without moving under a blanket. His face was pale and grey.

"How long?" I asked, proud of myself for getting two words out.

"You have been here for eight darks and seven suns." It was the woman again who spoke.

I looked back at Weoduye, and she followed my gaze, "They had him longer and he was beginning to turn. His legs and arms were quite grey, sickly grey. We covered the most damaged parts of his body in moss that was heavy with spillets. They are wonderful at sucking the essence of the shadows out; but it kills them. We must change the moss before every dark and at every dew light. It is working, and his color is returning."

"Spillets….me?" I said, keeping to two words, which seemed to be my boundary.

"Yes, we used the spillets on you as well, but not very long. We have to burn the moss afterwards, and the smell is horrendous." I didn't know what this word meant but it sounded bad. "Horrendous when you take it off and more horrendous when you burn it," she said, as if talking to herself. Back to me, she said, "But we must burn it. It doesn't completely die if you don't, and you can guess what could happen if it wasn't dealt with—shadows and all." She paused. "You must be wondering who I am." She looked into my eyes, but without waiting for a response, she said, "My name is

Chiffaa Oroser. I am from the land beyond Orzamond and I will be traveling with you to the city and maybe beyond." With another thought, she added, "The Camarod will have to determine that."

"Here?" Oh, no—back to one word.

"I came to Foul Lands with the Jannanons, but I couldn't cross." She laughed and covered her mouth. "I wouldn't have made it. They are clever creatures," she said, nodding at Sheios and Goyel, who were sitting beside Weoduye. "You and I are big and clumsy. We are just the kind of thing the shadows are waiting for, especially you. My, you would have been a prize—a real Tor'oc. To think of it, you will be a wonder for everyone now." Her eyes glazed; and she was in the time to come, seeing me in the city with people gazing at me, their mouths open, their eyes wide in surprise. "All the way here, and even while I waited, I doubted you existed. But here you are—big and strong and beautiful." She held her gaze on me and returned to talking to herself. "In all the tales, no one ever wrote how beautiful the Tor'ocs were. But then maybe you're not so beautiful when you're hacking off somebody's head."

"I never—"

"I know, I know. You're a peaceful people now. So I've heard. But how anyone can be certain of that is beyond my reason. I have to say, by the looks of those arms, you don't look peaceful." She stood and walked away.

I don't remember the fall to sleep, but after, I woke in the early dew light. I was no longer covered in mud. They had cleaned me, though I didn't know when. The pain inside me was a low thumping, a vibration I could just feel. As I pushed myself to sit, there were jabs, strikes of pain, but nothing that would stop me from rising. My body wanted to be up. I stood, and Bol came to me, nuzzling his face against my body. I rubbed him between his eyes, ant he closed them in the pleasure of my touch.

The others were still in their beds, asleep on the ground. Weoduye was in the same death-like pose that I'd seen him in before. I walked to him and knelt. His breath was light, and he was having trouble with it. Breathing was a hard thing for him to do, and there was a bad smell that rose off him—a sick, rotten smell. I pulled the cloth that covered him away, and the smell attacked me. It was the moss that had lost its natural brown-green tone and was now a black, crusty thing full of spoiled, dead spillets. I carried all the moss away and laid it in a pit where I thought they must have been burning it—a far distance away and upwind.

Walking back to Weoduye, I turned to Bol, who had accompanied me to the pit. "She is a healer, I think," I said, pointing to the woman asleep on the ground, "but she may not have the Touch."

Beside Weoduye again, I knelt down close to him, moving my hands against his arms and his legs and across several spots on his torso where there were large grey blisters. The pain jumped at me, but more importantly, I saw where the pain lived. There were strings inside him that twisted and turned, tiny snake-like pieces of shadow that burned and snapped just as the fire inside the walls of the Seap had.

    I leaned close to his ear and whispered, "We have to get the fire out. You have felt pain. This will be worse." Weoduye had no reaction, but I had to tell him whether he understood or not.

    I started with his feet, holding them, pressing my hands against the bony top of each foot, sending my message of wanting to pull the strings so that they came toward me, all the way to the surface of the skin where they wriggled and turned the skin even darker. I had them, though, and I could control them. I kept them there with my want and moved them up the legs, attracting all the strings as the twisting, burning, snapping mass passed above their fellows which then were pulled along too. My hands felt the burning and the pain pushing me to remove them from his body. Weoduye was hot, and my hands also felt as though they were burning.

    I moved all the strings and pulled them together to his mid. Keeping one hand pressed on the wriggling strings, I passed over each arm with my free hand and guided the strings there to join the others in the torso. Now a fist-sized ball of shadow strings undulated under his skin in a disturbing way. I had to force this mass through Weoduye, force it down into his stomach and then up through him and out of his mouth, pulling along whatever strings were left in the higher parts of his body. I had never done such a thing, but I knew that this was the moment that was going to hurt the little

Jannanon. It would be beyond pain—I have not a word for it. I hoped it would not end him.

I took a breath and said to myself, "Keep breathing."

Without another count I pushed with all the force of my soul--and as the squiggling ball dove down into him, he gasped, choked, and fought for air. His eyes exploded open in agony as this sensation beyond pain struck all points in his body. I had no more counts on my side. I grabbed the ball with my soul and forced it up, as the body was seizing, convulsing, tightening the path to his mouth. I had to be stronger than his small body with its own great strength—a surprising strength. The force of my soul and my flesh merged, and in an effort lasting no longer than a breath, the ball—wriggling, burning, snapping—tore up through his body, landing in his mouth, pushing it wide, wide open. I grabbed the snakes—for they truly looked like a tightly twisted, undulating ball of snakes; and as my hand took hold, it burned me. I didn't let go, and in that jiff, it was out of his mouth--and I tossed it far away from all of us. Weoduye's eyes closed, and his body shuddered in a series of three fits.

There were eyes on me, and I turned. Sheios and Goyel were standing, pale and unmoving in a kind of shock, staring at their companion. They must have felt something of what Weoduye had gone through. I had forgotten about their connection. The woman was still lying down, but she was looking at me, her face frozen in surprise. I stood and walked to her.

Wind

"He will need some mud," I said, not stopping, heading to my oro bow and arrows that I had spotted just past her. I wasn't going to take the snake ball into my hand, which now felt raw and branded. I would spear the ball with an arrow, ride to where I could see Foul Lands again and send the shadow snakes back to where they belonged.

Once I had it on the arrow, I mounted Bol, who flinched away from the ball of snakes that I held away from both of us. It was as light as anything made of the shadows. He knew what I wanted and where to go and ran at top speed so that Foul Lands showed itself in no counts at all. It was still a distance away, but I didn't want to get any nearer to it than we were. Bol stopped as he felt my resistance, and I jumped off him.

I unfolded my bow, notched the arrow, aimed it high and far, pulled the bow string back to my full strength, and let it go. The arrow with the pierced ball flew high, arched across the green land and well into the burnt Foul Lands. I could just see the arrow standing with its feathers toward the sky, its point in the earth, and the shadows bursting into fire a jiff after landing back in their homeland. The flames burned the shadow snakes as well as the arrow. 'It is better that all of it burns,' I thought.

Bol and I rode slowly back to camp. My hand throbbed. I was sure the woman, Chiffaa would have something to soothe it, but I needed time to be only with Bol. I was sad and lost in my thoughts, and I wanted to be lost.

The drops—we were made of the drops. I was made of them; Bol was made of them, as was the earth below his hoofs, the rocks, the grass, the trees, the air. Were the shadows made of them, too? I think they were made of the absence of drops, as my own shadow was made of the absence of light. This was what made them ruined things, things that could not be ended because they were not part of life. But maybe they could be transformed; they once had been something else before they had become shadows. The Out World had brought me off the Peninsula to save them—that I knew.

I reasoned that Soaad was my spirit mother and raised me to be the one to save them from the shadows, and that the Mothers probably saw the threat long before others had. Another knowing struck me that they had been waiting for me to arrive, a savior whom they fear, but in whom they rest all their hopes. Chiffaa had seen me save Weoduye, and for whatever reason the Out World had for needing my help, if she were to tell the people what she saw, they would think that I could cure them—person by person. I would try to help with whatever threat hung over them, but I would not be their healer. Even on the Peninsula, I hid the talent. There was a woman in the City in the Trees that had the Touch. She died, sick and shriveled; the Tor'ocs who struggled with diseases had sucked the life out of her. There are just so many drops any of us have, and I would not be spending mine on the people of the Out World.

I missed the Peninsula and my people and my life. I had been gone a short count and within this time

Wind

I was different, altered. I would never be the same, and if my reason was right, I would be changing and changing, shifting into someone else. Would they recognize the changes at home? Would they recognize me? Would I ever see the City in the Trees again? I had dreamed of Uthiriul being in this world I was in now but never had seen myself there in the dreams.

Sorrow and longing were in my mind when the first petals fell around and on me. They were white with edges of red. I looked up and into a rain of petals, falling from the sky. They had been blown from blooming trees, but I had not seen any trees in bloom. Petals circled and fell and fell as the land around us turned white with a tinge of red. They were falling so quickly and were so thick that even Bol seemed to be turning white. These trees were close to Foul Lands, and yet they bloomed. This was a wonder that pulled me away from my sorrow. It was a wonder I had never seen on the Peninsula. Yes, I was sad that I had left, but I knew at that jiff that I would not give back any of what I had done since the leaving. I would not even give back the shadows and the pain. There was a knowing in the pain that I needed.

The blooming trees surrounded us in an aroma that told me, "We are glad that you are in the world. Be glad to be among us." Was I touched by these new trees the same way as with Weoduye? Was that the gift of the pain? Whatever it was, trees could always cheer me, and this was even more special. My heart lifted, and I blew a blessing back to the sadly beautiful trees.

The falling of the petals stopped before we reached the camp. We were both covered in the white flower petals edged in red when we arrived, and I could see by the looks of the others that we were a vision – an unsettling one, but a vision. Weoduye was where I had left him, but now he was covered in mud, and his breathing was better. Sheios, Goyel, and Chiffa came to me as I slid off Bol. I led him into shade, where I hoped he might find sweet root. As we moved, the white flowers fell away from us.

Sheios and Goyel were beside me after I'd let go of Bol.

"Thank you," they said as Jannanons again—in their song like way.

"You were the ones who saved me; I should be thanking you."

"You fell into the tunnels to get Weoduye; we had to save you both. And now you brought him back to us." Then they knelt at my feet. "With our lives we are bent and bonded to you, Aeon."

I pulled them both up. "I will not take your bond. We are in balance—you do not owe me."

They started to kneel again, but I held them up. "If you had not saved me, I would not have been here for Weoduye; and I did nothing. I was there when the pain snake came out of him, and I grabbed it from his mouth. That was all. You would have done the same."

They looked at me, confused. This was not what they had seen, but my words were turning their memories into what the words told them.

"You have the Touch. I saw it," Chiffaa said from behind me.

I did not turn to her. "No, I do not. The things were traveling up through his body, and I didn't know what it was. I touched him to feel what was happening to him."

"You might deny it, but you made that happen," she said.

I turned then to look at her to change her mind. "It was an accident that I was there, or maybe I heard something. I don't recall. But it wasn't me. I am not a healer like you."

"Correct, you're not a healer like me—you have the Touch."

I shook my head and let out a frustrated breath. "Don't tell people I have the Touch. I don't have it. For all the waters in the world, I wish I did. I wish I were special, but I am just the Leaf. I am the only Tor'oc you have ever seen, so I am remarkable to you, but if you could see the City in the Trees and all the Tor'ocs there, you would know how un-special I am, how less than ordinary I really am."

I could not tell if she accepted this or if she was simply giving in for the moment. She stepped into me and took my burnt hand.

"I will take care of this," she said, looking closely at the burn, and then she looked up into my eyes and with a funny smile she added, "It is very special, your hand. We can't have anything happening to ruin it."

"Please," I pleaded. "I don't have...don't tell anyone..."

"I won't," she said, walking away to get the salve. And over her shoulder she threw, "Your secret is safe."

"There is no secret!" I screamed.

Later, Weoduye was eating and drinking, but not talking. His eyes were still not the light purple of before—purple, certainly, but they were darker with a cast of silver in them. Perhaps his eyes would be forever changed. For all I knew, my eyes had shifted too. He was the only one who understood the pain, and I wanted to talk to him about it. He was in it longer and might understand it better than I did, but even if he didn't, I needed to share it with him. The others wouldn't understand.

That dark, I asked permission to sleep in the boughs of a Weeper, the only tree nearby sturdy enough to hold me. There wasn't a forest this close to Foul Lands. It was open, grassy, rolling land with a few small trees and the one larger Weeper. I'd always liked being in a Weeper because it felt like sleeping in a curtain of long leaves. However, I could not find more than one spot for my bed sling because the limbs were too narrow and weak. I was still in pain, but falling to sleep in that curtain of leaves, with the sway of this wonderful tree—Weepers have a beautiful movement—and a new wind blowing kisses to me to help me rest, the pain eased a bit, and I dreamed of home.

I heard my name, and it was not in the dream; it was in the World. I woke and heard it again, a whisper that seemed to be coming from inside my head. Again, the voice spoke my name. It was Weoduye. I rose and looked out through the curtain to where Weoduye slept. He was lying where he had before. I climbed out of the sling, down the Weeper, and crossed quietly to the Jannanon, careful not to wake anyone. He was awake; his eyes opened. He stared at me, and I knelt beside him.

"You were there?" He asked but did his lips move? I wasn't certain in the dark.

"Yes, I tried to save you, but I didn't." I lowered myself closer so that he could hear my whispers. "We were both saved by Sheios, Goyel, and a woman who is here named Chiffaa."

He wanted to know the rest. Somehow, I told him without any more spoken words between us. I told him about the wriggling shadow snakes that were inside him and how I took them out. He would have known if I had lied to him. I asked him to keep this secret, that people would misunderstand, and would want me to heal the World.

"I am grateful." This time I saw from his unmoving lips that the words did not come through them.

"How?" I asked.

He knew that I was asking how it was that I could hear him and he hear me. "We are touched now. Touched through the shadow pain and touched because your force entered my body."

I smiled. "I'm almost a Jannanon then."

He forced a smile back. "By honor, yes. You are too big for anything more."

"Am I touched to Sheios and Goyel as well?"

"No, only to me."

"Where did you find yourself?" I asked, hoping he would know my meaning.

"You mean, inside the pain?" he asked, and I answered with a wordless 'yes' that the touch between us understood.

Weoduye took several breaths to let himself remember. "I was being pulled—my legs, my arms—pulled away from my body so far that I couldn't see my hands or my feet; and I couldn't see who was pulling me. All I could see was a swirling, grey cloud that engulfed me. Every time I took a breath the grey air rushed into my mouth and choked me, and as I gasped for air, more grey cloud rushed in. I looked down at my arms and legs as they turned grey, like the cloud that was all around me. At one moment, you were there in the cloud--and it was just at that moment that whatever had me, let go. My arms, my legs flew back at me, hitting me so hard pain and pain and pain shot through me. I was nothing but pain. Then I lost all sense of the grey cloud and all sense of my body. I was in black, and nothing was there. There was nothing to remember. I don't know if I was anything until a new pain built in my legs and moved up me and down my arms and up through my chest and into my mouth, and I tasted bitterness and something that I think was death. Then it was gone. The black became lighter, not grey but more like dew light just before the light. When I woke, I was covered in this mud."

He looked the most unhappy about the mud, and I didn't want to laugh, but I did—I knew the feeling. "This mud helps," I said, as someone who knows. "After the grey cloud and in the place where there was nothing, did you see a woman in white?"

His eyes became concerned as his mind wheeled back to the nothingness. Surprise came into his expression, "Yes." He was shocked that he had not remembered her.

"I will tell you what I know," I said.

Weoduye's eyes moved to me with this thought, "Tell me now."

"Her name is Soaad, and she is one of the Mothers—the fifth Mother. She does not show herself to everyone. Or maybe most cannot see her; but you have, and I have. She is the mother of those of us who can see and know beyond the plane of this earth. She will teach me to use what she gave me at my birth. There is a plan for me that I reason started before I was born."

Although his eyes asked, 'What plan?' there was something in his gaze that told me he had reasoned this as well.

"I don't know. But you have been touched by her, too. Because we were in the pain together and we are now touched, you will discover you have talents. I can help with them. Don't be afraid. We will need the talents in time, but for what?" I shrugged and became lost in the reason that I didn't know what was coming—

but certain that it would be more overwhelming than Foul Lands or the shadow creatures.

"Do you feel them, the shadows, can you feel them still?" His question came inside my head.

"I don't think so, not much, but they had hold of you longer," I answered.

"It is as though they are standing there and there and there." Neither his head nor his arms gave direction, but I knew he meant that he felt them all around him. When he said it, I felt them too.

"The feeling will be gone soon and soon." I guessed and I hoped to be right.

"Yes, maybe, but I want to be gone from here."

I looked to my big oryx, awake and watchful, standing under the Weeper. "If you can ride Bol, we can leave tomorrow."

"Like this, he may not want me to." I knew he meant because he was sick.

"He knows more than that." I nodded, knowing Bol's senses were truer than my words. "He will be fine with you."

I touched Weoduye's chest and pushed a wave of calmness into him. He sighed; his eyes closed; and he was back to walking the path of sleep. I made my way into the Weeper and my sling where I was visited by thoughts that wanted to keep me awake, but they lost the battle. I was thinking, then fighting not to think. The next breath it was dew light, and I was waking.

Wind

The other three were one in their reaction to leaving—they did not want to move, not until Weoduye was better, in another two lights, and not before. I understood that Far Road was only a light away, and my decision was simple. I wanted to be at that place.

The Jannanons were the first to ease, as Weoduye had silently talked to make them know what he was feeling, make them feel Foul Lands and shadows that he could still feel and wanted to lose. Chiffaa, angry and pouty about leaving so soon, helped to pack the camp and, surprisingly, made a bed of sorts on top of Bol, of whom she seemed to be slightly fearful, while all the time muttering to herself about the Jannanons and me.

I lifted Weoduye onto Bol, placed him on his back with his head resting on the hump, and tied him down safely. Bol wasn't happy about the twine being wrapped around and under him, but he let me, snorting while I did it, telling me that this may likely be a one-time assent. He walked gently with Weoduye, as he could sense the sickness in the Jannanon, who winced through the first steps of the journey. The movement increased the pain. Though we had only traveled half an arpent, I looked at Weoduye to make sure that he wanted to continue. He looked back, telling me to go on. Soon, he relaxed into Bol's walk and sway, and he seemed even to sleep.

Flowers—not everywhere, but there were small yellow flowers living among the small bushes and thin trees. As the land made a constant, slow rise stretching away from Foul Lands, flowers of color were able to grow again here and there in the rocky ground. The grasses began to look greener, the bushes fatter, and the trees stronger and bigger, though not quite big and strong enough yet to be called thriving.

Birds—I had not been aware of the lack of birds flying in the sky-- that was now constantly getting bluer-- but there were birds here. High above, birds of prey were searching for the small animals that must also have been there. I had last seen a bird long before Foul Lands where the sky turned grey. We passed under a small group of trees here, and I heard birdsong coming from the limbs, from small birds making a click song.

Like the rest of our group, I had lost the thought that there was no flowing water anywhere near Foul Lands. There had been the inky water that had stained our feet, but a stream of fresh water had not existed near us for long and long. Like hearing leaf-hidden birds in the trees, I heard the water here before I saw it. Bol stopped at the first stream and drank. We all did. Sheios and Goyel fed the fresh water to Weoduye, whose eyes took on a light that we had all been waiting to see, though I had been unaware of waiting. We ate beside a stream, and the sound of the water falling over the rocks was more beautiful than the bird song. As we passed over streams on our way, the smell of the water was clean and powerful and helped to bring us all back into the World.

The land had risen high, and it seemed to end in near sight. When we rested a moment, I looked back to where we had come and could see Foul Lands in the far. I saw how the land came back to life the farther my eyes traveled away from the burnt ground. It felt like a dream, remembering the battle with the Umɔrare and the tunnels and the Seap. I looked to my companions; the Jannanons and Bol were all faced away from the faraway Foul Lands. Chiffaa, however, was looking at me, studying me. I smiled at her and by her surprised look back, it must have been the first smile she had seen on my face.

The land didn't end where it seemed to; it flattened out into fields of tall grasses, wildflowers, waters big enough to be called rivers, with bushes deeply green growing beside them. In my far sight, there were forests, though the land was so flat the forest looked more like a wall of trees that may or may not have had more trees behind it. The air on this flat land was hot, and there was the sense that it had just rained, and the air was still holding water mixed with the smell of earth.

As we walked through fields, I could see that the ink that had stained Bol's legs was disappearing as the grasses cleaned us The flowers had all been white where we first met them, but now combinations of colors showed in flowers I had never seen, with insects new to me flying around them. Sheios picked some of these flowers and handed them to Weoduye, who laid them across his mid. This helped him regain his own color and his own breath. Foul Lands were at long last falling away from us. As we walked through fields, I could see that the ink that had stained Bol's legs was disappearing as the grasses cleaned us.

We reached the forest when the light was halfway to the edge of the earth. It was an old forest, though new to me. There were many trees I did not know, and I didn't feel that my companions would allow me the time to stop and know them. The trees were murmuring to one another about us, and their language was different, though I caught words. They mainly talked about Bol and Weoduye and what kind of animal I might be. I kept my tongue, wanting to hear more and understand more and learn more. The forest was dark with the trees, but I sensed that it was not wide and that there would be more open land soon.

We were through the forest in too short of time. I greatly favored the feeling of the trees again; I felt safe, and I felt home. I had wanted to stop and sleep in their boughs and find out what they knew, but we were quickly through it. Now, before us was what I had thought I would surely recognize but didn't—the Far Road--its edge just at the border of the forest.

What did I think it would look like? There were no roads, only bridges and walkways on the Peninsula. A road was something we had heard of in our myths. I had an idea and a vision of it, though the vision I had understood then was not a clear one, but a misty sense of what a road could be. I imagined it as a cleared long path that still had bushes and some trees and rocks, and animals living on it. What I saw before me here was hostile to animals and plants. No grass, no bush, or tree could be there. It was not exactly flat, but ever so slightly curved, and the earth beaten down to a shine.

I looked to my companions. They were smiling at seeing the road, and I was not. My reason told me that if Bol could smile, he would not be smiling either.

He and I did not like the look of the thing that stretched out far and far. I followed Chiffaa, Sheios, and Goyel, who seemed to want to be on the road just as much as I wanted to be back in the forest. Bol and I walked onto it, and both gazed down. The road was not dirt, at least not anymore. It was a deep brown shade with strips of dirty yellow veins, and its shine came from something that had been mixed into the dirt, a thing that made it hard and unforgiving. With Bol beside me, I walked away the length of a small tree so that we had left the road, hopefully forever.

"What are you doing?" Sheios and Goyel asked. Weoduye was still too ill to join them in talk.

I didn't answer but stayed along the side of the road with the good ground beneath me. I could not take my eyes off the shine of the road. I wondered why the people had to do such a thing. My feet were offended by the very few steps I had taken on it. People here all wore soles, and I knew why—they had to protect themselves from the road. Bol and I kept pace with the others, who came to understand that the road was not for us. This world was without reason, and I thought it was becoming stranger by each new light.

We kept our heads down, Bol and I. Neither of us wanted to see any new surprises, so we were very surprised when our companions stopped, and we looked up to see a house sitting on the ground beside the road. It was brown and shiny with yellow veins. It looked like part of the road but with walls and openings, and the top ended in a circle of six cones with one larger cone in the mid. It was a good-sized house, though not as large as a public kollokk in the City in the Trees, and it had not been grown there. It had been made by someone.

Chiffaa, Sheios, and Goyel stood waiting a short distance from the house. Part of the wall facing us opened, and I saw that this part was different from the rest. It was made of something different, and as it opened, one edge kept hold of the wall. The thing that had opened it stepped into the light. It was an older man who looked fit under his cloths. His hair was long and wrapped in a cloth that shimmered in many colors, colors changing as he moved. His beard covered the lower half of his face from his nose down and was colored burnt orange with flecks of light brown. He was a bit shorter than I was and thin. Everything about him was thin—his long nose, his eyes, his ears, his hands, his fingers. He looked sternly at our group, drinking me and Bol in with his eyes, and not seeing Weoduye at first. When he did, he crossed to us, and no one said a word. The man stopped a Tor'oc distance away and gazed at Weoduye, who returned the look, blinking as he strained to turn his head.

"You're alive," the old man said, as much a statement as it was a question.

"And breathing easier," Weoduye answered, and in response the man smiled, a relaxed smile, and everyone smiled but me and Bol.

The man turned to me. "May I approach?"

I nodded, and he came up to the side of Bol. As he did, I laid a hand on the oryx's neck to calm him.

Wind

"Did you meet the shadows?" The old man asked.

The answer came from behind us, from the road. "They were pulled into the Seap," said Chiffaa.

The man turned to her with awe and the stern look again and said, "All of you?"

Chiffaa shook her head, "No, only Weoduye, the Tor'oc, and Sheios."

Those words were new to me and hit me like a slap. How was it possible that Sheios had fought and defeated the shadows, then pulled Weoduye and me out of the Seap? He was either stronger than reason told me, or there was a truth missing.

"In truth," Chiffaa continued, "Weoduye was pulled in, and the Tor'oc followed to save him."

The old man turned to take me in. "How did you save him from the Seap?" He asked.

"I didn't," I said. and told him no more. It was a mystery that the old man would have to unravel. Maybe when he did, I would know something, too.

"I am the Sand Keeper," he said, and he extended his hand to me, holding it open and on its side. I didn't know what he wanted, but I reasoned he wanted me to respond. I followed his movement, bringing my hand up and hanging it in the air as he did. He stared at me and then at my hand. Our hands were mirrors of each other held a short distance apart.

"They don't greet with hand holds in the Tor'oc Prison," Sheios and Goyel said.

The Sand Keeper put his hand down. "Probably all for the best."

"I am Aeon the Leaf," I said, and by his look he was surprised that I had a name.

"Aeon the Leaf," he repeated. "Can you help me with Weoduye? He will be more comfortable inside."

I untied the Jannanon and lifted him off Bol, who shivered with the pleasure of his freedom. I held Weoduye like a small child, which was how he felt to me, and followed the Sand Keeper to his house, entering as he did. There was little light inside, but enough to see. Light came from the openings at the very top of each cone, and the cones were at the mid of the ceilings of seven rooms. The entire house was covered in something like the grass weavings called tallums that we made for the floors of our kollokks. Unlike our tallums, the floors inside the Sand Keeper's house were soft, and my steps melted into them. They were not made of grass, but of an animal's hair, as I learned later. It was cool inside; a light wind was moving through the house, up and out through the cones.

The Sand Keeper pointed to a high stack of tallums, and I laid Weoduye down on them. From behind me, Chiffaa appeared—her footsteps had been swallowed by these marvelous tallums. She knelt beside the youngest Jannanon and wiped his head and neck with a cloth that was wet with water or something like water. Weoduye sighed at the touch.

It was as dark in there as the Seap, however, it was welcoming and friendly, though there was no sway

Wind

to this house, and it did seem odd to me to be in a home without a sway. Anything made on the ground would not have the sway, and I felt a sorrow for those who would never know that they were missing so much. I could feel the Sand Keeper staring at me from a shadowed part of the room that we were in.

"Sand is what is found at the edge of great bodies of water," I said to him. "I have not seen anything like that here. What makes you the Sand Keeper?"

He signaled me to follow him out of the room and out of the house.

We found ourselves standing beside the road when he finally replied, "You are right. There are no great bodies of water near here, and there is no sand that is natural to this land. But there is sand to be found where water once was, and water covered everything once. In a land like this where there seems to be no sand, I bring the sand forth."

"For what?" I asked, not being able to reason a cause.

"First, it was to build the road; now, it is to keep it." He could see that I was not understanding. "I probably should be called the Road Keeper, because it is my responsibility to make sure the road is kept." He could see that I still was not following his meaning. "The road. It is made of sand, burnt sand, which we call rough glass, and it is softer and more giving than actual glass. You couldn't make a road of glass; it would crack and break and be much too slippery to walk on, of course. You do have glass on your island?"

I shook my head, "No, I reason we do not have anything like this thing you call glass."

"Well, they made the road of rough glass with the crushed shells of the Credo Tree nut, that gives it more strength as well as its softness."

"You name this soft?" I asked in awe.

"Soft enough to walk on or roll a wagon," he replied, and I shook my head to tell him that I disagreed, though I didn't know what rolling a wagon was.

"Wherever it breaks or wears away or is damaged in some fashion, I find the Credo Trees and the repairers use the sand I provide with the crushed nuts, that are readily available everywhere, as you can imagine."

I could not imagine because Credo Trees and the repairing and the road were all new to me. I thought maybe the Credo Trees grew in part of the forest where we had passed but now understood that I would meet more and was glad of that.

"But you will see all that in time. I'll be joining you on your way to Orzamond. It is the time of year for me to start out again, and there will be plenty of work along the way."

"Was the road here when my people came this way?"

"Oh, yes—oh, yes. The road is quite ancient, and thanks to all the Sand Keepers who came before me, it is still here and, if I can say so, it is as good as when it was first poured."

Wind

He gazed at the road with much fondness. I gazed at it with hate. I would not walk on it if I could help it, although everything that would come next was unknown to me. I reasoned that learning to walk on this horrible path might be something I would have to win.

Barry Alexander Brown

7

There was a pitch of trees a short distance away from the Sand Keeper's house, and that was where I decided Bol and I would spend our darks while waiting for Weoduye to heal. We rode there after the day-end meal as the light began to touch the edge of the land, and I was glad to be away from the road, even glad to be away from my companions who had saved me. We came slowly onto the grove and entered the most unusual woods I had seen since leaving the Peninsula.

They were strange, somewhat short trees holding many long, silvery-green leaves that did not fall toward the earth as Weeper leaves do, but struck out on their own, on limbs that twisted away from one another to cover as much of the air as possible and leave a large open space under the thick roof of the leaves. The bark was smooth but not slippery, looked easy to climb, and was a beautiful dark purple that set itself apart from the silver under-bottom of the leaves. I had the sense of entering a place of magic. The nuts of the trees were a yellow brown, the color that I had seen in the veins of the road, which made me reason that these were the Credo Trees.

I came down from Bol, knelt on the ground and bowed my head to these regal trees. "May I grow here?" I blew in my simplest way. There was no response.

Perhaps they did not use the wind to speak. I thumped the ground, and again the trees were mute. I either could not talk to these trees, or they did not want me here and were refusing to answer, or to see and hear me. If that were true, I would not stay against their will; but I wanted to touch one of them before leaving and traveling back. I walked up and placed my hand against the trunk of one, and the skin was pleasantly rough—so, as I had guessed, easy to climb. I was sorry that I would not be climbing and sleeping in it. My hand rested there as I felt the skin of my fingers tingle. In that tingling there were words.

"We understand the wind language, but we cannot use it. You may grow here."

Wind

For me to talk to them, I had to touch them. How I was able to understand the tingling of the skin was a mystery to me, but I accepted it and hoped in time I would learn how it worked.

"Are you the Credo Trees?" I asked.

"Credo? Is that the man-name for us?"

"I believe it is. They use nuts like yours to build the road," I told them, in case they did not know.

"Yes, we know they do this. We do not like it, but we do not stop it," they tingled back to me. "We call ourselves the 'Mondane', which simply means 'The Trees' in our ancient words."

"I will call you Mondane. May I grow among you for two or three darks?"

There was a hesitation before tingling, "We have a question for you first."

"Please," I said.

"What kind of beast are you? Are you man?"

"I am."

"Man is the most brutal of all the beasts. It steals the seeds without asking. It cuts us and burns us, though we turn our smell when we are cut to an odor man does not like." It was true that there was a musky smell to the trees that I was only beginning to breathe with ease.

"I will not cut you or burn you or take your fruit without asking." I bent my head down in full respect.

The leaves of all the Mondane rustled in a talk with one another that I could not follow and never would. The rustling slowed and came to a halt. I still had my hand resting on the trunk of my tree and I heard, "We have decided you must be a different man—a new man. We will give you pardon and let you grow here; but if you earn our distrust, we will toss you out."

"I will give you no reason for mistrust," I blew back, and bent even further.

"Then welcome; and if you please, we have questions." They were very curious about where I had come from and were fascinated with the story of the City in the Trees. They asked what I was called and, not being able to pronounce Aeon, they simply called me the Leaf, which they thought was a very good name and could not understand why I would go by any other. They asked about Bol and why he would let me ride him. They showed us where the sweet roots grew and, as the trees were different, these were different looking roots than I had ever seen. Based on how quickly Bol devoured them, I guessed they must have had a new taste as well—even oryx desire variety.

I climbed a tree that had invited me in once I had told how we slept on the Peninsula. The areas were wide and clean inside the trees, with more space around me than I had seen in trees before. Even though it was early, I tied my bed sling and lay in it to enjoy again the sway of a large tree. I had called the trees small compared to the Bent Trees, but they were large compared with what I had slept in since being near Foul Lands. Lying out, I felt my muscles let go, my breath soften, and the knot inside my head, that I'd been unaware of, loosened. I felt at home in this strange place among these beautiful trees, and the feeling made me sing a song that we sometimes sang to the trees at home. There were no words of meaning in the song, only music that began in our chests and quivered up through our throats, music that brought peace to us and peace to the trees. As I sang, the tree began to tremble. All the trees began trembling, and a hum filled the small forest, a musical hum that joined my song and changed it into their song. We sang together for long and long, longer than I had ever sung on the Peninsula. The music reached into me, swallowing the last remains of the shadows that were still hiding inside me, hiding where I was unaware. Before we left this place, I knew I would have to bring Weoduye here and sing with the trees to clear him from his own hidden shadows.

As sleep was coming to me, I lightly blew, "I look to the days and darks, and I am glad to be among you."

The tingling came down the limbs, through my sling, and into my entire body. "Good dark, Leaf. Take root, grow, and be strong." In it was an invitation for me to stay forever, and in the last moments before sleep, my wish came that I would grow there until I was old and bent.

In my dream that night, I am high in the boughs of the Mondane, but they are larger and grander than in my waking; and the forest is thick with them as far as I can see. As I gaze over the forest, a flock of black birds with blue heads, and wings that turn red as they flap, fly over the forest toward me, landing on the branches that surround me. They are not at ease in these trees, nervously moving back and forth, not resting, staring at me as if I am about do something unusual and violent. All of them look at me as they twitch and move.

They coo in their bird talk, yapping, talking over one another, none of them listening; and I can understand them as I can understand the trees.

"What is he doing?" "He's just sitting there?" "I can't stand his smell."

"What's the matter with him?" "Staring and staring, unpleasant."

"There's something wrong." "Jola—go and peck him."

"Why me?"

"Unpleasant"

"Look, this could happen to any of us."

"Kill him or help him."

"Kill him—we can't do that, that is against everything," the leader of the birds says, and they all quiet.

In the quiet I say, "Who are you?"

"Odd, odd," one of them says behind me.

"We are you, just like you," replies the leader kindly.

Wind

"You are nothing like me," I say, and I am upset that they might be right.

"Look at yourself." I do as the leader commands me. What I see are my arms and torso and legs. "You see—just like us," the leader states, as though it is feathers that I am looking at.

From below me a voice that I know yells, "Don't trust them!"

I look down, and Uthiriul is standing on a branch looking up at all of us. She has finnif knives in both hands, spinning finnif knives that she is ready to use.

"Don't listen—she is lost," the leader warns me.

"But I don't trust you and I am nothing like you," I tell him.

"You are exactly like us," he coos, and as if to show me, all the birds leap off the branches and swarm me like insects on rotten fruit. They surround me, covering my body with theirs, and what I see when I look down at myself are black feathers, blue heads, and flapping wings turning from black to red over and over as they hit my body in their convulsions.

"Come—let's fly," whispers the leader into my ear.

"I can't." It is a plea to him not to make me.

"You have feathers and wings. You can—you are one of us." The leader is insistent that I believe this.

"There is no return from this!" Uthiriul yells from below as her voice echoes through the tree.

At once, we are flying up, straight up, and hovering above the tree. The black birds release me, and I stay there among them, hovering and flying and wanting to be there. A cry breaks the sensation, a new, wonderful sensation of not wanting to be anywhere but here, of not wanting to be anything but a black bird. Two finnif knives swirl up through the tree, cutting into the flock in their aim to kill and maim.

"You don't know!" I scream back at Uthiriul. "They are us!"

Uthiriul howls--and the dream decays into pure sleep.

I woke a long time after at dew light and remembered the dream. I looked down to find Bol waiting for me.

Smiling at my oryx, I told him, "What a strange, strange dream I had this last dark. If we run into black birds with blue heads and wings that turn red when they fly, run me away from them." I laughed at the thought that this ever could come true. The light of this new day was beautiful, and this time, the dream surely was just a dream.

Bol and I remained among the Mondane for three more lights without seeing any of our companions. Bol found a new thorn bush that he liked almost as much as the new sweet roots. I hunted, cooked, and slept. Twice we took long rides across this new land that was flat and unchanging. On the fourth light, a woman's voice woke me from a pleasant dream about the Peninsula. When I looked out over my bed sling to see who it was, Chiffaa was below, gazing up and sitting on a large beast, the same sort that I had seen Uthiriul riding in my dreams. I climbed down to meet them—really to get a better look at the beast.

My eyes never left the animal, and when I reached the ground, Chiffaa told me, "It's called a Pallurino. You must have horses like them in the prison." I shook my head, no. "But your ancestors were famous riders."

"That might be, but almost everything died in the first flood," I said, walking up to the beast, laying my hands against its neck and running them along its body.

"I will teach you to ride, then." She smiled at me in some kind of teasing way.

"I have my beast," I said, nodding to Bol, who had kept his distance from the Pallurino.

"You should at least try it, but never mind. I've come to tell you how Weoduye is doing." Chiffaa easily changed the topic.

"I know how he's doing."

"And how's that? You haven't been seen in days."

"Weoduye and I are touched. He is doing well and thinks he's ready for travel, but he's not."

Chiffaa looked at me from an odd angle, her eyes nearly closing in her stare. "And why do you think he's not?"

"He has hidden shadows. You must bring him here to be cleared." I swung my arm to indicate the forest. "The Mondane will help me clear him."

She looked about to catch a sight of this thing called the Mondane. "And where are these Mondane?"

"You are under them."

Looking up, she said, "You mean the Credo Trees?"

"They don't like to be called that," I stated simply, and she gazed back at me as though I had swallowed the moon.

"And how would you know that? Are you touched with them, too?"

"Oh, if that were only possible." I smiled at the wonderful thought of that ever happening. "They can tell you a lot if you are willing to listen."

Wind

She laughed at this, and her look changed to some kind of wonderment. "You are nothing like I thought you would be."

"You mean from the Tor'ocs of legend?"

Her smile left her face, and a cloud of sorrow took its place. "Yes...the Legends." There was more to her words, something she did not want to say; and it made me curious about her. She shook herself to force a change and turned back to me. "After you eat, let's ride. I have something to show you."

We ate, or rather I ate, and she impatiently watched. I hurried through the meal, readied myself and Bol for the ride, and climbed on him. She was waiting for me on her Pallurino.

At a slow walk, we left the small patch of trees and headed onto the flat land. I could not imagine what could be seen that would interest me—Bol and I had been across this land, and it was same from one arpent to another.

"You must be happy to be away from the prison," Chiffaa said, not looking at me.

"It's not a prison to us. It's true that we cannot leave its boundaries, but it is home, and I am not happy to be away from it. It is much more beautiful than here, and it is a place with more reason to it." I found that there was a deep sadness and longing in me for the Peninsula.

She then looked at me, surprised at my words, "As a girl, I was sometimes sad for the Tor'ocs, who still had to pay for the crimes of their long-ago ancestors. I never thought you could be in any place but a dark, horrible prison, or on an island that was all rocks and desert. I was wrong."

"And the place you are from, what is it like?" I truly was curious.

"It's a city as unusual as your City in the Trees." Her face was all joy in remembering. "It's called Soos. It's a floating city that was built on unanchored islands that we made in the middle of a large, large lake — Lake Lier. Actually, your people forced us onto the lake."

I gave her a look that asked, 'How's that?'

"We were attacked and defeated and enslaved by Sumon and the original Tor'oc Nation when we were farmers and fishermen on the shores of the lake. When they were done with us, done with the killing and the burning and the terror, when they thought that my starved ancestors would not live long enough to fetch their next meal or mend their saddles or clean their tents, the army left. The people who lived decided to build a defense against the monsters who might return. One of our mystics foretold that a Tor'oc would return to destroy us. The Tor'ocs could not swim…"

"We still can't," I added.

She flinched at my words; it reminded her that she was telling the story to an actual Tor'oc, and maybe the Tor'oc the mystic had seen. She brought herself back to the story that was necessary for me hear.

"Well, as the Tor'ocs could not swim, a city built on floating islands in the middle of the lake was planned as the best defense against the Nation."

Wind

"The islands are large enough for a city?" I could not imagine it.

"No one island is, but the islands have been joined together by bridges that arch over the water. It is beautiful. The houses and buildings are built from a white wood that is light yet incredibly strong. In time, the white wood aged into shades of oranges and reds that were buried inside the white."

"How do you get the white wood?" I grimaced at the thought. "Do you kill trees to get it?"

"I suppose so—we chop them down and cut them up into long, long strips."

I turned pale at the thought of it, and my stomach turned. I was not sure I could look at this city of murdered trees.

"Couldn't they have made the city out of mud like the Sand Keeper's house?" I asked.

"It would have been too heavy and would have sunk the islands. Even normal wood would have been too much. We were lucky to have the White Forest."

"Is there anything left of it?" I asked, thinking they may have killed the entire forest for their homes.

"My city or the forest?" she replied, and before I could answer she went on. "The forest is as big as ever."

"How do you know it is as big as ever?" I asked with a touch of anger in my voice. I felt there was something more to be said that she was not telling me or did not know.

"We take great care of the forest, planting a tree for each one we take," Chiffaa said, but she seemed distracted and sad.

"And your city?" I asked.

"I don't know about Soos now," she said, and sorrow covered us like a fog. "We feared to be under siege when I left It could have happened by now."

"Siege—how? You live in the mid of a lake. How could anyone put you under siege?"

She stared at me a moment before saying, "I'm not allowed to tell you. You will find out at the Camarod."

Then the realization, "Does the siege have anything to do with why they came for me?"

"I have really told you too much." She was trying to shut herself to my questions, though she wanted to answer.

I thought I could change the topic but still learn something. "How far is Soos from where we are headed?"

"It takes many and many days to ride from Soos to Orzamond-- more days than you have traveled since leaving the prison. It is the farthest you can go in Aemira. Beyond Soos are mountains and beyond that a desert that's impassable, or at least we thought."

"So, your enemy has come from beyond the mountains." That was clear to me even though she refused to say another word.

Wind

"We're here," she said, her face brightening. I had been so lost in her story and my imagination of the floating city that I had not seen what we were approaching.

I looked about, and all I could see were the same bushes, same rocks, same brown grass that appeared to cover this entire land. She was smiling and excited as she got off her Pallurino and headed toward a large circle of fire bushes that I had not noticed. As she walked, she was taking off her cloths and letting them drop on a path that led down into the bushes. I jumped off Bol and followed. By the time I caught up to her, she was naked and standing at a bush a head taller than her, her back to me, pushing the branches away with her hands. She turned her head toward me, smiling, and said, "Come." She stepped through the bush and disappeared.

As I pushed the bush aside and stepped through, I was met with a mass of glittering silver white balls that filled the space from my feet to above my head.

"They're called Light Pearls." Chiffaa's voice came from somewhere inside the mass. "They love skin, and our skin loves them." Her hand appeared out of the mass and grabbed at my watchet. "You should have left that on the ground."

Unsure what I was looking at, I asked, "What are they?"

"Creatures—marvelous flying little creatures."

"They're flying?" I could not see their wings.

Guessing at my misunderstanding of these Light Pearl creatures, she said, "They spin—that's what keeps them up."

Looking quite closely, I saw that they were spinning—very, very quickly—and they made a slight sound as they spun.

"But I have been back and forth across this land and have never seen them once." I marveled at how I could have missed this.

"They never fly higher than the top of the fire bush. I don't know why—maybe they don't want to be seen. Take everything off and come in; it's too good not to feel this," she said, with a laugh in her voice.

I did as I was told and stepped further. There was almost no space between one Light Pearl and another. As I walked into them, they moved aside the way water moves away to let you into it. Light Pearls touched every fraction of my body. Their spinning pushed into my skin, not with a force, but as a caress that tickled and tingled.

"They eat everything unnecessary that you carry on your skin. That's what they're doing—it's a sort of delicacy for them." I heard her sigh with pleasure. "You will never feel cleaner."

I stretched my arms out to let the Light Pearls under. I must have been a delicacy for them, as they were certainly ravenous for me. If I could have slept in this place, it might have been as soothing as a tree. I had to admit to myself that there were many wonderful things about the Out World that I would have never

Wind

known if I had stayed in the City in the Trees. Knowing these wonders eased the sadness of missing home.

I had no sense of the count of how long we were in the place of the Light Pearls. I could hear Chiffaa but not often. She occasionally would sigh or laugh or giggle or simply breathe, but the general sense was that I was there alone with the Light Pearls. My eyes were closed and at some moment I sat down slowly, not wanting to crush any of them. I could have stayed like that for long and long, but decided it was time to leave the place of the Light Pearls—time to make certain that Bol was all right. I crawled through them and out, past the ring of fire bushes. On the side near where we had entered, I stood up and looked down at my skin that glowed and glistened. Chiffaa had been right about the clean feeling. But it was more than being clean. My skin had light in it, and maybe that was why they were called Light Pearls.

When Chiffaa reappeared, dressed and glowing, I was ready to head back to the Mondane. She was smiling and her hair was spread out from her head in every direction. I raised my arms to touch my hair as well. Chiffaa laughed and pointed.

"You look as though you've been hit by skyfire," she could barely say through her laughter.

"You should see yourself," I replied, also with a smile, and spread my hands out to show her what her own hair looked like. She felt the ends of her hair and howled with glee.

"We should bring Weoduye here after the clearing," I told her.

"It would do them all good, but the Sand Keeper would never come," she said, as she tried to wrestle her hair back into place.

"And why not?"

"Sand Keepers never take off their cloths." She frowned at the thought. "You never see one naked."

"Well, he can do it with cloths on," I suggested.

"Light Pearls don't like that, and when they don't like something, it is an entirely different experience." This made her laugh more. "They are very pleasant little creatures, but you don't want to make them angry."

We brought the Jannanons back to the place of the Light Pearls the next light, after the Mondanes, and after I sang a clearing to Weoduye. He came out of the Light Pearls clean, glowing, and free of the last threads of the shadows. One aspect of the Light Pearls was that no one wanted to put their clothes back on afterwards. The watchet and sit-upons and the long cloths felt dirty and clinging. The Jannanons and I sat naked for a long count at the edge of the fire bushes. Chiffaa stayed alone on the other side, either to let us resume our friendship or out of embarrassment, but it was good to spend those hours with just the Jannanons again.

The next dew light, we left from the Sand Keeper's house. Bol and I would not walk on the road, which I could see bothered the Sand Keeper. He was insulted because this was his good road, the best road, and his new companions wanted nothing to do with it.

Wind

I avoided looking at him, but I did study the road as we went, wanting to find the problem with it before he did. I never did. To me, the road was perfect, not a crack, not a dimple. The Sand Keeper walked along, looking down and, at times, bending down to look closely at some piece he had doubts about. For me it was an endless, seamless strip that looked as though it had been there no longer than a cycle of the moon. This was the road that my ancestors had traveled, and reason told me that they had seen it as I did, riding their beasts like Chiffaa's Pallurino and were probably glad to have this perfect line to ride on. The track along the side of the road was almost as well kept as the road itself—not a bush, not a rock, not even grass was allowed to stay and grow near the road. That was enough of a road for Bol and me, and it was easy to walk on.

We traveled that way for so many lights and darks that I lost count and only stopped once for the Sand Keeper—he had happily and unhappily found a place in need of repair. I wanted to see what he saw and walked onto the road to have a look. For the length and the width of one of my fingers, there was an open crack that exposed the underneath, that was darker as it was hidden from the light. The sign to repair the Sand Keeper made was a small temple built by leaning branches of a nearby tree, a tree that was made of only thorns that, as the tree grew, turned into gentler versions of themselves, though never entirely gentle. I have drawn a limb of the tree to show what it looked like, but I don't think I could describe it in a way that anyone could see it through my words. The tree must have attracted a great beast that liked its taste for the tree to maintain a defense like this.

The branches were as strong and sturdy as Sumon's spear, and the Sand Keeper drove them into the ground deep enough that harsh winds could not blow them about. I reasoned there were others who would find the sign as well as the sand and nuts that the Sand Keeper left sheltered under the temple of branches. These others would repair the road with the sand I had not seen the Sand Keeper find. I knew that he carried a satchel of nuts, but the sand was something he somehow brought out of the ground. I would have to pay closer attention the next time.

We ate while the Sand Keeper worked; and when he was done, we walked on. I had the feeling that there was a place my companions wanted to reach before the dark. They had not said so, but the feeling was deep.

The land continued to be level, and I could see that the road was leading us to a flat-topped mountain that was far, but not so far that we could not reach it that light. By the look of Chiffaa and the Jannanons, this was where we were headed and had been heading since the beginning.

"That is the city of Lul," the Jannanons told me. Weoduye had felt my desire to know our destination, and because he felt me, Goyel and Sheios understood.

"That mountain is a city?" I asked, gazing at the black thing that was growing as we came nearer and nearer to it.

"It's not a mountain. It's a wall." I looked to them, understanding even less. They could see my confusion and said, "A wall that surrounds the city. A wall that is very, very high."

I puzzled this, not knowing what a wall was. "Don't tell me any more about it. Let me see it when we come upon it."

I rode on Bol, not wanting to watch my step as we got close and close to this wall. My eyes were all for taking in this thing, taking in the skin of Lul and trying to understand it before anyone could make it easy for me. What I could make out was that the skin of Lul was made of stones stacked tightly together and bound to one another by mud that had hardened. Reaching higher than the tallest tree on the Peninsula, the rock skin looked smooth, with no places to find a grip. It rippled, much the way the land that led to Foul Lands had and was shaped in what I reasoned was a great circle surrounding something inside. It was hard to see what ended the skin at its highest point, but what I could see looked jagged and uneven, and between the uneven openings, it looked as though tiny, unmoving faces glared down at us.

Bol and I were so astonished by this mirage that I had not looked at the ground for some time. I was brought back to it when all my travelers screamed, "Stop!" We looked down and in front of us was a drop that would certainly have broken us if we had fallen into it. The drop was many Tor'ocs wide and deep and followed the same ripple as the wall. At the bottom of the drop was a forest of giant thorn trees that would have ripped us open before we hit the ground. I turned back to the Jannanons with a look of surprise and confusion, my face asking, 'Please tell me something so I understand.'

"Lul was a city without a wall before the Muons came and before the Tor'ocs followed them," the Jannanons began. "The people were devastated by the two armies. The first army ate them; and the second punished them for not being ready and able to tend to the Nation. Of the Luls who survived, there was a boy named Jieiwe who became their leader and their mystic. He had a vision of this." All three waved their arms and hands in the direction of the huge wall.

Gazing back at it, I saw that the top extended south from where the bottom started, the way a flower opens. Had it been like that before? How could I not have noticed?

"Why was it built like this, like rippled waves in the sea?" I asked, not able to see a reason for it although it had a beauty to it.

"The design was the mystic's vision, built so that no one could climb this wall or build a ladder or stairs. They could be attacked from at least three directions—straight above and from both sides. There have been armies that have traveled all the way to take the city and left on seeing the wall, understanding that the Luls would extinguish anyone trying to get in." The Jannanons looked at the wall with great regard. "No one has ever attempted it."

"So, there have been wars and armies since the Tor'ocs?" I understood that it had not been a thousand years of peace as I felt they had led me to believe.

Chiffaa's voice came from behind me. "Yes, there have been wars and armies and lords who wanted to rule Aemira."

"And none have?" I wondered out loud.

"Some have, but not for long. You see, we have the Mothers who do not allow these attacks to last."

"But they couldn't stop the Tor'oc Nation," I pointed out.

"They imprisoned you, didn't they?" She had me—they had done that.

I looked back at the wall, this massive, man-built circle of rocks that I could not even see the other side of in my mind's eye. "This must have taken generations and generations to build."

The Jannanons and Chiffaa and the Sand Keeper all exchanged glances that held a secret and a debate. They didn't want to tell me something. I stared at Weoduye and I thought I could get a thread of the secret from him. He resisted, but I got hold of something and pulled, the secret unraveling little by little until a vision was in front of my mind's eye. What I saw was a wonder that was greater than the wall itself. I gazed back at the looming, unclimbable, unconquerable wall and knew.

"It is not actually there at all," I said, as much to hear myself say it.

The Sand Keeper cursed in a language I did not know and pointed a finger at Weoduye. "You told him!"

The Jannanons responded, "No, he pulled it out."

"He shouldn't know this." The Sand Keeper fumed and shot me looks as though he wanted to end me where I stood.

"Aeon's not an enemy of the Luls," Chiffaa said, trying to soften the Sand Keeper's anger.

"He won't even walk on the road," the Sand Keeper said, pointing an accusing finger at me. "How can you trust him? You don't know what he'll do or not do. He's a Tor'oc! And not just a Tor'oc…he has the blood of Sumon in him. You see that spear on his back? There's the mark of Sumon on it. That Sumon blood means to use it, and not only on Shadows in the Seap. Which one of us is going to feel that point running through them? Maybe all of us when it's said and done." He gazed with hatred at me.

I stared back at the Sand Keeper, who would not hold my look. "I did not ask to be here, and I do not know why or to where we are going. I was told that Orzamond is our destination, but reason tells me that whatever it is you need me for is beyond that. I have trusted all of you and in that trust is my blood. You have all kept secrets from me, and if I wanted, I could pull those secrets out of this one." I nodded toward Weoduye, who looked guilty, as though it were his fault that we were touched. "I chose not to do that out of respect for whatever wishes you have for keeping these secrets. Now, not to trust me lacks reason. However, maybe your fear of the long-dead Tor'ocs of the legends is too great to see Aeon the Leaf."

I made my speech looking at the Sand Keeper, who never looked back at me once—he was too busy hanging onto his anger—but I felt other eyes on me and turned to see Chiffaa sensing me in a way she had never done. I had become another man standing before her, one that she knew better and at the same moment one who had become more of a mystery.

Her expression made me intensely aware of myself, and I turned back to the wall that was not there. "So, how long did it take them to make this?" I asked, and before they could answer I knew. "A single dark." Jieiwe had done it that quickly, and I was awed by him. "But how do they keep it?"

"The children are taught to keep it," the Jannanons said. "At a certain age, they are taught to see the wall and to believe in what they see and to make others believe in it as well. Their belief is so strong and is held so constant, it becomes true and as constant as their belief, which is unwavering. The belief of everyone inside the wall makes this real."

"And the drop," I said, looking down at the thorn trees that look as real as the wall. "Is this an illusion?"

"No, the drop is real, and it will kill you. That was one of the great insights of the mystic." Chiffaa wanted to insert herself to show me she was with me. "If one knows that the drop is real and deadly, the wall becomes unquestioned."

"And does everyone see the wall?" I asked.

"Yes, everyone sees it." And guessing at my next question they added, "Even if one knows it does not exist, you see it."

I gazed at the wall again and thought they were not right. If you knew it was not there, you wouldn't see it. It was in the belief that the wall existed. I knew it was not there, and in that moment of knowing, the wall shimmered and disappeared—not completely—but became an after-image of itself. What was left was a giant door made of metal and wood, with a city beyond the door that I could not understand well enough to see. It was like the cities we were told about in our own stories—cities where houses are built on top of one another, houses that are nothing like anything that is grown in the City in the Trees. I didn't like it and didn't want to see Lul anymore, so I let enough of my belief in the wall take hold so that the wall reappeared before me. I looked to the wooden structure that had remained when the wall disappeared. "That is real, isn't it?"

"It's the bridge that will let us cross the drop," Chiffaa said quietly. She was standing close.

It was like some bridges grown in the City in the Trees, but this one wasn't grown. They had built it with the bodies of slaughtered trees. I walked closer to take a better look. When I reached the edge of the drop where the bridge must fall, the metal door opened slightly, about an arm's length, and out of its opening two birds flew, brown and black birds of prey that circled above me. Their dark eyes that saw everything took me in. My sense was that they were determining if I were friend or foe. I went to my knees, as I would before the trees; and

Wind

I bent my head and laid my weapons on the ground around me. Riding the wind, the birds circled closer. My head remained bent with my eyes toward the ground where I could watch their shadows in the long light, shadows that grew smaller and stronger as their bodies, with wings fully extended, glided gracefully toward me. Finally, one of the birds touched the earth in front of me. Its head angled up; its eyes met mine; its penetrating gaze peered into me, marking my intention. It held that stare for a count that I can only guess now was thirty. I could feel it reading me and I did not want to interfere or influence it; I allowed it to see me as I am. It wouldn't care that I was a Tor'oc—I felt that. Satisfied that it knew me, the bird jumped back into the wind and by its shadow I saw it fly to the door. I looked up just as the two birds passed back through the opening to disappear into Lul.

My companions joined me at the place where I waited. I felt sure the people of Lul would recognize them; I was the one who made them uncertain. The door creaked, and I saw large ropes tied to the top of the door at both edges. The ropes moved, let loose from inside; and the door lowered gently toward us.

"Step back, Aeon," the Jannanons warned. "It will land exactly where you are standing."

I did as I was warned, while keeping my eyes on the door as I collected my weapons and put them back into place. Bol came beside me, and I rested my hand on his neck; he was nervous about the giant flat object slowly falling toward us.

"You'll be giving up that spear to the council when we get in," the Sand Keeper said, a sense of justice tinged with revenge in his voice.

I smiled back at him. "And what would I use to run you through with then?"

He glared at me. If he had been one of the birds, I would still be kneeling with my head bent as the door closed with a thud. But he was not, and the bridge reached the ground with the same light touch as the bird who had judged me. I climbed onto Bol and readied myself to enter the first Out World city of my knowledge.

"I think it might be better if you walked," Chiffaa suggested.

"Maybe," I nodded that this was probably true. "But Bol would feel better if I rode. I don't know if he can see the wall, but he can feel it, doesn't like it, and doesn't want to be inside of it."

"This will certainly create a stir," the Jannanons said, not without a little delight in their voices.

The Sand Keeper grumbled something to himself and walked past, out to the front of our group, and began to cross the flat, open bridge. Chiffaa followed, and I felt it was my turn next. The Jannanons would create the tail.

I could feel through Bol's body that the wood below us was different, but not unpleasant to us as the road had felt. My thoughts were on the bridge's wood as we entered the city, a city that I hated on first sight, but that caught me by surprise the moment I was inside and among it. As I had found the slaughtered wood, I found this not so unpleasant.

The city was made of houses not built on top of each other, as I had thought, but built on countless rolling hills that at first gave the impression they were on top of one another, as there was little space between them. The houses had the same shape as the hoods the Jannanons wore, pointed; and the tops fell away in a slope that rested on the shoulders of the land. I learned they were called roofs and these roofs made up nearly the entire house and were made of grass that resembled a thick, brown-grey mat. The marvel of each and every house was its large front side. The front side facing the light reached from the ground to the point at the top and was made of glass—at least a hundred glass sheets of different shapes, each a different color, and held together by some type of metal that looked as though it had just been poured, as it held the glisten of its moment as a liquid. The general shape of this glass front was a swirl, a shell-like swirl that in some houses became two or three swirls. Each house was different yet similar in its form. The entrance was as marvelous as the glass. The door was in the shape of a large shell, set on end with the wide opening facing out. To enter, you simply walked through the shell, circled around inside the shining pink and orange walls, and stepped out. You were then inside the house that was lit in every color, and these colors changed the feel and shape of the rooms as light traveled across the sky throughout the day.

It was in Lul that they gave me paper, and where Pit taught me to draw. I made a good drawing of a Lul house. As I drew, I wondered at the repeated shape of the shell that could be seen in almost everything made in Lul. The Peninsula was surrounded by water, and the water freely gave shells to us, shells that were found along the edges of the great seas. Here, however, there were no seas, no lakes, no large rivers. The mystery of the shell remained with me until my time with Jieiwe, the mystic who had died at the birth of the wall. I will come to that soon enough.

The houses were set on passageways they called, 'rules'. The smaller rules twisted around from the bottom to the top of every hill. The great Tied passageway did tie all the passageways together into a single unit. The Tied started at the bridge and, as the rules did, twisted around the city in tighter and tighter arcs until coming to a point in the mid. Once, I looked down on the city from a great height and I saw the whole city was shaped like a shell, with many small shells inside it. These passageways were not hard like the road surface, but dirt beaten down to a reflection that was soft to walk on.

When we first entered the city no one was to be seen, but I could feel their eyes on us. The Sand Keeper kept walking into the city, but I stopped Bol in the mid of the great opening after the bridge. I wanted to take in the city, and I wanted the unknown people to have time to take me in and to give them time to come to me. Chiffaa and the Jannanons stopped and waited with me. The Sand Keeper, sensing that he was continuing alone, turned and frowned at us with an expression that said, 'What now?'

It was unsettling to be in this place seemingly empty of people, but with nothing but signs of people all around. We had traveled that day from the Sand Keeper's house to here without seeing any evidence of man, except the road. Here we were surrounded by man, yet none could be seen. I had the sense of a collective hush around me.

"Now, now," the Sand Keeper yelled, turning about as he yelled, addressing the city. "Yes, it's a Tor'oc," he said, pointing at me, "as in the legends, and from my experience just as potentially dangerous, but he is only ONE. There is no reason to fear ONE. He is not a Nation; he cannot fight all of you. He will fear your numbers more than you fear him. Show yourselves!"

Out of the shell opening of one of the houses—a house at the curve after which was the rest of the city—came a miniature person. They were either farther away than I was judging or they were a very, very small people. In comparison, the Jannanons were giants. The person stood a moment, looked in our direction and, after a time deciding what to do, started to walk toward us. Unsure and walking as though walking was a new thing to it, it still walked with determination. As this person walked, in the open square around us there were flashes so short they were nothing more than impressions—a hand in the air, a piece of cloth a step later, a foot nearly appearing several steps again. The little person coming never noticed these impressions that appeared and disappeared as she passed them, her destination was me and her eyes never left me. I could see she was a girl.

As she neared me, I understood that it was small for good reason. She was a child and, by the looks of it, a child who was young and young. She held her gaze to me, but as soon as she came to a stop close enough to look straight up at me, she turned to Bol, who had lowered his head to smell her. She raised her hand, laid it on his nose and asked, "What is his name?"

Pleased with the wisdom of the question, I leaned over so that she could hear me as best she could and replied, "His name is Bol." She looked up at me with an expression that had the same question in it for me. "My name is Aeon the Leaf."

"The Leaf." She tasted the word and liked it.

"And what is your name?" I asked, remembering that I had been taught proper ways to meet a stranger when I had been her size.

"Sissase," she said, and looked back at my beast. "Bol—what is he?"

"He's an oryx."

Her eyes popped at the sound of the word.

"So, you've heard of oryx before?" She shook her head, no, she had never heard of one, but by the look of her she liked and liked the sound of the word. She grinned; her entire body grinned with the delight of the oryx that she was touching.

I thought I knew, but I wanted to make certain, so I asked, "How old are you?"

Wind

She held up two fists and from the fists two fingers from each hand shot out. "You are four," I said, and she nodded her head.

I felt certain that she liked us enough for me to ask, "Sissase, where is everybody? Are they hiding?"

She scrunched her face into a frown, puffed out her cheeks with air that she held, looked back up at me, and refused to answer. Somehow, I had the sense that I was being foolish or stupid, at least from the way Sissase saw things.

"Are they all around us and I just can't see them?"

She blew the air out and fluttered her lips. "What are you saying?" Reason told me that she didn't like this kind of joke, and that I didn't know what the joke was. I could feel my companions holding themselves back, waiting to see how this was going to play with me.

"Sissase, let's play a guessing game. Would you like to?" Children on the Peninsula loved games; my hope was that she was the same. She nodded that she would like to play and was eager for it.

"Do you live here in Lul all by yourself?" I asked, and she answered a silly question with a very long "Nooooooo." I could see that she was hoping the questions would get better.

"Are they all in their houses, afraid to come out?"

She looked at me as if I had gone from foolish to blind. There was no reason for her to answer; my questions were getting worse.

"Are they all gathered in one place inside this wall?" I gestured to the great wall that surrounded the city.

Her face followed my hand to the direction it pointed, and she asked, "What wall?" And then she laughed.

"You can't see the wall?" She laughed even harder at my joke. She really did not see it. "Sissase, you don't believe in the wall, do you?"

She smiled a shy smile. "I'm too little to believe. No one has taught me. I can't learn that, yet."

"Please," said the Sand Keeper, and took a step in our direction with the intention of coming between the little girl and me. Chiffaa held up a hand, a hand that stopped him from taking another step. I pretended to ignore him.

"Is everyone very, very close?" I asked. It was the first good question. She nodded and watched sharply for the next question. "If I held out my arms like this, could I touch them?"

She howled with her laughter, falling to the ground, "Noooooo."

"Do you see them—now?" My question made her stop laughing. She looked around the open area and nodded, still grinning, said, "Yes." So, that was it.

"Would you like to ride with me on Bol?" I extended a hand down to her, knowing the answer. There was a rustle of air that swirled around us and the sound of unhappy gasps. I reached down further; she grabbed my hand, and I pulled her up, setting her on the

Wind

hump in front of me. I turned Bol as though we were going to walk out of the city, out along the bridge. However, before we reached it, we turned, and my legs pressed on Bol signaling to run a circle around the big open space.

Before he could take four good steps, people exploded into being in front of us, running to save themselves. The entire open was full of people, jumping and moving and getting out of one another's way. My guess was that the entire population of Lul had been around us the entire time. I couldn't see them because they had made me believe they were not there.

Having stopped Bol in order to take in the sight of the Luls, I leaned down to whisper into Sissase's ear, "Do you know enough about believing to tell me something?"

Childishly, teasingly, she replied, "Maybe."

"Did they have to stand still to keep themselves from being seen?"

I had finally gotten it. She spun to me, and joy shook her body; her hands grabbed my face.

I sat on Bol as the crowd settled, waiting for Sissase's nervous parents to come and take her; they must have been worried to see her sitting on a legendary animal and in the arms of a legendary ghoul. But no one came.

"Where are your parents?" I asked Sissase.

"She hasn't any," a voice replied from below. There was a friendly-faced man, a little younger or a little older than I was. "Like mine, her parents are gone." He reached up with both hands, and she fell into them. "We live in the house just there. It's set aside for people like us, people with no one."

To him and to myself I added, as if I just knew it, "I have no one either."

Holding Sissase in his arms, the two of them regarded me as they would one of their own. "He can live with us," Sissase said to the young man; she wanted this.

"Do you have a tree?" I asked, and her eyes beamed.

"Yes! We have a big one. So, will you come and bring Bol?"

"I think you want Bol even more than you want me." I smiled at her.

"We will see," the man said in a soothing way. He raised a hand to me in the way the Jannanons had shown me people greet one another in the Out World. "My name is Pit. I apologize that we were rude. We have never seen anything like you. Everyone was scared. Me, too." I reached down with my flat open hand, imitating him, and he grabbed my hand and squeezed, and I squeezed back.

"Are you making friends?" Chiffaa was there and wanting to know.

"He's staying with us," Sissase told her—the girl was laying claim to me.

"I think the council may have different plans," Chiffaa said back to the little one, trying to make it gently clear that this was beyond a child's wishes. She had not considered mine.

"I decide in which tree I sling my bed," I said, making it not-so-gently clear who was going to make the final consideration. "I think I have an offer here that I like, as long as the tree accepts me."

Chiffaa was shocked but was not quick enough to reply before the Jannanons, and others who I guessed were the important people of the city, arrived.

"May we?" the Jannanons said, pushing past Chiffaa, Pit, and Sissase. "We would like to introduce you to the Council of Lul."

A woman who had to be the head of the Council, as the rest of them stood back just enough for her to be forward, bent her head in respect. "We welcome you. Stay and believe for as long as you wish."

'I wish to not believe at all,' is what I thought.

Barry Alexander Brown

8

The Spear of Sumon kept us in Lul longer than any of us wanted. The controversy was fueled by the Sand Keeper from the beginning. There were laws of lineal rights in Lul that were in direct contradiction to the laws of war regulating ancient found Tor'oc weapons and wares. The spear was mine by the right of blood, and I was the one who found it. What further complicated the law for the Council was the question of whether, as a Tor'oc, I was bound by any of their laws, especially ones about Tor'oc wares. I stood before the Council time and time again, and each time I felt that they wanted to dismiss the issue and see the last of me. On the other hand, the Sand Keeper, who felt their willingness not to judge for or against, agitated for a decision. In truth, he agitated for them to take the spear away by force if I didn't hand it over, and I had made it clear that, no matter their decision, I would not do that. To make the matter even harder for the Sand Keeper, the Council gave me a defender who argued my side for the single enjoyment of winning. In her heart she disliked me, disliked the spear, and sided with the Sand Keeper; however, there was something greater for her than me or my spear. She had a cunning and a craft to argue either side, and the very argument that seemed to put her in a corner was the one she liked to turn to her advantage, the one she transformed into a trap to ensnare the Sand Keeper and lay him low. However, low was not a place he would stay. Her cunning was met by his will and his anger, so in Lul we stayed and stayed.

  Throughout Lul, everyone wore white. The cloths were white while the people walked the rules and the Tied--but inside they were bathed in constantly changing blazes of color, as light streamed through the multi-colored windows of their buildings. As my defender stood to address the council, her long cloth would reflect the changing splashes of orange, blue, green. As she came back to me, splashes of red, purple, and yellow washed over her. I could not listen to her legal arguments anymore, but I could watch her without tiring, trying to decide in which point of the room I wanted her to remain because I liked the look. This light play was the only thing that kept me from running out of the room, jumping on Bol and leaving—that and because the Jannanons told me it would be a great, great mistake; although they refused to suffer through the arguments after sitting in the hall only two times. Strangely enough, the sessions were held in the hall the Luls had chosen to display the few Tor'oc weapons that their ancestors had kept or found from long and long ago. At times, the Sand Keeper would point to this or that wall to indicate where my spear should eventually rest. I never looked to see where he pointed.

    I had taken Sissase's invitation to sling my bed in their tree, a not-so-giant Seda at the rear of their house who was not-so-ready or willing to have me climb into it to make my temporary home. Still, the Seda was very fond of Sissase and, upon understanding that it was the little girl's request that I stay there, she let me sleep in her boughs. The tree must have looked big and big to Sissase, but the limbs were just large and strong enough to hold me, though I felt the Seda groan more than once when I let myself fall into bed at night. There were darks when Sissase wanted to sleep in the tree as well, and I made another little sling for her to sleep near me. On those darks I would tell her stories of the City in the Trees, stories of the life on the Peninsula, stories of our journey so far on our way to Orzamond. I asked her if she knew the Legends and had ever heard of Tor'ocs. She had not. In Lul, there was no one to tell her the stories or scare her into behaving by threatening unknown Tor'oc horror. I had become everything that Tor'oc meant to her, and she thought it was the best thing one could be. At least I had one champion in the Out World.

To Sissase, there was only one thing in the whole world better than a Tor'oc, and that was Bol. If she could have turned herself into an oryx, she would have. The door bridge stayed open, since the greatest threat to the Luls—me—was already inside the wall that was not there. Sissase and I crossed the bridge for rides on Bol out into the land. Secretly, I was hoping to find another deep bowl of Light Pearls. Sometimes Chiffaa would join us on her Pallurino, that I discovered was the name of only one type of this animal that all called 'horse'. The Luls had horses, and Sissase knew them, but she thought they were horrible compared to Bol. I marveled at the beautiful animals, though I could not make a vision of myself riding one.

Life was easy for me in Lul, and it was easy enough for me to learn new ways and new knowledge. My teachers were Sissase and Pit—especially Pit. The city was divided into groups or sodals—there were sodals for growing crops; as well as for making metal, furniture, cloths, sols, saddles, and glass; for designing and constructing their homes; for maintaining the rules and the Tied; for artists and musicians; and for hunting (to which Sissase's parents had belonged before their deaths). Luls were born into their parents' sodal, except for The Council, which was not a sodal that one could be born into. The Council was made of representatives from each group, and the head of it was a position that changed in cycles so that, at least for a time, each sodal became head of the Council.

I was interested in the hunter sodal, because I felt kinship with the group, and because it was what Sissase was born to. I was also interested in what had happened to the little girl's mother and father.

"There are small animals in the nearby lands," Pit began with a knowledge I already had, "but the great pursuits, the great animals, are in the mountains a two-day ride from here. You can see the peaks in the far and far." He pointed in a direction that I believed was where the road would lead us, where along the edge of the land I could see a jagged black line. "Sissase's parents hunted together. They were very good at it and often brought back a great variety and a large weight of meat. It was always a holiday when they returned from a hunt."

"They must have hunted for many lights and then took more lights returning." I was about to ask a question, but Pit knew what I wanted to know.

"They didn't travel alone," he continued. "There was the sodal who prepared the meat—smoked it, or cooked it, or dried it, or packed it in salt to keep the raw meat fresh. They would take three or four empty cassions with them that would come back full with the meat and animal skins."

"What happened to them?" The question I really wanted someone to answer.

"No one is certain," Pit looked off in the direction of the far and far jagged black line. "The mountains are dangerous. For most of the beasts, we are the predator; but for others we are the prey. There are animals that want to eat us in those high places, and then there are men who want other things." He gazed at me and knew I did not understand. "There's a band of Rovers who hide in the mountains, and Rovers are nothing but murderers and thieves."

"So, her parents just disappeared?"

"A search party was sent out for them; but all that was found were pieces of cloths, a broken bow and some arrows that had been fired in what looked like a fight," Pit said, but I could tell it was all just from the stories told by others. "I believe they were killed by something or somebody."

"Those mountains are where the road leads us," I said, as a fact and a question.

Pit nodded. "But they say that if you stay on the road, the big beasts will leave you alone."

"And the Rovers?" I asked, though I didn't think he would know.

He shook his head. "The Rovers are not afraid of the road."

"But won't they be afraid of a Tor'oc like the rest of you?" I smiled so he would know I was making light of his warning.

He remained grim. "I doubt they will know you're a Tor'oc, and they probably wouldn't believe it if they were told. You are a mythical creature that most of us doubt ever really existed." And then he smiled.

Pit was born as part of the artist sodal; and if anyone was born for a task, he was born for that. On paper or with clay, he could reproduce anything he saw, and it wasn't just the thing itself that was recreated but the way in which he saw it. Pit saw it differently and more beautifully than the rest of us. He made me see common things in an uncommon way; he showed me how to look at them. There were others who designed the houses and buildings and created the plans for them to be built, but it was the fine artists who designed the glass walls and chose the patterns for the colors.

He was drawing such a design one day when the light was young, and I was rising from bed. It was the first time I had seen paper or had ever seen ink in so many and many colors. On the Peninsula we had ink in only four colors—colors that we were able to extract from flowers that grew there. Pit was consumed by the work and didn't notice me until he was nearly done. I watched him give life to a glass wall that only he could see. He was shy that I had seen him do it.

Waving his hand over the drawing as if it were nothing, he said, "It is just a sketch."

It was marvelous, so perhaps a sketch was a way of saying that something was truly beautiful; that's how I understood what he told me.

"How did you learn to do this?" There was so much wonderment in my voice that he smiled.

"I suppose a certain amount of talent is necessary, but anyone can learn to draw," he said.

I shook my head. "Not me or anyone like me."

"And who is like you?" he said, still smiling, because in this world there was no one.

"There is an entire Peninsula of people just like me, and I don't think any one of them could learn to draw."

"But in your stories, you told us they learned how to do everything else—grow a city, talk to trees, find water, grow crops, make cloths. They taught themselves everything. They just didn't know about paper or they would have learned how to make that, too, and then they would have taught themselves to draw." He made it sound so easy. "That probably would have taken generations to accomplish, which is not the time we have, so I'm going to teach you." He picked up a long, thin stick that he used for drawing and dipped it into a bowl of red color. He handed it to me as he took out a clean sheet of paper that I hated to ruin. "We are going to start with a simple line."

I tried to draw lines and I did ruin that paper and many more after that. It was lights and lights before I could draw the cup that Pit and Sissase had given me to use while staying with them. Finally, the cup in the drawing had the right shape, the right color, the right feel of the real thing. From that moment I wanted to draw everything around me. Pit continued to teach, and I grew in my ability. He was patient and he knew the right thing to say to guide my hand; but in truth, he did not teach me to draw. He taught me to see. My hand followed my sight, and the better I saw, the better I drew. Pit said I had crafty, cunning fingers. He called it a gift that I was born with, though he never told who he thought had given me this gift.

Gifts come from someone—this one might have come from Soaad, but why did she not tell me about it? Perhaps this was the way I had to discover it. Perhaps my path, which I reasoned she helped guide, led me purposefully to Lul and to Pit. My path had certainly led me to the spear that I would not give up—I knew I would need it—and the feel was the same with drawing. I knew it was changing me for something; I didn't need to know what just then. I was content to see and to draw.

I wanted to give something to Pit in return for his efforts with me. I had nothing, but still I asked him what he wanted.

"Teach me weapons," he replied in the fraction of a count. "The hunters are taught weapons here in Lul, but not the rest of us. We are taught to believe."

Pit was lean and strong, but not strong enough to pull the strings on an oro bow, which was made for Tor'oc bodies. The oro bows are made to fire an arrow true and far, but at close range they're terrible. A rabbit will disappear into blood and hair if it is not hit from far enough away. So, I decided to teach him the finnif knife. The two blades always had given me problems, but because they had the same swirl design of Lul, I reasoned he would be good at it.

He liked the look of the knife. He liked that there were edges that could cut and slice on four sides. He also liked that he could spin it on a finger, spin it so it flew across a distance and into an aim. As all beginners do, he cut himself every time he picked it up and tossed it. However, the cuts didn't stop him from handling it and desiring it. I told him about throws that I never bothered with—two fingers on a single blade, the side spin, the reverse spin that's tossed from the hip.

Pit was as fiery about the knife as I was about drawing. Every moment I had that I could, I took paper, the ink, and the stick, and I drew. He threw every day and ignored his art. He got very good—not as good as Uthiriul, but if ever he met her, he would give her a challenge. I told him he had crafty, cunning fingers, but "Just don't cut any off!" He laughed. I made a bond with myself to give him one of the knives when I left.

Sissase wanted to learn weapons as well. I told her that she was not large enough yet, but when she was that I would teach her. I could not see how this would happen and I didn't like that I was untrue to her; but telling her what was bound to happen was worse. I had to leave. She would never see me again, never learn the ways of the Tor'oc, never ride Bol even one more time, never learn the weapons I had promised to teach her. My leaving was the future I saw. The vision that was reflected in her eyes was a different one—she would become a Tor'oc; she would find her own oryx; she would learn weapons; she would know me until I died; and I would never die, as far as her vision told her.

In the beginning, I was often taken to someone's house for an end-of-day meal in Lul. It was a tradition there to have guests come to houses to eat as the light grew long, to talk, to sing, to know each other's days. They pretended to want me to take part in this each dark. They did want to know much about me and what it was like to be a Tor'oc. At each house it was the same – the same wonderings of me, the same judgements, the same mistrust of me as a Tor'oc. They attempted to hide these feelings, but they were always there and always

Wind

appeared after much of their local drink was done. These were not meals of kinship. These were obligations that were thrust upon them. They did not want me in their houses for the meals, and in a very short handful of lights, I did not want to be there either. There were only two people in Lul who were mine and they were two orphans. I began to refuse the asking to come for meals and in a short time, they stopped asking. I was grateful for that. From then forward, I ate my meals with Pitt and Sissase and the Jannanons and sometimes Chiffaa; and we talked and shared songs and told each other of our days.

The light was staying longer every day, and the dark was smaller and smaller. Once when Sissase and I were in our bed slings, the light low in the sky, but with enough time to linger there for a while longer, she wanted a story about the Tor'ocs from long and long ago. I asked her what she wanted to hear, and she said she wanted to know about the seas. I didn't know much about them because we had stayed out of them and away from them, but I did know how they were named. So, I told her that story.

"The mother of the Tor'ocs was called Morla," I began.

"Yes—yes, Morla—she's our mother," Sissase couldn't help herself from adding.

"Morla named most things on the Peninsula. The sea to the north she named Sumon after her father," I said, but continued too slowly.

"The Warrior King, and you have his spear," she filled in the place where I took a breath.

"He was not a King, but you are right; I have his spear," I said. "The sea was always in a rage—what looked to us as a seething, angry rage—but it was not a rage. The sea was a warrior, always in battle, always fighting."

"Like Sumon, the Warrior King." He was an image that Sissase saw and wanted.

"That is what Morla thought too, so she named it the Sea of Sumon. The other sea was calm and beautiful, and when you saw it, you wanted to be in it."

She could feel that there was danger even in those words and so she asked, "What would happen if you went in it?"

"Sometimes nothing; but sometimes, most times, it would pull you in and under and drag you down to a place you could not come back from, a place you where could not breathe—you would die."

She pulled in her breath at the thought of the treacherous, beautiful water.

"Morla did not know what to name it, and everyone called it the Sea of Hidden Death, but she did not like that name."

"I don't like it either," Sissase wanted me to know.

"It was called that for long and long, until Morla's daughter had a daughter, who grew about to the age that you are now." I glanced to see the effect on my

Wind

friend—her sleepy eyes opened wide as she saw herself in the story.

"That little girl's name was O'bir."

"O'bir," Sissase whispered to herself.

"O'bir was very beautiful, like you, but unlike you she had light hair and light eyes. She was also very sweet, pleasant to be with, with a laugh that was music. One early light, she and a boy got into a fight—an argument, as you would call it here—and the boy called her stupid or ugly, no one was certain."

"That is not a good thing to say," said my companion, and I could see that she had been called that by some child at some time.

"Later, when the boy wasn't thinking about O'bir or about what he had said, and when he was not aware that she was nearby, she came on him quietly from behind and pushed him out of the tree."

"What?!" Sissase shot up in her bed.

"Yes, she pushed him out of the tree—a very, very bad thing to do in the City in the Trees, very forbidden."

"I won't do that when we are there." She was making me a bond, and in that moment, she took another piece of my soul. I forced myself to ignore the bond.

"I know you won't." I smiled. "The boy was hurt but not badly hurt. It was not a long fall. O'bir was punished, but from that day on she was known as the beautiful, sweet girl who would break you if you made her angry. It was thought that the threat was always there, no matter how gentle she seemed to be. Morla went to the sea and, in the naming ceremony, called it the Sea of O'bir."

"What happened to the little girl?" my little girl wanted to know.

"She grew up into a woman, very strong and beautiful. She was leader of the Tor'ocs in her time. She was fair, and some say she was gentle, but if you did her harm, she would break you in some way, quietly and secretly. Like the sea, they had to respect her and be careful with her. No one had a problem with calling the sea O'bir. To the people, they seemed to be one and the same, the sea and her. I sometimes went to the sea and stared at the water trying to see her in it."

"And did you?" Sissase asked, hoping that I did.

"In my way, I did." She looked at me, not understanding. "Her blood is in me. She had a daughter who had a son who also had a son who had a daughter who had a daughter who had a son; and this went on and on until the blood came down to me. I am the last of the line."

"And are you the King of the Tor'ocs now?"

"We don't have kings, and I am not the leader. I am the Leaf, the least of all the Tor'ocs."

She shook her head, which said that the least was far, far from true. She did not know me; she did not know that in soon and soon I would break her the way O'bir had broken the boy. But I was worse than O'bir, for she had been a little girl and knew only so much. I was grown and knew what I was doing. It seemed that

Wind

I was in true the blood of O'bir. These were my thoughts when I heard the easy breaths of Sissase. She was asleep, and for that moment and for lights to come, she would not be broken.

I lay in my sling not ready for sleep, so I picked up paper and the ink. I put the point of the stick to the paper and told it to draw anything that it wanted. I had pushed it and shoved it across papers and papers with purpose. Now I was giving it freedom—do what you want. The stick started to swirl. It swirled slowly, a large black swirl that covered the paper, gaining a speed that was turning the drawing into a giant black swirl resembling a hole, the kind the shadows leapt down into. I didn't like that, but I had given the stick its freedom.

"I am not losing myself in your hole," I told the stick. It paid me no attention.

As the hole got bigger and darker and more believable, I felt myself push away from it. I was not going to fall in. I became so concerned, that I was unaware of my rising away from it, higher and higher, up through the tree, past it, rising above the city and into the sky that was losing the light of that day. All I saw was the hole that remained a threat, though it looked smaller and smaller, farther and farther away. When I found myself at a certain height, the stick stopped. The hole was finished, and now I was able to look away from it.

That was when I saw the city of Lul from above. I saw the design of the one large shell formed by the Tied with the many little shells inside it. One would have had to see it from that height to make a design so perfect and marvelous. That was a wonder to me.

I wanted to remember this, to draw it, all the details as I saw them then, including the wall that was not there. I had seen the wall from below, but looking at it from above gave more of an impression of the kind of defense it could be if it had really existed. Something caught my eye; there was movement along the top of the wall. There was something or someone on it, but how could that be when the wall only existed because the Luls could make you believe it did? It wasn't real, and nobody could be on it. I moved closer to see what the illusion was.

No one could see me when I moved as spirit; I had no form, no width, no length, no weight to me. I moved toward the thing on top of the wall and as I did the thing stopped and turned to watch me come to it. I descended and it watched, and that made me wary.

It was a man who was standing there, arms dropped in front of him, hands holding each other in their patient wait for me to finally reach him. He was wearing some cloth that was hard to see in the last of the light. His hair was white and cut short, including the beard. From the solid white color of his hair, I guessed that he would be old and he looked old, with wrinkles on wrinkles, but when I came close to him, he was all of sudden young. His skin was healthy and without lines, and he had the blush of youth in his eyes and around his mouth. I had thought that perhaps he could only feel me, but when I was near him, it was clear that he was

Wind

seeing me and taking me in. I came to rest on the top of the wall beside him; it felt solid under my feet.

"Welcome," was all he said, and waited.

"Thank you," I replied, making it more a question than anything else.

"You are a Tor'oc, aren't you? You don't quite look like the rest of them, but I can see that it is what you are. There can't be many of you or I would have known." He said all this as much to himself as to me.

"I am what you see." I tried to make this as gentle as I could. The look of him said that he had seen Tor'ocs before, not just in the Legends, and that he had had dealings with them, unpleasant dealings. However, he was not afraid of me.

"What brings you to Lul?" he asked.

"Passing through or trying to pass through." It did not seem wise to mention the spear or the Council. "I am on my way to Orzamond for a Camarod."

"A Camarod." He was wary; the word gave him a shock. "Why would they hold a Camarod, and why would they ask a Tor'oc there? Has everything changed so much?"

"I don't know," I said. I felt the foolishness for doing everything I had done without a pebble of knowledge of why I was doing it. "I am new to the Out World. My people have been kept on an island away from everything for a thousand years. I am the first to cross back."

"A thousand years," he marveled at the distance of time. "Has it been that long?"

"May I ask you who you are? Are you a soul as I am at this moment?" I asked, bringing him back from what looked like a thousand years ago.

He gazed back at me as though he had forgotten I was there. "No, I am not a soul. I am Jieiwe."

"The Mystic, Jieiwe?" I was in true wonder.

He nodded. That was nothing to him and it should be nothing to me.

"The mystic who died the day the wall was created?" I wanted to make sure of what I was already certain was true.

"I did not die. I am the wall."

"The wall that is not there, that is what you are?"

"The wall is there," he said, defending himself and his creation. "If you think it isn't there then try getting through it or over it."

"But it's only made by belief, only made in the vision inside my head." I wanted him to acknowledge the truth.

"Yes, like everything else," he said.

"Other things are real." I pointed to what we were standing on, "But this is not." Though it felt real, even to my soul.

"Why are things real? Why, because you can touch them or see them or hear them? That is *all* happening inside your head. Yes, there are things that are real that can you see and touch and hear, and there are things that are not. But there's little chance that you will ever know the difference, whatever your name is."

"I am Aeon," I said, and that stopped him. He looked at me as if I were real for the first time, and then his gaze fell back again into the past.

"Oh, yes—now, I remember. I saw you. I knew you would come."

"And what was it that you saw?" Perhaps I would find out why I was standing on a wall that wasn't there.

"I saw a storm coming...a storm of black birds." As he said it, he could see it.

"The black birds with red wings." I wanted this not to be so, but his look back froze me.

He nodded. "A storm of black birds with red wings, and you are not prepared for it. Orzamond has called you in hope, but you are not their savior."

"Yes. As the fee said, I will let them down." I knew this to be the truth.

"Worse than that, Aeon...worse than that." There was deep sadness and hurt in those words of the mystic.

"What did you see? What is going to happen to me?"

He shook his head that he did not know. "I only saw that far. The rest was a feeling, a glimpse. I knew I was to see and to tell you. I don't know why."

"Perhaps to prepare me," I suggested.

"Nothing can prepare you." He was resigned, as I should have been.

I felt Sissase stir in the bed sling near my body. I did not like leaving her in the tree alone. She could get hurt. I had to return quickly. I faced away from the mystic and toward the city and the tree. I saw the design again and wanted to know. "Why the shell? Why this?" I gestured toward Lul.

"The shell is strong; it is a fortress in and of itself. My people are weak, but I wanted them to live in strength. So, I gave them a shell to live in."

I nodded and felt Sissase stir once more. "I wish we could talk further," I said to the mystic. "I must go."

His lips formed a smile, and he nodded. "Until we meet again."

I was surprised by that. Had he seen things further? I wanted to stay, to ask him, but Sissase was in the mid of something inside her dream that was troubling.

I sailed back to the tree, back to my body lying a half Tor'oc away from Sissase. She was moving and moaning in the mid of the dream as though under attack. I lay my hand across her chest and rested it there until she felt me and felt she was safe from the dream. She can dream about anything, I thought; just don't let it be about black birds with red wings.

The next light, the Lul Consul - who had been sent to Orzamond - returned. The Council had sent him to ask that Hasmapludi III, Gerent of the Middle and

Wind

High Bosagin, help them make the decision about my spear. The message back was a simple one:

Bring the Tor'oc and the Spear without delay.

The Sand Keeper, angry and defeated, could argue no more before the Council. My wish was that he would remain in Lul and let us leave without him. The Jannanons felt the same. It was Chiffaa who allowed and encouraged him to continue with us. She reasoned that we would need him.

I told Pit about the message from the Gerent and that the Jannanons wanted to leave immediately, as early as the next dew light. I thought he would be unhappy at the news, perhaps sad. But his response was in his expression, a determined frown. He looked down, thinking hard about what to say; and I waited.

"I want to come with you," he said, looking back up at me, expecting to see rejection. I hadn't predicted this, but as soon as it was said, I saw that I had known his intent for days. There were two people and one oryx that I had taken to my soul during this journey, and Pit was one of them. The Jannanons I was fond of, but they remained another thing to me, a thing apart that I would never feel one with, though I had the touch with Weoduye. Pit had changed me, and I had changed him. We had grown close enough that I felt he was a brother, that he was blood.

Smiling, I said, "I would like that."

Pit kept his frown. "But what will the others say? Won't they object?"

"They might, but I care less and less about their desires. They want me for something that they won't tell me about, though they know. There is a price for that, and part of the price is that they can now do what I want. I am doing enough of what they want and doing it without seeing."

Pit smiled. He could see himself leaving Lul and this life, leaving it for what he saw could only be better and more exciting. He would no longer be a person without anyone. He would be someone with a brother.

"I have one more request." Pit folded his hands in front of him, looking afraid to go on.

"What is it?" I felt I had to say, or we would still be standing there.

"Sissase." Pit looked up at me and I knew his meaning.

"She is only four," I said. "She has to remain here where people can take care of her, where she can grow up around her own."

"Aeon, I will tell you as someone who knows." Pit's voice was no longer afraid. He had to tell me so I would know. "When you grow up in Lul without anyone, the people will feed you and house you and educate you, but they won't care for you. Sissase at four already knows this. You and I care for her. She is ours. She has become yours even more than she was ever mine. And if I can say what I have seen between the two of you, you are hers as well! I am going with you—"

Wind

I cut him off. "Yes, that is said and set. However, we cannot bring a small child, someone who has barely left her mother's breast."

"This is not someone, this is Sissase." He was feeling his resolve to convince me.

"She belongs here." That was the notion I had of it.

"I am telling you that she doesn't." Pit stepped toward me.

"And what would have happened if I had not come along?"

"But you did," he interrupted.

I wouldn't be side trapped. "She would have grown up and become a Lul and married and been part of some sodal..."

"There are people who do not fit in Lul and they don't stay. They are forced to leave. There is no sodal for them, no partner, no life." I turned my head, as I didn't want to hear any more. "You have a happy vision for Sissase. I don't. There is no one here who will take her to train her to hunt like her parents would have. The other sodals won't see any reason to take notice of her. She will grow, as anyone will with care or without, but she will drift. Then someday they will show her the way to leave. I think we should be the ones to show her the way and take her with us."

The talk was beginning to make me confused and tense. "Then how will she grow up? What would become of her?"

"She will become a Tor'oc." He had a plan that set me off balance.

"She will become a what?"

"A Tor'oc—like you," he said, as calmly as if he were saying that it would rain later. "It's what she wants."

"You must be born a Tor'oc; you can't just become one," I said, though I wasn't actually sure that any of that was true. It just seemed that it was true because this idea had never existed for me before.

"How do you know you can't become one?" Pit asked and didn't wait for me to respond. "She will grow big, like you—big and naturally strong like her parents, who were not as big as you but close. I can't see how it's likely that every Tor'oc is the exact same height. Are they?" He was not sure.

"No, of course we are not all the same." I didn't like how this was going.

"And she is dark like you, again, not as dark, but if you're so concerned about that..."

I put up my hand to stop him. "This is not about how big she'll grow or how dark she will get. I cannot take her. I cannot raise her to be a Tor'oc."

"Raise who to be a Tor'oc?" Sissase's small voice came from behind me. I turned; her eyes were bright with anticipation and wonder. She was standing in the opening to the room. She came toward me and stopped. "Raise who?"

I knelt down to her and took my time before I said, "Sissase, it has come time for me to leave." Her expression froze. She wanted to hear but she didn't want to hear the worst, which I could she see knew was coming. "There is not much I know about the Out World, but there is danger there. I do know that. Pit has asked if he could join me when I leave, and I told him he could." She looked from me to Pit moving nothing but her eyes. She was holding herself for what else might be coming. She looked back at me.

"Who could be raised to be a Tor'oc?" She said again as though everything else I had said was unimportant.

"Everyone in the World thinks that a Tor'oc is the worst thing ever to become." I was finding my argument as my defender might have.

"I don't," she said, and my argument crumbled like a nut three seasons old.

I was not going to be won so easily. I would fight like the Sand Keeper had fought. "You have a wonderful, colorful, beautiful house here in Lul." My arm swept the room for her to look at. "A comfortable bed…"

"I like sleeping in trees." How could I argue with such wisdom as that?

"I don't know if I could keep you safe if you came with us," I said, and the possibility that she might come lit her face with a hope that she hadn't let herself believe.

This is wrong; I am giving her hope where none exists. That was my private thought. I resolved to make this quick, get it done, better for her. She will grow up safer and better in Lul, and in time she will not even remember me.

I took her by the shoulders and looked into her eyes so she would know as much from my look as by my words that this was final, "Sissase, you simply cannot come. There is no place for you. It may seem that this is worst, but it is the best I can do."

"Who will tell me stories?" She asked fighting not to show tears.

"I am certain there are many here in Lul who will tell stories to you each dark," I said and looked to Pit for his support. He returned my look and shook his head to mean, 'No, there won't be.'

"You will grow up happy here," I said to her. She was not looking at me now. She looked down and away from me. She had the gaze of someone lost.

"I know nothing about little girls, about what you need…"

"You know everything," she whispered in a way that said it was true and known, especially known to her.

The last of my resistance fell. In the instant before my next breath, it turned to dust more useless than a nut three seasons old. I was the one in wonder at myself and at this moment. She had defeated me, not so much with words as with something that radiated from her, something that was pure want with nothing held back.

"So, you wouldn't mind riding Bol for who knows how long? Wouldn't mind being raised to be a

Tor'oc? Because I don't know how to raise you to be anything else."

She threw her arms around my neck and buried her face in my skin. She was saying something that was muffled, and the words were being sucked into me. Did I hear or did I feel what she was saying? She was repeating over and over, "Yes, yes, yes, yes, yes, yes, yes, yes, yes."

I looked up at Pit. He was smiling. His eyes were wet. I had a brother, and I had a daughter, which I was not old enough or ready for her. Pit had been right. I was hers and she was mine.

"Are you sure they will let me take her?" The thought had just hit me.

Pit's smile grew larger and then he laughed. "If you tell them, they will probably want us to leave before the dark so that you won't change your mind."

Sissase jerked back away from me to search my eyes. Was it possible I would change my mind? I smiled to tell her I wouldn't. I was bent and bonded. I kissed her forehead so she would know that it was settled and set.

"Sissase the Tor'oc, that's what you'll be called from now on," I told her. Her mouth opened in awe of who she was becoming. She sighed, a sigh that had a fraction of a laugh in it. "There are two Tor'ocs in Aemira now. They hadn't planned for that."

She grinned; she was proud. My reason told me this could not be, but in that moment, I saw a flash of her grown. She was a Tor'oc. She was fierce. She was someone who knew herself, someone who commanded the eyes of others, someone who would lead and not be led. I thought maybe this was why I had been brought into the Out World, to find her, to raise her so that she could be their savior. I marveled at the possibility that this could be true.

After Sissase had gone to sleep, after all Lul had joined her, I wanted to feel myself high above this city again. I would never return and I wanted one last look at it as I had seen it once before. I relaxed myself into my sling and let my soul part from my body. Within a breath, I was gazing down at the wonder of Lul, and it was a wonder. Some houses had candles still burning inside throwing a color spray of light out onto the rules. I was not hovering above; I was standing on the wall. I had been pulled there. Jieiwe was not far away, gazing at me.

I did not have to speak loudly for him to hear me. "I reasoned I left my body to see Lul for the last and never again."

"Hmmmh," was what he grunted.

"Now, I reason that that was only a whisper of the truth", I said.

"Mmmm-hmmm," this grunt meant he reasoned that as well and wanted me to go on.

"Am I truly like you?" I asked.

"In what way?" he replied.

I gestured to the wall beneath us, "Can I create and make others believe?"

Wind

"Do you want to create? Do you want others to believe?" he asked.

I had never reasoned that one way or another.

"I can't reason if I want to or not," I finally said, and he shook his head.

"Creating and believing is in the want," he said. "How can you create if you don't want to? How could you make others believe if you don't care if they do? You can't."

"Then how am I like you?" I truly wanted to know.

"We are brothers, and like me, you were born with the gifts," he said. "You have the Touch even if you would like it to remain unknown. You have the Touch because you want it. You can leave the prison of your body because you want the freedom. At the beginning, I was like you, and I did not want to create for long and long. Then I wanted it. I wanted because we needed it; we needed protection. We were like babes set out on the ground for the beasts to eat. There was no other than me to protect us. And we were not going to be eaten! I wanted; I was filled with want -- and you see the result." He swept his arms out in the two directions of the wall. "When you are filled with want, you will use it."

I turned and looked down at the city, "Did you create Lul? Is it actually not there?"

'It is there. They built it. They poured the glass and mortared the walls," he said, "but it is my vision. I saw Lul long before it was built. I did not need the will or the want to create it because they had the want."

"Perhaps I will never have the will or the want," I said, as much to myself as to Jieiwe.

"That's not how it is or will be," he said. "You are walking a path that will be too much for you not to be filled with an overwhelming want. The want will come; and at that time, you'll find the will."

"Oh," I said, "And where is this overwhelming want going to come from?"

Without a breath he said, "From danger and fear and anger."

"So, I will have a want whether I desire or not," I said. It was not a question.

Jieiwe smiled, "Oh, to be so young again," he said. "The want has a will of its own."

"So before I'm ended, I'll have created a wall myself?" Again, I was not asking a question.

Jieiwe held his smile and said, "You will create something far grander."

"And why would you say that?" I asked.

"Because I am settled and set in Lul," he said. "All I wanted was a wall. You will want a world."

I shook my head, "I will not want a world. If I create that, I will have to rule it."

"You and others," he added.

"What others?" I asked, hoping he had the vision of what was to come.

"Live," he said softly and came close to lay a hand on my arm. "Want will come though you don't reason it. You need nothing more than to live. It will all come and you will be swallowed by it."

I don't remember leaving or flowing back to my body or even giving a word of farewell to Jieiwe but I recall a flash of a breath and in that flash the mystic was old – wrinkles upon wrinkles. The next breath I knew was the one that woke me in the dark. My first thought was that I needed to see Jieiwe again, and I could not reason when that would happen.

Later, in the dew light, the Jannanons, Chiffaa, and the Sand Keeper came to retrieve us and to leave. The sight that met them was Sissase sitting on Bol, Pit wearing a finnif knife and a satchel with his wares, and me, all calm and ready. Their shock and amazement that this could be was written on each of their faces. I didn't let them ask.

"They are coming with us." I turned Bol to head down the Tied toward the open gate, and Pit walked along beside me. I looked back at the five who had not moved and said, "Will you be coming as well?" Again, I didn't wait for them but continued. We were halfway to the gate before they caught us.

Chiffaa knew I wasn't going to stop. She came beside me and gestured toward Sissase, "Have you cleared this with the Council?"

I nodded. "I talked to my defender before my sleep. She said the Council had wished for this."

Chiffaa couldn't believe me and was certain I was telling her something untrue, but near the gate the Head of the Council herself was sitting, waiting at this early hour to see, to make certain that what she had heard was not a myth. She mistrusted the defender, who would try to convince her that fire is really the dark in disguise just to keep her tongue in practice.

The Head of the Council stood and forced a smile, which she was good at. "Good travels, and may the belief stay with you." She waved at Sissase, and my little girl waved back, both eager to see the last of each other.

Weoduye, who could feel what I felt for Sissase because we were touched, laid a hand on her leg as he walked beside Bol. She looked down at him as all three Jannanons said in unison, "Welcome." Then all three nodded to Pit.

Chiffaa, trying not to be left behind in the emotions of the moment, smiled in a way that said, 'I give up,' and lifted her eyes to add, 'and I am glad to do so.' The Sand Keeper, who knew that he was walking with us only because Chiffaa had fought for his cause, said and did nothing, as though all this were happening far and far away from him, though he did look unhappy about it or about something.

We traveled along the road through that day's light toward the mountains. The Jannanons had made it clear that we would sleep in the hills right before the mountains. Sissase rode Bol and looked around as though she were seeing this land for the first time. We had ridden this way together not so long before, but it was now the gateway to her life. She would forget these days as she grew older. She would forget that she had ever lived in a city called Lul. Now, for just this moment, she was keeping every instant as something precious that could disappear at any turn. She reached out to touch me at times to make certain that I was still real and still there.

The Sand Keeper kept to his road, his eyes looking down, where he was happy to forget me. We were almost to the hour of the mid-day meal when he found his crack. He was joyed to find it, joyed to find the thing that gave him reason to be. This was something pure, something no defender could argue him into a corner about, something he could win. He needed it. We stopped, and the Jannanons prepared the meal, while the Sand Keeper went to his task of bringing the sand.

I took Sissase off Bol and whispered to her, "I don't know how he does it, but there will be sand, just enough to fix the road, sand that the Sand Keeper finds in the earth. We have to watch him to see how he does it, if we can."

Sissase turned to the Sand Keeper with her focus burning into him. I didn't know if she could understand something that I didn't, but her sight was purer than mine. I could see him do it and not see it at the same time, even with my sight strengthened from my days drawing in Lul. Her strength was that she would not question what she saw.

Later, this was what she reported back to me: "The sand is everywhere. We are even made of it."

I was certain he didn't get it from any of us, so I asked, "Does he find it in the earth?"

"Some of it," she said. "The rest of it he takes from the wind, from bushes, from grass, from rocks, and from bones he finds in the earth."

"Why so many things," I wondered, not meaning to say the words.

"It's all different sand. He needs all of it." Sissase knew this but didn't know what it meant.

I could not have watched the Sand Keeper so carefully as she had. He would have thrown me glances to tell me his secrets were not for me. The little I had seen told me some of the things that Sissase knew. I did see him find a small animal's bones in the earth that he crushed in his hand and then poured the crushed powder into a bag. He knew where to find the bones, went to it without looking any other place, without a hesitant step. He also had taken a cloth that he had waved in the air, in the wind, and folded it as though capturing something.

I saw that the nearest trees were far and far. To wait for him to walk to them and back to make the house for the sand and the nuts would cause such a delay that we would be spending the dark not in the hills, but on the plain before the hills where there were few trees for sleeping.

"I will ride Bol to get your wood for you," I told the Sand Keeper, pointing to the trees that I could see but that he was having difficulty seeing.

I put Sissase on Bol and jumped up behind her. Weoduye came to me with his sword out to give it to me.

Wind

"You will need this to cut the limb," he said, and I had a vision of cutting a tree, that I had not realized I was promising to do. I would have to ask the trees which limbs I could cut and apologize to them. I hoped they would understand.

After the slow walk of the light, I could feel Bol wanting to run; and Sissase, who sat in front of me on his hump, wanted him to run. I projected myself out far in front of him, as far as the trees where we were headed. I yelled the command and let him have his speed. Sissase's hair flew back, and while I could not see her face, I could tell that she rode well. Her upright body told me her eyes were squints; her mouth was set. She looked straight ahead, taking in the speed, taking in the wind, taking in the passing land. I let my thoughts drift.

We reached the trees faster than I wanted. What I had to do was unpleasant. I had not talked to the thorn tree from earlier. I didn't know if I was about to meet trees that I could understand, but that could not understand me. Bol slowed to a natural walk. His instinct told him that we were where I wanted us to be. The trees were packed tightly together like the ones in the Drop outside the wall. Bol found an opening, and we entered their forest. I rested my hands on his fore flanks, and he stopped. I got off slowly and reached for Sissase. She was stiff in my arms.

"These are mean, bad trees," she said to me, softly enough for no one else to hear.

"There are no bad trees, Sissase." My voice had a seriousness that said she should pay attention. "They grow these thorns for protection."

"From what?"

I didn't know, but I would ask.

"I am going to try to talk to the trees," I told her, the beginning of her lessons in Tor'oc.

"Can you do that?" she wondered, wanting it to be so.

"I can for many trees, but I don't know about these. We will see. To become a Tor'oc, you will have to learn to speak wind and talk to trees."

She nodded, and the fierce look I had seen in the earlier flash took possession of her face. I sat her on the ground and turned to one tree. I knelt, bowed my head, and without considering, I said as I would to the Bent Trees on the Peninsula, "I am here as you are." I moved my arms in the way the greeting ends.

There was no response. I waited, looking down, considering what I should do next. A slight breeze blew through the trees, and I could feel the limbs above me directing it.

The wind, coming through the tree I faced, blew to me, "We are here as you are." My head jerked up. I could not believe what I heard. They spoke just as the Bent Trees spoke.

"Are they talking to you?" Sissase asked me in a very small voice. I nodded to her with a relaxed, thankful smile.

Wind

  The trees wanted to know much. Where I was from; where I was going; who were my companions; how is it that I knew how to speak wind, all the trees wanted to know this; and finally, why I was there? I told them of my task and asked their forgiveness for arriving among them with such a request. There was an old tree deep in their mid that was dying. He was old and remembered hearing of the passing of the Tor'oc Nation from the trees that had been there at that time. There were parts of him that had no feeling, he said, and from those parts I could take what I needed. It would not be rotten wood. It would still be strong and do what I needed of it. I also asked for leaves from parts that were still alive. He gave them to me, letting them fall to the ground where Sissase and I stood.

  After cutting enough limbs for the house that the Sand Keeper would make, I knelt beside Sissase. "We need to thank the tree for his sacrifice and for his gifts. I want you to thank him. Repeat this." I blew the salutation of gratitude softly into her ears for her to hear. She repeated it but had not quite understood. I blew again. She tried again, and on the third try she did it well, not exactly, but well enough for the tree to understand. I directed her toward the tree, and we both knelt. She blew her gratitude, and the entire forest laughed with their leaves. She felt this and knew they were laughing. She looked up and looked around her.

  I put my arm around her, pulling her toward me. "Done well."

  "I talked to the trees, and they laughed. Did I say something wrong?"

"No, you did it perfectly...that's why they laughed. They didn't expect it. The trees everywhere will know you now, Sissase, as the man-girl who can talk. As far as they know, there is only one of you."

"Is there only one, just me?"

I shook my head, "Here, yes, but you have many sisters in the City in the Trees."

"Tor'ocs," she said to herself. Her inner vision was creating a picture of her and her sisters. "Ask them about the thorns."

I had forgotten about that. The old tree told me that in long-forgotten times there was a large beast that loved the taste of their leaves and their fresh wood, the thin, new limbs. They had grown thorns as their cousins the bushes had, but even those thorns didn't stop the beast from eating them. They finally grew themselves into a shape where not a single place was not a thorn. Their very being was thorns, and the beast could not chew without being cut, could not swallow without bleeding.

"And the beast does not eat you now," I blew.

"The beasts are no longer here or anywhere that we know. They were driven to the far end of the land beyond the mountains."

I pointed toward the mountains that we could see, the mountains we would be crossing after the next dark. "They are beyond that?"

"Beyond and beyond. There are more mountains, greater mountains at the end of the land. The beasts were driven beyond those."

"Driven by who?"

"Driven by man, who were afraid of them. They were great, powerful beasts."

"I would like to see such a beast," I blew back to them.

"You should not wish that," the tree blew back.

We finished our talk about the land that was yet to come. The old tree knew a little, but only impressions. He knew there was a great forest somewhere beyond that had mysteries in it that the trees there did not want to share. He did not know if we would come to it.

We returned to the road where our companions waited and offered the limbs to the Sand Keeper. He took the wood and the leaves, saying something that I guessed was his thank you, a thank you that was hard for him to utter between his teeth that did not part.

We rode on a little faster than before. The Jannanons were eager to be in the hills before we lost the light. I could see Sissase watching the road and wondering something. I walked beside Bol, close enough for her to ask when she was ready.

"Why don't we walk on the road like the others do?"

"We don't like it," I said simply back to her.

"We don't?" And 'why not?' was the look in her eyes.

"Bol and I don't like the feel of it under our feet. The ground alongside is a perfectly good road for us."

She looked down at the cleared path that ran alongside the road and watched Bol's easy steps on the hard earth. She nodded, deciding to agree with me. "We don't like the road," she said, and I smiled. It was going to be difficult for me to explain that liking the road or not liking it would have nothing to do with her becoming a Tor'oc. I would have to be careful to separate what I liked from what she needed to learn.

"You may like the road, if you want." I wanted her to know that and be certain of it.

She shook her head with resolution. "We do not like the road."

"That might upset the Sand Keeper to hear you say that." I gestured toward the old man, who kept his eyes bent down to his beautiful road, trying to find the marks of age on it.

"We do not like the Sand Keeper," she said with a look that had knives in it.

"No," I had her look at me, "the Sand Keeper is not our enemy. He is afraid of the spear and of me, but he has no reason to be." She threw him a look, and if that look had held a knife there would have been blade in his back. I touched her leg for her to look away from him again and back to me. "Hear me. He is not our enemy."

She relaxed, and I thought of the story of O'bir. Sissase very much seemed like her great granddaughter. Maybe, as with Uthiriul, Sissase had more of the blood of my ancestors than I had.

Wind

We walked the first hill at the foot of the mountains as the shadows grew long. There was only enough light for us to reach the next highest hill which would take us into its taller cousins. The Jannanons stopped us and told us we could make camp and eat.

Pit, Sissase, and I took our walk among the trees as the meal was being prepared. I taught them how to choose a tree to sleep in, and what made it comfortable and welcoming. I taught Sissase how to blow a greeting, and I spotted Pit attempting to do the same. Maybe I was turning him into a Tor'oc as well. He was very good with a finnif knife, but he would never grow big enough to be a To'roc.

That dark, Sissase fell to sleep before I did, as always. I gazed at her peacefully sleeping body and wondered if she would ever dream in a bed in a house again, but my reason told me she wanted to be a Tor'oc too much to ever let that happen. She would not remember sleeping in a bed and probably in the years to come would deny it had ever happened.

The moon rose over the edge of the land and bathed the tree in its light. Just as it did, a course of tiny bells rang through the trees. We were surrounded by the ringing of the bells. I asked the tree if it had made the sound, and it told me it had not. I looked below to where Pit was resting. He saw me.

"Gruens," he said. "They are related to snakes, but they don't look like snakes. It's their song."

I fell asleep listening to the song of the Gruens, wondering about these singers who did not look like their snake relatives. That was not what I dreamed about.

Barry Alexander Brown

Wind

9

Soaad is waiting for me in the dream. We are standing on the Sand Keeper's road. Walls of rock rise up around us. The road is an arch, and we are at the top of it. I cannot see what is behind or what is ahead.

"They wait for you," Soaad says, a warning.

"Who?"

"The ones who want to take everything," she looks up to the top of the rock walls.

"Are we in the mountains?" I ask, but I know that we are. She nods.

"Do they know we are coming?"

She looks at me. "They know. They have seen, and they know how many you are; but they don't know who you are." She points at me.

"What am I to do?"

"You have to protect her--do not hesitate to protect."

"She's the savior, isn't she?" I know this. I am certain.

Soaad smiles. "She is one of them. You are her savior first."

"What should I do to protect her?"

"Do not hesitate. Do not be uncertain to strike."

"Will I be?" I fear I won't be.

"It is a challenge."

"I think I am ready for the challenge, whatever it is," I say, feeling a little foolish.

She looks at me as a mother looks at a child who is saying something silly but brave. "We all think we are ready until…."

"Until the moment," I finish her words.

"Until the moment," she repeats.

"I will wake ready and stay ready for the challenge all through the mountains. I will fight it when the moment comes."

"Will you kill?" she asks.

I do not have a quick word back. "If I have to."

Wind

"You will only know that then, and it won't ask you or wait for you."

"Will it attack with death?" I am asking more than she will tell me.

"You will only know that in the instant, and that instant will be all you'll have to see if it's death or not."

"I am not going to kill unless it's necessary."

"Yes, I know," she says; this is why she is here.

"Can't you tell me if it's necessary?"

"Only the instant can tell you," she says sadly. She wants to tell me more, but there is a boundary to what she can say. This is more than a warning; this is about me.

There is nothing more to say. The dream is done in the way dreams end; it is simply gone.

I woke remembering the dream as though it had been a meeting that we'd had on the top of the mountain, not a dream.

After the early meal, I asked the Jannanons to walk with me. I led them to a place where we could see the mountain we had to cross.

"Is there a way around and not over?" I asked them, pointing toward the highest peak.

They were surprised by my question and looked at the giant in front of us. They considered my question, not truly considering it, but wondering why I had asked it.

"There is no way around," they said. Goyel pointed one way, Sheios the other. "The mountains stretch beyond and beyond. We cannot go around them."

"Is it like the lake? Because I did reach one end with Bol." I asked.

"No, it is greater than the lake. The lake is nothing. The mountains have lakes in them that are larger than that one. We have to cross." They looked concerned. "Why do you have to know this?"

"I've been warned about the mountain—about what waits inside of it for us."

"Warned by who?" They could not believe that I could have a warning that they did not know about.

"Soaad came to me last night. She said there is something up there that is already hunting us. I think whatever it is has been watching and waiting and planning."

"Who warned you?" They had never heard of Soaad; I had never told them.

"Soaad—the fifth mother."

"There are only four mothers." They were certain of that.

I held up five fingers as if that were proof. "There are five. She came to my dream and told me to be ready."

"For what—for Rovers?" They were alarmed.

"I don't know. Maybe Rovers and maybe a beast. She couldn't tell me."

They were dismayed and didn't know what to do with the warning. "When we crossed with Chiffaa, we saw no signs of Rovers or of any great beasts," they said, knowing that this meant little or nothing.

"It won't be like that." My dreams are not wrong—that was the way it would be. "We have to be ready."

"Because it is coming," they said.

"No, because we are going to it." I gazed back at the mountain, asking silently for it to show us the danger that was hiding there.

The Sand Keeper led the way as he often did, with his head down. I felt that we were using him as the lure to attract whatever was coming. He would be the first thing they saw and the first they would strike. I did not feel easy about that. Behind the Sand Keeper were the three Jannanons, walking in line. Sheios was at one edge of the road looking, searching for the unknown in that direction. Weoduye was at the center, his eyes cast ahead. Goyel was on the other side of him, a mirror image of Sheios. Chiffaa walked behind them and saw that they were on great alert, which put her on edge. Sissase was riding Bol. I was next to them, and Pit was next to me. Chiffaa would glance back at me, her face stern, fear in her eyes. When she looked away from me for a moment, I handed Pit the second finnif knife.

"Take this," I whispered. "Be on guard." I nodded toward the mountain that we were just reaching.

He took the knife. "What is it?"

I shook my head. "We don't know."

He tied the knife in its sheaf around his mid and touched it, readying himself.

"Can't you tell me?" He whispered back to me, knowing that Chiffaa and Sissase were not supposed to hear.

"Just be ready," I said quietly to him.

Chiffaa caught some of our words and snapped her head around, shooting a look that said, 'What aren't you telling us?' She put her hand inside of the cloth she wore and rested it there. I wondered if she had a hidden weapon. I hoped so.

We walked until the mid-meal. The Sand Keeper had earlier found a crack, pulled forth sand, even there out of rock. He had made the house for the sand, and crushed nuts from the limbs he had found earlier. The Jannanons and I stood facing away from him, waiting for something to happen. I chose the place for the meal. It was inside a group of rocks arranged so that it would be impossible for a beast or man to surprise us. Still, my eyes never left that one opening where something could enter.

The thought was that we could cross the mountain in a single light; and once over it, we would be out of danger—or so I thought, based on the warning. We were near the top of the mountain where I could see the road arching over and disappearing on the other side. As in the dream, the road ran between rock walls, out of which enough space was carved for the road and a small path beside it. On the approach, there were boulders stacked on one another, with giant cracks between the rocks that could be easy walkways. All was quiet. There was not a tree or a bush at this height, and it would have been cold except that the light warmed us. I was tired from the winding walk up this mountain and tired from the constant fear that we were prey ready to be taken.

For a moment I looked down--and that was when it happened. Chiffaa gasped and I looked up.

There was someone on the road before us. It wasn't just one someone; it was three in front, four behind us, and four on the boulders to either side of us, all with weapons in hand. There was a roughness and meanness in their stance and their cloths. They were dirty, and none of their cloths fit them well.

The Sand Keeper was the last to see them, as he walked with eyes only for the road; and he nearly collided with the man in the mid of the three blocking our way. That man took his long sword and touched the Sand Keeper's head with the point. The old man jerked up in surprise.

"I think you stop here," the leader of the band of thieves said.

Pit turned slightly toward me but kept his gaze on one of the men near us on the rocks. "Rovers," was all he said, and his hands had already taken out the two knives that had been hidden at his sides.

The leader turned slightly toward one of his men and said, "So, what do you think we have here?"

The rough man addressed replied, "Travelers—using our road without paying."

The leader repeated it as though it were a thought he had never had or heard. "Travelers—using our road—and not paying."

"It is not your road." The Sand Keeper couldn't help himself. The leader smacked the old man with the side of his sword, knocking him down and shutting him up.

Sissase jumped when it happened. I pressed my hand on her back and lightly pushed her down toward Bol.

"Lie against Bol. Hold tight; don't look up." She closed her eyes tight, gripped Bol with her hands and legs, and took a piece of Bol's mane hair in her teeth.

I felt eyes on me and looked up to see the leader staring. "What are you saying back there?" he yelled across the Sand Keeper, the Jannanons, and Chiffaa.

"I was talking to the girl," I said. "She's afraid."

The leader nodded. "Wise." He stared at me, taking me in. He seemed to recognize something, and he said out loud, "What are you?"

A man on a rock nearby yelled to the leader, "He looks like the other one…the one who…." The leader stopped him with a look.

"I'm a Tor'oc," I yelled to the leader, whose look back at me was surprise, then amusement. He laughed.

"There are many things you might be, but that is the one you're not. But that is clever," he said chuckling. "Tor'oc…very good. Well, we could joke here all day, but there is business to do."

Wind

"Business?" I heard the Sand Keeper say in a small voice.

The leader looked down at him. "Yes, business. There's a fine to pay. A fine for using our road without permission."

"No one..." said the Sand Keeper.

Chiffaa quickly cut him off by calling his name, and asking, "How much is this fine?"

"Whatever you have—that seems fair," said the leader, and all his men agreed. "Let us start with your weapons. Lay them down." He pointed to a place on the road where he would be able to see our weapons piled on top of one another, but none of us moved to put them there.

"Let us pass," the three Jannanons said. "We are wanted at the Camarod in Orzamond. If we do not arrive soon and soon, they will look for us; and they will discover that we got no farther than this mountain. They will know. They will hunt you and they will find you."

"It is a pretty story," said the leader, "but I have only heard of a Camarod in the Legends. It's like that Tor'oc you have there—simply unbelievable. Lay down your weapons." He commanded that time.

At that, all three Jannanons unsheathed their swords in a single motion, ready for the fight. Without another thought, I grabbed the spear and pulled it around to hold it, point aimed straight at the leader himself.

The leader grabbed the Sand Keeper by his hair and pulled him off the ground. The edge of his long sword pressed against the old man's bared throat.

"Lay those weapons down or I'll slice this one open," the leader cried out. His men stiffened, as ready for the fight as the Jannanons.

The Sand Keeper was crying and saying over and over, "No!"

"We don't want death here," I called out to the leader.

"Death is here already," the leader said back to me, almost as a song. "Do it!" he yelled to the men.

The Rovers charged and everything slowed. I seemed to be the only one moving at normal speed. I looked behind, as I had felt the Rovers there moving closer during our talk. Bol kicked the nearest one, who flew back down the road and was never seen again. Then my oryx spun around on the other two, lowering his head to point his horns toward the mid of their bodies where he wanted to cut them. They fell back, and Sissase held on as Bol jumped at them.

Pit was throwing a knife underhand at a Rover on the rock just above us. The knife spun backwards, up toward the man to catch him just under his chin—I didn't need to see it. The Jannanons had chosen a man each and were already fighting them. With one hand, Chiffaa held a flute, or something like it, pressed against her lips. Her cheeks were two balls of air, and she was blowing into the flute. This was aimed at one of the men.

Wind

The leader wanted to see the fight and how it faired, and he had not yet cut the throat of the Sand Keeper. He looked to me, saw that my spear was meant for him, that I was frozen, and that the spear was ready. The Sand Keeper was yelling something—everyone seemed to be yelling—while the voice of the Sand Keeper was calling, "Help!" His eyes were on me, too. The blade of the leader's sword moved against the throat of the Sand Keeper, and I saw blood—and everything stopped.

Soaad was beside me, just behind me, leaning into me. "You must act, Aeon," she said in a soft voice.

"But he's a man. I can't kill him." I was pleading for her to understand.

"He dies or the Sand Keeper dies. Death is already here."

"Death is not here at my hands." I was making my case.

"Death doesn't care."

"I can't," I cried.

"Then that is your decision," I heard sadness and loss.

In the next count everything was moving, including my arm that was tossing the spear; it flew fast and sure. Pit and I had practiced against aims in Lul for lights and lights, but this time the aim was the leader's chest. He was struck with a sound that I can still hear, a sound of cracking bone and flesh ripping open. The force knocked him back from the Sand Keeper, who grabbed his throat that had been cut but not badly.

The leader dropped his sword, stumbled backward with the spear sticking out of him on both sides. He stumbled and he fell as I ran to him. The fighting all around me was over. I reached the leader, who lay with his back arched. The point of the spear was stuck in the ground underneath him; his hands grasped the body of the spear; his fingers moved around the sybil on it. His eyes showed shock, surprise, pain, and wonder as they moved across the sybil.

"What is…" he said, blood filling his mouth.

I tasted blood in mine as well. "It's the Mark of Sumon."

He gasped and looked at me, frightened, alarmed, confused. "Tor'oc." I nodded and laid my hand on my chest.

"I am sorry." I wanted to pull the spear out but didn't know how I could.

He put a blood-soaked hand on my face and felt it. "You are not supposed to be real."

"Do you think you can stand?" I asked him. "I might be able to pull the spear out…"

His smile stopped me mid-word; he thought it was funny that I thought he might be able to stand. That is the way he died.

By instinct, I bowed my head and sang the death song. When I looked up, I found the Jannanons standing near, their swords put away. Chiffaa was on her knees tending to the Sand Keeper. At Bol's side was Pit, holding Sissase, who was clinging to his body and his neck. He was rocking her and singing to her.

Wind

On the ground were five other bodies. The living Rovers were gone; the dead ones remained. I saw the one Pit had killed and guessed at the ones the Jannanons had beaten, but there was one that lay dead without a mark, without blood. I reasoned that this was the one Chiffaa had killed with her flute. I didn't even want to know how it happened. We had all killed, and I was feeling sick at the horror of killing.

I rose to walk to Pit and Sissase, and as I passed, the Sand Keeper reached out to touch my leg to stop me from passing. I looked down; there was gratitude in his eyes.

"Do not thank me for this, not for killing," I said, and moved on.

When I reached Pit and Sissase, she sensed me and pushed herself up from the boy she had known since she could remember. Tears streaked her face.

"Forgive me," I whispered to the little girl for whom I would have done anything.

She motioned for me to come close to her; and when I did, she kissed my cheek. She forgave me—she would always forgive me.

The earth was too hard to dig, so we buried the Rovers in rocks. I asked for their forgiveness as well.

After the burials were done, the Jannanons had us push ahead quickly. I was glad to be gone from that place; I wanted off the mountain. I wanted a tree to put my sling in. I wanted Sissase to begin to forget what had happened. The Sand Keeper was too shaken to travel, so he rode behind Sissase on Bol and, for that time, ignored the road. We walked down, down the far side of the mountain faster than we needed, but it was what we all wanted.

The hills at the far side had a stream where I bathed to wash the blood from my body, from my watchet and sit upons. The hills had Bent Trees—beautiful, welcoming Bent Trees—and that dark when Sissase and I lay in my bed sling, as she wouldn't sleep in hers, I told her a story from the City in the Trees.

"This is a story about O'bir's daughter, Okjolik, who finished the understanding of the wind language and who gave the Tor'ocs the written word. Do you want to know how to spell Sissase with our marks?" I asked Sissase, whose head rested against my chest. She nodded, rubbing her head up and down against my skin.

On her back, I traced the marks we called the Nom to spell Sissase. She held her breath as I did this; she was feeling and trying to see the marks. "There are forty-one marks in the Nom. I will teach them to you. Would you like that?" She nodded again. "On the Peninsula we can make paper from a tall grass that grows there but the paper does not last long and long. Most of our written words are carved into the skin of the Bent Trees – their skin is tough and thick. If you don't cut too deeply, it does not hurt the tree. Still, the skin is a living thing, so it grows; and if the words are not carved again and again, they disappear into the tree. There are Tor'ocs whose lifelong work is to keep the words from disappearing. They know the history of our people better than anyone because they write it over and over.

"As great as the written word is, Okjolik is not well known for that. She is known for something we Tor'ocs think is even greater — the hanging way. Would you like to hear about that?" She didn't nod this time but pressed her small hands into me to tell me to continue.

"Do you remember what the hanging way is?" Her hands pressed into my chest, that time with a little more force to tell not to stop again. I went on. "For three generations, the Tor'ocs used the large branches of the trees for a way to walk from one tree to another as the city grew with more and more people. Okjolik had visions; and in her visions, she saw the city grow, grow as far as the farthest tree in the forest, grow to include great halls and balconies in trees that were too far apart to walk to except on the ground and that she visioned was not the way. The way to move in this grand new city had to be in the trees."

"She said that whenever she had a problem with a vision, a part that she couldn't see or understand, she would go on great walks to free her mind of thought. On these walks the problem would solve itself. It was how she came to see the forty-one marks of the Nom and understand them and know them. She couldn't see how the city could grow beyond the trees that were already used, but she knew that the city needed to grow.

"She began in the dew light and walked without a place to walk to, without noticing where she walked, without seeing, without hearing, without thought. The Tor'ocs of the time recognized when Okjolik was on one of her walks, and they let her be. She walked through the dew light, into mid light, and into the shadows that grew long. Coming out of the walk, she found herself standing in the mid of a small lake no bigger than the width of this tree we're in now. She was standing in the mid of water that she was sure was deeper than she was, but the water reached no higher than her ankles, and only her feet were wet. It was as though the water itself was holding her up. She gazed down to see what below her was keeping her up and saw two strands of vines that had fallen into the water from a tree above. The vines had grown down from the tree, wound through the water, and then grown back up into another tree. There it was, the way that she had been looking for, a way to weave and grow bridges throughout the forest.

"In parts of the forest there were many vines that had grown long and close to one another. Those vines could be pulled up from where their ends reached the ground, then twisted around, tied together, and stretched to create a walkway. She did this in the lights and lights and lights after her walk in the water. This was what became the first hanging way and one of the only ones that could be made so quickly because the vines were already close and in line. Later hanging ways had to be planned, and the vines had to be shown how to grow across and not down. To grow any part of the hanging way took a long time; but by the time Okjolik was old, there were hanging ways throughout the trees, even to trees that were far apart. The first of the great halls was grown as well, in a far tree that we never could have reached without the way. That first way she made has lasted until today. They called it Okjolik Way, and it has been our tradition that when you could not solve a problem, you could go lie on the Okjolik Way and, the answer to the problem would come to you."

I could not see her face, but my feeling was that Sissase was smiling at the knowing of Okjolik Way. She raised herself up to look at me, and her smile faded into a look that was more serious.

"He was a bad, wasn't he?" She didn't have to tell me the one she meant.

"It seemed he was," I said.

"He would have done bad to us," she stated simply.

I nodded. "He meant to do bad."

She took in a big breath and pressed her hands into me again, as though making sure I was really there. "You cannot let them do bad things to you. You cannot die."

Like a punch, I was knocked back by how much she understood of that fight, of how much she knew of what had happened to her mother and her father. I had thought she was too young to know, but she knew. I put my arms around her and held her close so she could hear my heart.

"We are safe, and I am safe. I will be for you forever and forever." It was a bond I could not make, but I did. Her body relaxed on me for the first time since we had climbed into my sling, and soon her breath evened into a smooth sleep. I was still sick from the death and the killing, from what I had done. The small body that rested against me, that wanted nothing bad to ever happen to me, was the best cure for the sickness. She was my savior as much as I was hers. I nearly left her in Lul, and I was shocked that I had come so close to a giant misstep. I was fearful of my stupidity and foolishness. Sissase was the life of my heart, my eyes.

"Soaad, if you can hear me, help me not to come to such a misstep again," I said in voice that was scant above a whisper.

The wind blew through the trees, and even though it should have been the Bent Trees talking, it sounded like my second mother.

"We are always with you."

This helped me sleep, helped me not to dream again of the killing. It was enough that this horror was in my every breath throughout the light—I could be without it in the dark.

In the next lights, the walk to the Jannanons' city that they called Jielada followed a steady down slope. We saw the city from far, and, as we got closer, I was glad to see that it did not have a wall, real or just belief. On the light we finally arrived, I saw the city had grown around three small lakes with tall thin rocks in the mid of each of the waters. At the top of each rock was a dwelling. Impressed, Pit drew a picture of it.

Weoduye came beside me. He saw and he could feel that I was taken by the tall rocks with houses on top.

"They are called Kirks, and the three living Fanes serve their lives in them. The Fanes are those who give us the touch. You will meet them soon and soon," he told me through our touch, his eyes never leaving the Kirks themselves, a smile playing upon his lips. I looked at him long enough for him to hear my question.

"There are never more than three Fanes at a time. They are Jannanons, but not like us. You will see that. When a Fane dies, a new Fane is born to a regular family. No one knows who it will be or how a family is chosen, but it is clear and clear when a Fane is born. Fanes cannot give birth themselves, though they are both of male and female, each and every one of them. When the new Fane baby is recognized, it is taken by the Prioresses, young women of the city who have to serve for six seasons in the Kirks to take care of the Fanes. All the women have to serve before they are fully grown. During this time, they gain their spiritual knowledge, and because all the women serve, there is never an argument when a baby is chosen and taken—the mother knows this is an honor and is proud that she has given birth to a Fane."

"Do they have names?" I asked.

"No. We only call them the Fanes, but because they give us the touch, we feel each of them as their selves. There is never confusion, though they all grow to be identical in look, only changing with great age."

I heard music long before I saw that a crowd of Jannanons was there below us to greet and welcome. At the head of the large crowd were three extremely tall, thin people with white, white hair that flowed longer than I was tall. They were moving to the music, tossing their long strands of hair up and down as they leaned like young thin Weepers swaying in a wind.

Pit and Sissase were mesmerized by the image of the Fanes and wanted to know what they were. I told them as much as I understood.

The three Fanes were dancing toward us, and we were walking faster and faster toward them. I had thought they were tall like me, but they were taller. In height, I was to them as the Jannanons were to me. I came to their mid chest. They moved to us, swaying and tossing their hair, surrounding Pit, Bol, Sissase, and me. They were chanting something, and as their long, thin arms waved, their hands moved in gestures that seemed to be saying, 'Come,' while they circled round us.

Sissase was grinning, on the edge of laughing. No one had to explain to her that they were dancing their welcome. She could see and feel it and smell it.

I had not noticed at first that Sheios, Goyel, and Weoduye were dancing also, and that the entire Jannanon people were on the road, dancing, playing music, and making music with their throats. Chiffaa was imitating the stomping step the Jannanons did to their music, as she laughed and clapped. Even the Sand Keeper was smiling. The Jannanons' joy was a cloud that covered us, that we happily breathed in, a cloud of healing.

Soon and soon, my Jannanon companions disappeared into the embraces of their wives and their children and their friends. I took Sissase off Bol—I wanted to hold someone, too, and wanted to be held. Pit draped his arm around Bol, who was the only one of us who needed calming. Chiffaa danced to us, putting her arms around me, pressing her body against Sissase. She kissed both of us and laughed, which made Sissase laugh.

We stayed in Jielada only twelve darks. Waiting for us was an emissary from the Camarod who wanted—who said that he *needed*—us to leave as soon as we were rested and able.

Sheios, Goyel, and Weoduye had planned that they would be replaced by other Jannanons and stay in Jielada, but they decided that they could not stay. They wanted to continue with me to the Camarod, and for whatever it was they wanted me for, perhaps to continue beyond that. They wanted to continue, and, by chance or by destiny, the Fanes had told them it was their haza, foreseen in a secret ceremony held while they had been traveling with me.

I liked the Jannanon people. Maybe I had grown used to my companions who were so like the rest of the people. I was touched with Weoduye; and Sheios had saved me, if not Goyel as well. They lived in dwellings built on top of one another, as we had been taught people did in the Out World. The houses were square, sharp-cornered structures framed to overlap, each seeming to have fallen into place slightly off center from the one below it. This pattern allowed their connecting stairways to link the city together. The entire city of Jielada was a pale blue, like the flowers that bloomed early in the year. In the greying dew light, the city took on the cold look of ice, though still a beautiful color from my vantage in the tree where Sissase and I slept. The firelight that colored the windows in the blue walls gave the city a warm, inviting feel as the light fell low in the sky each day. I learned they were burning the old dead wood they found in the forests. We did the same on the Peninsula. Pit, Chiffaa, and the Sand Keeper had been given rooms in a house built only for travelers, where there were always Jannanons waiting to meet their needs.

For many lights, Sissase would not leave me, wanting to ride my shoulders the way she rode Bol. Her constant presence helped to rid me of the sickness that had stayed with me, the sickness that pressed my thoughts, my head, my stomach, my heart. She would eat at times sitting on me, using the top of my head as a table, leaving crumbs of whatever it was she had eaten in my hair. I should have been angry of that, but there were few things that gave me more pleasure or peace than having her on me.

Word came to me one late light that the Fanes wanted me to come to them. They wanted to hold something called a Rassat with me alone. No one could tell me what this was. It was known that the Fanes would hold Rassats among themselves, but never with normal Jannanons and never with travelers of any kind or with anyone else. The people knew the name only, not what it was. They knew only that the Fanes were given wisdom and sight during the Rassats.

Wind

Sissase had begun to spend time on her own, time with Pit, and time with Chiffaa away from me, so I thought I could go to the Fanes for however long the Rassat would take. I was assured it would not be long and long.

A small boyt took me to one of the Kirks in the lake on the side of the city where we had entered. The boyt man left me on a small landing. There was a door just above the water level. The door opened as the boyt pushed away. A young woman half my height held the door. She smiled and nodded, and with a tilt of her head, asked me to come inside.

She motioned me up the long stone staircase leading to the top of the Kirk. The walls were lit by candles set far enough apart to hide a view of the next candle, though its light always lit the way. The ancient stairs wound round inside the tall rock. Each step had been worn down and curves carved in the center by countless footfalls. My feet slid into these grooves, and they guided me to walk where all had walked before me through the ages.

I reached the first grand hall of the Kirk with little breath left in me. Waiting at the top were three young Jannanon women standing beside a chair that seemed to be made of clouds as I fell into it. They laughed to see how grateful I was for the chair and handed me a drink they said would help restore me. There was no urgency for me to be quickly up and alert, so I lingered in the chair until I felt stronger.

Waiting for me in a higher room whose windows looked out in all directions, the three Fanes were seated on the floor in the mid of the room, their legs crossed, their long white hair spreading onto the floor around them like tallums or what they called mats. The three Fanes sat facing one another but far apart in a triad, three points like the sharpened stone that makes the head of an arrow. It struck me that the city of Jielada rested in the mid of three tall rocks that formed the same shape as the twenty-third mark of the Nom. It was known in the Peninsula that the mid of the twenty-third mark was a place of strength, and I think this was known here as well. The young women who led me into the room took me to the Fanes, into the mid of them, asked me to sit there, and told me to face any way I wanted. I located where I thought the tree I had slept in was and faced that. I was looking out the windows past two of the Fanes as the women left us.

"Brother," one of the Fanes said, "you may grow here among us."

It was the greeting of the ancient trees yet spoken in the words of men. I blew back gratitude in wind, and the three blew back a welcome.

"You call me brother." I looked from one to another. "How is that?"

"We share the same mother," the second Fane said.

"We are family," the third Fane added.

"Soaad," I stated and asked in the same breath. They smiled in return. "But I am not a Fane."

"No, but nearer than you think you are." I was losing track of which Fane was talking, as they sounded alike. I was also losing the sense that it was important to know.

"Then what am I?" I asked, wondering if it were a simple question to answer.

"You are like your brother, Jieiwe."

"The Mystic from Lul?"

They smiled in return.

"I don't believe that I am a mystic." I knew I was not special enough to be one. "I have dreams, but they are only dreams."

They smiled in return.

"We rarely have a brother among us," one of the Fanes said.

Another continued, "The Rassat is special with the fourth. It is stronger and clearer."

The third Fane added, "We have waited long and long for you."

"The Rassat foretells the future?" I wanted to make sure I understood the purpose.

They shook their heads, still smiling. "It does not. It is a window into the present. The future is untold, but its birth is the now that is just as difficult to see. If you are willing, you can help us see it and keep it."

"I am willing," I said these words before I was certain, but the words moved me to be.

They smiled in return. They lowered their heads. It was beginning.

A wind circled the room, taking the flames from the candles that lined the walls. Holding the fire inside it, the wind swirled around us. The fire grew into an unbroken circle that burned at the level of the shoulders of the Fanes. The circle burned without touching the floor, without touching anything. The Fanes had closed their eyes. I closed mine.

Soaad was there for us in a place that was all light, beaming as any mother would to see four of her children united. She looked to me.

"This one's heart is not yet mended. The Rassat will make you whole." She appeared far away, but her hand was caressing my face.

The fire had followed us into this place of all light. It surrounded us still. I wanted to touch it, though it was a circle on the other side of the Fanes. I stretched my arms toward it. The fire responded, drawing in its circle and moving toward me. It moved through the Fanes, and tightened as it swirled round me. It tightened more as it engulfed me, tightened until there were only flames, and I was the fire. The place of all light exploded into images and colors and sounds, all cascading, popping, swirling, undulating, melting, appearing, disappearing, liquid, solid, wispy, loud, silent, faces, land, stars, hands, roads, trees, rivers, cities, beasts, ice, rocks, swords, feet, fires, windows, paths, black birds. It was a tempest that knocked me, that went in and out of

Wind

me, that I could not turn away from. The tempest had me, yet it didn't want me.

Inside the whirlwind of color, sound, images, I had felt all time; and I had not been alone. The Fanes had been there with me. When it had blown itself gone, we were in the room again, sitting just as before. I fell back, more exhausted than from the steep walk up the stone steps. I looked at my brothers and could see that their eyes were still closed, their faces serious, their wild hair the only sign of the storm we had witnessed. Strands of their hair were still sticking out, blown by the strong winds into disarray, and so long that they touched the hair of the next sitting Fane. It helped me to see clear signs that the whirlwind had been real.

As they opened their eyes, each of the Fanes turned onto their hands and knees and crawled to me, placing their palms with long thin fingers on my chest and torso, their hands big enough to cover my entire mid.

"The world is more than I know and more than I can understand," I whispered to them.

"You have shown us much and much," one said.

"You understood?" It was difficult for me to see how it was anything more than fleeting moments.

"We will," another said.

"You brought us more of the present than we have ever seen," the third one added. "We will know it soon and soon."

"But not the future." I remembered that the storm was the now.

"The present shines the light on the future," said the first one.

"And is that important?"

"It seems to be, until the future comes," said the second.

"And then it's the present." I was beginning to see.

The three smiled.

The third one ended the Rassat with, "You are hungry and thirsty. Let us eat."

Riding on the boyt back to the city, I felt better than I had since before my dream about the Rovers. Soaad had been true. The Rassat had made me whole again.

The days left in Jielada were a celebration of return and also farewell. Meals followed meals. There were demonstrations of the oro bow by me and of the finnif knife by Pit. The attention poured on Bol made him nervous, though he was calmer when Sissase rode him through the town to show off her riding and her oryx. Whenever anyone asked her what the Tor'oc was like that she was traveling with, she would answer, "We live in trees; and we can talk to trees; and they can talk back."

"But isn't it scary?" they would ultimately ask.

She would shake her head and say, "You should not be afraid of us."

Wind

She had reached the point where she was forgetting very, very quickly that she hadn't been born a Tor'oc, and there was something in that I liked.

One dew light, several of the young Prioresses were waiting for me at the bottom of my tree when I woke. They told me the Fanes were eager to talk to me and asked me to come meet with them when I was ready.

They waited for me to eat my morning meal with Sissase and Pit, who would stay with her while I was gone. The Prioresses led me to another lake where a boyt took us to the Kirk in the mid. This Kirk was similar to the first one, with differences in the door that led to the stairs that were also lighter in color than the other Kirk, but they led just as far up the rock, and had the same sort of grooves worn down from their use over a long time. The main hall, however, was quite different. The first one had been all red. This hall was yellow with many mirrors. There was a soft chair as in the first, that swallowed me up; and there were three young women waiting with the drink to revive me.

In a higher room that also had yellow walls and rugs, I met the Fanes. The three were not seated but reclining on cushions thrown on a deep carpet. They gestured for me to choose a spot and lean back as they had.

"It is so good to see you," the first Fane smiled.

"We have done much work since the Rassat," said the second.

"Much we've learned, more than ever," added the third.

"So, you see the future now," I said, wanting to say something.

"The future always has several paths it can take from the present," the second replied.

"There is one path that concerns us…yours," said the first.

"You see my future."

"We see your death," the third added flatly.

"And when am I to die?" I asked slowly.

"Soon and soon," said the third, as that was the Fane I was facing.

"One of your companions means to harm you," said the first.

I smiled. "No, the Sand Keeper was angry and afraid before; but since the fight on the mountain, he looks at me as the one who saved him. I don't think he means me harm if that's what you saw from the past. You see on his face that he wants to repay me or show his gratitude but there is nothing he can do. He is a frustrated and a sorrowful character."

"It's another," said the second Fane, "the woman from Soos—Chiffaa Oroser. She is on a task to end you."

"But she has had many opportunities if that had been her task." I did not believe them.

"Her task is greater than that. She had to learn and know as much about the Tor'oc as possible, but she cannot let you enter the city of Orzamond. That is the command of her city," said the third.

"And how will she end me? I am much stronger than her," I said.

"She carries a hidden batana through which she can blow a small arrow with poison from the curare," said the second.

"A batana? I don't know what that is."

"It is made from a hollow cane plant. It's sometimes longer than the hunter himself; or it can be as small as your hand. The hunter has small arrows that he can put into the batana and then blow it so it travels far and fast."

"I reason that is what killed the Rover on the mountain," I said, thinking my thoughts aloud. "There wasn't a mark or blood on him. But why would the leaders of her city want to end me?"

"Because of their prophesy. You will lead an army to destroy their city," said the first.

"That is not possible," I said in wonder.

"It is more than possible—we agree with the prophesy," said the third.

I had no words to respond. I let myself fall back into the cushion and stared at the ceiling of the yellow room. Finally, I slowly said, "So, she will end me, and her city will be saved."

"No," said all three Fanes together.

I looked to them, not understanding.

"Another will end her or come close," said the first. "Goyel saw her end the Rover on the mountain. She hid her batana again quickly, thinking no one had seen. Our three had been suspicious of Chiffaa from the moment the emissary from Soos demanded she accompany them on their journey to bring you. When he saw the weapon and saw how she wanted to keep a secret of it, he knew her task."

"They have watched her, and all the Jannanons in Jielada have watched her because they know what Goyel knows," added the third.

"So, she will be ended instead of me." I wanted to make clear that I understood.

"No," the three Fanes said together.

"But there could be another path," added the third.

"Another path?" Was there another way the future could go?

"She could become your mate," said the second.

"The woman who wants to end me also wants my children?"

"She does not want to end you," explained the first. "That is her task. She has found something she did not expect—she desires to touch you, to be with you, to lie with you. She wants to be the life of your heart."

"But there has never been a sign of that," I protested.

"Think again—is that true?" said the second.

Wind

Remembering our journey, our time in Lul, I saw that there had been times she would look at me, times when her hand would move across my arm or shoulder or back, times when she would bring me something that her reason told her I would not know of on our path along the road. Often, she would be near me when we ate. She leaned across me once at a meal, her hair and her body close; and I remembered that the smell of her was pleasant, more than pleasant—I wanted more. I wanted to take her in; I wanted to breathe her.

"Then what will happen?" I was confused and lost.

"All of it."

"That can't be." Can reason be a river that flows against itself? That was senseless.

I didn't want to hear or try to understand more. We talked of other knowledge they had because of the Rassat. We talked of a storm that was coming. We talked of a child that was coming to Weoduye—his first, which would be born while he was away, but which was just starting life now. We talked of Pit, who would become a great leader but not soon and soon. We talked of the Sand Keeper, who would defend me when others wanted my end. We talked of Uthiriul, who they said was waiting for me. We finally talked of Sissase, who would be safe and grow to be a Tor'oc, a Tor'oc as fierce and fair as my vision.

The Fanes were still unraveling the present. It would take them many lights and darks before they could clearly see the future. The storm was a human one, and that made it difficult to see and understand.

PART THREE

BLOOD MOON

Barry Alexander Brown

10

As much celebration flowed out to honor our leaving Jielada as happened on our arrival. All the souls of the city poured onto the road dancing and singing. Longing and some worry showed in the eyes of the families of my three Jannanon travelers who were leaving them again so quickly. Sissase had become well known and well liked in the city, and many Jannanons that I didn't recognize danced around Bol and Sissase. She laughed because the people wanted her to laugh and to leave happy. Pit and I were walking beside each other; in front of us walked the Sand Keeper, and then Chiffaa. Without thinking much, I had placed her there where I could watch her. When the Fanes appeared, they wrapped themselves around me for a moment, and I felt like a child being held softly against them.

They were saying to me, "Soon and soon we will see you, brother. Death will not stop you." They were smiling, but I was not.

"Don't be troubled," the first Fane whispered to me, as the second Fane caressed my head and hair, and the third Fane placed a hand against my chest.

Pit looked confused and wary. He had heard the line about death. In his eyes was a question to me about the meaning, and he could see I understood. I shook my head at him to tell him it was nothing. He didn't believe me.

The dancing and celebrations continued for many and many arpents. It began to feel as though the entire city was going to accompany us to Orzamond, but little by little, the Jannanon people dropped away to walk back to Jielada. The final ones left were the families who did not want to say goodbye, though they did in time, and we were once again the small group with one added member—the emissary from the Camarod.

He rode an epus. I will try to refer to it as a horse as everyone in the Out World does. He rode much like Chiffaa who was often on her own horse, the Pallurino, but just as often she walked beside it. I believe she walked to keep the Sand Keeper company, though he didn't seem to notice as his eyes were nearly always on the road searching for the cracks that gave him much pleasure to find.

I never learned his name. 'The emissary' was what I knew him as and how I referred to him. He was sent from Orzamond only to make sure that I was delivered from one place to another. I was cargo to him, nothing more, and, like cargo, I responded to him in the dumb and uninterested way that cargo would. He was not strongly unlikeable or likeable. He was simply there, contented with himself, certain that we were all eager to know about him, at the same time that he was eager not to share any more information than he thought we should have. He dressed in fine cloths that were very impressive, and he had more fine cloths packed in two large satchels that his horse carried tied behind the saddle. He rode in the front of our band and never looked back.

The land we crossed was lined with deep crevasses where long-flowing rivers had slowly worn away the earth. The road crossed these drops— beautiful and wondrous scars in the earth. Each time we came upon one of the deep falls, we had to walk single file because the bridges over the divides were just wide enough for two people to cross. The view of the drop kept my mind sharp, and I did not notice the road beneath me. The only things I saw were the walls of the crevasse, the trees and bushes that hung on and grew there, and the rivers below crashing over huge rocks that lay in them. When not viewing the deep divides, I was careful to keep watch of Chiffaa's movements.

It would take five darks to cross the land to even see Orzamond from a distance. I was wary of the darks, wary that Chiffaa might try to end me during one of them. I chose my sleeping trees carefully, asking the trees to help protect me, to warn me if anyone approached. I also took high limbs that were covered from the ground by the lower limbs, making it difficult, if not impossible, to fire at me from below. She would have had to climb to reach a place to even see me, and the trees would toss her if she tried. I told them of my fear. I felt the safest in the trees, yet it remained difficult for me to rest my mind and sleep.

As we neared Orzamond, many and many signs of man appeared—homes, cattle, horses behind fences, crops that would soon be ready to take, crops that looked newly planted, other roads that met the Sand Keeper's road, and roads that ran off to the far reaches of the land where I was told other people lived in other cities. There were several small towns as well that the road ran through, towns where the people came out to see the Tor'oc and the oryx and the little girl who rode the great beast as if it were the most natural thing to do. In some of the towns, we stopped for the mid meal and sometimes for the day-end meal. Each town made and served food I had never reasoned existed, and most often it was very tasty and good. At the end of each meal, after the emissary had eaten it completely, he would state that the food was inferior to that in

Orzamond, that it would, in his words, "barely sustain us until we reach a decent edible meal."

The people in each town could not take enough of me. They would stare, and some of the younger ones would touch me or want to touch me but were too frightened. I was the thing of myth and legend come to life, but was I the thing hiding in dark places ready to punish them? That's what they wanted to know, even for the older ones and some of the much older ones. When Sissase noticed their glaring stares, she wanted to be glared at, too. She was a Tor'oc as well, the thing of legends and myth. When we sat for the meals, she would take my lap; and the way that I ate with my fingers, she would eat with hers. She liked doing those things anyway, but her imitation of me had to be perfect for the staring, glaring crowd. The emissary made a comment loud enough for us to hear, that "only people who were nothing more than the untamed ate with their fingers." Sissase threw the food she held in her hands at him after that remark, and the food landed on his fine cloths.

He glared at her as he cleaned it away from his cloths.

I shrugged and said, "Untamed. What can you expect?"

After meals, Goyel would secretly wipe a bit of greenish brown mud on my fingers, which he insisted I eat—not exactly eat, but let melt away on my tongue. The mud was bitter, made from the leaves and roots of plants and bushes that were new to me. The first day of eating the mud made me uneasy. I wanted to vomit it, but he stood by me, telling me to hold it in. He said it was for my health, that it would get less uncomfortable to eat, and it did, though it was never easy. Goyel did not tell me to hide this herbal medicine from the others, but I knew that I should.

Orzamond finally appeared in the far and far, At first, it looked like a mountain in the distance with a hat sitting on its top. We saw it not long after the first meal.

"We should reach it in the next light, if the road doesn't stop us," the Sand Keeper announced for the benefit of those of us who had never come this way.

We were walking on a slight rise, and this gave us sight of the world between us and the city, the place I had been heading toward since I fell into the river with Iz. Before us, the land was open, with tall, light brown grass, bushes scattered here and there, and then a thick, dark forest that devoured the road a short distance before the mountain. I was not eager to get to Orzamond, where I would find out why I had been called into the Out World. I had liked the easy, unending discovery of these new lands. I felt this time fading with each steady step we took toward Orzamond where a different kind of discovery was waiting.

Chiffaa had stayed at the front of our group with the Sand Keeper and the emissary, who hardly seemed to notice any of us in the rear. I had kept a constant watch on her. We would reach Orzamond soon and soon, yet she had not tried to end me, had not even appeared interested that I was there. The Fanes derived their sense of the future from the reading of the present. Perhaps they had misread it. Could they ever be wrong? I was feeling less and less in danger, and felt that once we entered Orzamond, I would be free of the prophesy that she would end me. Perhaps there were worse things waiting, but at least that would be over. We had not shared another moment like the one we had at the Light Pearls, and that alone was enough to make a difference for me. I felt hurt that she could possibly be against me and glad that, so far, she had shown she wasn't.

As we neared the forest, that looked thicker as we got closer, Orzamond took the shape of a city built on the side of a mountain. A heavy line circled from the top to the bottom of the mountain city. Though I only knew three cities—the City in the Trees, Lul, and Jielada— each of them had a look and colour that belonged to it. Orzamond was every color with no seeming reason to its makeup. The houses and other structures were dots of reds and blues and greens and yellows and every combination of those colors. I could not make out the shapes of their buildings, but reason told me that if they were free with the color, they would be free with the shapes.

I called the Jannanons to me and pointed toward Orzamond. "The line there, is that a road like the Tied in Lul?"

"In some ways," the Jannanons answered. "But it is not a road; it is a river that will be the way we reach the Grand Hall at the center of Orzamond." They were all three pointing to the hat shape at the top of the mountain.

There was a law that I knew had to be true not only on the Peninsula, but everywhere: water flowed from high to low. I reasoned there were two ways to travel a boyt up a river, up a mountain—they either pulled the boyts up or were strong enough to push them.

Gazing at the city that I could not yet see clearly, I thought out loud, "They must be very strong, the people of Orzamond."

The Jannanons followed my gaze to see what I was seeing and then looked back at me confused. "Why?" they said in unison.

"To push or pull a boyt up that river," I said, thinking it was clear what I meant.

"They don't do either," the Jannanons said earnestly. "The boyts are taken by the current up and through the city."

I laughed, knowing that wasn't true. "So, the river starts at the bottom and flows to the top." How ridiculous.

They nodded. "The river Irienik was a gift from the Four Mothers to a Gerent whom one of the Mothers—Liuf—loved. He was a true leader—visionary, handsome, brave. He ruled and lived much and much longer than any other Gerent, which was another gift. He and Liuf were secretly married and, as a present to her husband, she gave him a river that would take him wherever he wanted, even up a mountain. During his life, the river flowed whichever direction he wished. If he wanted to boyt to the bottom, it took him, and of course the other way as well. When he died at the age of 211, Liuf flowed the river in only one direction—up to where she had left her heart. He is entombed there. The people of Orzamond named the river after him in tribute. It is rumored that she calls it something else."

I stared back at the line that wound up the mountain and tried to vision a river that flowed up. "Will we boyt up the river to the top?" I asked.

"The only other ways are the many staircases that line the city, and none of us wants to take them." The Jannanons smiled in some knowing way.

I was happy and interested to take a boyt in the wrong direction.

We were nearing the opening of the forest. It had an opening in a way that other forests do not have. The road ran under an arch made by limbs crossing over it, and what was beyond was impossible to see. It was dark as any dark I've slept in. The Sand Keeper caught me staring at the opening and he reasoned my thoughts. He held something up in one of his hands. It was a small, deeply blue ball.

"We will get through the Niedlmae with this." He held the blue ball up for me to see. "You could walk through without any light, but it is unnerving to be in such dark. Believe me, it is darker than any night in there." He pointed to the forest.

I looked to the Jannanons. "Why do they call it that—Niedlmae?"

"An ancient tongue—means the black woods," they explained to me.

A little hand reached out and touched my shoulder. I turned to see that Sissase didn't like the sound or the look of where we were heading.

"It is only dark, nothing else—just trees, and they won't harm us," I said to reassure her. She looked from me to the opening and wasn't reassured. I nodded to Pit and gestured toward Sissase and Bol. "Why don't you ride with Sissase?" Pit had been riding on and off with Sissase. In two steps, he was up on Bol, putting his arms around her; and she leaned back into him, comforted.

The Sand Keeper entered the forest first. Chiffaa and the emissary—both on their horses—held back. The Jannanons stopped, which made me put my hand on Bol to halt him. The Sand Keeper stepped far enough up the road that the dark had nearly taken him. He stopped, turned to show the ball again in his hand—I reasoned it was for me to see—and then he walked further to where he was gone from the light, gone from our view. Suddenly there was a burst of light, and he was bathed in a warm glow that hung above him. He held his hand out again to show me that it was now empty. The blue ball had exploded into light and hung there on its own. He waved for us to come.

Chiffaa and the emissary rode into the Niedlmae, and we followed. The Sand Keeper was waiting to explain something to me as his eyes never left me; he was smiling and his empty hand reached into a satchel and took out another blue ball.

"These are marvelous things." He showed me the ball again as I came to him. "They don't last long but without them, the woods are a scary place, and a Sand Keeper can't do his job. Although this part of the road is really somebody else's responsibility, we all still try to help out. I will show you how the little balls work when that one is almost done," he said, pointing to the light above.

"Do they have a name?" I asked, as everything in the Out World was called a word that I had never heard.

"They are called beedles." The name seemed to please him.

We walked down the road, and I kept to it. The path along the road was lost in shadow. Our one source of light gave the trees a look of something evil, menacing, but it was only the light. The air under the trees was moist and thick and held the smell of long and long ago. I knelt on the road and, not facing any one tree, I blew to them the greeting I knew. They blew back a welcome and filled the air with visions with their aroma.

The vision that they wanted to share with me was of the upper reaches of the trees, where light still penetrated. They understood that neither I nor any other man would know this. The upper branches were thick and twisted around one another, even more so than in the Bent Trees. There were birds there and plants that grew off the trees, and there were also other creatures that were happy enough never to ever see the earth. These creatures looked like thin, hairy men, but were smaller, with longer arms and legs. They moved through the trees with grace, with ease. These little beasts bathed themselves in the light of day on the very tops of the trees where the leaves were thick enough to give them a bed. They ate fruit from the plants growing on the trees, played with one another, had a language that no man had ever learned, and never bothered with man, who had only given them trouble when the two kinds met. The trees invited me to climb them when I could, to meet the creatures, to see the world above. I blew back a promise that I would be happy to when my time in Orzamond was over.

The vision was so strong for me that I hardly noticed that the light of the first beedle was dying. The Sand Keeper nudged me to pay attention. I shook the visions away to see him. He was holding the blue ball out for me to clearly see what he was about to do.

"Watch closely," he said, lifting his hand with the ball in it above his head and throwing the beedle down to smash against the road. The ball hit with the sound of a huge slap. It bounced once and flew up past us as light poured out of it. The ball came to a slow stop about a Tor'oc higher than us and hung there. The Sand Keeper pointed up to it as if he had invented the thing. "Remarkable, wouldn't you say?" He smiled and looked to me, wanting me to smile, but I was too amazed by it to grin. I did shake my head to show him I thought it was a thing of wonder.

Wind

"What keeps it up?" I asked.

The Sand Keeper shook his head, "I don't know—it has something to do with the air inside this place. It only works like that here. Shall we?" he said, indicating moving forward.

We walked on. The road curved around and soon we would be out of the light, so the Sand Keeper would have the joy of smashing another beedle against the road and smiling up at the light. He took a ball from his satchel, moved it in his fingers, raised his arm, and as he was about to throw the beedle with enough might to smash it, Chiffaa's horse turned abruptly, its forelegs hitting the Sand Keeper, knocking the beedle loose from his grip. It fell and rolled away as the light of the last beedle was dying. Chiffaa reached inside of her cloth and looked at me.

"Forgive me," she whispered, a whisper that sounded as close as if she were at my ear. She raised something to her mouth and blew—I had a moment to raise my arm at the small arrow heading toward me. It hit me in my upper arm. I lost balance and fell back, as the light died, and we were thrown into darkness.

I heard Pit's yell, a horse galloping, the Jannanons' steps coming toward me, the Sand Keeper cursing, and the emissary asking over and over "What's happening?" Sissase was screaming—a terrible, terrible piercing scream. The trees blew around me asking if I were hurt. I tried to stand and couldn't. There was a ringing in my ears. My senses were fading. I could not hear the sounds around me and I could not make my body rise—in fact, I could not act to my will at all. I was alone in the dark. Then the black of the dark changed, and I felt my head lying in somebody's lap—perhaps one of the Jannanons. Were my eyes closed or was the light still dead? The hand stroked my forehead—a woman's hand. There were lips that touched my brow.

Light crept in; my eyes were open. Above me was Soaad, who held me, held my head, smiling at me, smiling to be able to see me and to feel me.

"Are you here in the forest?" I was surprised that she was there.

She shook her head. "No."

"Am I not there either?" I was confused.

"You are and you're not," she gently explained.

I remembered. "Chiffaa shot me. With what?" I looked into her eyes for the answer.

"A poisoned pendle." She saw I didn't know what that was. "A small arrow."

"And why am I here with you?"

"You died," she said simply.

I shot up to sit. "I'm dead?"

A voice from behind me said, "Now, now—fast conclusions will leave you where you are." I looked around. The other four Mothers were there with us in a place that seemed all dark except for the light that lit us. The Mother who spoke was tall, and I recognized her from the stories; she was Diluhao. Completely lost in understanding, I looked at her as she said, "Died and dead are not the same."

"I died—I must be dead." It was reasonable.

"They die once and they think they know everything," the Mother named Viem Hels said.

"I am not dead?" I looked from Mother to Mother for an answer; there was none in their looks.

"Stop reasoning so much," said the Mother Keoen Fam. "Don't think. Experience."

Liuf, the Mother who loved the ancient Gerent, stepped to me. "You are lucky. They will take your body up the River of My Eyes."

"The River of My Eyes – is that what you named it?" I asked. "They will bury me there?" I didn't want to hear that they would. I didn't want this at all.

"No one will bury you anywhere—not for long and long," said Soaad softly to me.

"The Fanes knew this was coming. They warned me," I said, feeling sorrow for myself, sorrow for my death.

"It was not a warning." Soaad continued to speak softly to me.

"It was to aid you," said Liuf.

"To prepare you," added Diluhao.

"To make you ready." Viem Hels was close to me when she said this. They had all come closer.

"You knew what the Fanes told me. You knew this would happen." My reason was leading me. "You could have stopped this."

"We could have," said Keoen Fam. "But without dying…"

Soaad shrugged as though I should I understand. "...no rebirth."

Viem Hels knelt down to me. "You have been heading to this death for long and long."

"I don't want to be dead," I snapped back to her.

"What did I say about died and dead?" Diluhao knelt beside her sister.

"Aren't you speaking and reasoning?" Liuf wanted me to consider this.

"The river that flows against itself," I whispered to myself in confusion; I truly did not understand. "I died but I'm not..."

The five Mothers shared a look that said, 'He just might understand.'

"Of the present, what do you want to see?" asked Keoen Fam.

I didn't have to consider long and said, "I want to see what is happening to me, to my friends."

"Then take us there," commanded Diluhao.

"How?" I didn't know, didn't even understand the meaning of those words.

Liuf leaned toward me, "Show us how."

I looked to Soaad for some guidance, and she nodded. 'Go on,' her nod was saying. 'Show us the way.'

They all were certain I could do something, and I had no idea of how or what to do. They were not going to guide me. I had to feel this to know it. I had answered before thinking it out, but, really, I did want to know how Pit and the Jannanons, Bol and Sissase were taking the attack, taking what had happened to me. I wanted to see myself, to see how fearful I was in death, hoping to see I wasn't dead at all, hoping to see that I was only in the deep sleep that happens to people in a fall or when bitten by a poisonous snake or spider.

Soaad put her hand on my chest, her hand over my heart. "Don't think."

I took in a breath, though I wasn't aware of breathing, and thought that where I was, I shouldn't need to breathe; but the act helped bring me to find myself. I let go of my confusion, let go of not understanding. I fell into my want, into feeling for the touch I had with my companions. The touch I had with Weoduye could be a path, but the natural touch I had with Sissase was a stronger path. It was a path of emotion, of the heart, of the soul. I could feel her, feel her panic, her fear, and loss.

The black that the Mothers and I were in shifted, grew grey, shimmered and sparkled. The grey grew to a deep, dark green, and I was able to see large flat leaves growing out of thick tree branches. We were in the Niedlmae, up in the limbs of the forest. Far below us were people leaning over someone, picking up the someone limp and unhelping, placing the someone down on a long flat mat made of wood and leaves. The mat was tied to an oryx, to Bol. I felt something alive close to me, something that wasn't a tree or the Mothers. I turned away from what was happening below, finding that I was surrounded by small, hairy, brown creatures that also were looking down at the people. As I stared at the strange little man-like beasts, one of them looked up and into my eyes. It wasn't a clear gaze, and there was a look of wonder in those eyes, as though he could not see me, but he could feel me there in front of him. He said something to his group of hairy man-beasts, and they scurried away as one, back up the trees where they stopped at a height to stare back down at the people below.

I looked down again as well, looked down and was pulled down to Sissase. My little girl wore a terrible glare. She was staring at the someone on the mat who was behind me. I wanted to touch her, to hold her, to make her know that she did not have to be afraid; but I was not in my body, and my soul could not touch her. She reached out; her hand went to the someone lying on the mat. She was grabbing the someone's hand, holding it and climbing up onto the tallum to be close to the body the hand belonged to. The body was me lying there.

"You can't stay there, Sissase," Pit said to her with kindness and softness. "We have to take him to the city." He pointed to the road in front, where beyond was Orzamond. Sissase shook her head and lay her body against the me on the mat, clutching it with all of herself.

I moved in to look at me, to look at her. I moved to a short-length away from my own face. What I looked at was not breathing; it was as still and unmoving as the earth. They all must think that I am dead. I had certainly died, but I was not dead. I was beginning to understand. I was the river that flowed against itself.

Wind

I moved closer to Sissase, whose pain gripped her heart the way she gripped my body. There was no need for her pain, for the ache and the panic and the sorrow.

I kissed her forehead and whispered into her ear, "I will return to you."

She looked up in a snap and glared into the dead face. She had heard me and knew it was me and not her mind. She took on a look of fierceness, serious and hopeful. She crawled up onto the chest and stared into the face again. She crawled up further, slowly leaned down, kissed the chin just below the lip and laid her head softly against the body.

"Yes, yes, yes, yes," she whispered.

She turned to Pit and said, "We have to go; he needs help." She raised her arms for him to take her. As he did, he wore the heavy burden of the man who would have to tell her that I was beyond help, that I was gone forever. For now, though, he would cradle her in his arms, and he would lead Bol, who would drag the mat carrying my body to the city. The emissary said something to the Jannanons, turned his horse, and rode at speed toward the city.

The Mothers were tied to me as firmly as the mat was tied to Bol. Where Bol went, my soul would follow.

However, the Mothers seemed to have had enough of this slow, grim march.

"Do we have to watch the trek?" Liuf said. With an explosion of exasperated air, Liuf puffed, "Let's get to My Love!"

Time was changeable. She waved an arm or a hand, and we were transported, along with my companions, who were not so much rushed through the walk as felt that the walk happened and didn't happen at the same moment.

In two steps, everyone arrived at the gate of Orzamond—a journey that should have taken five hundred steps. They walked through the gate to see a low rock wall bordering a group of large boulders inside a wide courtyard. A waterfall flowing upward bubbled over the rocks.

There were many people, mainly men, dressed in long cloths of red with double yellow strips from top to bottom along the openings where they were bound. They were waiting for us at the gate near the birth of the river. Under the Jannanon's instructions, they lifted my body off the mat, and carried me gently and solemnly to a boyt that was tied at the top of the falls. There was a bed in the boyt, and they laid me there as Sissase crawled into the boyt after me. All the town's people looked down at me with troubled faces lost in a sadness, a sorrow for a person whom they didn't know.

One of the men bent down and pulled a cloth up over my feet, my legs, my torso and my face. Sissase screamed. Yanking the cloth off my face she yelled, "No!" She moved fast to place her small body next to my head, shoving a hand into my hair as she stared back at the men, daring them to try that again. I felt the face of my soul smile. The little one truly had the blood of Tor'oc in her.

Wind

She looked down at me and said, "I won't let them, caru." I had never heard the word but knew it was her name for father.

The Jannanons sat next to my body. After untying the rope that held the boyt, the men withdrew. Pit was leading Bol up a winding path that would take them to the top of the city, along the way the river flowed, along the way the boyt was beginning to move. The River of My Eyes that had looked grey green turned to a blue slightly darker than the sky, then back to green, depending on something in the water that I could not make out. Inside the river were slivers of silver currents that grabbed the boyt and pushed it. The boyt was flat with low sides. It seemed to ride on the river rather than in it, like the boyt that took us across the lake. There was no one guiding the boyt; the river knew where to take us and how fast to take us; no need for a boyt man. I looked at Liuf, who was next to me. She was serene, a happiness in her I had not felt before.

"My Love will see to it that you are fine," she said to me.

At that, Sissase leaned to the side of the boyt and put her hand into the water, cupping a small palm of water that she carried back to my body. She knelt near my head, letting the water fall on my brow and gently rubbing the wet into my skin, into my hair. My little girl leaned closer still and kissed my forehead, kissed my eyes, kissed my cheeks, kissed my nose, sat back up, and gazed down to my face.

The flat boyt moved slowly, steadily up the river, not quite rocking because the river was smooth and easy; but there was a gentle sway of the boyt, almost the sway of a tree.

I wanted to be on the boyt and next to Sissase. I wanted to feel the river beneath me.

"You can go," whispered Soaad to me. I looked from Mother to Mother. They all agreed.

"You have learned enough for now," said Keoen Fam.

"Will I have to die again?" I felt I did not want to, though it had only been painful for my companions.

"No, this death will stay with you," said Diluhao.

"It will keep teaching," added Viem Hels.

"Then I want to go." They smiled their blessing back to me, and I fell into myself.

I laid with my eyes closed, my breath shallow, feeling the small hand move slowly, gently through my hair, at times touching the skin under the hair with the tips of her fingers. The boyt underneath me rocked back and forth slightly, as though a light wind blew it. In that wind was a separate movement, the movement of the silver current that not only flowed in the river, it flowed up through the boyt, up into me. Part of Liuf's soul energy was in that current. It felt healing and comforting, but also gave out a heat for something lost. The heat and the current filled me.

A small sting in my arm where the pendle had struck took my notice. The prick of pain helped to bring me back into my body, though I wanted to lie still for a while longer.

Somewhere beyond the edge of sleep, I drifted — suspended in a world where the river's hush and the touch of hands blended with a current brighter than daylight, drawing me gently out of unbeing. There were voices, distant at first, echoing softly with concern and care. The warmth of Sissase lingered, a memory pressed into my skin, while the river's pulse faded into the rhythms of living bodies and urgent motion.

I felt the subtle shift from dream to waking, as if every sensation returned in its own time — first the weight of my own bones, then the pressure of the boards beneath me, then the brush of fingers, the cadence of breath not my own. The light through my eyelids glowed red and gold, as if dawn itself hovered at the edge of consciousness, promising that the world continued.

The presence of others gathered, thickening in the air — a hush broken by a flurry of movements as I was drawn closer to waking. Suspended between memory and the present, I became aware of voices, of a trembling beneath my body, and the sudden return of urgency and life.

The boyt underneath, the hand through my hair, the heat of Liuf healing me was enough. I fell into a simple sleep that would not last long but would give me what renewal sleep gives.

I woke hearing the words, "You be careful." Hands were touching me, pushing hands that went under me and around me. I took in a breath and opened my eyes a little to see who the hands were attached to. There were several men in long red cloths.

"Stop, stop, stop!" Sissase was loud, louder than she had ever been. Moving between two of the red cloths, she landed on me. We were chest to chest, her hands pressed against me to push herself up high enough to look into my eyes. She saw that I was looking back.

Sissase's mouth opened, and the sound of happy air escaped. She let herself fall into me, hugging my torso with her entire body as she whispered, "Caru." Faces came down around my body, including Sheios, Goyel, and Weoduye.

"He's alive," Weoduye announced on his own, as he felt it in the way that others could only see. "I sensed it before but reasoned it was only my hope that was speaking."

Weoduye grabbed my hand to hold. Goyel was saying a prayer of thanks. Sheios was grinning, surprise mixed with tears in his eyes.

"I thought it had not worked," he said, but he didn't seem to be speaking to me.

I reasoned I would try my voice to see if I still had one. "What...what worked?" The sound was like a growl—my throat was dry—but even that was good to feel.

"We gave you an anti-venom." He looked kindly at me. "The green mud you were eating for three days."

"Why would you do that?" 'How did he know?' was what I was reasoning.

"The Fanes." He gestured as though he was sorry he had not told me. "They predicted Chiffaa would end you. They told us of her poison and told us the counter to it. We had always suspected her—there was no other reason for her to travel with us and her people had forced it on us. We kept an eye on her except for that moment." He had failed in his guarding of me and felt the worse for that.

Another thing struck me. "How are you speaking separately—just you and just Sheios and Weoduye?"

"In great emotion we lose the touch of one another, and we are happy to lose it for you." He reached out and placed his hand across my eyes. He held it there for several breaths. In that touch was a bond of friendship that was there already, but now he meant it to be known that he was bent to it.

He drew his hand away to show me the earnest feeling he held for me. I asked him to bend to me. He did, and I put my hand across his eyes as he had done to mine.

"I am bent and bonded," I said so low only he could hear, but Shieos and Weoduye looked up, startled at the words. They understood what was moving between Goyel and me, and among all of us.

A voice directed into my chest also said, "Bent and bonded." Yes, Sissase was part of this as well. I put my hands on her to let her know that I wanted to rise. She sat up, and I followed.

We had reached the top of the river, the top of the mountain, the top of the city of Orzamond. I could see the deep blue roofs of the city buildings below, roofs made of some kind of dried earth colored blue. I could see the river that wound its way up through the city. I could see the land that we had traveled, the Niedlmae still dark and green, the road disappearing into the forest and reappearing on its other side. The world looked different to me. It looked new, as though I had not seen or traveled through it—it looked like a marvel. I looked at Sissase, who didn't look new to me, only precious.

"You are a wonder," a familiar voice spoke from the land behind our boyt. "The whole city has heard and knows the Tor'oc is dead, ended on the eve of arriving, yet here you are sitting and chatting." The emissary came around to show himself, and I was glad to see him.

"And were they really happy with that?" I was certain that some were not.

"No, no. Great, great mourning and fear." He came closer to the boyt and signaled to men in the red cloths to help us out. "A myth surrounds you that has grown from the few stories they've heard of your journey here. They have heard that you are larger and stronger and fiercer than any Tor'oc in the Legends, larger than any man who walks. Your skin is as black as the dark." He stopped and smiled, as this was far and far from true. "Your weapons are so menacing only you can handle them. I let it be known that it was all lies except one thing that is true and true—you carry the spear of your far-flung grandfather. So, with all that, if you can be ended, what hope is there for them?" He opened his palms toward me to say, 'Can you blame them?'

I was helped up by the red cloths, and following Sissase, I stepped off the boyt.

"So, when they see me, I will disappoint them."

"Oh, no. Coming back to life trumps everything they've heard; I can assure you of that." The emissary bowed. "Welcome to Orzamond."

Behind him I saw the hat-shaped thing that sat on the top of the mountain. It was a building but not a building, a remnant of some ancient giant creature close to the look of small creatures that we have near and in the Divul. They are not fish, but they swim. They have a head and tail like a snake, legs like a beast, and a hard house that grows with them, a house that is round and angled, and is as much a part of them as their legs, head, and tail. We called them 'vums', but reason told me that had been a name the survivors called them. Here, they would be called something else. This something else was gigantic—the entire city in the trees could be kept inside the walls of this one. The look of it was of a grand dome which was what they called it.

At our level, the Grand Dome of Orzamond was a series of arches that led into countless numbers of entrances. I was being helped toward one of them while Sissase held my hand, clinging close to me.

"What has happened to Chiffaa?" I asked the emissary, who walked on the other side of one of the red cloths.

His face grew grey. He hissed, "She is with her city men. The emissaries from Soos are keeping her in their quarters and refusing entrance to anyone. But when we can get her…"

I held my hand up to stop him. "No, no harm for her."

Sissase gripped her hand into a ball, and I looked down to her. "No, none of us will harm her. I want this settled between us." I looked to all of them. Harm was what they wanted. "No harm," I repeated, to make it true and clear, demanding by my gaze that they agree. They did, mainly by looking away from me, but their bodies told me they agreed. They didn't want to, but they agreed.

The emissary, frustrated and bewildered, stepped toward me. "But she tried to end you."

"She, in fact, ended me!" I replied without further explanation.

He sputtered at my senseless reasoning. "She has to pay for this."

"She has, and she will." I knew this was true, but it was a haze to me how it was true.

"This is not up to you alone," the emissary was still sputtering.

"That is true and true, but if I can keep her from harm, I will," I told them all so they would know my aim.

I was feeling strain on my body and my spirit from everything that had happened since my waking that dew light. I picked Sissase up and held her. "Let's find a tree to rest in." She nodded her head—yes, yes, yes.

"A tree?" The emissary appeared to be more undone by my every word. "We have wonderful chambers for you, beautiful beds."

I cocked my head at him. "You know we don't sleep in beds."

"We're Tor'ocs." Sissase finished my thought. "We need a tree."

He was flustered beyond speech. "But...but." Lost for anything else, he said, "The only trees are in the garden of the Gerent. You won't be safe there."

"He will be safe," the Jannanons said, together again.

"The Gerent may not allow it." He was hoping that was true.

"If he doesn't, we can return to the Niedlmae," the Jannanons said as a jest and a warning. The emissary cried out in pain. There is a game we play on the Peninsula in which the aim is to trap somebody in a part of a tree where they can't climb down or across or up. That moment is called axiled. He may not have known the word, but he knew the feeling. Axiled, he stormed away from us. My guess was that he went to tell the Gerent the unfortunate news.

I looked to the two red cloths who were propping me up. "Which way to the garden?"

Before we could take two steps, a wonderful bellow filled my ears. Bol had arrived and seen me or smelled me. I was being held under my arms by two red cloths, so I turned my head to the sound. Pit was running just behind Bol, who was making his way at speed toward me.

I felt the bodies in the red cloths jump, drop their hands and dash back as Bol reached us. He slid to a stop—the floor underneath was as smooth as the road—his big head down, his horns surrounding me as he hit me just softly enough to lift my body onto the brow between his eyes. I hugged him around his head, and he made a growl that rose deep from his belly. He was glad to see me.

The next body to hit me was Pit, who pulled me down off Bol and hugged me as though I might disappear if he let go. "Up! Up!" Sissase called from below—she was shoving on our legs, but all she wanted was to be a part of this. Pit reached down, grabbed her, and she up where she belonged, hugging Pit and me around our necks.

"How is it? I saw you dead." He gazed at me with wonder, happiness, and thanks. "Was I wrong?"

"I died but I wasn't ended." I gestured toward myself to say, 'Clearly'. "The good Jannanons had prepared my body. I can't reason it myself, but their awful tasting mud worked. They brought me back."

A tongue appeared on my face and licked me—an oryx tongue is rough, and I have never seen them use their tongues for affection, but I supposed then that they did in private.

Pit turned to Sheios, Goyel, and Weoduye, and his look told them that he was their man from that moment on. He took a step away from me and pushed his hand toward them.

"In the past I have suspected bad things of you, wrong things." He knelt down to them and bent his head. "You have my ever gratitude. Whatever your wish, demand it of me."

They placed a hand each on the top of Pit's head. "He is our brother, too. You owe us nothing more than we owe you for your love of him."

"Can we make our way to rest?" I asked them.

Bol understood and could tell that I was weak. He bent his front legs down to position himself low enough for me fall onto him. Sissase sat in front of his hump, turned with her back to Bol's head, and she stroked my hair as I laid myself against Bol's big, great, wonderful body. I was glad to see him, too.

I looked and saw the people of the city of Orzamond were standing silently around us; they had witnessed my rebirth – they were frozen by the sight of it. The red cloths stood a distance away from us, staring and gawking, shuddering with fear. "Can you lead us to the garden?"

They all stared as one at the body of Bol, clear that they did not think it appropriate to let a beast like him into the Grand Dome on top of their city.

I said with as much command and authority as I had ever mustered, "Please. Lead us. Now!"

They jumped, turned, and we followed.

We walked through an arch to what I thought was an entrance, but on the other side of the arch appeared a grand plateau. The huge dome was positioned two Tor'ocs high off of the plateau floor. From the floor, there were ramps leading up into the dome, dozens of ramps made of stones so smooth and fitted so well together that they appeared to be one single thing. Up close to them, I could see the individual rocks. I gazed up high to see what was reflecting the golden light onto us. It was the underbelly of the great dome that was much like the underside of the vums. There were soft-looking yellow plates, big enough that each plate was larger than the largest public kollokk in the City in the Trees.

The small group of red cloths that we were following took one of the far ramps into the dome. I was thankful for the ramps, as Bol would have had a hard time walking on steps; and I could not reason that Bol would have let me down easily after finding me again.

The golden light increased in intensity as we entered the first floor of the dome. It was a genius use of the natural light from outside, reflected and transformed through the walls of the dome to make the light soft and bright and warm. This first room had the same basic shape of the entire dome, long and round with sharp angles that created smaller domes that were all flat angles in a beautiful, complex pattern, as in the shell of the vum.

The center of the ceiling of this room caught Pit's eye, and I looked up to see as well. In the center of the dome ceiling was a drawing, but not a drawing—it was what I learned later was a tableau not made of ink but of pigment called 'paint'. The picture was of a hunt of a great beast that I had never seen before—an angry, hairy beast with long white horns that came from the sides of its mouth. Hunters surrounded it with their spears and arrows, and some arrows had hit the great beast, who was fighting back against the hunt. It was an impressive scene that caught the movement of the hunters, their horses, and the beast.

I did not look back until we had crossed this small domed room to wide doors that opened onto a green space with bushes, flowers, grass, and trees. The garden grew on a grand balcony that ran the distance of the great dome. The balcony was wide, but longer than wide. It gave a view of the other side of the city, widening out onto a valley that stretched before us, with hills like the waves of the sea that disappeared far and far into the distance. The rolling land below and away was filled with rivers and forests and open fields and fields used by farmers for their crops. It was a land that birds would admire and want to live in. The balcony garden was a wonder, but the land beyond had a magic that could not be built by the hands of man.

The garden was a made place, tended so that it was well groomed, with low-cut grass, trees that were shorn to give them shape, and bushes arranged for the colors and sizes of their flowers. It was beautiful, but too man-formed for me. For now, however, it would do well for Sissase, Bol, and me. I was hoping that Pit and the Jannanons would take comfortable beds in the dome somewhere, but I knew they wouldn't. If they could have slept comfortably in the trees beside Sissase and me, they would have. For this dark, they would sleep beneath us on the ground, on the short grass that I had found soft and easy under my feet when I had stepped off Bol.

"Welcome to my garden!" A man's voice boomed out from someplace slightly higher than us.

On another balcony, at the level of the top of the trees, stood a man of some age in glowing cloths of gold and purple. He wore a smile and a crown. This was the Gerent.

The smaller man beside him was our friend, the emissary, who appeared to be bent into a permanent bow.

The emissary, waving his arms, said, "Hasmapludi III, Gerent of the Middle and High Bosagin! Please bow!"

We did as we were told in order to show respect, as I later would to the trees as soon as I could present myself to them.

The Gerent made his way to us down a curved ramp; there didn't appear to be any stairs in the dome. I liked that.

"Please, please, up, up!" the Gerent was calling out to us.

Wind

We rose just as he reached us. His eyes were on me, never left me. He came close, bowed his head, and took my hand in both of his, cupping them in a greeting that overflowed in delight and welcoming.

"Aeon, thank you for living, thank you for coming." It was a hearted gratitude, true and moving to me.

I nodded my head. "Thank you for allowing the use of your Garden and your trees."

He laughed. "Yes, yes. My emissary was quite nervous about that. He argued the impossibility of my allowing it, until I stopped him." He leaned over to whisper to me, "He can be as unbending as a rock." We shared a smile at the emissary's discomfort.

"He has goodness in him though." I wanted to point out a thing I liked about the emissary.

The Gerent took a long, serious look at me, though he still smiled. "If you win him, which you have, he is true and trustful like no other... just stiff." He laughed again, and I laughed, too.

The Gerent turned away from me to address the rest. "This is Bol." He turned back to me with raised eyebrows. "An impressive animal." He knelt down to Sissase. "And you are the other Tor'oc that we were not expecting. Sissase—yes?"

Sissase nodded her head, barely hiding her glee in being recognized as what she was—a Tor'oc.

The Gerent next shook Pit's hand. "You are the artist and the knife thrower that the entire city is talking about. Pit, I believe is your name. You made quite an impression, leading the great oryx up through our town. I wouldn't be surprised to see a statue erected for the sheer remembrance at the sight of the two of you."

Pit bowed but said nothing.

The Gerent took the Jannanons in with one long look and a sincere smile that was all gratitude. He knelt down on one knee to them.

"My friends. You have done what you said you would, what none of us thought was truly possible. You may have yet saved us. There is nothing I can do to repay you for this. Know that we are all in your debt and we are at your service."

I heard something shaking beside me. It was the emissary. He was staring at the Gerent on one knee. He was shocked, and breathing hard, and holding himself back from rushing to pull the Gerent up onto his feet.

The Gerent reached out with both hands to the Jannanons. The three knelt down as he had done, touching the royal hands with one hand each.

The emissary had had enough. "My Worthiness, it should be time to choose a tree, as you said before. You would like to do that."

The emissary stumbled his way to the Gerent, finally reaching him and lifting him up.

"Absolutely, the time," the Gerent said, bringing himself back to the moment. "I have heard you prefer trees to beds. I would like to suggest a special tree—my favorite."

Wind

He led us to a large tree with open branches, small, well tapered dark green leaves, and smooth skin, which he told us had come on a grand boyt from an island far and far into the seas. The tree had grown there since the time of his grand and grandfathers. He called it a Figure Tree, sometimes only called The Fig. It was great and beautiful and belonged in the garden of a great leader.

At The Fig, I bent down on both knees, and Sissase did the same beside me. We both lowered our heads, and I blew a greeting. "May we grow here?"

Every leaf on the tree shuddered. It blew back, "Oh, beast who can speak, and how beautifully you speak. You may grow, and please grow among us for long and long. Does the little beast speak as well?"

Sissase blew back, "Yes." I looked at her and marveled—how did she learn so quickly?

"I am called Aeon the Leaf, and she is simply Sissase," I blew to tell the old tree.

"The Leaf, good. We will have to find a name to add to hers. Trees here do not have names, as you know, but where I am from, we have names of our own," the tree blew back. "Mine is Fiernd, but nothing has been able to call me that for long and long."

"Fiernd," Sissase blew back, and the leaves shuddered even more. "We wish to be in your branches."

To correct her, I added, "We are beasts who rest in trees for the dark. We ask to be among your limbs and branches."

"I would be shamed if you slept anywhere else," Fiernd blew back. I would have to get used to a tree with a name.

I thanked the tree and rose, turning to the Gerent and my friends. The Gerent was staring at me.

He simply said, "You talk to trees; is that right?"

He wasn't asking me; he had turned to the emissary, who shook his head, yes. The Gerent looked up, and his eyes swept over the leaves that had shuddered twice.

"And they talk back," the Gerent was saying to hear himself say it. He looked back at me. "You are a wonder."

It was enough for the Gerent for that moment. He turned and walked back to the ramp that would lead him up again. He stopped, turned to give one last look at me and Sissase and the Figure Tree.

He called back to me so that I would not be hurt or confused. "It is a lot to gather—a Tor'oc in the flesh who rises from the dead and talks to trees who talk back. A lot to gather, but I will gather it and hold it in my heart. Understand, I need to sleep on this. It will be gathered in me, and if it takes sleeping in a tree with you to do so, I will. I give my word."

He turned and disappeared up the ramp and into the rooms above.

11

"The orza beast was a giant, giant tortoise that lived in the sea when this land was covered by waters," the Gerent said, starting his history as we sat and lounged on the pillows of his rooms for the dew light meal of odd fruits and familiar meats. He took a bite of a fruit that had a covering of spikes, which he handled carefully, skillfully. "It's believed the ancient shell was preserved by the sand at the bottom of the sea, which presumably covered it. You can find remnants of other orza shells here and there, but its bits and pieces at best." He gestured to the ceiling and walls surrounding us. "This is the only known intact shell." He was proud of that.

"The founders of Orzamond discovered this mountain with the shell sitting on top of it and, of course, here it was—a fortress ready-made. They cleared off the dirt, and light filled the whole of the shell inside. The panels," he pointed to a large yellow glowing window in the wall of the dome, "naturally let light in throughout the shell. At the time of discovery, the shell was dark brown, with some yellow lamina in the center of each section. It wasn't painted gold and white until later, but I think it's that lacquer that has helped preserve it through these many, many centuries. And the general maintenance of the dome has helped keep it, as well. The real genius was in the floors and ceilings." He looked up above; we all looked. "You see, it looks like a ceiling that is just under the sky and not, in fact, many rooms below it. In my thoughts, it's even a bit more beautiful than most ceilings."

It was beautiful—a tarnished light brown finish to a smooth surface, with veins of light yellow, like the road. The Gerent turned to the red cloths who stood at the far edge of the large room. He gestured and they pulled ropes that were already in their hands. Something slid with a soft, gentle sound through the ceiling above and light filled the space where the thing they moved had blocked the light.

"Using reflection and refraction--I can't explain how it's done, though it's been told to me countless times. Light is thrown into the floors, which are also ceilings. If you want dark, you close the floor above you. You want it lighter," again he gestured to the red cloths, "you open the floor – in truth, a floor beneath the floor." He smiled up at the lighted ceiling that threw a warm glow across all of us. "So, you see, we are in the mid of a gigantic dome, lit without the use of candle or torch to see. Frankly, whenever I am anywhere in the country, I can't understand how they breathe with those torches burning day and night. And you can see that the torch smoke leaves its mark on those poor people's skin. Look closely during the Camarod today; you'll see what I mean."

"The Camarod is immediately today?" I could not believe it.

The Gerent looked at me, surprised that I was unaware. "Yes, today. We have all been waiting, but here you are now. So, why wait longer? And you yourself must be eager to find out what the trouble is all about."

I nodded. "I have been told nothing."

The Gerent looked with a satisfied and thankful smile to the Jannanons, who would have liked to have smiled back but were embarrassed that they had hid so much from me.

"Well, you will find out all today," said the Gerent. "I want this Camarod to be said and done with." He leaned over to me for effect. "There are over three hundred commissions here, and most eat as if they have never seen decent food before. Oh, and beyond that, of some of these envoys I have had my limit. It's too much to even look or hear them again with their complaints and ideas and wants. No, let's get on with the Camarod, get on with the business and send these natives home."

"What is it you want of me in this Camarod?" I asked him and pinned him with my eyes.

"Just to listen," he said, but it was not the truth, and his face grew tight, letting me know there was more. "Listen, and once you know and understand, you will be asked to accept or deny us."

"I don't know what any of you think I have to give." I opened my arms to indicate that what I had was sitting before them. "I have very little."

The Gerent looked uncomfortable with that and, gazing away from me, he said, "We'll see; we'll see."

"Am I going to the Camarod?" Sissase asked me, looking at no one else.

I reached over, took her, and placed her in my lap. "I won't go without you. After all, I believe they must have Tor'ocs there. I don't think there's a Camarod without me, and I am not there without you."

The Gerent swung back to me, hearing the implied threat that we might not come. I had traveled this distance. I was certainly going to come, but I was tired of everyone else's certainty that I was their Tor'oc who would dance when they wanted me to dance.

Before the events of the day that they called a Camarod, the emissary took Pit, Sissase, and me on a walk through the city. I had made it a condition that I see it and see it before anything else. I felt that my future was about to be unmade that day. I wanted to see the city where this dividing line was being drawn.

There wasn't a single straight road or path in the city. The streets that ran from the bottom were snake-like passages carved so it would be easier to make your way up or down. There were cross streets that wound around the mountain; they were often wide streets built on earth that was terraced to make the roads flat. The up/down streets that crossed these ways came in on unlikely angles and exited again like that. It gave me the feel of roads that were at odds with one another.

The houses were just as mismatched — each a different color, as I had seen from the land below, each built by someone who wanted it known that the house next to theirs had no influence in any way on their own design. There were tall houses with sharp lines that met the next house like it without any space in between them. There were also round structures with oval windows wedged next to a shell-like place that would have fit almost perfectly in Lul.

The entire city was threaded together by tiny markets opened to the streets – the markets built into many of the mismatched houses that opened to the street. The markets were small, some no larger than my kollokk in the City in the Trees. Each market specialized in a single thing — candles, fruit, bread, knives, bowls, cloths, head dresses, soles, beddings, meat, saddles, weapons, mirrors, glass, floor coverings. The people of

Orzamond were market keepers; and I thought they must trade among one another, but they did not. One had to buy the things with as'ash—the copper I had made fun of in the boyt. This as'ash was given to me over and over in the cities that we had visited. Often it was given to "help us on our journey" but the as'ash had never been of any help. Even more copper had been laid on us that morning. I still could hardly believe that a market keeper would trade me anything for a few small pieces of copper; but they did and were happy to trade, eager to trade, and each trade filled them with a kind of joy. They would quickly take the copper and hide it even more quickly in locked boxes. I felt sorrow and felt badly that I was cheating these people of their leather goods, their knives, their candles that I took. I thought they might be under a spell that made them believe the copper was worth more than it was, but they appeared to all be under the same spell, which, I reasoned made—in their world—the copper meaningful. I was never under that spell and am still not under it.

One market keeper offered me a sack of copper for anything I had brought from the Peninsula—my satchel, my finnif knife, my sit upons. I laughed and refused him. The emissary, eyes popping in shock, pulled me aside.

"Do you understand that is a great deal he's offering to you?" the emissary whispered to me. "You could buy anything with that much as'ash."

Another strange word, which they called trading—buying and sometimes selling—that I got wrong every time I tried to use the words buying, selling.

I smiled at his foolishness. "What are you talking about? You couldn't even make a decent-sized bowl out of that little amount of copper." I held up the small sack of copper that I still had. "I am trying to rid myself of these little discs, not get more of them."

I walked away from the market keeper and the emissary, thinking that I was far less a fool than the two of them took me for.

The Camarod was to start when the light of the day was directly above. I'd had enough of trading, selling, and buying, and, with my hands full, we made our way up to the dome.

We first returned to the Gerent's gardens where I had left Bol. The Gerent was not quite happy at having an oryx on his terrace. I fed Bol the purple roots for which I had traded copper inside a market that took up the entire first level of a very squat, square, purple house. I thought he would like the roots that were the same color as the market house, and he did. It was in that market that they had attempted to give me back even smaller pieces of copper that they had said were mine. I had given them too much of something, though the emissary had been clear which discs I needed for the roots. I also had refused that market keeper. I did not know what game she was playing with me, but I didn't want to play.

We entered the large hall at the very top of the dome through a tunnel that the emissary told me would make it easier for us to reach the center of the hall, where everyone would expect me to be with the Gerent. He called it a dais. As the room opened to us, we found ourselves on the floor of a great round hall; and the dais was a raised round span that sat in the mid of the hall. There two winding pathways began, spiraling, swirling up to near the top of the dome. The path flattened in many places, with seats on those landings where my reason told me that the commissions could sit during long sessions. I reasoned this would be such a session.

We were the first to arrive. That had been my request. The emissary gestured to chairs on the dais for Pit, Sissase, and me to take. The chairs moved when we sat in them. Sissase was the first to discover that each chair could turn in a circle to face any part of the great hall, and they also tilted a little to allow a view of the upper reaches of the hall without us having to strain to gaze up.

The different commissions entered separately through the many doors at the highest height of the hall. Each group arrived as one, all dressed alike, in the same colors and the same style of dress that were theirs and no other's. They knew where they belonged and made their way to the landing meant for them. Often, they would enter, begin to walk the spirals down to their place, and then see us staring up at them. This always broke them of their solemn march. Upon seeing us, some would stumble into the person in front, others

Wind

would stop to stare back, always in silence dissolving into murmuring and pointing which they tried to hide from us as they finally began their walk again, this time with less assurance. I could see that Sissase was enjoying this show and was trying to figure out ways to make them stop and bump into one another more by simply moving her legs, stretching, bending forward, and once falling out of her chair, seemingly by accident. I could not hold back my laugh as that group fell over one another, almost in imitation.

At that, the emissary bent over to pick Sissase back up and place her in her chair. "Please, don't do that," he said.

She looked to me with a smile, and I nodded that he was right, though I did enjoy it as well.

The emissary had been giving us a commentary on each of the regions as the members entered. The first group wore yellow cloths with red stripes that draped from the top of the heads to cover their entire body except the face.

"They are always first, the Kadjafrees—very surprised to see you and just as surprised that we beat them here." The emissary was talking just loud enough for Pit, Sissase, and me to hear him; any louder and his voice would have reverberated around the great hall. One of the marvels of the design was that sound traveled in that room with ease and grace. "They are from the lowlands that grow many crops, but their red grasses and yellow grasses make soft and delicious bread that is almost like cake. It is what they are most proud of." He gestured for us to notice the colors they wore.

The groups that followed were the Damus, who fished fish from the rivers and lakes and wore silver-blue watchets, long, loose sit upons, and necklaces of golden-brown feathers from eagles that took the fish as well. The Eeunes wore little but leather strips to cover their strong bodies, as they were hunters and warriors and guards from many different regions who had adopted a way that belonged only to them. The Melopalins were the metal workers who mined the ore and turned it into whatever they wanted.

"They wear white, though the mines they work in are black and grey," the emissary explained to us. "They want us to know that they are clean. There was a lot of prejudice against them for many generations." He thought that was enough for us to understand the significance of the white.

"Are they the ones who also make the as'ash?" I wanted to get a look at the people who did that.

"No, that would be them." The emissary pointed to another group that had just entered above us. "They are the Seleuks. Very crafty, excellent eyes, wonderful artists. That is how they can carve the molds for the gold and silver lurm as'ash."

"You mean copper," I corrected him.

"Oh, only little of the lurm as'ash is copper—most of what you have is gold and silver, and everything in that sack the merchant offered you was gold with diamond eyes in the faces of the lions on the coyns. That was a fortune you turned away,"

I made a thought for myself to remember to find the meaning of gold that is more than a color, and of diamond eyes, and fortune, that I understood had to do with the seeing of the future, though I was not so certain that was what the emissary meant.

There were many commissions flowing in at that moment, and it was difficult for me to gather who was who, where they had come from, and what their purpose was in Aemira, but I heard the names and purposes. There were commissions that had traveled as far as I had who wore black that shimmered blue as they moved, and also dark green ones who gave the Out World fruit. The red cloths I finally understood were spirit guides and servants. Road-colored commissions carried goods from one town to another. The Sand Keepers dressed just like our Sand Keeper, who was among that group, and he gave us a nod and a smile.

I recognized the Luls when they entered, led by the Head of the Council, along with my defender and my prosecutor and a host of others following her. They stared in a different way at us—we were familiar to them, but we were not the same as their memories. Pit and Sissase had become strangers, no longer souls from Lul; and I had died.

The commissions that filled the other landings were from far-flung and nearby regions and cities, wearing blues, purples, water greens, light browns, clay earth reds, and shades of all these colors combined in stripes and dots of whites, blacks, reds, blues, greens, and yellows. I looked up at the hall and understood what I had seen that light, understood Orzamond—the city grown from all these people, all the people of the Out World. They had built their homes to reflect where they had traveled from, and they traded the goods and wares of their origins, each special in their own markets. Orzamond was not a city in itself, but a city made of everywhere.

Two last groups entered at the same moment from opposite ends of the hall, walking down the two spirals at similar paces, but with opposing emotions driving them. The Jannanons in their grey, hooded cloths smiled and waved to us. The people from Soos, in white and sea blue, frowned, looked fearful, angry, resistant. I saw Chiffaa in that group. We met eyes for an instant before she had to look away, looked down, attempted to hide herself among her people, attempted to disappear. They sat in the mid of one of the spirals, as the Jannanons took a place at the bottom very near us. I was glad to see my friends and companions, glad that they had been placed at our side.

Tinkling of bells echoed through the hall that was full of people. All the commissions quieted and looked with anticipation in our direction; the focus was on us, us alone. From the tunnel where we had entered the hall, an instrument of beauty blew a single note that bent into another; and the Gerent entered the hall in a cloth of white and gold that reflected the warm light falling through the panels above. His head was covered in a wrap of cloth fitted with stones and feathers with a thin band of blue leathered lizard skin that wound in and out of the wrap.

The assemblage sang back the note that bent into another in response, over and over, not in unison, but as a hall filled with individuals. The sound had harmony and power to it; it was impressive and moved something in me. I saw that Sissase was feeling something as well, and her eyes scanned the people in awe. Pit was smiling.

The Gerent reached the dais, held his hands up in greeting, and the hall slowly came to quiet again.

"Fen der Aemira," the Gerent cried out, and the commissions answered as one, "Fen der Na Leen."

I looked to the emissary, and he whispered, "An ancient greeting, 'Peace to Aemira,' and they answered, 'Peace to Our Own.'" He slyly pointed to the Gerent. "He is Our Own." The emissary sat back to listen to the Gerent.

"As your humble servant in the office of Gerent of the Middle and High Bosagin, I, Hasmapludi III, ask for your permission to bring back into session this Camarod of Susceptible Nations, which has been suspended one hundred and ninety-three darks and lights, suspended as we waited for the result of our charge to the brave and resilient Jannanons—Goyel, Sheios, and Weoduye. They traveled to the very end of this world on our wish, to return with a guest that knew nothing of Aemira, knew nothing of why he was summoned, a guest we ourselves feared could possibly be the end of us, if we believed the Damnation Legends-which I do."

The assembled laughed because he made the last three words funny; desperately wanting to laugh, they jumped on his attempt.

"I have met with this guest in my own rooms without guards and I am most proud to tell you that he is impressive and possibly dangerous, but I don't believe to us. We have wanted for this day. Let me bring before you our most awaited guest, Aeon the Tor'oc."

He gestured to me as the emissary leaned and whispered, "Stand up."

I did stand, and the assembled did not sing a note or laugh—they took a breath in as though I might attack them in the next moment. The Gerent felt the held breaths as I did, and he moved to the next moment to release them.

"Next to Aeon is a surprise, a thing not to be expected and not to take lightly—Sissase the Tor'oc," the Gerent said, while his arm swung open to the little girl whose eyes were large and proud and who took to her feet to stand beside me. "The last in the entourage before you is the orphaned artist Pit. I have seen him handle the finnif knife, and I believe he just might be a little bit Tor'oc himself."

Again, the assembled laughed, a laugh of relief.

Wind

"We welcome them here," the Gerent said, not as a question or statement but a command. The assembled sang a note that bent, this time together, and the power of so many voices as one put me back into my chair. Sissase climbed up onto me where she felt the safest. I liked that she was there, my arms around her, as we both stared back at the sea of unusual faces that didn't appear welcoming at all.

As the note ended, I said, just loud enough for all to hear, "Why?"

The Gerent swung his body round to look at me. The question in his look said, 'Why what?'

"Why did you bring us here?" I asked.

I had wanted that answer, and I would wait no longer. He saw in me that I was not going to be patient for whatever further he had planned to say to the assembled. I was not going to wait for more greetings and pleasantry. I was not going to wait for whatever else they felt they must play out before feeding me the meat of the meal. The moment had arrived before they wanted it to, but there was nothing in me that cared for that. I held the Gerent in my stare and demanded he tell me, yet he still wanted to put off the moment, to ease into it in the way he had imagined he would. He fumbled and muttered and turned back to the hall of commissions.

"As we have seen…" the Gerent started, and I looked down to Sissase.

"Let's go," I said to her as I moved to stand, holding her, she holding me.

The Gerent was quickly onto me, his hands at my shoulders, gently pushing me back to sit.

"No, no, no," he was pleading with me. "I will get to it; I will get to it now—I will."

The hall murmured, upset at me, unbalanced by me.

"The Tor'oc has a right," the Gerent said loudly back to the hall. "We have kept him blind, and he came willing and blindly to us. We thank him for that."

I waited for the Gerent to gather his way to tell me.

"We have brought you to us to lead our armies against an enemy that we have not the knowledge to fight—an enemy that will lay us low, that will destroy our cities, our towns, our farms, that will kill many and enslave those that survive."

The Gerent already looked beaten as he talked.

"Where is this enemy?" I asked. In the many days of travel, I had not a seen a single sign of war or conflict or warriors, threating or not threating.

He pointed in the direction away from where we had come, "They are in the far mountains—a treacherous place, difficult to pass, some thought impossible, but they are coming, an army of thousands with enormous weapons and beasts to pull those weapons across the passes. Certainly, it has been slow for them, but they are coming, deliberately coming."

"Who are they?" I asked in a bewildered voice.

"Tor'ocs," was the Gerent's answer, that threw me into blindness, silent and confused.

"A thousand years ago, when your ancestors were cut off from the world by the raging river, a small band of your warriors were left on the wrong side of the river—our side. There were no more than fifty; but they were Tor'ocs, and fifty can fight like five hundred. They fought and were chased back across the land, chased far away from the prison that held you, chased across to the mountains, across the mountains to a vast desert so large no one has ever known if there was another side to it or what lies on that side. Some of the fifty died, but not all of them. To all of our surprise they somehow survived the crossing of that desert and, as we know now, found a land that has nourished them for the last thousand years.

"We have kept the time of the Tor'ocs alive in our memory with the Damnation Legends, and they have evidently done the same. They have grown back into a nation, and unlike the Tor'ocs of the prison island, they are a warrior nation like your ancestors—every man, woman, and child. Unlike your ancestors, they are skilled with weapons that no one has seen before, weapons they either found with the people on the other side of the desert or ones they have created themselves.

"They know that there is a place called Aemira on this side of the mountains. They know that their ancestors conquered this land. They know that most of the Tor'ocs from that time were destroyed, and that their own ancestors were the few who lived to father and mother a new Tor'oc Nation. That Nation has lived and grown for a thousand years for one purpose, to return across the mountains to us, to conquer us, to destroy us, to punish us.

"We have not the skill or the knowledge of Tor'oc warfare, modern or ancient. Your people, though you've grown peaceful in these long times, have still maintained the weapons and the skills and, by the look of you, the very bodies that are born for war. You have the blood of Sumon in you. We ask you to lead us."

"Lead you against Tor'ocs?" I said to the Gerent, wondering if he knew that was not a thing a Tor'oc could do.

"They are not Tor'ocs as you know what Tor'ocs are." The Gerent was ready with his answer. "You are more like the people here. You are peaceful; you reason; you care; you have skills beyond warfare." He pointed in the direction of the mountains again. "They are warriors. They know how to destroy, how to kill. They know nothing else. If we cannot stop them, everything you have seen in your travels will be wiped away. Every person you have known will be murdered. Every part of this world will become a thing ruined."

Wind

"How do you know any of what you are telling me?" Reason told me he was beyond his own knowledge. "This mysterious Tor'oc Nation has been on the other side of a desert that you cannot cross, and you know no one who has. You say that they are in mountains now that are impassable, and yet you tell me that they are a horde bent on your destruction. How do you know this?"

"The Great Rods have told us what we know." The Gerent nearly collapsed upon telling me this. "There was a high mountain city called Heiudsom, a fortress city built before memory, built on a high plain that overlooked the world. It was a city of people with ancient knowledge and ways removed from us. Few people ever traveled to it. Fewer ever left Heiudsom to travel to us, but there are some here who have seen the city and knew its wonders." He looked out into the hall at a section close by, where a man in mid age stood up to address me.

"My name is Ardrum. I am a trader, a buyer and seller, a traveler who has been to every corner of Aemira and corners beyond. I have been to Heiudsom," he held up three fingers, "...three times."

My eyes adjusted to the light where he stood. He was rough looking, with a deeply lined face, dark matted hair, dark eyes, a close-cropped beard, and course cloths making his watchet. In short, he looked honest.

"The Somans—as they were called—were masters of light." He threw up a handful of small balls that burst in colors and hung in the air around the great hall, like the one the Sand Keeper had carried in the Niedlmae.

I looked up at the lights. "Beedles," I said out loud.

"Yes, beedles. You know them." Ardrum was addressing me directly. I nodded back to him. "You will know them no more. The craft that made them is gone. And it was not just for the beedles the Somans were known." He pointed toward the Gerent. "They gave us gold. They wove it into their cloth from a cotton grown nowhere else and woven so fine that many people said that fees actually made it with magic. Our Own is wearing Soman cloth."

I looked to see the cloth that hung near me. It was simple and fine just as the trader described.

"It is all gone forever. Those who held the knowledge, who could have passed it to the next in line, are gone. Even the next are gone. I did not witness their going. But I have someone who did."

He put his hand on a boy's shoulder, and the boy looked up. Ardrum motioned for the boy to stand. He was a boy who was still a handful of years away from the end of growing and becoming a man. His hair was long and sand colored. His skin was several shades lighter than mine. He had spent long and long in the light of the day and would probably whiten to a color like the Gerent if he remained inside. His eyes were a sky blue and reflected the lights of the beedles in a pleasant, magical way. His one unusual feature was a large nose that did not fit his face. Hopefully, that face might eventually grow to fit the nose. As he talked, his voice crackled into shrill, high sounds that embarrassed him.

"I would like you all to meet the survivor of Heiudsom—Yeoal. He can tell you better of their going. He is the only one who can tell you," Ardrum said, as he looked to the boy to urge him to have the courage to describe what happened in his city.

Yeoal took some moments before speaking. "I am the last," he said, then held himself and finally gazed at Ardrum, who nodded for him to continue. "My friend Ardrum Keililosji found me, saved me in the Pleiseu Ravine after my escape. I am the last. My people have been murdered—my sisters, my parents, the seers, and the knowers—everyone."

"How did it happen?" the Gerent said, standing beside me. I reasoned he knew, but he sounded as if he were hearing this for the first time, as I was.

"Heidusom was untouchable—we had a wall, a high, thick wall that kept out the beasts that hunted in the high mountains. The wall was made in the time of wars so long and long ago that no one knew who the wars were with or why there were wars, but our great fathers built the wall; and the wall always protected us, until the Red Blacks came. They were dark like you."

He pointed at me. "They looked like you; but they wore red, and they wore black. They had large-wheeled weapons that could throw massive stones that broke our wall. When the wall broke, the Red Blacks poured into our city and killed with their swords and their spears and their knives anyone who was not kneeling or lying and crying. Anyone who ran, anyone who stood, they died that day. I was one of those who cried and cringed low in a house, hoping they would not find me. They found everyone and brought us to the Ocalo."

Ardrum stood to interrupt. "The town center—a large open plaza." He sat back down to give the space back to Yeoal who began again.

"A woman, a Red Black who had painted her face white—she was too frightening to look at—quieted us with her calls for silence. She then told us that our great fathers had killed in battle a Tor'oc boy of sixteen named Ropin, and that we would pay for his death with our deaths, with the removal of all the Somans from this life. They said they had waited a thousand years to take our lives, and that among the first to be taken would be the ones the age of Ropin.

"I was taken in that first group. They took us to the high plain that could be seen from anywhere in the Ocalo. They had also taken the younger children onto the plain and kept them a short way from us. My sisters were there. All the children were crying. The Red Black in white face told us that their children would end the lives of the children of Heidusom. She said their children needed the training. My sisters and the others were held at the point of short swords and knives that were held in the hands of the Red Black children the same age, the same size. I remember thinking they looked like they were going to play with my sisters, but they did not. The woman warrior in the white face told us all that the parents and the elders would watch their next in line die and know that the world of Heidusom was dying before them.

"She yelled a word and the Red Black children jumped and swung their swords and cut the little ones. I saw my sister Treo—two girls her same size stabbed her—one with a sword, one with a knife. She was crying, crying for our mother, and the little Red Black kept stabbing her. She was bleeding, bleeding; she fell to a place I couldn't see. The white-faced woman yelled again and the young who were like me and my friends ran into us with their blades and their screams and there was blood and I tried to run but something hit me and knocked me to the ground."

"Show them," Ardrum encouraged the boy who should have been dead. Yeoal did not want to show us and stood like a stone. Ardrum rose next to him, whispered to him, and then the boy cocked his head to the side. The trader raised the hair off of the boy's head to show us a red, raw scar that ran from his ear to the back of his skull. The hall gasped.

"Yeoal was struck by a sword that was meant to crush his skull and kill him," Ardrum yelled out to all of us. He whispered something again to Yeoal and sat. Yeoal took many breaths before speaking. We waited –

no one wanted to make him say more, to remember more, but truly wanted to hear more, wanted him to remember everything.

"When I woke...I was among the bodies of everyone I knew. I didn't want to see them, but I was under them; I had to climb out. There was fire; they were burning us. We were not in the Ocalo now; we were outside in a hole, and the bodies were all on fire. The smell made me lose everything in my stomach. It was bad, even for the Red Blacks; they could not stay near the smell. I crawled from the hole and ran."

"How long did you run?" Ardrum was up again. Yeoal held up two fingers. "Yeoal ran for two darks. I found him in the ravine. He was almost dead. I was headed to Heidusom for trading but had been delayed, as can happen. Fortune was on my side."

"By the time Ardrum had arrived in Orzamond with Yeoal we had already been told of the ruin of Heidusom by the Great Rods, who had flown to it because of the smoke, the burning bodies." The Gerent was speaking to me. "At that time, we only knew the city had been destroyed and the people murdered, and that there was a great army moving from that city in our direction."

"But how do you know they are Tor'ocs, these Red Blacks?" I did not want to believe they were Tor'ocs like me.

"The name Ropin. Have you never heard it?" the Gerent asked

Wind

It was a common name among the Tor'ocs on the Peninsula. Even when I heard it said in the story, I knew they had to be who they were. I still did not want to believe. "But it must be a name used throughout the Out World."

"Only in the Damnation Legends is the name known. There was a Ropin who murdered an entire Council by cutting them up, little by little, and feeding them to pigs," the Gerent said. "We would not even name a pig or a rat Ropin."

"How long before this Tor'oc army reaches the edge of Aemira?" I asked.

"We have a season. And so, you do admit that they are Tor'ocs?" The Gerent wanted to make this a certainty for me.

"I do not admit it. This might well be a Tor'oc nation that has regrown like we have in the City in the Trees. And it might be some murderous army that uses a story they heard. What other proof do you have?"

The Gerent turned to Yeoal and asked, "Did these Red Blacks have bows?"

The boy nodded and held up his two arms, which he crossed at his elbows. "They had a great bow that was like two bows put together. The arrows would fly right through a person. Children were torn in half if they were hit."

The Gerent was back to me. "Can you hand me your bow, Aeon—just for a moment?

I reached to the floor, where I had laid my own, and gave it to the Gerent. He faced the assembled again and yelled to the Eeunes, "Can you send someone down?"

A strong young man was on his feet and down to us in three breaths. The Gerent handed him the oro bow and an arrow that he had taken from me while the Eeune was coming. "Load that arrow and fire it anywhere you like."

The young man grinned and opened the bow into the X-shape the boy had demonstrated with his arms— the hall gasped again. The young Eeune raised the bow as if to fire the arrow over the heads of all and pulled-- or tried to pull. As strong as he was, he could not pull the strings back beyond making it tight. He could not bend the bow in order to fire the arrow. The wood from which the bow is made is like iron. We are raised to fire the oro bow; he was not. The young man could build his body to shoot with the oro bow, but it would take time.

As he took the oro bow away from the Eeune, the Gerent said to me, "You can shoot with this?" I nodded and took the bow back. "Would you like to show them?" He indicated everyone around us. I laid the bow down and ignored his gaze on me.

"Aeon, these are Tor'ocs who use the same weapons and have the same names. You see that is true."

Wind

I was still not ready to agree with him. "I am a Tor'oc." I held up a finger, "One Tor'oc. You are asking me to fight a nation. Whether they are Tor'ocs or not, how can only one do that?"

"We are asking you to train us, so that young Eeunes can fire that oro bow soon and soon. We need you to lead us against an army you will know how to fight," said the Gerent.

"How do you know I can lead you?"

"The Mothers told us you could," the Gerent said, and I was silent. "They told us you were born for this."

I stood to look out among the gathered commissions who had pinned so much hope on me. I told them, "There is a code by which we are raised on the Peninsula, a code that we trace back to the birth of the Tor'oc people. This code made us strong; it preserved us when the Out World tried to destroy us; it is a code we breathe in and breathe out, and it runs through me like my blood. We are forbidden to kill Tor'ocs, no matter the want or desire or reason to kill. I cannot raise an army to kill my brothers and sisters, even ones from the other side of the world. I cannot, and I will not."

I bowed my head. I wanted to help them. I could not.

A voice rang up from high above. "I will defeat them!" It was a voice I knew. Uthiriul was standing at a spot near the top of the hall. She was wearing a long brown cloth with a hood on her head. She pushed the hood back off her face and glared down at me.

"I am Uthiriul—a Tor'oc. I come from the Peninsula, and like my brother Tor'oc Aeon the Leaf, I grew in the City in the Trees."

She took out from under her robe an oro bow that was hidden there, arrowed the bow in a breath, aimed it at the dais and fired. The arrow flew through the hall faster than most of the commissions could follow, struck the chair the Gerent should have been sitting in, exploding it into shards of wood and torn cloth, leaving the arrow shaking in the floor of the dais beyond, a bit of chair wood hanging mid arrow.

"I will train you. I will lead you. I am not afraid of this murderous army that you call Tor'ocs." She began to walk down toward us as she pointed to me. "He may be convinced that these are brothers and sisters—I am not. They may have oro bows and they may know Tor'oc names, but they are not Tor'ocs. They are worse than Muons. They are murderous hyenas that teach their youngest ones to kill young ones. They are not Tor'ocs, and if they dare to call themselves Tor'ocs, I am bent on their destruction to the last of them. They are cowards who have not fought anyone; they have murdered the defenseless. But when they reach Aemira, they will have me to fight; they will have us to fight; and we will leave them lying in their own blood."

Sissase turned to me and asked, "Who is she?"

Wind

I whispered back, "Uthiriul. She is a Tor'oc, as she said. I cannot reason how she got here."

"You know her?" Sissase looked back at Uthiriul in wonder and awe.

"I have known her since anyone knew her." I could not stop myself smiling at the marvel of Uthiriul. She was as angry as she had been since she was little, and I was happy to see her.

"You know they call him the Leaf, but do you know why?" Uthiriul burst out again as she grew closer. "He tried to grab a leaf to stop himself from the Fall. He has always been afraid. He is afraid now, and that is why he does not want to lead you or to fight these Red Black murderers. When I last saw him, he was afraid to travel across the Divul. He was afraid of the Out World. He was afraid of what he would find where you find him now. He looks strong enough and brave enough." She reached the dais and walked onto it, crossing to me. "I am here to tell you that he is not what he seems to be, but he has told you that in his own words. He hides behind our code, but I do not hide. I will fight."

She held her oro bow aloft, and the commissions jumped to their feet, singing the single note that bent sounding over and over on top of one another. The Gerent was just behind Uthiriul, his eyes wide, his mouth open. He looked down to his ruined chair, to the arrow in the floor, and then up to me with eyes that asked me if she was real, if this was a true thing happening before him.

Uthiriul gazed down at the boy Yeoal and held her hands up to quiet the hall. Everyone saw that she wanted to speak to the survivor.

When the room was quiet enough for her, Uthiriul asked, "What were the names of your sisters?"

Yeoal was surprised, but he answered, "Treo and Ae."

"Can you come to me?" she asked, beckoning the boy to her, to be with her on the dais.

The boy came and stood beside her; he looked like a small and small child next to the large, strong Tor'oc woman. She put an arm around him.

"Treo and Ae—beautiful names that are new to me," Uthiriul began. "The Red Blacks have killed many beyond those two young ones, but it is their names we will remember. It is their names we will cry on the war field. It is their names the murderers will hear in their dying breaths." And then she yelled the two dead girl's names; and she made the names a war cry.

Uthiriul had become something I had only heard of in the stories of the long and long ago. She was a myth already—she was like the mothers of the Tor'ocs in the City in the Trees. She was as I had imagined Morla and Orl'isjud and O'bir. Maybe she had been correct that their blood flowed in her, too.

The Gerent had regained himself. He had lost the dais to Uthiriul, a woman he knew nothing of until a flash of a breath ago. He moved to the center of the dais, just behind her, and pulled the arrow from the floor with some difficulty.

He walked the few steps to Uthiriul and handed her the arrow.

"With all the talk of war," he said to her, "I believe you will want this."

He had the commissions back to him again.

"Uthiriul—yet another Tor'oc—is a surprise, and by the reaction of the commissions, a welcome surprise. We thank you for surprising us." He turned and took steps away from her. "Here in Aemira we live by rules and laws. Someone doesn't just appoint themselves leader of the armies, the Grand Commander. You are impressive, but we must meet on everything that has happened today. We will discuss; we will decide the course best suited for Aemira."

Uthiriul and the Gerent held each other in a look that neither wanted to lose. A cry lost it for them. From the mid of the spirals, from where the commissions of Soos were seated, there were cries and shouts and struggles. I saw Pit in the mid of it. Without thinking, I was on my feet and running to him.

I don't remember the flight from the dais to the melee; it seemed as if I were in one place one moment and in the fight the next. Pit was the center of the struggles; one older commission made the error of grabbing his arm and felt the strike of Pit's free hand in his mid-face, knocking the old man back into others. Pit was silent and fierce, fighting as though there were many of him, while all of Soos was trying to get hold of him and screaming, "Assassin! Unheard of! Of all places! Kill him! Not at a Camarod! Thief! Murderer!" There was something in the hand that had hit the old commission, but before I could move close enough, a young man who nearly had the same face as Chiffaa screamed something at me and pointed. On the ground lay Chiffaa, white and cold looking, one of her own pendles sticking from her chest. I swung again to Pit. That was what he was holding—Chiffaa's batana.

I was surrounded by screaming men and women, their screams so mingled that I couldn't hear what they yelled. It was accusing and threatening, and I cared not at all to hear it. I pushed them from me, like the rest of Aemira they were smaller than me, none of them had grown any higher than my chin. I wanted to get to the path to Chiffaa, but they still tried to block me. They were like children trying to hold back a wild cat, but there were enough of them to keep me from her.

"Back away!" my three Jannanons were shouting and pushing the Soos people back. Weoduye had felt my intent and led the two others to me. I was free. He had my thanks and knew it.

I dropped to my knees and leaned over Chiffaa. Life was escaping her. Her hands, her arms, her legs were losing color and warmth. Her face was chalk white; her eyes rolled open and shut and open again, and she saw me. There was confusion for a moment as she focused. Then her eyes rolled into the poison once more, and she was being dragged under by a strong current. I put one hand against her chest and with the other I pulled the pendle from her neck. Gasps from her fellows filled the place around us.

"Let her die!" screamed Pit from somewhere farther back.

I bent down to Chiffaa's torso and put my face against her mid where the poison would have to exit. A finnif knife was in my free hand, and I cut into her, a small cut but bloody; and the gasps were big with screams inside them. My mouth found the cut, my tongue tasting her blood as I sucked, pulling poison from her but not just by swallowing, but with something greater, with my spirit, with my own death that knew the poison and knew the half place where she already was.

Chiffaa sucked in air. Her hands grasped the back of my neck and shoulders. She arched, pushing her mid up to me. Foul, shattered blood with spikes of poison that pricked my lips, my mouth, my throat was making my stomach turn in revolt. The flow was fast; the poison had no strong anchor in her yet to keep it from coming. I would vomit in a moment; but the draining was long enough to release her, to pull enough poison to stop it from ending her. I would be ill for a short time, and she would be ill for longer. Yet we would both be alive, and I could feel the touch was already between us.

Many hands pulled me up and I vomited, which made them let me go. Pit was screaming, a howl angry and vengeful. If none of the rest had, he saw that I had saved her.

"Caru," a young, beautiful voice cried out, and Sissase landed on me. She was crying and gripping me. In my life, there was never a better feeling than her body on mine. Her force that was larger and older than her body and age healed me through my cloths, through my skin. I was weak from the poison now in me, but I raised both arms enough to caress my little girl.

"Don't cry," I said. "I will be fine."

Sissase looked into my eyes and saw that it was true, that this was a short damage. Next to us, Chiffaa coughed; her eyes flickered open; her breath was shallow and steady. This woman turned to see me, to see Sissase staring back at her with murder in her eyes. Chiffaa, with little strength, reached over to touch me.

"Forgive me," she whispered.

Sissase grabbed the hand and pushed it back. "No!" I held Sissase tighter.

"We forgive, Sissase...we do," I told her, told both of them.

Sissase looked back at me, still angry, still not wanting to forgive. I could see that Chiffaa was bleeding still from the wound. I laid a hand over it and with my waning power closed it, not healed, but closed to stop the outflow of life.

The rest of the commissions were in an array of confusion and concern. No one knew exactly what had happened. They knew Chiffaa had been attacked; some thought she was dead. Word flew that I was dead, too. Pit was blamed, but they didn't know how he had killed both of us. The truth hit them harder.

Chiffaa was not dead, though she should have been. Pit had shot her with her own pendle. I had saved her somehow by cutting her; the proof of her blood was all over her and me, the blood drying hideously on my face and body. The Soos commission lifted Chiffaa and took her after they saw the bleeding had stopped. I stayed lying on the floor with Sissase on top of me. That was where I belonged. There was murder, and there was magic; and no one knew what was greater. They had all seen more than I wanted them to see. I would not answer their questions, not even to Uthiriul would I answer.

Uthiriul appeared as others came to see about me, to see how bad I was hurt, to see where I should be taken. Her eyes did not question; they demanded an explanation.

I also wanted to know. "How?"

She knew I meant, how was it possible that she was there.

She knelt down to me. "I won't tell you here — later, when it is just us, Tor'oc to Tor'oc."

"Me, too, then," Sissase said.

Uthiriul looked sternly at the little girl, but I felt that she was already taken by her charm.

"Who is this?" Uthiriul asked me, as though Sissase couldn't answer for herself.

"I am Tor'oc, just like you," Sissase spat back.

I caressed Sissase's hair and smiled at Uthiriul. "Just like you."

"I don't know where you're from, but there are only two Tor'ocs in the Out World." Uthiriul was not ready to take in this little one.

"I speak wind. Only Tor'ocs speak to the trees." Sissase demonstrated by blowing a greeting, "I look to the days and darks and am I glad to be among you." Uthiriul forced herself not to smile, and in those moments, she studied Sissase.

"This is a surprising light for all of us," Uthiriul said. "The three of us will talk later when you are able," she added, looking back at me.

"Where is Pit?" I asked, hoping Uthiriul would know.

"Oh, the young killer." Uthiriul finally smiled. She pointed back down toward the dais. Pit was sitting in a chair just off the platform. He was being held there by a band of Eeunes, who were big enough and strong enough to keep him. He was staring up at us. All anger had left him; he looked weak, as though he had sucked the poison himself.

Behind them, on the dais, the Gerent was talking to Yeoal, the boy from the slaughtered city. Many of the commissions had left, and the few remaining had lost their panic and their talk had come to a murmur. I heard the Gerent and the boy.

"What do you mean by that?" the Gerent asked Yeoal.

"Well, we called them the Red Blacks, but their cloths weren't black," the boy replied.

"What color were they?" the Gerent asked, as though there was an importance in this that he felt but could not gather.

"Blue…a very dark, dark blue." The boy was lost, back in his city, "I saw that when they came at us, when they were close and striking out. I should have been crying, but my last thought was that their cloths were not black."

The birds in my dream were not black. I remembered my dream as though I had just woken from it. The birds I saw were a very, very dark blue. How did I not know that before?

Barry Alexander Brown

12

Sissase led the way, followed by Uthiriul, and the red cloths who carried me to Fiernd in the Gerent's garden. They could get me there, but not up and through the limbs. The Figure Tree helped as much as he could, and when he couldn't, Uthiriul was there to push me up enough so that I could get a footing on the next limb. I climbed knowing that no matter the struggle, it would be best for me to be in the tree in my bed sling. To keep my mind from the pain and the lack of strength, I blew the story of what had happened at the Camarod to the old tree as I moved from one branch to another. I finished telling what he wanted to know just as I reached my bed sling and fell into it.

Sissase put herself on a branch near my head, a branch that had a smaller limb growing from it, giving her a natural seat to lean against. Uthiriul took a place on a limb slightly higher and facing us. She blew a greeting to the tree, who, in wonder, asked if the entire world now spoke wind.

Sissase blew back, "No, she is Tor'oc like us." Uthiriul was annoyed that a child of four, and one she didn't consider a Tor'oc, was speaking on her behalf to a tree.

"How?" I asked Uthiriul when she looked to me. "How did you even cross the Divul?"

"To begin before that," Uthiriul started, "I went to my kollokk, gathered what I needed, and waited behind the Iven."

The Iven was one of the oldest trees in our city, near the edge, near the Divul. It had been struck by skyfire that split it to make it grow in two directions. In the place where the old tree had split, there was a mark, a mark that was the perfect picture of the skyfire itself. It had grown with the tree to be three lengths of a grown Tor'oc. For luck, during a storm, a Tor'oc might stand in that place, their back against the mark as the skyfire and thunder struck around us. Some also thought it would fulfill a desire they wanted above everything, especially if the light struck very, very nearby.

Wind

"I saw you carry the bucket to the old kollokk above the Divul and I knew you were leaving. I was going to stop you. I was going to take your place, and you were not seeing or hearing so I didn't need to be careful. I ran up that old tree, but just when I reached you, you fell." Uthiriul looked down, as though seeing me fall from the tree just then. "I saw the wonder beneath, the water circling you and holding you. It was many and many of the water fees turning themselves into something else. I should not have, but I stood and watched. As they were closing around you, my reason hit me, and I jumped--but I missed, or it moved. I landed in the water, and the fees that held you moved fast; and I was caught by that current and dragged through the water. Then there were fees also around me, doing what they had done to you, and we were running fast through the Divul. I was certain I would drown, but there was air somehow. I was breathing, but I was wet. The water rushed about me; and I didn't know where I was until I washed onto a grassy riverbank. The fees had left me on the other side of the Divul somewhere. I think it was far from you. I was alive and in the Out World."

As she told the story, she lived the story. I could see her before me wet and frightened, climbing out of the Divul, falling on the ground of the Out World, regretting that she had been fool enough to do what she had done. I could see her rise to her feet and take in the sight of the land. Then she took a breath and accepted that she was alone in a world unknown and dangerous.

"Fentesimal," I said.

She looked at me and smiled at the word, 'fentesimal'. She repeated it in a way that told me she did not use the word anymore.

"I found a good and kind tree that I slept in that night. The grove made me feel better. They showed me the fruits and bushes that the animals ate. They warned me of the Muon. They showed the direction to find the city of Orzamond. They pointed me to the road."

"The road." Sissase made a face and a sound to go with it. Uthiriul looked to the little girl, and her eyes smiled, though nothing else did. I believe it was the start of the grown Tor'oc accepting the little one.

"Yes, the road, a monster of ugliness." Uthiriul nodded. "But it was safe to travel."

"It wasn't safe before?" I asked.

"You should know it wasn't safe." Uthiriul looked back at me. "The Muon attacked on my third night. I was sleeping in a tree with strong, low branches, easy to climb. It was the second time the fees saved me."

"Was the tree standing in water?" I was having trouble seeing water fees in a tree.

"There are many kinds of fees," said Uthiriul, understanding my meaning. "There are wood and bush fees, earth fees, and fees in the air even now around us. There are fees that ride the wind and fire fees. The wood fees living in the tree saved me that third dark. The Muon had been tracking me. When he saw I was in a place close to the ground, a place he could climb, he came once I was asleep.

"The wood under me cracked." Uthiriul slapped her hands together, and her listeners jumped. "I jumped, just like you. Then the wood fees yelled 'Muuuuon!' I was up, and around me were fees like the water fee, but in wood; and at my feet was the Muon, grabbing my bed sling, fighting the wood fees. I was out of my sling and landing on the ground when I saw the fighting above me, near where I had been. The Muon could not eat the wood fees, but he could destroy them. He was shattering them, grabbing one and shattering another with it.

"Somehow, I had grabbed a finnif knife as I jumped. I threw the knife, hitting him in the back and cutting him. It howled, rolled off that branch, and hit the ground not far away from me. Earlier that light I had cut a good limb for walking from a newly dead ironwood tree I had come across. The limb was leaning against my tree. I grabbed it and hit the Muon across the face." Uthiriul gestured to her nose as the place she hit him. She was moving in the Figure Tree as she would have on the ground with the Muon, both hands held out holding an invisible limb, moving forward, striking again and again.

"I hit around his head, at his knees, across the back of a hand, anywhere that would hurt. He got to his feet but was faced away from me. I used the moment to get back in my tree and climb higher, taking my bow and satchel and the knives. The wood fees were with me. We all climbed high and high. The Muon yelled and climbed as far as before, but he got no further. He looked and saw me, and there was vengeance in those eyes. I wanted to throw a knife that would land between them." She pointed to the space between her own eyes. "I wanted to end him, but my reason told me there was too much tree in the way, and I would lose another knife to his shoulder or his back or in the tree itself, which I didn't want to do.

"He left after staying long and yelling and wanting to climb up, but he couldn't. I did not have my sling, so the wood fees made a bowl out of themselves for me to sleep in. It was hard but shaped for me, so I slept. In the dew light I had my first talk with the fees."

"Were they like the one who had come for me?" I reasoned they must be.

'No, they were different. Every sort of fee is different. Not so much in size but always in speech. Some can speak as we do and speak well, and others barely and others not at all, though I always understood them.

"How big are they?" Sissase had found her tongue again, and her eyes were returning to their usual size after being large and excited throughout Uthiriul's story of the Muon and the wood fees.

Uthiriul showed the size a fee would be between her two hands. It was not big. Sissase looked at the empty space, thinking of a fee there, wanting to truly see a fee there.

Wind

"So, the wood fees are nothing like the water fees except in size and they can speak," I said, making certain I knew.

"They also move in and through and out of the wood like the water fees move through water," Uthiriul said. "Their voices are low and deep, and they can use the wood in the trees to speak to one another across huge distances. Their favorite way to travel is through the roots underground where the trees are tangled and tangled, more tangled than the limbs in our city. They travel faster there than above ground."

"And what did you talk with them about?" I was getting more and more drawn to the wood fees and wanted to see them, too.

"They thanked me, and I thanked them. They saw that I could have run when I first had gotten away from the Muon, but that I stayed to fight because they were in the fight and in the fight because of me. They had saved me to begin with."

"There was nothing else you could have done." I nodded. Seeing me nod, Sissase nodded as well.

"We pledged to one another; and from there to here, all fees have been with me."

"You had companions," I said, understanding more of how she could have done what she did.

"The best companions, who taught me much, and were never unsure of me," Uthiriul said this, knowing something of my story, I reasoned.

445

"Did they help you fight the Muon when you met him again?"

She looked suspiciously at me. "How do you know I fought him again?"

"I am certain you fought at the lake edge—I heard it."

Her eyes rolled, remembering that moment.

"Yes, he was there at the water when I got there." Uthiriul thought back to her time at the lake, just as she had when she remembered fighting the Muon in the other tree. "I think he had been tracking you but found me. He was upwind from me, and I smelled him before he smelled me. An awful smell. I can smell him in my sleep at times, which I hate."

"What does he smell like?" Sissase wanted to know and didn't want to know.

Uthiriul thought a moment, or maybe she was bringing the smell back to her. "Do you know the smell of the inside of an animal who has been cut open and its insides lie on the ground? Mix that with soured eggs and human dung and a rotting, dying man's breath—that is the perfume of a Muon."

From my memory, that was a very good description. Though I had never smelled it near, his stink had reached me.

"We had a boyt. How did you get across that lake?" I was trying to see her journey.

"I did not get across it. I went around it."

"Did you lose the Muon at the water edge then?"

"I never lost him." Uthiriul's eyes gazed out to the world beyond Orzamond. "He followed me. He is there somewhere." She gestured to the land that lay out away from us.

"Did you fight him many times?"

"No, I did not fight him again after the lake, but I have seen him three times since," Uthiriul said. "The last time was in the woods where you died."

"You know about that," I said, feeling too aware of myself.

"Everyone knows of it. The One Who Cannot Die, they call you in some ancient language that everyone seems to know. I cannot say the words, but they all think you did die, so the name's confusing. Did you die?"

I spread my arms. "Does it look like I did?"

"At the moment, yes."

"Fentesimal," I said, and smiled. She smiled back.

"Why did you save her?" Uthiriul asked.

"She didn't want to end me, and she didn't, no matter what I look like."

"Ocer, what do you think?" Uthiriul looked to Sissase, using the Tor'oc word for a good child.

"Pit was right to end her," Sissase said, but was shy about it. She knew I would not like the answer.

"She saved me in Foul Lands," I said, trying to push myself up and failing. "She ran into the Seap and pulled me out."

"So, you think you owe her," Uthiriul said.

"I do still," I answered.

"She did not pull you from the Seap," Uthiriul said, certain of that.

"How would you know?"

"I was there." She dropped that in between us like a stick of wood on fire.

I was struck. I knew she was not there. "What do you know?"

"I was the one who pulled you from the Seap," she said, letting that sink into me. "You and the Jannanons had cleared Foul Lands just as I was running from the Muon across that burnt place. I saw the Jannanon, Sheios, from far, and knew he wasn't a shadow. I went to him and asked what he was doing there in the mid of that place. Once he told me, the two of us went down into the Seap; and there you were, looking worse than you do now. I pulled you out. You are heavy when you are almost dead."

I found my voice after moments of confusion. "Why didn't you stay?"

Wind

"I had a Muon who wanted me. You could not fight, and none of your companions could travel without leaving you and the other one. You would have all died, so I pulled the Muon away from you."

"I traveled toward where the light rises. Your friends told me I would find a city there where I could find rest and safety and food. I let the Muon see me once before I lost him again. He followed, as I knew he would."

"Did the Jannanons not see that you were Tor'oc?" I asked, thinking that they knew and did not tell me.

"They knew—I told them."

"So, they knew you escaped the Peninsula and were headed for the Camarod?"

"Yes, they knew that."

"Why did they not tell me?"

"Because I saved you, and they owed me. I told them that silence was their payment," Uthiriul said with such strength it even silenced me. "The two Jannanons argued with me. My answer was that I would stay among them until the Muon came and then there would be nothing to argue. I would live—they would not unless they hid. I had heard they were very good at hiding but that would have left you as a meal for the Muon. They agreed, and they were Jannanons at their word. The Soos girl never cared to tell you or not tell you. I cannot believe you thought that stick of a woman could pull you from the Seap."

As hard as this was to reason her story as true, nothing else made reason.

"Did you find the city where the light rises?" Sissase asked. I was surprised to hear her voice. I had forgotten she was there in the shock of what I was knowing.

Uthiriul smiled. "I did find the city, the first city I had ever seen not built in trees." She said that for Sissase. "It was in a bowl of land, a perfect bowl, and all the houses and buildings looked liked bowls turned upside down. The city is J'kal, formed in a circle like the land around it." She wanted to tell us, yet she was holding back. She never liked showing her excitement. "They're horse people. I learned to take a horse and ride it, just like in your dreams of me." She pointed at me with her foot.

"It was my horse who put me far ahead of the Muon and why he got close enough again," Uthiriul said. "There were times in the darks on my way to J'kal when I heard him, felt him close to me. But as the Jannanons did, I hid well enough but he was learning me. In the last fight at the lake, he almost took me."

"I heard a howl," I told her.

Uthiriul nodded. "When I stabbed him with an arrow." She held up a hand as if it were wrapped around a shaft. "I didn't have time to arrow the bow.

He was already on me. I walked right up on him where he was waiting."

She lowered her watchet to show a scar on her shoulder, a deep knife scar in the shape of a mouth of teeth.

"He had me on the ground, biting into me, his nails digging into my mid. I had just a jiff to pull an arrow and stab. It took his eye." Uthiriul was back there under the Muon, and I saw him as she saw him. "That was luck. In another jiff, he would have ended me."

"I understand how well you can hide, but he's a hunter. How did he not smell you on those darks?"

"The Jannanons have tricks. As they said, it doesn't help to hide your body if you cannot hide your smell. They have a salve they rub on six points of their bodies. It doesn't take much." She pointed to her wrists, her ankles, two points on her neck. "The salve does not alter your smell, but it makes any beast think the smell is coming from behind them, always from behind them. They are led to turn to find you. They turn and turn and turn. They go mad from turning. Then they run to leave your smell to stop the turning if they can. I heard the Muon turning one night beneath me. He hates the madness, but it has not stopped him from coming for me. The salve doesn't alter the trail left from your feet."

"He knew I was in the city in the bowl. He was afraid of the city, but he stalked it. Some people went missing, and some horses and other beasts that they raised to eat. He ate them, too. I spotted him one night on the edge of the bowl above us. Once I learned to ride the horse, I left J'kal by the road; and he followed."

"He could smell you on the horse?" I could not reason that.

"No, I made a show of leaving. He saw me that first light. Afterwards, I was hardly on the ground, so it was hard for him to find me, but he always did in his time, and he kept coming. He was never close except in the mountain pass beyond Jielada. He's a beast but a clever hunter. He was in the rocks when I met a band of thieves."

"Rovers," Sissase said, remembering them.

"Is that what they were named?" Uthiriul asked, knowing that it was by sound of the little girl's voice. "Well, these Rovers thought they had me. They were in front of me and to my sides and behind me. They hadn't seen the Muon hiding. Maybe the Muon thought they were going to take his prize. He was on them before any of them could speak. In the confusion, I ended two of them, and I saw the Muon end three in the breath it takes to say that." She was back watching the beast. "He must have stayed and feasted." She said to herself, shook her head and brought herself back. "Once the thief blocking my way was flattened by an arrow, Diye took her speed, and we were gone to leave the Muon doing his work."

"Diye is that what you call your horse?" asked Sissase. Uthiriul nodded and smiled at the sound of the horse's name. "Diye is not as good a name as Bol."

Wind

"Oh, is that the name of the oryx?" Uthiriul asked of me. "That beast is more known than even the One Who Cannot Die. There are drawings of your oryx everywhere. What an ugly beast to ride."

"I prefer my Bol over anything else," I said.

'You would. You are too taken with the past," Uthiriul said.

"No, I just like oryx over epus," I said.

"Epus—you see? No one has used that word since the Great One was naming the Seas, at least not in the Out World. They are horses and they are fast, and the ride is like taking the hanging way. Oryx are hard and slow and clumsy; it's like walking on rocks."

"Bol killed a Rover with his horns. Does Diye have horns?" Sissase screamed at Uthiriul.

Uthiriul looked at Sissase, liking the little girl more and more with each new word from her. Sissase was not born Tor'oc, but she was Tor'oc to her heart and beyond.

"You have me. Diye does not have horns, and horns are very useful," Uthiriul said with reverence to Sissase. "But Sissase, you need to learn to ride horses as well as oryx. There are simply not many oryx in this part of the Out World."

"I will find my own Bol someday when I'm big." Sissase had just pledged to travel the world to find her own beast. "But I can ride epus too."

"Good, because I won't be able to lead these Out Worlders forever; and they will need you, sometime, someday on horseback."

"And you truly mean to lead them against these other Tor'ocs?" I asked.

"You should not call them Tor'ocs. They may have once been, but they are no longer. Just as Sissase is gaining Tor'oc, they have lost it." Uthirul was angry and vengeful. "They are beasts like the Muon, who kill the unknowing."

"What happened?" I sensed something beyond my reason.

Uthiriul flashed a look at me and then away, not wanting me to see what her eyes wanted to show. She fought not to tell me, but she began. "I knew a girl, too…in J'kal. Her name was Ruiosi. She had only her mother's mother."

"Her parents had died?" Sissase asked, already taken by the other girl. Uthiriul's look to Sissase told her yes. "Like me," Sissase said, as she reached to touch my arm.

"I lived with Ruiosi and her ancient mother's mother. In those short and short days, I was more a mother to her than her own blood. Three darks before I left, my little one was gone. We found part of her, a part the Muon did not eat. I will end the Muon someday, and I will end those human beasts that call themselves

Tor'ocs. They will be wiped from the land as though they never existed."

"What was Ruiosi like?" Perhaps I should not have asked, but I wanted to see her. Uthiriul was strong as she saw her again.

"She is older than you." Uthiriul looked at Sissase. "Not much, but she has that selfsame fierceness. She has grey eyes and hair the color of white straw and skin that glows with the blood underneath it. Her smile is all smiles, and it lights a room better than any candle. She moves like a cat when she wants to. And she laughs. The best part of her is that she is simply her and her in the most way possible."

The Muon had killed her little girl, and now this Nation of Tor'ocs was going to pay for that.

Uthiriul came back to us and gazed at Sissase with more warmth than I thought was in her. "I told Ruiosi I would return and take her to the Peninsula, where she would gain Tor'oc. She wanted that, as you do. The Muon took that from her and took that from me."

"You and Aeon and I can go to the Peninsula. You can take me," Sissase said.

A tear rolled down Uthiriul's cheek, and she smiled at Sissase. "I will, ocer. You have my bond. Bent and bonded."

"Didn't you have a chance to end the Muon in the mountains?" I asked.

"I didn't. He surprised us, and by the time I could turn the oro bow, Diye had us over the ridge." Uthiriul sighed. "But I saw him one more time and nearly had him then, in the forest..."

"Where I died."

"Yes. Where you died, the Muon should have," Uthiriul was putting herself again in the Niedlemae.

"The Muon got the scent of my horse, so he knew I was on the road. He could not keep up with Diye. I was going to have to wait for him to end him. I let Diye graze in a field this side of the woods so the Muon would keep going through the trees. Then I found the spot where I would end him. The road rises to a turn where the light was just starting to come in. I could hide on his blind side there and watch him approach. I reasoned a single arrow through his heart would be what I needed.

"He came as the light was low, as I thought he might. He likes to walk in the dark. That forest is dark at the brightest hours, but my eyes had gotten used to the light that was there. I saw him. I had my bow crossed and ready with an arrow. He was my aim, and I had the Muon when a screech warned him. I shot. The arrow drove through him and out, but not where I wanted. It hit him here." She put her hand to her shoulder, just above her heart. "It tore him badly, but he lived and ran. I ran after him, but I never got another aim. Then I lost him in the dark, dark of those woods."

"What screeched?" Sissase asked, in awe of the story.

"I don't know. It came from above."

But I did know—it was one of the little man-beasts that lived in those trees screeching a warning. I would keep that from Uthiriul or she would wipe them from the world as well. They would carry the curse and the punishment for the death of Ruiosi if she knew. That was the first secret I had kept from her.

"Did they know you as a Tor'oc in J'kal?" Or did the Jannanons keep their news of the other Tor'oc in the cities from me, even when the World knew it?

Uthiriul shook her head. "No one knew, and I did not tell them. When I was asked, I said I was for the Camarod and needed to get there. The good horsemen of J'kal wondered about me, wondered where someone so unknowing of the world had come from. But they liked me enough not to wonder too much, and I liked them, better than any of these other commissions. It was their people who got me into the Camarod in that hood and cloth. They knew the horse I rode and knew the names I gave them. They gave me their trust, and I will have to talk to them after this to ask their forgiveness for my deceit.

"After J'kal, I avoided the other cities." She looked to Sissase. "I missed Lul, as I was on another road until I was past it. That is where you are from, isn't it?"

"I was once from Lul, but not now," Sissase said, perhaps not understanding well the meaning of being from somewhere.

"I nearly came to Jielada, but the Fanes met me on the road and warned me not to go. They said all the Jannanons would know I was Tor'oc. Then the entire Out World would know soon after, and I would never be allowed near Orzamond if I were known. My companions were the fees in those days on the road. They came, as they had heard of me from the wood fees. We spent the fire lights together, and I told them of the Peninsula. They told me of the World as they knew it. The ones who did not speak as we speak showed me the natural world, which I thought I knew, but saw soon that I had known very little."

Uthiriul turned and gazed at me with me with a fierce look, "The fees—and the fees are many—are bent and bonded to me in this war. I knew long before what the Camarod was about, and I have heard the stories the fees have heard from fees that saw the slaughter. The Fanes told me my haza – I'll lead an army against these killers. They told me that when I was finished, that nation would be a whisper in the wind and nothing more than ashes. They told me you would fight me."

"Fight is a strong word, though I am against you in this. We are not sure whether they are Tor'ocs or not, no matter what they've done. For me, I must see them and judge them for myself. No story or tale is going to start me to war and killing, especially against a Tor'oc army."

"Your words sound courageous and reasoned, but I hear fear in them," Uthiriul said, and jumped to the ground three Tor'ocs away. She looked up, not to me but to Sissase. "You may grow here," Uthiriul blew back to the girl. Sissase glowed. Another Tor'oc had taken her in.

Uthiriul walked away, taking steps out of her way to pass Bol and give him her hand as she walked, moving her hand across his side. Whatever she had said about oryx, she was glad to see one again. Sissase watched Uthiriul as the grown female Tor'oc disappeared into the Grand Dome.

"You want to be like her, don't you?"

Sissase snapped her head around to me. "I want to be like you!"

"But you will grow and be like her; I can see it."

"I won't—she does not like you, and you are mine."

"You are wrong. Uthiriul likes me, and she is as bent and bonded to me as I am to her. It is just her way, and she has always been that way. She is true, and she is honest, and she is fierce, like you, my lovely one."

"She will fight those other Tor'ocs, and you don't want her to."

"If they are Tor'ocs, I don't. If they are Tor'ocs, then this is a fight for others, not us."

"But why, if they are killing everybody?"

"It is our code, and the code has kept us strong and kept our peace among our own. Without it, I would not be here, and Uthiriul would not be here, and you would not be here. Our ancestors would have destroyed one another. We would have been lost to the wind. But the code is all, and the code can't be broken."

"She will break the code," said Sissase after a time of thinking about the code.

"She has told herself that she won't be breaking the code, but I am not sure she has convinced herself, though she does say it with anger and conviction." I smiled at the part Uthiriul was playing. "She has to keep telling herself that they are not Tor'ocs."

Sissase was staring at me, frowning at me. She wanted to say something, and she was not saying it.

"What is it?" I asked.

"You said you wanted to see these Tor'ocs yourself. How are you going to do that?" Sissase looked at me as fiercely as Uthiriul ever had.

"I will have to go and see them, but they will never see me."

"If you go, I go, too." Her fists were balled, ready to fight.

I smiled at her. "The way I go, no one can come with me; but you will be with me always, even when I am there."

Wind

This sounded good to Sissase, and she didn't question how that could be true.

"I am feeling strong enough to go get Pit," I said, sitting up. "How about you?"

Sissase's eyes popped. "Will they let him go?"

"He didn't end her, and she tried to end me and didn't; so, all is in balance," I said, holding my two hands up to the same height as each other.

We swung down from the tree, not jumping as Uthiriul had. We found Pit being held in a room where they put the ones they didn't know what else to do with. I reasoned with the emissary and the Gerent and, not wanting this story to continue, they let Pit go into Sissase's arms.

Once back at our Figure Tree, I cornered Pit to bond forgiveness for Chiffaa. All was in the past. He was relieved and glad to bend.

Of all the lights, this had been the longest. We were tired and took to our bed slings, with mats on the ground for Pit. I listened to Sissase's easy breaths of sleep. I heard Pit's uneasy restlessness, and I reasoned he was dreaming of the shooting of Chiffaa again and again. Fiernd held me safely in its limbs, my breaths quieted, and I prepared myself for a new journey.

Barry Alexander Brown

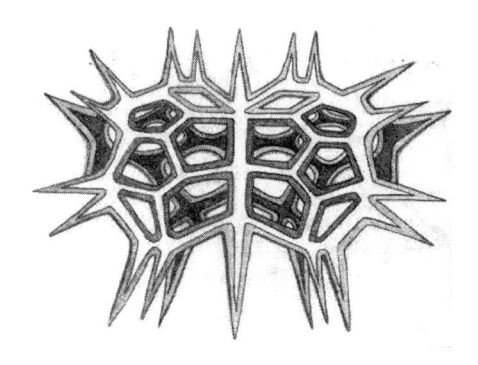

13

Where? Journey where? The Tor'ocs were in the mountains beyond Orzamond, somewhere beyond; and the mountains weren't a single thing but many and many that could hide thousands, as if they had never been there and weren't there then. A place to fly to was what I needed and wanted, a place to be drawn to, a place for my soul's eye to see. I did not have that place and could not see a way to have it. "Do not search for them," my mind whispered.

Let them find me, I thought. I would be easy to find. I let my muscles go, relaxed, fell deeper into my sling. As tired as I was, I was aware that sleep could take me too far before the journey began. I set my body against deep sleep, wished for it not to come; there was the feeling that my consciousness in twilight sleep held the gateway to the path I had to take. It would be easy to miss the gate and the path, to fall unconscious into deeper sleep.

I drifted into the twilight, the weightless, dreamless place where there is no light and no dark. The one thought I held was Tor'ocs—not my Tor'ocs, but the others.

"Pull me to you. Take me," I said over and over to the twilight place. "Find me."

Slowly, I feel the marks on my body before I can see them. I feel them push their way up through the skin of my neck and my face and head. I open my eyes just enough to look, to see my feet and legs being branded, covered with the sybils and marks of the Tor'ocs. So many they are, one on top of another, appearing and climbing up my body across my torso. They want me and they have me. I close my eyes.

In the twilight there is no time. It could be no length of time; it could be the entire dark. It seems that I am somewhere different than the Gerent's garden. I hear before I can see —a great mass, the footsteps of men and beasts, an army moving, metal hitting metal, metal hitting wood, leather brushing leather, and leather brushing skin, a thousand, thousand times in every breath. It is around me; I am in the midst of it, or rather, I am at the head of it. Then I can smell them, and then I can see them, the sight of them slowly coming to me as the dark exits to let me see the great Tor'oc Nation.

Wind

I am on horseback, and the whole head of the army is on horse. Behind us, many and many are on foot. I look about. To the person, the Tor'ocs are dressed for fighting—long swords in belts around their mids, oro bows ready on their backs, spears in hands or held by straps that could easily release the spear. Some only have swords, some only have bows or spears, and some wear all three.

The line of Tor'ocs at the head is an impressive sight of men and women who stare ahead as their horses walk. Gazing forward, they are looking for something. I turn to see what it could be. The land is familiar and different from what I thought I recognized. Before me stretches the Peninsula—I am certain of that, but we are on the Out World side, staring at it without a Divul to divide us from it. The great grassland we are walking through will no longer be there in my time. The Father Tree has not yet been grown, nor have any of the trees I first met. The land is open in this time, only grass, and the grass grows to the height of the underbelly of the horses.

The man riding beside me stops his horse, and the entire mass next to him and behind him stops. I stop. It feels as though a hand is pressing against my chest telling me, 'No further.' The man is still; his eyes are on the Peninsula. He is trying to see it; he is taking it in, weighing what is there, looking for what is waiting for his army. I look to him. He is large and strong, but there is something larger and stronger about him than his size. It is his presence; it radiates off him and surrounds him and surrounds those close to him. It surrounds me. I have to see him then in a way that would let me into the secrets that I want from him.

His face is covered in a beard, his head hair is long and hangs around and out and has an unmade look to it, but it fits him and his power. Because they are so dark, I do not notice his ears at first, though his hair does not cover them. They are ink marked. I lean a little to see them better. I see a sybil I know—it is the mark of Sumon. I turn away from him and to the others around me—all their ears are ink marked; each has their own uncommon sybil. The sybils are again marked on the upper arms of each Tor'oc. I look back at the leader who sits with his thoughts on the land before us. Then I see him as I have seen him before in the battle on the mountain top and at the grave of his son. This is Sumon, my blood.

I have been pulled to Sumon and the ancient Tor'oc Nation. I am among them, one of them, and before us is the Peninsula. There is a dip in the land in front of us; this is the place where the Divul will be someday, but now it is land that leads to the last conquest.

"Morla," Sumon says, not loud, but with enough command for anyone to hear.

A horse moves behind me and a woman of twenty rides easily to her father and leader. He hears her approach and feels her but does not turn to her. I stare in awe at the Mother of the Tor'ocs of the City in the Trees. She is young and fresh; she is not beautiful at first sight, but the strength in her is beautiful. Her ears are ink marked, too. Someday, I would see that mark in the oldest trees in our city, but the trees would grow so that those marks would become a mangled distort of her sybil.

"I see something moving in those trees and bushes— there are men," Sumon says to her. "Take ten and find out who's waiting for us."

She turns her horse and yells, "Aoerr!"

A small band of men and women rides to her; and once they arrive, she kicks her horse, and they ride with speed down the dip and into the Peninsula where they disappear in the forest. She is gone only a jif when she appears again, returning with someone thrown over the horse in front of her. Reaching us, she throws down the package, the man landing before Sumon. The rest of the ten follow close behind Morla; a few carry captives as well.

The man is not big but he is sturdy, dressed in animal skins; his hair is matted and dirty; his skin is light, though caked in dust and earth, making it appear darker. He wears no soles, and that is when I notice the soles on all the feet of the Tor'ocs around me. They are long soles tied tightly around the legs.

The man gets to his feet and stares at Sumon, who is staring back. The man says something in a language unknown to all of us.

"They were yelling to each other in those woods," Morla says to her father. "We are not going to be able to talk to these. They don't understand us; they talk a different tongue."

"They'll understand us enough," Sumon said. He gestures for the man to come to him, and the man walks forward.

Sumon leans down and touches the man at the place between the eyes. He then grabs the man by the top of the head and turns him, turning his entire body to face the Peninsula. Releasing his grip, Sumon sits back up, raises a foot away from the horse saddle and gently pushes the back of the man to make him stumble forward. Sumon moves his horse to a walk. The man understands. He is being commanded to lead the Tor'oc Nation to where his own live. The army walks, following the small line of captives. We cross the place where the Divul someday will be, crossing into the forest; and I am home again among the Bent Trees; some I recognize, though they are smaller and younger. I cannot help but blow a greeting, though they do not answer. Perhaps they are too surprised; perhaps I am only there as a soul, yet it feels as though I am riding a horse; it feels as though I have a body.

We travel through the forest and finally come to a stop at the other side, where animal skin huts are laid out in a strange order, making a village of sorts. There are open fires burning, but no one is there to be seen. Sumon jumps from his horse and lands softly on the ground—it is a graceful movement. He walks about this part of the village and then turns to one of his men on horse.

"Get the cooks," Sumon commands. "We eat here."

The cooks are not Tor'ocs, they are people captured as slaves, taken from the Out World as the army passed through it. Most of these slaves are women, but not all. They busy themselves with making use of the open fires and build new ones to cook the enormous supply of meat that is appearing from deep within the mass of the army.

Sumon sits at one of the fires, staring into it. He is joined by Morla and a few others who, I reason, are the commanders of the army. He says nothing; he is in his own thoughts. The Sumon fire is the first ready with cooked food, and he is the first to be fed. He eats thoughtlessly, his reason still elsewhere.

"There is nothing here," Sumon whispers, but they all hear. "We were lied to; they made us fools."

"What about these people?" Morla asks, gesturing to the empty village.

"Them? They are nothing; they have nothing. They are primits, barely above the beasts," Sumon said.

A Tor'oc from behind asks, "Shall we take them or end them?"

"No," Sumon said, looking at the huts near us. "Look how they live. They can't do anything for us, these are not slaves. I will not end them; I will not waste my revenge, and they have done nothing against us, not even raising a fight when we were on them. We will punish the ones who made us fools. These," and he gestured to the captives not far away, "are living in enough punishment as it is."

"What is your wish, then?" Morla asks.

"Leave. I don't want to spend even one dark here," Sumon replies. He turns to one of the men sitting close to him. "Biel, take your kin and make sure there is no attack coming from our rear. This smells like that. I cannot reason why they wanted us here except to win the advantage."

Biel rises to his feet and calls to a group at a fire not far away. "Ropin! You come with us."

Biel looks over as the boy in his mid-teens looks up—the boy whose death will be avenged a thousand years later. He is thin and long, but not full-grown and not yet old enough to have ink-marked ears. He leaves with Biel's kin to be on the other side when the river is born.

Sumon is coming to the end of his meal as he speaks to Morla. "Let us ride and see what we can of this place before we leave it."

On horse, we walk back toward the Divul that is not yet there. We walk under a canopy of trees, and our horses shy away from the center of a group of trees. I look up. It is the falling place. I can see the spot where Lijkose will fall, where I will fall, but in this time the falling place is much lower. I look back at the gathering of the Tor'oc Nation; she must be there somewhere, a younger, smaller Lijkose.

The place our horses avoid is soft ground. Those beasts feel it there, feel that they would sink into it and have trouble getting out of it. The horses may not be as smart as oryx, but they have instinct.

We ride on, and I see the last tree I will climb someday in the Peninsula. It is strong and young and is not the last tree in the forest; the ones beyond it would be gone soon and soon. Oddly enough, Sumon turns his horse at that tree to head back to other parts of the Peninsula--and just as he does, the ground shatters at our feet. The earth cracks, falls, and blows dust and dirt into the air as our horses run.

Sumon pulls his frightened horse to a stop and turns to see the newly made canyon where water is already swirling in. It is the fierce water from both seas that does not meet in friendship now but in hate and rivalry, fighting and losing and winning and giving violent birth to the Divul. Sumon stares in awe, surprise, and anger. He sees that the Out World has been cut from him, that the canyon is too deep and the water too wild to cross.

"Aoerr!" Sumon yells and rides full speed away from the new river. We all follow. He yells back to Morla, "We have to find a way out."

We ride along the edge of the O'bir Sea, arpent after arpent, until we reach the point of the Peninsula, the high ground that gives a view of the land now imprisoning us. Here, Sumon stops and takes stock of the land and sea around us. There is no escape except by boyt, which the native tribe does not seem to have and which the Tor'ocs could not carve.

A movement not far off catches his sense, and Sumon is off his horse, running toward the bushes where he spots something. Out of the bush runs a man exactly like the first captive; and I would have thought he was the same but the other is arpents and arpents away. Without losing speed, Sumon draws his sword and swings it high above him. The new man screams at the sight of the blade and stumbles. Sumon is on him. He hacks the man, cutting his head, his arms, his torso, slicing him into pieces.

Afterward, Sumon turns to us, the blood of his victim dripping off his sword. "I was wrong about these primits. They are sorcerers. They mean to trap us here, but they are the ones who will be trapped. Hunt them and end them; leave them all like this." His sword sways in the direction of the pieces of head, torso, arms, and legs that once were human. "Before this dark, I do not want to find one of them breathing."

I want to tell him that he was right at first about the natives; and killing them would be like killing himself. They were primits, not conjurors. I reason the Four Mothers counted on that. Extermination of the Tor'oc Nation was the goal, and theirs was a classic three-stage attack—cut the enemy off, deny them food and shelter, and then finish them with an overwhelming assault for which the enemy had no defense. The Tor'ocs were playing their parts as the Mothers reasoned they would. The native tribe would have supplied the food, known where to find the fresh water, hunt the small animals, build the fires, and erect the shelters. But these people would be murdered to the last, and my people would suffer in a deep way unknown to them.

In that jiff of a realization, time becomes formless; and I witness the time that I follow as I would the current in a river. I see the time after the slaughter of the primits. The days grow smaller, and the Tor'ocs grow weaker; but some of my people are beginning to change, learning to forage for plants that can be eaten, trapping and killing small animals, constructing the barest refuges from the cold and rain.

On a blue-sky morning, the sun warmer than in many lights, two storms begin to rage in the seas to the north and south. The storms rise out of the seas themselves, sucking seawater into gigantic swirling cyclones that become larger and larger as they converge, moving slowly toward land in one monstrous killing force: the Mad'la. This is not just from what I see, but from my own experience, as this same storm rages and floods us every year. I have seen it all my life. It is not a thing of nature. A conjured craft creates it, and it is a craft that drives it. Now on this bright blue morning, I see the craft begin its work.

A wall of water two Tor'ocs high rushes across the land, a crazed living thing that takes anything and everything not rooted firmly in the ground. As in my time, the flood is quick and vicious and clever. As it reaches the Divul, it turns back onto the Tor'ocs who survived the first assault. Returning, it is smaller, more cunning, and ruthless, as it uses the broken ground and trees and plants inside itself to grab the water-tossed, nearly drowning Tor'ocs, and carry them back to the sea from which it came. Most die by the time they reach the shores. The others soon die in the deep.

As the waters swirl around me, I look to the trees – "Save us," I blow in wind. The large tree beside me turns its leaves to gaze down.

"You are of us?" The tree blows back.

"I am," I call back. I stare into the limbs and see the City in the Trees and blow the image. For three breaths, the City in the Trees is before me and above me – I see my kollokk among many others; I see the hanging ways, and the large, round community kollokks – I see the center of our lives. I am back in my home, and someone is beside me, also gazing up – Morla, her eyes are wide, and wonder fills them. She sees what I see, and it freezes her as though she were made of stone – even the rushing water is forced around this stone creature. She does not breathe and then she sucks in the vision of the City in the Trees in one deep breath.

"Take to the trees," I whisper to her. She looks to see me, but there is only water and air where she looks – I am there and not there. When we both look back up, the City in the Trees is gone.

Wind

Morla grabs a boy being swept past her. "Take to the trees," she cries out to all the bodies in the water. She takes the boy and pushes him onto the lowest limb of the nearest tree, grabbing that limb to pull herself free of the torrent. She turns back to the water just below and grabs a girl, then screams again, "Take to the trees!"

In this way, the arms and hands of the yet living Tor'ocs learn to grab for the low limbs to save themselves. The water rushes and rushes, and the trees fill with Tor'ocs until the water is gone.

I am in the high trees with Morla beside me. The land below us is clean new earth. There are no bodies and no horses and no shelters and no food and no fires or remnants of where fires once burned. There is nothing left of the Tor'ocs below. Morla looks to the trees and branches that surround us. She calls out and waits for the others to call back, and they do. Slowly, small bodies make their way along limbs and branches to us—children, they are all children. They are all that is left of the Great Tor'oc Nation—two hundred frightened and weary children.

We are in the branches of six bent trees so large and tightly intertwined that they form a balcony large enough that the children can sit and rest. A wall of vines falls around this place on three sides, creating natural shelters in nooks and crannies along the edges of the balcony. Morla is the Mother and the Savior; a young, resilient, headstrong, fair, intuitive leader who has a natural affinity for the trees.

"You can talk to them." I use the wind to speak into her ear. She touches her ear in surprise.

"How?" she asks.

I put my hand on a large branch and ask the tree to speak to her. He blows her the welcome, "We are here as you are." And then many and many trees together blow, "Set your roots – you may grow here."

She hears something but she cannot understand. It takes her the rest of her life and the lives of three more generations—daughter, granddaughter, and great granddaughter—to fully hear what they are saying. We take this for granted in my time; only a fool can't hear and understand the language of the trees.

I cross the balcony to the place where we fall, where we celebrate Lijkose Iant An Acu, where I am named 'the Leaf'. I look down; it is not so high a fall as later when I have one-hundred-and-one moons, perhaps because I was smaller, or perhaps because the trees will grow much and much in a thousand years; perhaps it's both. I have the urge to fall as I look down and wonder if I could. I lean, let myself lean further and fall. Unlike during Lijkose Iant An Acu, now I have no fear and enjoy the fall. It is slow, and I see the trees see me as I fall. I blow to them, and they gasp. The light of colors that I see when I hit the soft ground is around me as I fall; it encircles me, holds me, and pierces me with its warmth and knowledge. We normally cannot see it when we fall, but this is happening; this is what changes us. The last light is blue and red and black—black is the

Wind

color of the light, or maybe a very, very dark blue. I hit the ground, and it is not the ground I expect. It is hard—I feel it in my soul state, but it does not hurt me.

I look about from my place on the ground. I am not on the Peninsula. I am in a colder, harsher place, a rock-bound place where the earth is as unforgiving as the Sand Keeper's road. I stand up. I can see far and far; I am in a place that is high above most of the land.

I am in the mountains on flat land at the top of one of the peaks; a little more of the mountain rises above me; the flat land runs a circle around the end that juts to a sharp final point. There are large and large boulders, a field of them in this high place. At first, I do not see, but then I am struck with the knowledge that the rocks next to me are not just rocks. They are large, large carved-rock sculptures. There are carved heads an arm's length bigger than I am. One rock forms a bird's head; the next is a man with a beard; the third is a woman—a warrior. The head of the man and woman have marks on their ears. They resemble Tor'oc faces. There is a fourth rock farther away that is half rock and half face.

Sounds rise from below me. People—many and many—are walking my way and singing. It is a joyous song, but not loud and not fast, a quiet, joyous song coming from the voices of a great, great many. I don't want to be seen by these strangers, but I reason that since I was not able to be seen by Sumon or Morla--though perhaps visible to Biel--then I won't be seen here. I climb on a rock head to be higher, to see everything, to watch and wait.

The first group appears up a path as wide as four Tor'ocs' high. They are body to body, and they fill the entire width of the path. Behind them are more and more, tightly walking together, singing and swaying to their songs, taking their steps as one. There is not a breath of space between one person and another. They are one thing made of many.

One top of this moving, walking, swaying mass, someone is crawling on hands and knees using the bodies below as a floor. As they get close to the rock head where I sit, I see that the crawler is a man, a naked young man who has probably just reached his growth. The light is low in the sky, and I think the warm end of light has lit him to make it appear that his ears are red and bleeding; but he is too far away to know if it is the light or real blood. There are other naked crawlers further down the mass, some are women, some are men—perhaps two handfuls of them, ten in all.

The mass is almost reaching the rock I am on, the closest sculpture to them, the head of the warrior woman. They get only a few steps away from my rock, and the first line of walkers falls. Behind them, others rush forward to fall on top of the first ones. Now more move forward fast, falling onto the ones already prone. They are landing and lying on one another, making a bridge, sloping from the ground to the top of the head where I am. They continue singing; the song is shaking the rock, and I feel it up through my soul. The sloping

Wind

bridge of people has reached the height of my rock—I could touch the hands of the very top people. Their fingers grip the rock.

In the next moment, rays from the last light of day hit a glass object that I had not seen. The glass is half the size of my head and cut into sharp angles. It sits on a smaller rock at the edge of where we are, the edge that is closest to the dying light. We are all illuminated by its reflected brightness that splits into rainbow lines of color— a blinding, glowing array of color.

Just as the light brightens, the first crawler springs to his feet and dashes toward us, running over prone bodies that compress to help the runner to find a footing. The bodies push the runner forward with small jerks and undulations. He picks up speed and hits the bodies of the slope, running fast enough to nearly throw him onto the top, his feet touching next to me, his body a blur, his speed never slowing. He runs over the first of the stone heads in two steps and runs off. I am not watching the people below as they surround the rocks, but there are bodies and bodies between the heads, making a surface to run by holding their arms up, the hands flat. The runner runs off the first head, across the hands which are strong and hold fast. He lands on the second head and across that one, running over more hands, finally jumping onto the last head, never slowing. There are no more hands or people beyond that head. Instead of stopping—which I think his speed would make difficult—his foot catches the rock, and he spins. He spins fast on the top of the head, his hands and arms flying out at his sides. I am so taken by the sight that the next runner—a woman—blurs past, surprising me. She runs along the hands, across the next head, over hands again, and hits the spinner in full speed, grabbing him and laughing, joining the spin with her body and arms, and causing the spin to go faster.

I turn back to the mass and see that the other crawlers have all become runners, all running toward my rock, each hitting the human slope and running up and across and dashing through the color lines of light, smashing into the spinners, joining them, spinning, laughing; and the spin group grows larger one person at a moment, the spin not slowing but gaining speed. The song changes with each new spinner; it is quicker and louder, and I hear names inside the song. I want to join the song; I want to be a runner; I want to be among the hands below the runner. I want to hit the spinners at my full speed to melt into them, be one in them, and spin. I want all of it.

I see the last of the runners coming and I jump to my feet. As her foot hits my rock, I step with her, running across the hands that I push to feel, running across the second head and onto the waiting mass of hands. I can feel the hands pushing me upwards, warmth and power coming through them. The song is in the hands, and I hear my name—they are chanting me; they feel me as I feel them. We are at the farthest rock, and the bodies spinning have thrown the legs of the outward spinners into the air. The runner next to me hits the mass a breath before I do. She clings to them,

Wind

and I cling, grabbing and holding, and magically a place opens just for us within the spin. The spinners are not spinning to me now—the world is spinning and can't be seen in the spin; it is all light beyond us, colors and colors of light. I look from face to face in our group; their ears are red and bleeding, and beneath the blood are black lines—their ears marked with their own sybils. I envy their marked ears. We are laughing in the joy of the spin; and our kinship and joy light us from somewhere deep within and without.

The colors outside of us are dimming and in a single jiff are gone. Our spin loses its speed and, as though responding to a single command, we let go of one another; and the spin flings us off the last head, the head of the bird. The spinners are caught by the waiting arms of the mass, arms that held them before, held them when they crawled and held them when they ran. As I move, I am only a soul; no one has to catch me.

Now a disturbing thought invades my trance—I recall that deep in the Seap, the shadows were spinners too. Does a line connect this spinning and theirs? The spinning in the Seap was slow and troubled; it was the spin for those lost forever. These mountain spinners are not lost; they are spinning into life, bound to one another, spinning into belonging.

Little light is left in the sky. The dark is creeping back, but new light flickers on as torches are lit, not many and many, just enough for each of the spinners to take. The torches are pushed into hands that are waiting to take them. The mass is bathed in the torchlight, and the spinners sit down on cloths of black and red waiting for them. The people around them put the cloths on the spinners as they move the torch from one hand to another. They put their arms through the new watchets and their legs step into new sit-upons, as their feet are covered with new soles. Every cloth is red and black, shimmering in the fire light that at moments bathes the people in a fiery red—black flashes to red and back to black again.

The spinners meet again at the glass sculpture that split the last light of day into colors. They circle the glass, which is grabbing the firelight and twisting it into a pure white light that glows around the spinners. I see that the black of their cloths is actually dark, dark blue, just as Yeoal said. A single male voice sings out behind and above us. On the peak of the mountain, not far above us, stands a man ringed in light that swirls around him from the ground. He sings a song also handed down to us on the Peninsula, an ancient song with ancient words that I do not understand. It is the Song of Beginning. We sing it at births; we sing it alone when we feel change; we sing it the day of union when two people join. There is something sad in the song because forever something ends as something begins.

As the last words of the song ring out above us, the whole mass of people moves with the spinners, leading all down to what must be their camp below. A new song rises from them, easier, more joyful—I want to call it the Song of Life; it feels like life, their life, their new life as full Tor'ocs sybiled and marked. The feel of

Wind

the mass has changed from the moment I first saw them—they were in ceremony then; now they are in life. They move freely to the new song, their bodies laughing with their dance.

The camp is not far but it is in darkness. I can see silhouettes of tents; there are unseen fires ready to be lit throughout the city. As soon as these fires burst into flames, the tents seem to sway as the people come near them. The tents are smooth, light brown animal skins marked in careful designs made of the inked marks of the people who possess them.

The tents are laid in circles that grow larger as they form farther from the center. This is surely for defense. An enemy could attack only from a direction or two, but the dwellers could defend and counter an attack from many directions. And if an enemy found themselves in the mid of the camp, the tent inhabitants could strike from every direction.

Now in the mid of the camp, all stop. We are in the mid of flames that mark the edge of a giant circle. In the mid of the mid, two people stand—nearly identical looking people, but one is male, the other female, older than I am, but not a generation older.

"Ah Bieyah...Ah Bieyah," the two yell out to the mass, who begin to quiet themselves to hear them speak.

I bend down to a girl near me—she is so close in her look that she could be Sissase's sister. I hope that she is as open. I lean in close and ask, "Who are they?"

She moves to look in my direction; she hears me but cannot see me.

"Tell me—I don't know them. Who are they?" I ask again.

She is careful about answering, and copying my talking low, she whispers back with a tone that says that I should know this already.

"Bansid and A'kasja."

"Who are they?" I ask one more time.

"They are the Vonders of the Nor," she replies, and looks hard to see me. "Where are you? Aren't you a Nor?"

"I'm a Tor'oc," I tell her.

"Me too," she says, as if that were known. "I'm a Nor Tor'oc. You're not? You're a lurer. Where are you?"

"And does Vonder mean 'leader'?" I ask. She looks as though she has never heard the word before, and maybe she hasn't. "Also tell me further, are Bansid and A'kasja of the same mother and the same day?"

"Yes, don't you know that?" She says this louder than she had said anything else. People look to her and look to the empty space she is staring into.

The entire mass quiets, which takes my attention away from the girl. I look up and to the mid, where the twin brother and sister are staring at me from the far place where they stand. It is clear that no one else has seen my soul; perhaps they are staring like the others, at

Wind

the empty space, but it doesn't feel that way. The sister, whom I reasoned was A'kasja, turns to her brother and twists her head just a notch. It is enough for him to turn away and look to the spinners who have grouped themselves nearby.

"Oedju," he says to the group, and looks fondly at them. "There is only one night that you are an Oedju, and Sumon has chosen you as special, for this is a chosen night. You are spinning on the best of the darks—the dark of the Blood Moon. It is the moon of endings and beginnings. You are Blood Moon Oedju, and your haza is to be Vonders in the land of Aemira. You will take cities; you will take their armies and make them yours; you will take their good lands and their lakes; and in time one of you will be Vonder of Aemira. This is your haza; this is our haza. This is the foretold—one of those who has spun this Blood Moon will hold the greatest power yet seen in this world. Then they will know the Nor and will remember the Tor'ocs. We will rule justly as Sumon had and as the others had before him. We will bring knowledge to Aemira. We will bring the light. We will forgive them their crimes against us and the generations long before us."

The mass moans together in happiness at the words.

A'kasja leans into the brother and says something to him. He looks up at the far reaches of the mass, slows his look as his eyes cross mine. He nods ever so slightly to his sister. She steps to where he had been standing.

"This is a special Blood Moon, more so than any other," she begins. "We have someone among us. He is not of body, but he is of our blood. He is our brother, long lost."

There is an uneasiness in the mass; they cannot follow her meaning.

"I have tried to gain his name, but I have not. He is the Spere; that is all I know of him," she says, looking across the mass.

That's it. They were chanting 'Spere' for the breathes that I was running, and I heard it as my name.

"He is among you now, but do not look for him; you will not see him," she says. "He does not want to be seen and he has the power not to be. We welcome you, Spere. We welcome and want you among us. You are not here by chance on this Blood Moon, on this Moon of the Oedju. Sumon has sent you to us on this night of beginning. You must feel that you are a part of this, a part of the new light."

"I spoke to him," the Sissase sister calls out.

"Who said this?" A'kasja yells back. "Bring her to me."

Hands grab her and lift her, passing the girl from one body to another until she is placed in front of the twin. A'kasja looks down to the girl.

"You said you spoke to him?" A'kasja asks, and the little girl nods. "How do you know it was the Spere?"

Wind

"Because I heard him but could not see him," the girl replies.

"And what did he say to you?"

"He said he was a Tor'oc," the girl says, and the people purr. "He wanted to know about you, and he didn't know about us Nor Tor'ocs."

Bansid, appearing next to his sister, smiles. "No, he would not know about the Nor." He looks up in my direction and holds his arms up in a gesture of welcome. "Spere! You hide from us, but there is no reason in that. We are blood. We do not judge why you hesitate; we accept you have reason for this. When you are ready...brother, come to us."

Over the peak of the mountain, behind the brother and sister, a large white moon is rising, lighting us with its brightness, even bright enough to cast sharp shadows and dim the effect of the fire around us. We all look to it. Then the light falls on the clouds that are blowing in, clouds that cover the moon. The mass groans at this.

"No, no!" Bansid cries out, holding hands up and smiling. "The clouds are trying to fool you, as they want to do on these nights, but we know the moon and the prankster clouds. The moon will blow them away as it always does, but maybe not until it begins to bleed, and that will not be for many counts." Bansid looks out and across, taking in everyone. "Who will tell the story of the first Oedju?" Many answer, but he chooses one of the spinners, a young woman with dark red hair. I have never seen a Tor'oc with hair like that. Maybe Nor Tor'ocs aren't pure; maybe it is not her true color. When she arrives next to Bansid, who lays both his hands on her shoulders and bows his head, she bows back. He lets go as he turns her toward the mass. Some cry out her name. 'Erema' is what it sounds to me. She smiles back at them.

"This is a blessed place," she begins, and the mass agrees. "We are in the mountains of the first Oedju. We know this is not the true place, for no one knows that place, the place where Dia spun herself to Oedju. Dia, the one pledged to join Ropin before he was lost. Dia, whose blood runs in many of us. Dia, who mourned Ropin but could not mourn for three lights and darks. As we know, they were running away from an army that had attacked them and would end them if they were found.

"It was on the third dark that she tells her elders that she wants to be marked with a sybil given to her by Ropin. They tell her she is yet too young; she must wait another twelve cycles of the moon. She tells them, "I may not be with you in twelve moons. We may all be with Ropin then. I do not want to die unmarked." They are moved and understand the reason and agree. She is marked that night, and once the marking is finished, her mourning for Ropin takes her. She runs up a mountain to a place of large and large rocks. She runs up one of the rocks that is many heights higher than her; she runs across the rock and runs to the next rock and the next, though there is only air between the rocks.

Wind

"She runs until she comes to a rock where there are no rocks beyond, and those who see her see her spin while holding something, but none could see what she is holding. She laughs. Whatever holds her lets her go, and she is flung from the rock, and the people catch her. They ask, "How did you run between the rocks?" and she answers, "I ran on the hands of the Tor'ocs who have died in battle.' They ask, "How did you spin, what were you holding?" She tells them, "Ropin was waiting for me at the last rock, as he waits for us even now." She tells them, "He spun me, and in the spin; he told me that I was Oedju now like him—he an Oedju in death, me an Oedju in life." They do not know what an Oedju is, and she tells them, "A new person—a person remade."

"We spin to become Oedju, to be remade," she says, bows her head, and takes steps back.

Someone makes a sound, a noise that takes our attention back to the moon. The lower part of the moon disappears into black, and the black is growing, taking more and more of the moon. Inside the black, which could not be seen at first, is copper red. As the black grows, the red also grows; so, as the moon grows darker, it becomes redder. It is bleeding. The moon is ending and beginning.

I feel a tugging of my soul being pulled away from the moon. I know it. I am being drawn back to my body. My body is pulling me; it wants me; it wants to wake. It wants to wake Sissase; she should see this to witness this vision of the Oedju ceremony of long before; but I do not want to leave. I do not want to be gone when the moon is full of blood.

In a flick, I was in the tree, in my body, Sissase asleep close to me. I moved to the girl and touched her. I looked to the sky, and there the moon was still getting darker, still bloodier. I took Sissase out of her sling and she stirred. I held her, and she felt me, and she slowly came to wake.

Whispering to her, I said, "The moon is bleeding. You must see."

Her eyes opened for a jiff and closed again. "The moon is bleeding?" she said.

"It is the blood moon—the ending and the beginning. You should see it," I said quietly to her.

She opened her eyes and looked into mine. She knew this was important and that she had to try to wake. She took a long breath and held it and then looked into the sky to see the moon that had become completely red.

"Is it really bleeding?" she asked.

"I don't think so," I said. "I think it is the ending that turns it red; the beginning will bring it back to the light."

"What is it? What is ending?" she asked.

"That is different for everyone," I told her. "For us, the path I have taken you on is ending."

"What is beginning, then?"

Wind

"We are beginning," I said, and did not know the meaning of my own words.

"Did you go somewhere?" she asked, remembering what I had told her earlier.

"I did," I answered, not wanting to tell her more.

"What did you see?"

"Family," I said simply, and I looked to her so that she would look at me and hear my words. "We belong someplace, and it is not here."

"Are we going to go, then?"

"We will go, or they will come to us," I said. "This is our haza."

"If you go, I will go," Sissase said, and fell against me.

We may have had a place in the Out World, but not a fruitful and happy one while Tor'ocs were thought to be monsters, the enemy, evil things to be imprisoned and shunned. The Out World was not ours. Sissase was Tor'oc as I was Tor'oc, and there were Tor'ocs wanting and waiting for us.

Finally, I knew why I had been brought from the City in the Trees, and it was not why the Out World reasoned they had brought me. I had been brought to be a Tor'oc among Tor'ocs. That was what I would be.

Barry Alexander Brown

REFERENCES

Barry Alexander Brown

THE AUTHOR

Barry Alexander Brown

I wrote a lot of the novel WIND while on location in Uganda working on the film, *Queen of Katwe* for Mira Nair and Disney. I would rise early, drink coffee on my hotel room terrace at the edge of Lake Victoria and write a few pages every day. I was compelled to write. This story was coming to me like a thing demanding to be born. I'm a filmmaker and I love the process of making movies. In writing WIND, I discovered that I loved the creation of a novel even more. It was an adventure for me to dive into this unknown world – it always took me somewhere and it was nearly always a pleasure. Many times, it felt as if the story was writing itself, and I was the bystander who had been chosen to put it to paper.

To me, the Peninsula, where the Tor'ocs have been imprisoned for a thousand years, and the world of Aemira, are real. I can visit these places, hear the people talk, watch them move and interact. I'm there with them in all the surprising cities and landscapes. The details of this world are vivid because I experience them. Like Aeon the Leaf, I was not in control of where this story took me. Halfway through the book, a four-year-old orphan girl kicks her way into the story. Her name is Sissase. She falls in love with Aeon and adopts him as her father. When it comes time for him to depart from the city in which she lives, she demands to be taken with him. Both of us – Aeon and myself – were shocked at the demand. "Under no circumstance can she come," we both said. We were both frightened and unnerved by the demand. But finally, leaving her was harder than taking her with us. So, she came. To my surprise and my wonder, Sissase became the linchpin of this story called WIND. I cannot imagine the book without her – in fact, it cannot be told without her. And yet she was not a part of this story until the page where she wandered down the street and into the book. That's the sort of thing that's impossible with making a feature film. No orphan girls show up and kick their way into a movie.

During the writing of this book, my wife Verane was very ill. To recuperate, we rented a house in Scottsdale, Arizona for her. As I said, I was away in Uganda working with Mira Nair. As I finished a chapter, I would email it to her – it was a way of giving her gifts during her long recovery. I was inspired to keep writing to keep sending her the chapters which she ate up and loved. In this last year, Verane has translated this book into French with her sister Ariane. They were incredibly dedicated to deliver the spirit and unique voice of this novel. What I witnessed was a work of love and dedication. I have heard over and over how gorgeous the writing is in French. Verane continues to work to get the word out about this book.

Wind

The other person I have to acknowledge is Kent Rush. She is an instrumental part of this book. First, she was the editor. I did not want anyone else to edit the book. She did an amazing job of cleaning up the writing while finding a way to make the sometimes awkwardness of the voice of Aeon the Leaf pleasant and readable. That was only the beginning. When I wanted a map of Aemira, it was Kent who created the map – in English and in French. I also wanted the Tor'oc alphabet to become a real thing – a complete alphabet. Kent looked at the history of alphabets. She then created a Tor'oc alphabet based on that history, an alphabet that made sense if a people were cut from the world and had never had the written word for themselves. I had not thought about needing numbers but she created that, too. The two together made it complete and it felt so much like the Tor'ocs I had come to know. The two of us came up with the idea of creating a scarf that was based on the map. She took it much further – she designed a beautiful scarf using the map, the alphabet, the numbers and a new element that took images from the story and placed them on a field of blue that made up most of the body of the scarf. Even as I write this, she continues to add more and more to the world of Wind. I feel so blessed to have both of these women as collaborators on this novel.

I'm in the midst of finishing the second volume of the trilogy. I feared that it would become like many second books of a trilogy – just a bridge to get us from Vol. I to Vol. III. But THE UN-WINDING has been just as much a delight and mystery unfolding as WIND. I am amazed how much it has its own personality and worth. I'm still not completely certain how the last few chapters of this new book are going to go. The process remains exciting to me, including sharing these worlds with you.

Welcome.

WIND GLOSSARY

A.

Acu – ancient word for the moon
Aemira – name of the Out World
Aeon the Leaf – last descendent of Sumon, Morla, her daughters, & grand-daughters
Aerema – red-haired Tor'oc who tells stories of the first Oedju
Ah Bieyah – ancient Tor'oc greeting meaning, "My People"
Aim – target
Antelopes – oryx, Anilless, Jiooiun
Aper – giant boar
Ardrum Keililosji – traveling trader who has visited Aemira & beyond
Arpent – measure of land much like an acre
As'ash – general term for money
Axiled – cornered, checkmated in a game

B.

Bale of arrows – case for carrying arrows over the shoulder

Bansid & A'kasja – twin brother and sister, leaders of the Nor Tor'oc
Batana – blow gun
Bed sling – hammock
Beedle – light implement Somans invented; tiny blue ball that can bounce & hang in the air emitting warm light
Bent & Bonded – pledged to someone by verbal contract
Blood Moon – rare red eclipse phase, time for initiation ceremonies
Bol – Aeon's tamed oryx

C.

Camarod of Susceptible Nations – special meeting of all people of Aemira
Capitalization – Capitalize city & tribe names, not species or item names.
Cassion - wagon
Chiffaa – consul from Soos, sent to shoot Aeon
City of Trees – name Tor'ocs call their village of treehouses
Consuls – elected leaders
Counts – way of marking time

D.

Dair Tree – tree very similar to modern Oak tree

Wind
Damnation Legends – folk tales of the banishment of Tor'ocs & Muons
Dark – a night
Dat – money
Dew Light – morning
Dia – the love of Ropin
Diye – Uthiriul's horse
Divul – river created by Four Mothers to keep Tor'ocs on Peninsula

E.

Ecus – horses
Epus – beasts for riding
Eeunes – corps of armed guardians in Aemira

F.

Fanes – Jannanon holy triad, men who guard & decipher omens in Jielada
Fastholds – castles
Fee – magical creature made of material from where it lives, able to move freely through its material
Fentesimal – exclamation of surprise & extremity
Fiernd – name of Figure Tree in Gerent's garden
Figure Tree – fig tree
Finnif knife – two bladed, S-shaped knife the Tor'ocs invented
Fire bush – plant that can withstand fire

Barry Alexander Brown

Fire-lights – nightly gathering around camp fires
Four Mothers -

G.

Gerent – leader of Aemira
Goyel – one of Aeon's close Jannanon companions across Aemira
Great Rod – giant intelligent bird; keeps distant from man but enjoys company of The Mothers
Gruens – round, flat, legless relative of snakes; makes a night song noise

H.

Hanging Way – living bridge made from growing vines in trees
Hasmapludi III, Gerent of the Middle & High Bosagsin – Aemira's leader, usually called Gerent
Haza – destiny
Heiudsom – ancient mountainous city

I.

Iven – old tree on the Penninsula struck by lightning long ago - Tor'ocs stand on its roots to make their desires come true.
Iz – name of water fee sprite that calls Aeon to Out World

J.

Jannanons – small Aemira people, from Jielada, can blend & disappear into their environment
Jieiwe – mystic of the city of Lul, created invisible city wall
Jielada – city of the Jannanons
Jiff – a moment in time
Jka'l – name of city where Uthiriul learned to ride horses
Junjun – herbal bush with leaves with healing properties

K.

Keoen Fam – dignitaries who held all ceremonies
Kirks – temples where the Fanes of Jielada live
Kollokk – habitats for living that Tor'ocs grow in trees

L.

Lake Lier – lake where Soos village floats
Last Man Run – a race held in war games that Tor'ocs created on the Peninsula
Legends – folk tales of the banishment of Tor'ocs & Muons
Light pearls – Aemira creatures; soft, spinning balls; can clean better than soap & water
Lijkose Iant An Acu – Tor'oc ceremony for night of a child's 144th full moon, in which they fall far down through a special opening in trees
Limp – limb

Liuf – one who carries out the physical feats
Lul – city of Aemira, walled a thousand years ago by their mystic, Jiewe
Lurer – conjuror, wizard
Lurm as'ash – type of money

M.

Mad'la – a yearly tsunami-like flood originally created by the four Mothers that keeps the waters across the Peninsula so high that the Tor'ocs are stranded and have to live in trees
Marks – tattoos, symbols each ancient Tor'oc chooses from images in nature
Mondane, or Credo Trees – its nut is used to build & repair roads in Aemira.
Morla – mother of Tor'ocs on the Peninsula who survived first flood & took others into to trees to survive future floods; founder of Tor'ocs' skill, tradition, & way of life since the end of their warring ways
The Mothers –
  Diluhao – who spoke to the people for The Four
  Keoen Fam – who held all ceremonies
  Viem Hels – who performed all rituals
  Liuf – who carried out the physical feats
  Soaad – fifth mother, unknown by the people, Aeon's spiritual mother
Muon – a devolved man-beast that hunts & eats other men

N.

Niedlmae – dark, thick forest on the outskirts of Orzamond
The Nom – Peninsula Tor'oc alphabet made of 32 characters
Nor Tor'oc – Tor'ocs from the other side of the world

O.

O'bir – Morla's grand-daughter
O'bir Sea – southern sea, Sea of Hidden Death
Observer's Eye – The Eye; ability to see the future or other places
Ocalo – town square of Heiudsom city
Ocer – slang for good children on the Peninsula
Oedju – a Nor Tor'oc who comes of age in their Moon Ceremony
Okjolik – O'bir's daughter; finished the understanding of wind language; gave Tor'ocs the written word; invented the hanging way
The One Who Cannot Die – ancient Orzamondi language name for Aeon
Orl'isjud – Morla's daughter
Oro bow – double-arch, X-hinged bow with power of two bows
Oryx – type of antelope
Orza – giant sea tortoise
Orzamond – capital city of Aemira
Out World – what Tor'ocs call Aemira

P.

Pallurino – breed of horse that Chiffaa rides
Pendle – blow gun dart dipped in poison from curare bush
Peninsula – Tor'oc's ancestral island homeland
Pleiseu Ravine – canyon in the mountains
Po – unit of money
Primits – primitive people
Prioress – young Jannanon woman with religious training who serves Fanes

Q.

Quatre Meres – the four spiritual guardians of Aemira

R.

Rassat – mystical rite Jielada's Fanes conduct to learn future through complex present
Red Robes – semi-religious order of guards in Orzamond
River Divul – a water boundary of Tor'oc lands
River Irienik – river that runs up mountain where Orzamond is built
Ropin – sixteen-year-old Tor'oc whose death the Nor Tor'oc nation pledge to avenge
Round ribbon – game like chase in which one player corners another

Rovers – thieves living in mountains between Lul & city of the Jannanons
Ruiosi – boy Uthiriul falls in love with in Jka'l
Rule – passageway
Ryt – a money coin

S.

Sand Keeper – man or woman charged with repairing roads
Seap – dungeons where shadow creatures live deep under Foul Lands
Settled & set – having promised to fulfil a pledge
Sheios – elder Jannanon who helps Aeon cross Aemira
Sit upons – pants
Soaad – Aeon's spiritual mother, fifth mother, unknown by most people
Sodals – trade guilds in city of Lul
Soles – shoes
Somans – people of Heiudsom
Soos – floating city
Spere – nickname Nor Tor'ocs call Aeon
Spillets – tiny creatures living in moss that absorb other beings' energy & give off light
Sumon – ancient Tor'oc war chief, father of Morla, grandfather of Aeon
Sweet root – plant oryx really like to eat
Sybils – marks & tattoos of ancient Tor'ocs, designs with meaning

T.

Tallum – woven grass panel
Tied – large passageway in city of Lul
Treo and Ae – Yeoal's sister; the war cry of Uthiriul
Tor'oc - tribal name for Aeon's people
Trow – a thing very close or small, measure unit for small distances
<u>Tree Greetings & Sayings:</u>
– *I look to the days and darks and am glad to be among you. May we grow strong together.*
– *I am here as you are.*
– *In all my rings…*
– *May I grow here?*
– *We know you and you may grow here.*
– *You are the one with the wind to his back.*

U.

Uthiriul – Aeon's childhood friend from Peninsula
Umbrare – banished eternal shadow beings
Ungratefuls – the Mothers' name for Tor'ocs

V.

Viem Hels – who performed all of the rituals
Vonder – leaders in the Nor Tor'ocs nation
Vum – name for tortoise on the Peninsula

W.

War Chief - Tor'oc military leader
Watchet – shirt
Weepers – type of tree, similar to a willow
Weoduye – purple-eyed, youngest of three Jannanons with Aeon crossing Aemira
Worthiness (Your) – common title of Gerent of Aemira

X.

X-shaped bow – special Tor'oc weapon

Y.

Yeoal – lone boy survivor of Heiudsom

Z.

Barry Alexander Brown

Writing in the WINDREAD ALPHABET

WINDREAD: The written form of the Tor'oc people's language was originally created eleven thousand years ago by O'jolique, great granddaughter of Morla, and found in the form of messages carved onto trees in the ancient land of Aemira. The WINDREAD alphabet, or Elementa, is a complete system, & several simple guidelines make it fully functional for writing:

29 letters: WINDREAD has the same 26 letters listed in the same sequence as in standard A-to-Z Latin alphabets, plus the three combo-letters of double-o, th, gh.

Capitals: All letters are the same height; there are no capitals.

Punctuation & spacing: A double dash -- functions as a period. A single dash - functions as a comma. A question mark is a dot with a triangle below. There are no other punctuation marks. Regular text lines have one line of spacing between them. Use two lines of spacing to indicate the start of a new paragraph.

Plurals: Rather than adding the letter "s" to a word, multiples are shown by ending the word in a letter-size asterisk. There are no different plural spellings, such as mouse & mice.

Titles & key aspects: Titles & aspects appear as symbols placed before the individual's name, as seen in the list shown on the next page: plural, plant, animal, spiritual leader, civic leader, male, female, past, future, question, comma, greetings/blessings.

Numbers: The Wind number system starts with zero, is mainly structured around multiples of twelve, & includes several mystic, ritual numbers, such as 101 and 144, composed of unique glyphs. On the next page, the numbers are: 0 to 13, 24, 48, 101, 144.

Typing: The WINDREAD Alphabet app is in development, to be announced on the website:

www.WINDTRILOGY.com

"As always, all the players and all possible plays were already in flight,"

Wind

WINDREAD - *The Tor'oc Alphabet*

The 29-letter alphabet consists of the same 26 letters, A to Z, as in other Latin languages, plus the three compound letters of double-O, th, & gh.

Punctuation

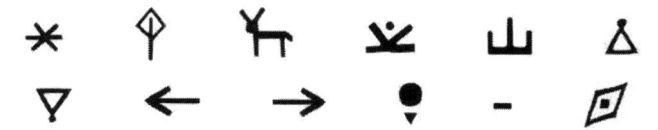

Several picture glyphs are used to indicate rank, sex, & character. There are no capital letters; 1 dash = comma; 2 dashes = period; diamond "eye" = greetings & blessings.

Numbers

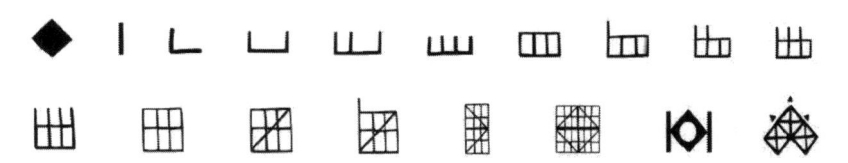

The number system focuses on multiples of 12.

Alphabet Design: Anne Kent Rush
@Copyright Barry Alexander Brown 2025

Barry Alexander Brown

WIND
The Tor'oc Trilogy

CONTACTS

Visit the Wind Website:
www.WindTrilogy.com

Retail Book Orders:
Amazon Books
or
Your favorite local bookstore

Wholesale Book Orders:
www.IngramSpark.com

English Edition
Intellect Publishing, LLC
Point Clear, Alabama
www.IntellectPublishing.com

French Edition:
Editions Massot
17 rue de Buci
75006 Paris, France
www.librairiemassot.com

Barry Alexander Brown

Made in the USA
Middletown, DE
01 October 2025